This Body

A NOVEL OF REINCARNATION

Laurel Doud

LITTLE, BROWN AND COMPANY

Boston • New York • London

AUTHOR'S ACKNOWLEDGMENTS

This work embodies the premise that the writing of a first novel is often by group process, so it is with orgasmic delight that I am able to publicly acknowledge and thank the following people:

My agent, Leigh Feldman, who saw what it could be; my editor, Sarah Burnes, who helped me make it what it is — organically; and my copyeditor, Stephen Lamont, who was "professional fussbudget" par excellence.

My readers: Linda Carroll for her rational view and her unwavering support in all my endeavors; Claudia Parker for her no-nonsense approach and her perceptive advice; and Terri and Eric Peterson and Robert McKenna for being there at the very beginning — and at the end.

My fellow writers (and subsequent readers) at Hedgebrook Cottages: Mylène Dressler for her lyrical beauty and encouragement; Roxanne Ray for her playwright's eye; and Stephanie Grant, who taught an old dog new tricks with her gentle and insightful guidance on two reads.

But, most of all, to my Muse, Lee Reilly, who loaned me her brain, her heart, and her courage so I could tell this story in the way that I had hoped to.

See a penni pick it up, all the day you'll have good luck.

Originally published in hardcover by Little, Brown and Company, 1998
First Back Bay paperback edition, 2000

The author is grateful for permission to include the following previously copyrighted material:

Burma-Shave advertisement from *The Verse by the Side of the Road: The Story of the Burma-Shave Signs and Jingles* by Frank Rowsome, Jr. Copyright © 1965 by Frank Rowsome, Jr. Reprinted by permission of Stephen Greene Press.

Excerpt from "Spilt Milk" by Will Doud-Martin. Copyright © 1998 by Will Doud-Martin. Reprinted by permission of the author.

The characters and events in this book are fictitious. Any similarity to real persons, living or dead, is coincidental and not intended by the author.

Library of Congress Cataloging-in-Publication Data

Doud, Laurel Marian.
This body : a novel / Laurel Doud. — 1st ed.
p.   cm.
ISBN 0-316-19675-4 (hc) / 0-316-19661-4 (pb)
I. Title.
PS3554.O815T48   1998
813'.54 — dc21
97-45573

10 9 8 7 6 5 4 3 2
QWV
Printed in the United States of America

PRAISE FOR LAUREL DOUD'S

This Body

"Laurel Doud has a genuine talent. . . . She plots ingeniously, draws her two very different central characters, Katharine and Thisby, with great skill, and handles some weighty themes with astonishing sureness."
— Charles Matthews, *San Jose Mercury News*

"An entertaining first novel that combines humor with sticky issues of identity. . . . An amusing novel."
— Elizabeth Bukowski, *Wall Street Journal*

"A fresh, thoughtful spin on the well-worn fantasy of inhabiting another body, this offbeat debut borrows the cast of A *Midsummer Night's Dream* and submits them to a very 1990s enchantment. . . . Crisply written, wry, and intelligent."
— *Publishers Weekly*

"Laurel Doud's humorous and engaging story of a woman who dies and regains consciousness in another's body, *This Body* captures the reader's imagination from the first. . . . Doud writes with such grace and conviction that the impossible seems quite plausible."
— Lynn Harnett, *Herald Sunday*
(Portsmouth, NH)

"The richness and intricacy of the plot propel the reader swiftly toward its satisfying conclusion."
— Judith Kicinski, *Library Journal*

"A fascinating and thought-provoking story. . . . A compassionate first novel of reincarnation."
— *San Francisco Chronicle*

You had much ado to make [my] anchor hold.

— William Shakespeare, *The Winter's Tale*, 1.2.213

"Some don't like the roller coaster; they go on the merry-go-round.

That just goes around. Nothing. I like the roller coaster. You get more out of it."

So, thanks, Danner and Will. I wouldn't have missed

the Giant Dipper for anything.

— with apologies to Lowell Ganz and Babaloo Mandel,

Parenthood

THIS BODY

Prologue ᴄ❧

Write me a prologue; and let the prologue seem to say, we will do no harm . . . this will put them out of fear.

— NICK BOTTOM, *A Midsummer Night's Dream*, 3.1.15

"*Wait* . . . ," she cried.
> But Death took her anyway.

After she regained consciousness and was able to think a bit more clearly, she wondered if "wait" was the reason it happened the way it did. Her "hocus pocus." Her "abracadabra." Her "presto chango."
> "Say the magic word, Sparky."
> *Wait* . . .

It couldn't have been a fluke, though; somebody else — somewhere, somehow — must have stumbled upon it too. But in all the years of waiting in grocery store checkout lines, she never saw any such headline in the *National Enquirer* or the *Star* or the *Globe*. She read only the headlines, of course; she never actually opened any of those tabloids. Well, maybe once, when actor Harrison Ford secretly wedded Melissa Mathison, the screenwriter for the movie E.T., in a private ceremony at the Santa Monica courthouse.

But in all the years she had stood there, pretending not to read even those headlines, she never saw THE BRAIN THAT WOULDN'T DIE! MIND OF DECEASED WOMAN TELEPORTS 400 MILES INTO BRAIN-DEAD GIRL. POSITIVE ID ON BRAIN-WAVE PATTERNS. FAMILIES CLASH OVER CUSTODY AND FILM RIGHTS.

Act 1, Scene 1 🐒

What's past is prologue, what to come
In yours and my discharge.

— ANTONIO, *The Tempest*, 2.1.253

Fade in.

Pain in her eyes is the first sensation.

Too bright. Too bright.

Waves of disorientation swell and roll underneath her. She squeezes her eyes shut and waits for the buckling to subside. When the surface firms, she forces her stiff eyelids to roll up over blistered pupils and wills her vision to track. As the shapes in front of her stabilize and come into focus, she realizes she is lying on a bathroom floor.

That much she can tell.

She is up close and personal with one of the squat porcelain knobs that cover the bolts at the bottom of a toilet — the ones that never stay on, though this one looks as though it's never come off. A halo of rust barnacles grows solid around its rim. The side of her face is sticking to the floor, and when she tries to shift her jaw back and forth, the skin stretches and pulls. There are oatmeal-like clumps in her mouth, and it's hard to breathe; her nostrils are packed tight. She spits out what she can and pulls her head — ever so gently — from the floor. There is a soft rubber-soled sucking sound. The movement sends her head spinning, and she grabs the toilet seat. Body and mind seem to connect, and even through her clogged nose, she smells a foul odor rising up like a fog from the bathroom floor. She gags, the muscles in her stomach and buttocks cramping spasmodically. The misery of it jolts her to her feet. Before she can faint, she blindly pushes herself out of the bathroom and away from the smell.

She moves from one room into another. The stink lessens, but she has brought much of it with her. Finding a kitchen sink with a plastic tub full of dirty dishes, she fumbles with the knobs and gets a stream of water going, rubbing her face while digging into her nostrils with her fingernails. She washes out her mouth and, when most of the slime is gone, leans under the faucet and drinks. She straightens up, and the maneuver sends her head whirling away from her again. She sinks down to the floor, and the ceiling above her fades out.

When she wakes up, cold and clammy and in the dim light of fading day, it takes her a while to realize that the sink is overflowing and that she is soaked through. It's easier to stand up this time, though she has to hold on to the rim of the sink. The knobs ripple slightly when she reaches out to turn them off. She pulls some dingy-looking towels from the handle of the refrigerator and throws them on the floor to sop up the water.

It's hard to think. She has never felt so sick in her life — not even after that wedding banquet, when she drank an entire bottle of champagne after coming off three months of strenuous dieting. Her husband and their three-year-old son had left to take the babysitter home, and her daughter, who was almost a year old and very mobile, stayed with her. She thought she was just fine, but suddenly the champagne hit her stomach and her head with a double-impact punch. She vaguely remembered her daughter coming into the bathroom as she was draped over the toilet bowl, but when she woke up later almost delirious on the cold floor, she had no idea how long she had been passed out or where her daughter was.

That was a picnic compared with this.

Her heart races and it hurts to breathe deeply. Her body shakes, and she feels an anxiousness that threatens to overwhelm her. Her clothes are stuck hard to her like an old-fashioned corn plaster bandage, and her hair is stiff with caked vomit. The only thing she can think of is to shower, and to shower means going back into that cesspool of a bathroom. But she can't think of anything else. She knows she doesn't know where she is or how she got there, but these questions will have to be deferred for the moment.

She walks deliberately, one foot placed slowly in front of the other as if on a tightrope, back through the only open door, into a bedroom. She grabs the scrunched-up bedspread at the foot of the mattress and throws it on the floor of the bathroom. It will have to do for now.

She yanks aside the mildew-spotted shower curtain to reveal the small, sliding window above the tiled wall. Stepping into the bathtub and breathing through her mouth, she opens the window as wide as it will go, letting in a slight breeze. She turns on the water and, hardly waiting for it to get lukewarm, twists the handle to redirect the stream to the showerhead. The bong that is slamming from side to side in her head crescendos, and the pain that is flashing across her forehead forces her eyes shut. She strips off her clothes and leaves them at the other end of the tub, the sodden mess sending rivulets of murky water running toward the drain.

She wets her clumpy hair and washes it with some shampoo, its perfumed smell almost turning her stomach again. She manages to get through two rinses before the thin veneer of her strength sloughs down the drain. Turning the water off, she steps onto the bedspread and wraps slightly crusty but thickly woven towels around her torso and her hair.

She heads straight for the bed in the next room and lies down, the towels still around her. It is almost dark. The vertigo settles slowly, and this time she falls asleep.

When she awakens, there is morning light, but she has a sense that she has slept a long time, perhaps through another entire day. Her body is dead weight, that sensation that comes with sleeping so deeply and in one position for too long. It takes all her strength to break the inertia and sit up, her body aching as if it has been clipped and spun up over the hood of a car. She touches her head, and feels that her hair is dry, but her scalp is thick with layers of sweat. Her mouth is dried out almost to cracking, and her stomach feels as though it has dropped down into the base of her spine. Her head still throbs, but her mind is beginning to clear — it's time to find out exactly what's going on.

She gets up, and the towels unravel around her, remaining on the bed. She looks down the length of her body and is hit with another attack of vertigo, so strong that she has to sit down on the edge of the bed. She doesn't want to move — ever again — but she makes herself slowly stretch out her arms and hands in front of her.

They are not hers.

The arms are pale, thin but shapely, the long fingers tipped with ragged nails. *Dancer's hands* — even she can make them pirouette like butterflies. She looks down, and the almost non-existent breasts with the very dark nipples are not hers. The flat — nay, concave — stomach, the thin thighs, the knees, are not hers. She stumbles into the bathroom, closes the medicine cabinet door, and stares at the reflection in the mirror.

The face, the hair, the eyes, are not hers.

This is not Katharine.

Act 1, Scene 2 ᕫᔓ

Where's the rest of me?

— RONALD REAGAN, *Kings Row* (1942)

Katharine watched as the hands that were not her hands touched the face that was not her face. She walked the fingers across the cheeks, up the nose, and across the forehead as if she were a blind person reading some new acquaintance's visage. This face was sharp and drawn, the skin the color and texture of bleached linen. The impossibly flat black hair sprang matted and tangled from the head like yarn from an old and grubby puppet. *Whose body is this?* She ran the hands down over the breasts and stomach and between the thighs. She could put both hands together as if in prayer and still not touch the inside of the thighs. She couldn't remember if she had ever in her adult life been able to do that with her own body. *Whose body is this?*

She jerked herself back into the bedroom and started looking for some sort of purse, flinging things off the dresser and the night tables that flanked the queen-size bed. On the desk, she found a brightly colored pocketbook and snatched at it as if it might scuttle away.

There was a driver's license — its photograph a version of the reflection that had stared back at her from the bathroom mirror, albeit a healthier one. Thisby Flute Bennet, the license read. *Is that a name?* 1125 Hillcrest Heights, Beverly Hills, CA

90210. *Geezus, only in LA.* She looked at the birth date listed; this body was seventeen years younger than her own. She turned over the license, and handwritten on the back was "155 Bruin Circle, #33, LA 90049."

This must be some sort of hallucination.

She stood up awkwardly, as if there were loose connections, a short circuit, in this body, and she had to consciously dictate orders to the extremities.

This must be a dream.

She had always dreamed vividly and with such clarity that she would wake up and not be sure whether the dream had actually happened. But there was no disputing the bites of this reality. This was not a dream. Every filament of this body screamed. Every neuron in her brain was on fire.

"What am I going to do?" she said out loud, hoarsely at first, but then with enough strength to hear the accent and cadence of the voice. It was not hers.

Is nothing mine but my mind? Returning to silence to hear her own voice in her own brain.

She quickly rummaged through the dresser drawers to find some clothes to cover this strange naked flesh. The jeans looked terribly thin — there would be no way she could fit into them, but this body did, obscenely easily. She felt more composed now, though — and less like a voyeur.

What do I remember last about me, in my own body? she thought as she slumped down on the bed. *Work?* Yes, she remembered it had been a workday, and a long one. She had been tired and not feeling very well, though that was not unusual. She hadn't been feeling well for a long time. Years, it seemed. Doctors pronounced her healthy, yet she still didn't feel good. So tired, so out of sync. She would have settled for feeling okay. Feeling good was for the young. She didn't remember anything unusual happening that night. It was a bit of a blur, though she was sure alcohol hadn't been involved — at least, not any more than the usual two glasses of wine before dinner. She had gone to bed early. She did remember that, suddenly. There had been a fight with her son, and she had ached to steal awhile into the oblivion of sleep. The fight was over something — *something, no doubt, like school or grades.* He was going to be a junior in the fall, and he was avoiding his required summer reading. His first-semester grades would be incredibly important for college. *Didn't he realize that?* She had lost her temper and said some things, and as he slammed out of the house, her daughter's bedroom door sounding in sympathetic echo, she had immediately wanted to take back her words.

She hadn't then called after him to be careful, to drive defensively, as if it were a conferred blessing, as if it would keep him from harm. Would the one time she forgot to warn him be the time he would do something stupid?

And she really hadn't forgotten — the caveat had been in her mind and on her lips, but that last burst of energy needed to purse her lips forward failed her. She had worried about it as she went to sleep, and that was the last thing she remembered.

No, that's not right. There was something else.

She woke up. Yes, she woke up, and something was wrong. She felt bad. Worse than she did now. She felt her rib cage expand from the inside, as if something alien had incubated inside of her and wanted to be born. She was going to explode. She heard, more than sensed, her husband beside her — his snores like the sound of clothespinned playing cards being shuffled against bicycle-wheel spokes. She had this schizoid need to gently nudge him under the shoulder blade as she had done countless times in their two decades of marriage, and to flail at him like a windmill. *How can you sleep while I'm dying?* He dropped away from her then, and she knew.

In the last second of life, she had cried, "Wait . . ."

What was she supposed to do now? *Phone home?* Yes, that's exactly what she would do. That would ground her. She would talk to her son or daughter or husband, and then everything would be all right.

There was a phone by the bed. She leaned over slowly, ignoring the insistent blink of the message-machine light, and picked up the receiver. She dialed her area code first; she would assume she was in LA. *What else do I have to go on?*

The phone rang. *Pick up!* Five heartbeats and someone answered, the greeting too truncated for Katharine to catch who it was.

"Is this the Ashley residence?" Katharine heard herself say in this other body's voice.

"Yes, it is. Who's calling, please?" It was a woman, and Katharine did not recognize her.

"Kath — " *Katharine Ashley? Was she? Really?*

She hung up and stared at the phone. What was she going to do? If only her head and stomach would stop lurching. There was an ache in this body that sometimes felt like hunger, but the thought of food made her tilt. The ache was like desire, and it seemed to be pulling at her, pulling her apart, stretching her over and under like saltwater taffy on metal arms at the Boardwalk.

She sat there on the bed and kicked at a sweater that was on the floor. Underneath it was a plastic Baggie weighted down in one corner by white powder.

Is this withdrawal? From drugs? Was this Thisby Flute Bennet an addict then? Katharine stiffened. *Had she . . . OD'd? Fried her brain and left this poor body directorless?*

Her skin itched, and she raked the torn nails down her arms, leaving traces of red. *I can't be an addict. Not me. I got through the Woodstock era unscathed. I never even liked marijuana.*

Katharine pulled up sharply on her panic. Did that mean they had made some sort of switch, some sort of transfer? *Traded places?*

She had to know. Before she could even begin to think or do anything else, she had to know if some drugged-out doppelgänger was inhabiting Katharine's body, wearing Katharine's clothes, looking at Katharine's face in the mirror, wondering where her own had gone? Saying, "I'm all, you know, like, really freaked out."

I'll call work, she thought and dialed her number. *Maybe she's there.*

"Ryerson-Connors Insurance. Ned Ryerson's office."

Disappointed, Katharine recognized the voice as belonging to Rita, one of the new girls they had hired recently.

"Katharine Ashley, please," she said, trying to stay under control, afraid she would be recognized, afraid she wouldn't be.

There was a longer silence than normal until Rita responded. "May I ask who's calling?"

Katharine fought down the urge to scream, *What are you doing at my desk? You're not trained for my job!* "I'm a personal friend," she said.

There was another long interval. "I think you should call their home."

"I can't get through," she lied. "Please tell me."

"I'm sorry, but Katharine died a year ago. Of a heart attack."

Act 1, Scene 3 🦎

What is the body when the head is off?

—KING EDWARD, *Henry VI, Part III*, 5.1.41

Katharine hung up the phone, not knowing whether she had said anything or not. She sat with her hands in her lap. *My hands? My God, they aren't mine. They'll never be mine. They're some dead girl's hands.*

A year? She died a year ago? But it was June. She couldn't remember the exact date, but it was definitely the month of June. She rubbed her forehead. It was so hard to concentrate. Was this body rejecting her as a brain donor?

She picked up a stiff and riffled-through newspaper from the floor. The masthead read *Los Angeles Times*, the front page story, POLICE DOUBT FIRE IS ACCIDENTAL, the dateline, Wednesday, June 21. She relaxed, but then she saw the year.

It was one year in her mind, but the next in this body.

Dead a whole year.

How could they live without her?

No one even knows how to load the dishwasher properly. They probably do the dishes twice as often, and you know no one has put a new roll of toilet paper on the holder in a year. No one has probably even thrown away the old ones. They're probably still there — cardboard tubes lined up on the windowsill, old soldiers with wisps of toilet paper stuck to their cylinders as if to staunch shaving nicks.

One whole year? Who would be giving Rathbone his pills and walking him every other day? And the bills? Her husband was terrible at paying bills. *Oh dear. He saw the Nordstrom's charge . . .*

As if it really matters now.

Did I die with clean underwear on? She snorted out loud. *I missed Ben's junior year, his junior prom, if he deigned to go, and Marion's graduation from junior high. She started to like that Jones boy. I missed all of that. I missed the spring, the bulbs I would have planted. I was planning to have the best spring garden: the crocuses, the tulips, then the Dutch hyacinths and irises.*

So much missing . . .

Does Philip miss me?

In the spring — *last spring?* — she had gone away for a weekend by herself. When she came back, the house was a complete disaster. Her husband's only comment was that nobody died; they'd survived, as if that were the best to be expected of them. He said he missed her, though. She knew he was a little hurt when she didn't reciprocate. It wasn't as if she didn't miss him and the kids, but the respite from their lives and their emotions and their schedules and needs and wants was . . . *such a relief.*

The minute she walked in the house, it was as if she had never left, and after she got readjusted, got the house back in order, she realized she had missed Philip.

Was he missing her now?

Has he fallen in love again? Was that woman who answered the phone his new love? Katharine saw them at the kitchen table, all together, an unusual event in her day, laughing at some dumb pun Ben made, Marion eyeing her milk glass as if it were filled with hemlock, Philip having concocted some new vegetable pasta and exclaiming, "I can't wait until you guys go away to college. Then you'll be begging to come home to eat my fettuccine," Rathbone munching happily on some dinner scraps slipped to him not very surreptitiously by that new woman. *You'll kill him with that kind of food!*

Breathless, Katharine rubbed her chest with stiff fingers,

feeling the sharp ridges of the breastbone beneath the thin layer of skin. Panic yawned and threatened to swallow her insides like the sucking mouth of a black hole. Katharine felt herself being drawn down into it.

I'll think about it tomorrow! I'll think about it when I'm stronger. I've got to stay sane. . . .

She was going to have to be practical, or lose her mind for the second time. She had always been a practical sort of person. This would be her greatest trial. But she needed to act. She needed to postpone the unanswered and unthinkable.

What she needed to do was to clean this apartment. She would never be able to focus in a mess like this. It would never do.

She felt like a stagehand working quickly to get ready for the next scene. By the front door, she stacked the newspapers that were scattered over the couches in the living room. She piled the beer cans and the whiskey bottles in the kitchen to be taken out later.

Tucked underneath sofa cushions and the general rubbage, she found more plastic bags of marijuana and the white powder she assumed was cocaine. She dumped them into the garbage can with such a strong combination of regret and viciousness, she was unwilling to analyze either emotion.

The predominant brand of cigarettes in the overflowing ashtrays was Marlboro, but there were other brands as well. *TB's friends, no doubt.* "TB" was Katharine's mental signature for this body, this Thisby Bennet. She wondered if the apartment reeked of cigarette smoke; she couldn't smell anything. *Perhaps this body's nasal passages are so irritated they can't detect it — and that means the stink in the bathroom is really bad.*

On the bookshelves in the living room, she found stacks of black-and-white photographs of strangely focused street scenes, their perspectives so off-balance that they made her stomach whirl. She replaced them facedown on the shelves.

Behind a cabinet door was a TV, VCR, and stereo system. The cassette left in the VCR was a Quentin Tarantino film that Katharine had never heard of — she had missed that too.

Katharine wasn't really a fan of Tarantino's films — too violent, too bloody, too strange — and watched them only because she wanted to know what Ben was watching, and only in video when she could use the remote control to fast-forward.

The artists on the CDs and tapes sounded familiar, and some she knew she had heard blaring from Ben's room. Ben had gone through numerous musical styles and had been a fan of grunge, industrial, ska, hardcore, heavy metal, speed metal, death metal. Until he stopped talking to her, she had been regaled with facts about various groups — who trashed their instruments, who taught himself to play, who wrote their own songs. Marion was a classic-rock listener: Crosby, Stills and Nash, The Who, Led Zeppelin, The Doobie Brothers. Sometimes Marion would come racing into the living room to pump up the volume on the stereo. "Oh, I just love this song," she would gush, and Katharine would find herself in a kind of time machine, seeing herself at the very same age, gushing over the very same song.

She felt a pinioning stab of homesickness. She fended it off.

The kitchen table was stacked with mail and grocery bags with food still in them. One bag had an opened box of Frosted Flakes. The eater had obviously just reached in and pulled out handfuls of the stuff, as flakes skittered across the bottom of the bag when Katharine moved it.

There wasn't much in the cupboards: some canned goods, condiments, and bottles of scotch, vermouth, and bitters. In another cabinet were plastic vials of prescription medicines, antibiotics generally, but there were also a couple whose curative powers remained a mystery to her. It didn't surprise her that TB would be a sickly person, but it surprised her that she would bother with doctors. *Or is he her pusher? Amphetamines and depressants and such things.* The doctor's name on all the labels, some with expiration dates long past, was the same: Dr. Elliot Mantle, Beverly Hills. She should probably remember that. Maybe she should start a list of the things she knew about

Thisby — just in case someone showed up: family, friends, boyfriends, and she had to be her. *Her dead ringer.* She could just imagine what type of boyfriend a person of her obvious habits would attract. It made her shudder.

She pulled open drawers that rattled with useless inventory. The child did not seem to own a pen or a sheet of paper. She found a stubby yellow pencil like the ones available at miniature golf or at the library — *no doubt, this was a golfing acquisition* — and ripped up a grocery bag into strips. She wrote awkwardly — her hand not responding well to commands — at the top of one sheet, "Elliot Mantle — doctor — Beverly Hills — 555–8411." She stacked the prescription labels neatly for future reference.

The contents of the refrigerator were hardly more nourishing. There was beer, Coke, an empty carton of juice, five jars of maraschino cherries (which she had always hated), and a bucket of Kentucky Fried Chicken, the thought of which twitched her stomach counterclockwise. She pitched everything out while gulping down a Coke, which made her throat tingle.

Katharine stood in front of the opened refrigerator. She liked bare refrigerators, one of those small contentions with Philip she had discovered early in their marriage. He loved them bulging with food and drink, a sign of wealth and prosperity. Of course, he wasn't the one to discover two-month-old leftovers, growing black-and-green fungus and smelling of putrid decay in their Tupperware containers.

She closed the door, leaned over the sink, and threw up, her stomach muscles barely strong enough to send the stinging soda back up her throat.

Katharine sat at the kitchen table with a small pile of mail in front of her. She had feebly frisbeed the junk mail, including a UCLA summer schedule of classes, into the garbage can and had separated the bills from the personal letters. There was only one of the latter, its envelope handwritten with no return address, Los Angeles on the canceled stamp. It read:

T —
Home-keeping youth have ever homely wits.
I want out of this fucking place. Call around 3 on
Tuesday/Thursday.
You know she's never here then.
Q

She gingerly sipped another Coke. She took up a piece of brown-bag stationery and wrote "friends/family" at the top. She listed "Q," but with a large question mark after it.

The bills were pretty straightforward — a phone bill, a rent-hike notice. *Geezus, the place looks nice, cleaned up and all, but the rent is our entire house payment up north.* There were no credit card bills. *No gas card bills. There's only eighty dollars in her wallet and no checkbook.* Katharine stopped. How was she going to pay for things like rent and food? How did TB pay for them? Did she have a job? Did she sell drugs for a living? *Maybe she gets paid for casual sex? What do I know?* Tears leaked from the corners of her eyes and slipped down her cheeks. She quickly wiped them away with the back of her hand. *Come on. Buck up. You can cry tomorrow.*

She figured she could do a reconnaissance of the bedroom before having to lie down again but then realized the search would have to be postponed until she cleaned the bathroom; the overwhelming stench had started to attack her precarious stomach.

Katharine didn't know quite where to start but decided to mop up as much of the offending purge as possible with the bedspread. She would have given anything for her large-capacity, four-cycle, heavy-duty Maytag washing machine, with its electronic sensors and infinitely adjustable water-level control. . . . *Stop it. Move on.*

There was a balcony off the kitchen nook, and she put the bedspread there until she could wash it. The crud would harden like little cement patties, but there was nothing else to be done.

Underneath the sink were basic cleaning supplies with labels so faded that if it weren't for their distinctive shapes, she wouldn't have known what they were. With these, she managed to get the worst of the topsoil off and left the heavy stuff for the next cleaning. Her arm and shoulder ached, she was so weak. She couldn't smell anything but Comet and Mr. Clean.

Seeping fatigue had slowly but steadily wormed its way up her fingers and into her soul. She tried to marshal strength, but couldn't. *I'm running on empty.* Her head and the back of her neck were thick and stiff with pain, and thunderbolts stabbed periodically behind her eyes. The sun had set some time before, and it was now quite dark outside. She barely had the energy to find a sweater to put on, as she was beginning to shake from a cold that seemed to emanate from within. The nagging hunger that wasn't for food pulled at her too. She crawled into bed and tugged the covers up and the pillow down until she was positively cocooned.

She wondered what her family was doing. Were they preparing for bed too? It was probably way too early for Ben, who even on restriction would rattle around the house, eating cereal, watching videos, until the wee hours of the morning. Would Philip be in bed? If he was, he'd be asleep already; the man was able to attain unconsciousness in less than a minute, something she was continually awed at as she lay in bed, her brain rumbling with half-finished conversations, lists of things to do, scenarios and worries of what might happen and to whom.

She suddenly had a vision of Philip when they were first married, how he would come to bed wearing a folded bandanna to keep his hair from frizzing into a hair ball around his head; he wouldn't let that happen on purpose until the next year, when Afros became fashionable. He was wearing that headband the first time she saw him. December 1, 1969. He was playing touch football with his friends on one of the grass fields on campus. He had tied the bandanna across his forehead to keep his long, curly hair out of his face and to sop up the sweat that streamed from his hairline. He looked like a medieval knight. His dog, a small shepherd mix, wore a matching scarf around his neck and waited patiently on the sidelines. A boy and his dog. The dog's name was Siddhartha. Philip was really into existentialism then. She pretended she understood Hesse and Sartre and Camus, but she never saw what all the fuss was about. Later, she wondered whether Philip had pretended too. He never reread those books, and man's essential isolation never seemed to concern him again.

Katharine had noticed Sid — even his master quickly forgot his more lofty name — before she noticed Philip. Sid had a pleasant grin, and even though Katharine wasn't much good at it, he let her throw the Frisbee for him — probably, she suspected, because nobody else would. When Philip and his friends somehow decided that their game was finished, he came over to retrieve Sid, who was happily stationed on her feet.

"He's a nice dog" was the only thing she could think to say.

Philip agreed, quickly dismissing her.

But they ended up walking in the same direction. Katharine lagged behind, so he wouldn't have to feel like he had to escort her, but Sid trotted by her side, forcing Philip to drop back and join them. He told her that he and his friends were trying to forget what was going to happen that night — the draft lottery. He had tried to get a deferment, a medical discharge, but nothing worked. His birth date was in the glass jug, and his balls were on the chopping block.

That night she waited and listened to the dates being drawn. March 9, Philip's birthday, was called at number 317; he would not be drafted. The next day she baked chocolate chip cookies and, marveling at her courage, took them to him in congratulations. She woke him up. He and his friends had gotten totally blotto — in celebration of good numbers, in denial of bad ones — after the draw. She sat on the edge of his bed while he tried to focus. He ate a couple of cookies and rebounded, telling her that cookies were a great cure for hangovers. They sat on his bed all that day talking — about the war, the meaning of life, the future of mankind — and in the early evening, she utterly amazed herself by crawling under the covers with him.

Then he said, *That was the best cure for a hangover.*

For a long time afterward, whenever he woke up with a hangover, she baked him chocolate chip cookies.

She hadn't baked him chocolate chip cookies in years.

No, I can't think about that now. It was best that she go to sleep, and with the dawning of a new day, she would awake feeling fine. She would attack the bedroom and find out exactly what day it was. It was a Plan.

She woke up, clutching her stomach as it spasmed. She tried to pull herself protectively into the fetal position, but both calves cramped and jerked her legs into a full extension. She quickly flexed her heels to ease the cramps. When there was a lull in the pain, Katharine realized it was long past dawn. *And I feel like shit. So much for the Plan.*

She lay in bed and wanted to stay there, but she was cold. She had sweat through her clothes, the bedsheets were damp, and she stank like some sort of feral animal.

She ached for the smell of coffee; Philip was always up before the rest of the family to start a pot and read the sports page in peace and quiet. The light of day was all wrong here too, coming from the left through Thisby's bedroom window instead of like at home, slowly approaching the foot of the bed, only to slant off down the hallway before reaching the covers. She looked away.

The sun was streaming onto the kitchen table from the balcony glass door. She was sure it was already terribly smoggy outside, but the heat felt good. She thought fleetingly that she might go outside on the balcony but was afraid of the smell from the bedspread. She couldn't tell what the balcony looked down on, but across the way was another apartment complex, five stories high, with balconies jutting out like the ends of Lincoln Logs.

She pulled out an Eggo waffle from the freezer, but after heating it, she eyed it warily. She couldn't trust this body. What seemed like hunger might not be real hunger, and this body was liable to take retribution. She carefully ate the waffle over the kitchen sink and waited, feeling the sun rays penetrate and ease her stiffness. Her stomach seemed to accept the food with only a mild aftershock of queasiness, so she tempted fate and took some aspirin.

Back in the bedroom, she checked out the telephone's answering machine. There were four messages. She pressed the GREETING button first and listened to a surly version of the voice that Katharine was able to produce from this body.

"Talk to me," the message said. There was a long pause and then a click.

Katharine felt her blood heat. *God, she sounds just like Ben.*

She pressed the PLAY MESSAGES button and a male voice slurred sluggishly, "Hey, this is Marko. You know, David's friend? You know, we met . . . where the fuck were we? Oh yeah, at the rave down in Pasadena. I think. It was a couple of months ago. Around there, I guess. I hang with Laddie and Greg. Anyway, I was thinking about you. Call me, you know, if you want to. My number is . . ."

Katharine couldn't imagine ever calling this lost boy, but she wrote down his name, phone number, and his friends' names on her brown paper.

The last three calls were from the same person, a man whose voice was intimate yet demanding. "I need to talk to you. Call me."

"I told you to call me. You said you were going to call in for messages. What, no phones down there? Call me."

"I'll be out of town for a day or two. Leave me a message where I can reach you."

He sounded as if he had a claim on Thisby, and Katharine hugged herself protectively. *But he said he was going out of town for a while.* She had some time. She erased the messages.

No more excuses. It's time to tackle the mess in this room.

Katharine sat at the kitchen table surrounded by the loot she had brought in from the bedroom. The watch she now twirled on Thisby's wrist was deceptively simple, gold with a thin expansion bracelet. The word "Cartier" was elegantly scripted across the face. She had found it on the floor under a pile of clothes she'd sorted through, hanging up the decent-looking ones and throwing the obviously dirty clothes in a corner for washing later. The style of most of the clothing was too weird and trendy. Many were in colors Katharine never wore. They had names in mail-order catalogs like coffee bean, mint julep, and hydrangea, though Thisby's favorite seemed to be varying shades of the color purple. There was a great deal of black clothing, though, that Katharine wouldn't mind wearing. She had often worn black herself. She had read that it made a body look ten pounds thinner.

Katharine found a pair of hiphugger, bell-bottom Levis and a halter top made from a pair of cut-up denim jeans wadded together under the dresser. These were original relics from Katharine's own teenage years. As she shook out the clothes, the smell of musk oil escaped from the creases. The scent dazed and then slightly confused her until the image of herself in 1970 materialized in her brain. She was dressed in similar garb, perfumed in musk oil, and planted in front of one of the last picture shows that featured a concave screen that stretched from one side of the theater to the other, surrounded by the sights and sounds of *Woodstock* — Stephen Stills of Crosby, Stills, Nash and Young, confessing to a half a million people, "This is our second gig. This is the second time we've ever played in front of people, man. We're scared shitless." Katharine had watched paisley-clad young people cavort on the ground and in the ponds, making love, drinking, smoking, dancing. She had watched Sly Stone admonish the crowd for waiting for the approval of their neighbors to let it all hang down and then work them into a sea of arms raised in salute, ironically reminiscent of World War II footage Katharine had seen of Hitler's political rallies. She had watched in sexual excitement as bare-chested Roger Daltrey of The Who pleaded with the audience to see him, feel him, touch him, heal him. She saw *Woodstock* five times the summer of 1970.

She put the clothes in a closet to be given away to the Goodwill.

Small pieces of paper — matchbooks, torn corners of menus, crispy napkins with the outline of once-wet bar glasses in their centers — were laid out like a solitaire hand on the kitchen table. Written on them were phone numbers. Katharine had found them in the drawer of one of Thisby's night tables. She had also found a set of keys and a checkbook. There was no ending balance listed in the account ledger, and the checks were so haphazardly recorded and out of sequence that nothing could be inferred. The keys had no identifying marks — no automobile insignia, no company logos. It was as if Thisby had lost every original key and had to replace them with generic ones.

The address book she had found at the bottom of a night table drawer was obviously old but well used, the cardboard showing through the cracked and broken pink vinyl. It was a time line of Thisby's life, the handwriting illustrating the evolution from child to young adult.

The first entry, under B, was written in block printing:

ANNE & ROBERT BENNET
1125 HILLCREST HEIGHTS
BEVERLY HILLS, CALIFORNIA 90210
555-1230

Then, in progressively maturing styles, were phone numbers for "Mom's work," "Dad's work."

Underneath all of that was "Rob," first with a dorm address at UCLA, then one for the SAE fraternity house, then listings for a couple of apartments. The last entry was just a phone number, written with a heavily pressed hand.

There were other Bennets listed, including a "Kewpie" with a local number and an Uncle Roy with an address in Central America, but no one with a name beginning with Q.

Or is "Q" also Kewpie?

In the desk, Katharine had found white lined paper and was now writing out names and their possible relationships to Thisby. *At least I know the names of Thisby's parents, and I assume there is an older brother named Rob who graduated from UCLA some years back.*

It was early evening, and she was stiff and sore. She had forgotten the pain in her head for a while, but now became acutely aware of it again. The list she had made wasn't as long as she thought it would be. There were almost more names of bars she compiled from the cocktail napkins and matchbooks — Goodbars, The Rapture, TechNoir, Potters, and F/X — than of friends who weren't crossed off and out of Thisby's life. Katharine vowed never to set foot in any of the bars. *And the friends? Well, I certainly can do without them too.* She folded the list and put it in her back pocket. *This is your life, Thisby Flute, reduced to names on wide-ruled school paper. Pretty pathetic, isn't it?*

That's when the phone rang.

It rang virtually in her left ear, and she was discombobulated until she realized that the drapes flanking the sliding glass door obscured a telephone.

She waited four rings — *I'm not ready* — but the answering machine didn't pick up. She began to shake, and as the ringing went on, each sound jolted her as if she were being given electroshock treatment.

She grabbed the receiver even as her brain screamed, *I'm not ready!* "Hello?" she demanded.

There was a silence, then a voice, sounding disgusted and hostile. "So you are there. What happened? Police run you out?"

"No" was all she could think of to say. *Run out of where?*

There was another pause. "Or didn't you go? I saw one of your so-called friends, and he said he thought you might be gone for a couple of weeks."

If TB had really died, no one would have come over to find her for weeks. And what a gruesome find. Poor thing. "I didn't go. I've been pretty sick."

"Yeah, I'll bet." There was the sound of inhaled breath. "Someday you're going to kill yourself, you know. What you do to yourself is your own business. I don't care. But when what you do affects Mom and Dad, then it's my business. And Quince's got it in her head that you're some sort of cult figure. Like Sid and Nancy."

So. This is brother Rob and . . . Quincey? . . . is the little sister; obviously the "Q" in the letter. So Thisby's the bad influence? What a surprise.

She began to feel a bit more confident. If she wanted to get back to her family, she had to stay sane and convince others she was sane too. *I'll cleanse this body. Cold turkey. I'm not mentally addicted.* She was going to have to try and play the part of Thisby Flute Bennet on the smallest of clues. *I'm a quick study.* Maybe she could pull this off. *At least he thinks I'm his sister.* "I got real close this time to killing myself." She waited a moment and then continued, "But things have changed. I'm different." *How different, hopefully, you'll never know.*

"Yeah, right."

"But I've drawn a blank on some parts of my life." *Like a total blank.*

"Well, no doubt you've killed off whole sections of your brain, so it doesn't surprise me."

Like the whole casaba. "Well, it really scared me this time. I'm different. I'm clean."

"I've heard that before," he said, but Katharine could hear the faintest hint of hope in his sarcasm. "Let's see if you can stay clean through the weekend. It was Mom and Dad's anniversary last week — you know, Midsummer Night and all, not that I expected you to remember that — but they asked me to see if I couldn't get you to come over Saturday to celebrate a little late. They're also hoping you'll spend the night."

Katharine drew a breath and steadied herself. "Okay."

"Okay? Okay? Like hell, okay. I'll believe it when I see it."

Katharine felt her temper rise. She didn't care what the history was between this girl and her brother, he didn't need to be so rude. "I said I'd be there. In fact, why don't you come over and pick me up?"

There was another pause. "What do you want?"

Katharine was beginning to get exasperated. "A ride."

"Hock your Porsche?"

Porsche? Geezus, how'd she afford that? "No. I just want a ride." The thought of trying to find her way around LA, the labyrinth of freeways, made her sweat. *Harbor, San Diego, Long Beach, Hollywood, Artesia . . . I'll take a wrong turn, or get forced into a detour, and end up in a really bad area and maybe even get attacked by thugs.*

"You be ready at one o'clock. And I mean one o'clock. If

you're not, you can find your own way there. Hey," he added, as if he were speaking as he was thinking, "you still got your driver's license, don't you?"

"Of course I do." *Did she?* She hadn't checked to see if the license was valid.

"Is the Porsche all right? You didn't wreck it, did you?"

Katharine was beginning to ripple. *I take it all back. This isn't going to be easy.* "Listen, Rob, I'll be ready at one — "

"Rob?" he barked.

Oh, hell, what have I said now?

"What do you really want?" he demanded.

Katharine felt exhausted. She could hardly answer. "I'll be ready at one. Bye."

She hung up the phone and dissolved into tears. Her head hurt. Her eyes hurt. The muscles across her chest and shoulders hurt. *These aren't even my pains. I didn't do anything to deserve this. I want to go home. I can't handle this. They'll probably put me away. Maybe I am insane. But I want to go home. I want to see my family.*

She stopped crying, too depleted to continue. She would go home. She would find this Porsche of TB's and drive home. She'd somehow make them realize who she was. She knew things about them only she could know. They would have to believe her. *So their mother returns after being dead a year, in the body of a twenty-two-year-old drug addict from LA.* It was weird, of course. But they couldn't deny who she was. Her kids would have a young-looking mother. Her husband would have an old wife in a new body. *Maybe cleaned up, this body wouldn't be so bad. He might even like it.* Going home. It sounded so soothing. But something kept tweaking her. *That woman. That woman on the phone. Who is she?*

She picked up the phone again and dialed home. That woman answered. She was laughing.

"Is Mrs. Ashley home?" Katharine asked almost belligerently.

The woman laughed again, her mouth not quite on the receiver. "Stop that." There was a muffled chuckle. "I'm sorry," she said into the mouthpiece. "This is Mrs. Ashley."

"Mrs. Katharine Ashley?" Katharine was getting mad. It kept the panic at bay.

"No. This is Diana Ashley," and her voice took on a more formal tone. "I'm sorry, Katharine died a year ago."

Oh, God. It's true. I'm dead and gone, and he's remarried. Why did they let me live if they planned on taking my life away?

"Would you like to speak with my husband? He's right here." Katharine heard Philip chuckle again. The woman's voice spun away from the receiver. "Hon, it's someone asking for Katharine."

"No," Katharine gasped. "No," she repeated and hung up. *My husband. My husband.* She felt her heart shrivel — two sizes too small — then picked up the phone again and dialed 411.

"What city, please," said the voice.

"I need to know the date and the day of the week."

"June twenty-seventh. Tuesday," the voice said without hesitation.

What a city, LA. No one bats an eye.

Katharine put the receiver down with measured control. She had three and a half days to prepare to meet her new family.

Act 1, Scene 4 🦎

"A lot of people enjoy being dead."

"But they're not dead really. They're just backing away from life."

—BUD CORT AND RUTH GORDON, *Harold and Maude* (1971)

Katharine ran on white rage. She was a dilithium crystal, glowing hardcold with righteous anger and jealousy. A halo of betrayal surrounded her, and she felt as though she could blind people with her incandescence. *He couldn't even wait a year to get married.*

She found and stalked the laundry room — *just let anyone confront me as Thisby. I'll blow right through them* — but apparently TB had not been the friendliest person in the complex. People said hello, but they did not start up any conversations.

Well, that's just fine with me.

By Thursday morning, she decided it was time to go out into the big city. She walked along the outskirts of UCLA and at Westwood Boulevard turned away from the school and headed into the business section decorated in the blue, white, and red of the upcoming Independence Day. The shops were small, mostly record and clothing stores catering to students, fast-food restaurants, bars, bakeries. She propelled herself away from the smell of the doughnuts, bought a bagel in a delicatessen, and picked at it while she continued down the street.

She went through the sidewalk bins of pulp fiction and used textbooks at Prospero's Books and bought a street map of LA and a dog-eared *Sunset Western Garden Book*, which armed her with a small measure of self.

She stopped in front of a small beauty salon called, simply, Hair. She was worried about spending all the money in Thisby's wallet, but the reflection in the glass was more than she could stand. She looked drawn and unhealthy, and she didn't know what to do about Thisby's hair. She had tried to comb it flat, but it just ended up looking like some sort of nonregulation pith helmet.

She entered, and the smell of perm solution and hairspray dimly penetrated her dilithium-hard shell. Katharine had been a teenager in the late sixties, when no self-respecting girl with long straight hair would be caught dead in a beauty salon. Natural was the only way. But after Marion was born and twenty pounds stayed on and on, Katharine treated herself to an afternoon away from the kids and, hopefully, to a new look. It was bliss. It was heaven. Somebody shampooed her hair. Somebody offered her a drink. Somebody massaged the oak-hard knots in her neck and shoulders. She didn't have to do anything. She didn't read the women's magazines or the gossip weeklies, she just sat there until she was nothing but cartilage. Philip didn't much like the new do. She didn't either, really, but it didn't matter. She had found a place where she could let go. Other people hated the smell of perms, but to Katharine it meant pampering and —

I don't have time for this. She breathed tightly through her mouth.

The only man in the salon, wearing the seemingly requisite slicked-back hair in a short ponytail, seated her and looked at her somewhat quizzically, like, What in the hell am I supposed to do with this?

When she told him to cut off just the damaged parts, he took an electric shaver and held it flat to her scalp. "About here. Are you into the juvenile authority look, luv?"

Katharine contemplated the buzz cut. She had always liked the tactile feel of hair on her shoulders, but not now. She didn't want any hair touching her. She didn't want to feel it at all. When the hairdresser realized that she was actually considering it, he amended his diagnosis. He fussed about and, after lifting a great deal of the flat black color until a pale brown sheen could be seen, left two or three inches all over her head. It stuck straight out, but Katharine liked it. It reminded her of the crimson bottlebrush they had had in the front yard of their first house. Thisby looked like some sort of futuristic punk assassin, tall and thin with all hard edges, but for the first time since she had died, Katharine felt the outside and the inside matching up. Here was no priss. This was something she could have never gotten away with as Katharine but now . . . *I like it.* She also felt protected, as if she were in a masquerade. It was a brilliant disguise.

But not totally.

On the way home from the store, a car going in the opposite direction honked at her, and a voice called, "Hey, Thiz!" She turned quickly down the next street and hid in the doorway of The Devil's Own, a head shop displaying leather, silver, and incense, until she felt it was safe to continue.

She prowled the rooms of the apartment after she put away the food and ate half the candy she had bought. She had spent almost all the money and now was furious at herself for succumbing to the grocery store's candy display with the sign overhead that said LIFE IS LIKE A BOX OF CHOCOLATES.

The white rage blazed.

She had never before felt this intense, this irrational, this volatile. But it pleased her. She didn't have to think while she was burning this hot, a constant film of strange-smelling sweat trying to cool her skin. She muscled control over this body. She fed it what it didn't want and made the food stay down by sheer willpower. She was a drill sergeant, whipping the new recruits into shape. *No mercy.*

It felt good because it didn't feel at all.

When the flame inside her periodically trimmed to a leaner, steadier glow, she was able to continue her inventory of the apartment. It was during one of these respites that she found the pictures in the utility closet. The closet was long and narrow with shelves butting up to a black wall. Boxes with a progressive range of years marked on the sides in felt pen lined the shelves. She reached up for one of them and her arm was so weak, she could hardly pull it off the shelf. It fell against her chest and she steadied it with her left arm until she had to drop it heavily to the ground. There were photographs inside — a lot of them.

She dragged the box into the kitchen and went back into the closet to get another one. As she pulled down a box near the back wall, she banged her hip against something. She looked down and, when her eyes adjusted, realized that the wall was really a door, and it was a doorknob that she had hit.

The beat of her heart staggered. What was beyond the door? Why would TB paint it black? Her hand reached for the knob. Was the audience behind her yelling, "Don't go in there, you stupid fool!"? And indeed it was like watching a movie, her hand slowly reaching for the knob, expecting it to be jerked away by some knife-wielding psycho standing framed in the lurid backlight.

At first the door seemed locked, until Katharine turned the knob harder. *Boy, you're really fearless.* She shoved the door aside. She couldn't see a thing. The feeble light from behind her shadowed a pull chain hanging just below the door header in front of her face. She jerked it hard and flinched as a red, leering light flooded the room. *It's a little whorehouse. . . .* No, it was her son's bedroom when he went through a phase of colored lights and folded Indian-print bedspreads nailed over the windows like blackout curtains.

A drug-processing operation?

No, a photographer's darkroom, narrow and deep, with counters running the length of the space. Cardboard boxes and plastic jugs lined the shelves below both counters. A sink was surrounded by trays and round containers, and a clothesline was strung at an angle from one wall to another.

The room was clean and neat and, therefore, seemed unused. There were no pictures on the corkboard, no negatives pinned like streamers from the clothesline. There was a very light film of dust on the countertops, undisturbed by finger-prints. TB had obviously abandoned this place, so Katharine turned off the light, closed the door, and went back into the kitchen, taking another box with her.

There was more in the boxes than she could have expected, yet less than she could have wished for. One box held a black case with padded shoulder straps. Inside was a camera, beauti-ful even to Katharine's untrained eye. The name on it was Nikon FM2, and there were lenses and other paraphernalia in a matching case. The other boxes were filled with photographs, negatives, 8 x 10 sheets with rows of small pictures, and a small spiral notebook filled with dates, numbers, and symbols like mathematical formulas written in Thisby's juvenile hand.

The real find was a stack of photo albums. The first one began when Thisby was a newborn. It looked like something her mother had started for her, half baby book, half photo album. A birth announcement was taped to the first page:

Thisby Flute Bennet
Wednesday, December 24
"There was a star danc'd, and under that she was born."

Katharine watched Thisby grow from a pretty baby to a chunky toddler to a waifish young child, performing in ballet recitals and acting in plays, though Thisby was always in the back with the chorus, not in front with the leads. There were photographs of the family, mostly of Rob and Thisby clowning around together. One was always next to the other, linked arm in arm, grinning identical smiles, the right side of their lips slanted up and out. Thisby's parents always appeared together too. They were a beautiful couple, smiling and confident and proud. Anne Bennet had the look of fine china, fragile yet stronger than might be expected. *If Thisby could grow into an Anne Bennet, there might be hope.*

When Thisby was seven or eight, a vague baby appeared — sister "Kewpie," as Thisby captioned her. The baby was always out of focus, but she did look like a Kewpie doll, with a topknot of hair tied with a thin ribbon above a round face.

From then on, the album was strictly Thisby's, and it looked as if she had taken to photography with a vengeance. She took pictures of everything and everyone, though the baby disappeared quickly from the photoplay. If Rob hadn't talked about Quincey in the present tense, Katharine might have thought she had died in infancy.

Sometimes the photos had captions, sometimes not. Katharine found out that Thisby had a dog named Snout and a best friend named Maxie Glenn. Her neighborhood cronies were named Curt and Steve and Laurie and Falfa — the most interesting of their photos, a lineup against a mural of the American flag almost obscured by gangland graffiti. There were pictures of cousins and aunts and uncles and grandparents and various boyfriends she captioned "Jack," "Ryan," and "Jake."

Rob was often a subject by himself, hamming it up with odd postures or silly faces. Sometimes the captions underneath read "The Merry Wanderer" or "Goodfellow" or what looked like a P with a great flourish underneath. But the pictures of Rob slowly decreased. By the time he looked to be in high school, there were hardly any at all, and it appeared as if Thisby had gone out of her way to distort the ones she did take of him. Sometimes he looked to have a tree sprouting from his head, or a shadow like a cancerous growth crawled up his face. Sometimes he looked like a mannequin. One photograph she had entitled "The Freshman," and he had shadows like thick horn-rimmed glasses around his eyes. He looked like some sort of diddlebockian nerd, and Katharine couldn't tell if the effect had been intentional.

People were replaced by buildings in the last album. The photographs were even more distorted by strange lighting and odd angles. Katharine realized the photos in the living room had been taken by Thisby, and these were their precursors. They were black-and-white, but Katharine had a sense that color wouldn't have mattered; everything was made up of grays: dirty, smoggy skies, grimy concrete and stone buildings, rubbled streets. It took Katharine a while to realize, however, that there were people in the photographs, but they could be mistaken for a part of the landscape, the architecture. They were slouched against the walls of buildings like rumpled gargoyles or stood stock-still like extra support for the columns. One photograph, taken at a slant, was of a low billboard with one side sagging to the ground. The advertisement was for a housing community called Pacific Heights, and in the corner a palm tree waved in the breeze over the swimming complex. Only it wasn't a palm tree but a wafer-thin black man who stood leaning against the billboard, his dreadlocks sticking out in a frond of spikes.

She was reminded of a children's perception game she used to like to play — Hidden Pictures. The goal was to find the incongruous items hidden in a larger landscape. Find the barnyard animals drawn into a city street. Find the kitchen appliances in a forest.

Find the vagrant.

It was as if humanity were hidden, masquerading as the inanimate, and unless viewers wanted to take the time and effort to find it, they didn't have to.

And I don't.

Act 1, Scene 5 ✍

I am a feather for each wind that blows.

— LEONTES, *The Winter's Tale*, 2.3.154

By the time Katharine woke up Saturday morning, the flame that had burned since Tuesday had consumed the insides of this body. The fury had turned her entrails to ash, and they swirled away in the hot summer breeze. Now there was nothing — no emotion, no feeling — and she felt as calm and logical as a mentat. She could fill this body, this husk, with any emotions or feelings she so chose. *I can be forgiving. I can be vindictive. I can be . . . Oh, the hell with this . . . I need to know what I'm going to do. I need a Plan. I need a goal. A mission.*

I need money and I need to know where I stand. With my family. With my husband. Was she going to fight for her husband? Could she even win him back, if she wanted to? She did have some rights, some claim to his affections. But whether she could wrest him from this Diana would have to be decided by trial. Did she want to do that? *Yes. Yes.* What else was there for her to do? *He is the only man I have ever known. He is the only man I have ever loved, who ever loved me . . . I don't know anyone else but him. I don't know anything else but him.*

She remembered how Philip looked the first time he held Ben in his arms, how amazingly comfortable and confident he looked, already rocking from side to side, a motion, even seventeen years later, he duplicated if he held anything in his arms for long. Philip had looked down at Ben, then over to her, and there was such incredible awe in his face. "We created this," they said to each other virtually simultaneously, which made them laugh, though Katharine's lower half protested such use. Katharine had loved Philip so then. It was a moment in her life she had framed and reverently centered on the mantelpiece of her mind.

That's what she wanted back.

Katharine could feel the fury seeping back into her, but it had a direction. *To go back home.* She would be the lioness fighting for her family. She would be out for blood. She would tear the interloper limb from limb. What else was there for her to do? She needed to arm herself, though, with information and money. She would infiltrate Thisby's family, find out how to finance herself back into the world, and find out what that world had become. *And go back home.*

What else was there for her to do?

She worried about what to wear for her introduction into Thisby's family. Out of habit she had looked for a dress and stockings, namely Hanes Alive to help alleviate the varicose veins that had plagued her as a result of her two pregnancies. But this body had no varicose veins, as Katharine had discovered while shaving in the shower, one heel propped up on the soapdish. These legs were not webbed with the purple lumps she had hated so much that she wore midcalf styles and pants — never shorts or miniskirts. She had run her hands up the inside of Thisby's smooth calves, feeling an almost absurd sense of joy. *To be rid of those . . . It's almost worth it.*

She had to root through the dresser to find a decent bra — not that Thisby really needed one. Her breasts barely stuck out from beyond her rib cage. Perhaps with a bit more flesh, they would be more prominent. In Katharine's teenage days, her peers didn't wear bras regardless of their breast mass, but Katharine had taken to heart the articles she read in the more conservative fashion magazines. If she could not pass the pencil test — if her breast sagged low enough to hold a pencil between it and her rib cage — she must wear a bra. Almost right after puberty she could put practically a whole box of pencils under her breasts, and they would be held fast. *Okay, an exaggeration.* She had tried to go without a bra a couple of times, but it had always felt so uncomfortable that it wasn't worth it. Her husband never seemed to mind her less-than-upright boobs, but she often eyed with envy the actresses on the screen. Even as large as they were, their uplifted breasts would have passed the pencil test. *What kind of breasts does that Diana have?*

Well, now she had breasts that could pass the pencil test — *they could pass a toothpick test; be careful what you wish for, you just might get it* — but it still felt uncomfortable to Katharine to go braless. She found one that looked like a training bra and put it on. The feel of the straps, the closure hooks, felt *right.*

She couldn't bring herself to dress as she imagined Thisby would, yet she couldn't make herself dress as Katharine would have. That was for a body that . . . *sleeps with the fishes.* She finally settled on an outfit her daughter would have liked: jeans, a white T-shirt, an oversized sport coat with contrasting turned-up sleeves, and white socks and penny loafers she found in the back of the closet. She looked at TB's reflection in the full-length mirror hung on the inside of the closet door and felt she was looking at a catalog ad. *Studied casualness,* but it suddenly seemed to fit the current symbiosis between this body and her mind.

The doorbell rang at twenty minutes to one. The airy sensation she had felt all morning suddenly solidified, and she crashed jarringly to the ground. She looked through the aperture in the front door, and the fish-eye lens revealed a young man, tight-jawed and rigid, half turned back toward the elevator. This was another version of the brother in Thisby's photographs.

This is it. This is not a screen test. This is real life.

She opened the door, and Rob turned around. He had grown into a handsome young man, though he still retained that stiff, controlled look that was evident in the last of Thisby's pictures. His blondish hair was thick and slightly curly. It was brushed back off his forehead and looked as though it often had ideas of its own, no matter what the cut or the volume of hair mousse. He was taller by half a head than TB and was dressed somewhat similarly to herself: jeans, a maroon T-shirt, and worn deck shoes over bare feet. *At least, I'm close.*

"So you didn't skip," he said, and walked into the apartment. He looked around, and there was thinly veiled surprise on his face. "I figured I'd better catch you before you did." He turned toward her and raked her up and down. "Don't you ever eat?"

Katharine opened her mouth to speak but then realized there was no answer he wanted to hear.

"Well, at least you don't look like one of the brides of Dracula like usual."

His sanctimonious tone bit hard. He had no right to speak to her like that, or to Thisby for that matter.

"You don't have to be so rude," Katharine demanded before she could check herself.

He turned and stared coldly at her. "What do you mean? I'm the very pink of courtesy." He turned once more as if to check out the apartment. "Come, recreant, come thou child. I'm parked illegally."

She grabbed Thisby's purse and followed him out.

His car was electric blue and looked as though it could ride the slipstream easily. *Marion would love it.* When she felt the band around her heart start to squeeze, she shook herself. *Not now.*

"Do you want the top down?" he asked.

"No." They had to talk. She didn't want to postpone it. She didn't want to get cold feet. She needed to know now whether she was going to be able to pull this off. *How much do these people really know about Thisby? Will they see me as the impostor that I am? Probably not, considering what I've seen . . . How much do I know about my own children? Would I know them? . . . Of course I would. A mother can sense these things. She knows. . . . Then perhaps Anne Bennet will be my ultimate challenge.*

"So, Rob," she began but stopped when she saw his face freeze up. *Oh, wonderful. This is not a great way to start.*

"Listen, Flute"— he said it as if it were an obscenity — "I didn't agree to drive you to Mom and Dad's so we could kill each other on the way. I am not my father, no matter how you see it."

"I am not my father." Geezus, does that mean more than the obvious? Father . . . Father . . . Robert Bennet. Ohhh. Robert. Rob. I'm not supposed to call him Rob.

"Well, what should I call you?" It was out of her mouth before she could stop it.

He glared over at her. "You know, you can be such a bitch," and he fell into a rigid silence.

Well, so much for Attempt Number One, but at least he hasn't called the men in the white coats. Thisby-as-bitch is obviously within character.

They turned left onto Hillcrest Road from Santa Monica Boulevard. The street was lined with grand houses in a hodge-podge of architectural styles, and palm trees flanked the side-walks like security guards.

The houses on Hillcrest Heights were set farther back from the street, hidden behind tall trees and scrub. They turned into a gravel driveway, drove around tall boxwood hedges, and stopped under an attached overhang. Honeysuckle twined in and out of the latticework, its sweet yet heavy fragrance spilling into the warm air. Katharine walked to the front of the house and stared up at its facade. It was two stories tall with a steeply pitched roofline. The lower level was brick, and the top story had cream-colored plastered walls with dark crisscrossing half-timbers. Small diamond-shaped panes in the long, narrow windows glittered in the afternoon sunlight. The flower beds bordering the house were filled with pansies, violets, daisies, primroses, and cowslips.

I would have loved to have been able to plant a flower garden like this at home.

She followed Rob through a side door into a kitchen filled with soft pale light. Honey-colored cabinets lined the walls, contrasting with the gray slate flooring and the gray-blue walls. There was a freestanding island sporting a double sink and a large cutting board. Copper pots hung overhead from a dropped-lighting fixture surrounded by batten. A cook's kitchen. The counters were tiled with large apricot-colored squares, and everywhere there were flowers and herbs in hanging baskets and in pots on shelves. Katharine could identify parsley, rosemary, and thyme amid the profusion.

Anne Bennet was leaning against a counter. She wasn't as tall or as thin — well, who would be — as Thisby, but she was an attractive woman, though older than Katharine by six or seven years. Her hair was salt-and-pepper — Katharine's would never have grayed this elegantly — and pulled back in a short ponytail that accentuated her green eyes. Her slightly crooked nose was dotted with freckles. She had an air of genuine casualness — something that always seemed to turn into sloppiness in Katharine — and Katharine was envious and surprised. She had expected, well, someone more affected, more staged.

A fire lit up in Anne Bennet's eyes when she saw Thisby, and a smile, shy and hesitant, appeared on her face. She put down her coffee mug on the sideboard and approached.

"Welcome ever smiles," she said, and looked liked she didn't know what to do with her hands.

As Anne came closer, Katharine almost reeled with the hunger radiating from her — the wanting, the longing to touch Thisby, yet the fear she would send her daughter flying away like an autistic child. Katharine recognized the look with a sickening feeling in her heart. Emotions she thought she had burned away, but had merely banked, sprang from the ashes like mythical phoenixes, and with their talons tore down her barriers as if they were mere celluloid. *Haven't I seen that very same face looking back at me in the mirror when my children pulled away from me, jerked away from me, ran screaming away from me?* Katharine stepped forward and embraced Thisby's mother.

Anne stiffened in surprise and pulled back first. "You look . . . nice." Her eyes strafed over Thisby's hair, and Katharine watched her bite back a comment. Katharine was awed by her control.

But if everyone is going to be nervous about what they say around Thisby, then maybe they won't pay attention to what I say. . . . This may not be a bad thing.

Anne turned to her son and, with a hand on his upper arm, kissed him on the cheek. "Thanks, Puck."

He made a noncommittal sound in his throat.

Puck? His name is Puck? She looked at him closely. *What kind of name is that?*

"So how are you?" Thisby's mother asked brightly, turning to Katharine.

I . . . I . . . "I'm okay."

"Good. I hope so. I mean, of course you are." Her face flushed, and she hurried on, recklessly, nervously, without hearing what she was saying. "Puck said you said you were better. I'm sure you are."

Katharine opened her mouth, but no sound came out.

Rob's — no, *Puck's* — face hardened. He snorted and left the room. The women continued to look at the door long after he left.

"Of course, we're all still worried about you. Puck especially."

Yeah, I bet he is.

"So how've you been? Have you eaten?" Katharine could see that Anne Bennet was beginning to crack, the dam threatening to burst. "You know," she continued, "maybe you'd like to visit that treatment center we talked about before. I mean, maybe they could help you fill in the blanks. Puck tells us you've forgotten some things."

Katharine's own panic began to rise and drew near to spilling over. *Oh, Jesus. Oh, Jesus. Oh, Jesus. Treatment center. Discovery. Mental hospital. The funny farm.*

"No . . . Mom." The word was stiff in her mouth. Her parents had died two years apart, her father only last year. *I guess it's been two years now.* Both had slowly wasted away while Katharine frantically tried to make their decline more comfortable. To call this woman "Mom" seemed as if she were defaming her own mother's memory. *But it has to be done. To get back, it has to be done.* "I'm okay. Really. It's just temporary. I'm sure. I'll remember after a while."

Anne was sizing up that answer critically when the phone rang, and she reluctantly turned to answer it. "Well, for only a moment, Edwina. I have family here," she said in a professional voice. "Yes, for that moment, you may have all of me." She turned toward the kitchen sink. "Yes, I understand that, but I also told you that they were not hardy and had to be treated delicately. . . ."

Katharine looked around and quickly went through the door that Puck had used. It led into a large, overstated dining room. The table, one that could easily seat eight without leaves, was stained the same shade as the dark paneling, and at its center was a magnificent arrangement of blood red roses in a crystal vase. This room was more what Katharine had expected. It was beautiful, elegant, and coordinated. She had always thought she would like to live in a house that looked like this — perfect down to the last detail — but she thought, *You don't live in a house that looks like this, you show a house that looks like this.*

Around the corner, out of sight, Katharine heard a female voice. "Well, hello, every mother's son. Are we all here to rehearse our parts?" The voice made Katharine's skin ripple. It was a voice of cultured sarcasm and practiced indifference.

"Shut up, Quince" Katharine heard Puck respond in tired anger.

"Did she really come?" Katharine thought for a moment that this was another person speaking but then realized it was the same voice, stripped of the precious tones.

"In the kitchen," Puck said.

There was the sound of feet, and a slight figure almost bowled Katharine over. The figure pulled up, and Katharine watched a mask drop over the young face that was filled with anticipation and excitement.

The girl stepped back and called loudly to the invisible Puck, "Comb down her hair! Look, look! It stands upright," and then, after squinting exaggeratedly, called again, "No, it's okay. It's only Thisby of the odious flowers." She paused at what sounded like the front door slamming and then spoke directly to Katharine. "I never figured you'd agree to come for something like this."

Jesus. She's Marion's age. Fourteen. Fifteen. She was dressed in faded jeans that threatened to slip off her hips and a plain white T-shirt. Her hair, flat black at the roots and bleached stark white at the ends, lay on her head in spiked clumps like a wilted sea anemone. Her makeup was severe, the mascara dark around the eyes and her lips were raisin-colored. She wore silver hoop earrings, to which she had attached additional pieces, like a charm bracelet, up the entire curve of both ears. A nose ring skewered her lower septum and was worn, perhaps, to camouflage the stretched upper lip and the slight but telltale scar of a cleft lip. *She must have had a good surgeon —* unlike Katharine's older cousin Rachel, whose cleft lip remained visible despite numerous cosmetic surgeries. *The young girl's nose still had the look of something not quite finished, though.*

"Why shouldn't I come?" Katharine asked, trying to get on the offensive.

"Jesters do oft prove prophets. Why should you come? Empty pocket?"

"I think so," Katharine agreed.

The girl grinned maliciously. "I knew it had to be something like that." She stopped a moment and looked at Katharine intently. "You look different, you know. I mean, not just the clothes, though if the soul of a man is his clothes, you're in deep shit. You look like you've been sick."

"Dead sick," Katharine said, and suddenly realized how tired she was. *I can't will this body any longer. What a charade.*

"He that dies pays all debts."

What am I missing here? Why is she talking like some costume drama?

Thisby's mother came into the dining room. "That woman. I swear. Oh, Quincey, you're home. Good." The girl gave her mother a vicious look, and Anne sighed. "I'm sorry. I forgot. *Quince.* It will take me a while to change over completely."

"It's not as if it isn't my real name or anything."

"I know, Quince. I'm sorry. I'll try harder."

Not Quincey? Quince . . . As in the fruit?

Anne turned to Katharine. "Your father's down at the studio, but he'll be home shortly. He'll be so pleased to see you."

Katharine watched Quince roll her eyes.

"So come on back into the kitchen. We'll talk there."

"Things are often spoke and seldom meant," Quince quipped.

Anne ignored her, and they returned to the kitchen. This was a talking kitchen; Katharine could almost see Anne leaning against the counters, laughing, Quince sitting on them Indian-style like Marion preferred, Puck up on one of the tall stools. *Who would want to talk anyplace else?* Katharine sat down at the breakfast table and worried about how much talking she was going to be required to do.

"Quince, why don't you get something to drink for your sister?"

"A soda would be great," Katharine told her.

Quince eyed her narrowly but then handed her one from the refrigerator. She then sat down at the table. Her mother obviously wished her gone but realized she wasn't leaving and decided it would be too draining to try to oust her. It had been very similar with Marion, though Marion was so quiet, so unobtrusive, it was hard to remember she was even there. Consequently, she had heard a great deal more than she should have. Katharine and Philip spoke about Ben in front of her, and Katharine never knew how much Marion passed on. Ben and Marion were growing closer as Ben was severing as many ties, real and imaginary, between his parents and himself as he could find or manufacture. As children, Marion and Ben had fought like normal siblings, assuming the other had meant the worst in whatever was said, but now they hardly ever argued. Often she'd pass by Marion's room, and she would be at her desk doing homework while Ben would be lying on the bed, daydreaming. At the beginning, Katharine had suggested that Ben go back to his own room and do his homework, or bring it in and do it in Marion's. For her troubles, they shut the door on her.

"Shooting anything new?"

Katharine finally heard Thisby's mother through her reverie, and it took her a few moments to figure out she meant shooting pictures. "No, I'm not. Haven't for a while."

"Well, I'm sure your father's offer is still good. We'd love to have an exhibit."

"I'd take the money and run," Quince said.

Anne ignored her. "Well, you think about it," she said, and seemed to gather her courage. "So, what do you think about school in the fall? Ready to go back?"

Katharine struggled to think how to answer. "I don't know," she stalled. "I'd like to get healthy first." *Then money.*

Quince muttered, but not too quietly to avoid notice, "Assume a virtue, if you have it not." This finally elicited a stern look from Anne, though she herself had been almost squinting at Katharine, as if that would allow her to see her daughter better and truer. Quince held up her hands in acquiescence.

Quince is aptly named. Like the fruit, inedible until cooked.

Through the kitchen window, Katharine saw a man exit a detached building and head toward the house. As he got closer, Katharine knew this was Robert Bennet — *patriarch of the Bonkers Bennet clan.*

He walked into the kitchen, searching for one face. When he saw Thisby's, he beamed. Katharine could see Quince stiffen as she noticed it too. It seemed to Katharine that Quince had even watched and waited for it, as if it would confirm yet again everything she had ever felt. *Oh dear.*

Katharine felt herself blush. *He's a good-looking man, isn't he? Anne said he was at the studio. Is he an actor?* A few years older than Philip, Robert Bennet had the look of one who could wear white while gardening and never get dirty. His silvery blond hair, although artfully cut, was beginning to thin. He wasn't as tall as his son and was slighter, though he obviously stuck to some sort of exercise regimen. *All of them look like they frequent the gym on a daily basis. Well, except, of course, for Thisby and Quince. They're a couple of scarecrows.* He was tanned, and his blue irises were circled in black like some sort of ocular eyeliner, which made them stand out like separate entities from the rest of his face. His smile was hypnotic, and Katharine felt almost forced to respond in kind.

She didn't quite know what to do now. Her own father, the quintessential quiet man, had never been this young, this vital, with this much presence. She stood up clumsily, but Robert Bennet felt no awkwardness. He closed the space between them and hugged her unreservedly. And Katharine found that it felt good. It felt good to have strong arms around her.

"It's so good to see you, Thiz. You look marv'lous. Mar-ve-los," he concluded in an exaggerated Latin accent.

Death becomes her? Ha, ha.

Quince was standing behind her father, sticking her finger down her throat in pantomime.

"It's nice to be here . . . Dad." Katharine pulled away self-consciously.

Robert Bennet held his daughter's body at the shoulders. "You look good. You really look good. The hair? Well," he gestured noncommittally and turned to his wife. "Doesn't she look good?" His wife agreed with a smile, but the truth was still in her eyes.

Katharine realized that to him, TB probably did look good. The fact that he wasn't seeing her waxen and stiff in a coffin — anything other than that — was "looking good." Katharine felt sorry for him.

Robert turned to his wife and asked in an almost disapproving tone, "Is Puck around?"

Katharine was mad at him then. *You just don't get it, do you? Your daughter's dead and this is the extent of your greeting? I bet you didn't even know how bad things had gotten with Thisby.* They must have known something was wrong; at least, Anne should have. But that didn't seem fair either. Thisby had obviously left home some years ago, and her parents didn't see much of her. How could they know the extent of it? Thisby wasn't going to tell them. Katharine could tell Puck knew more, but she didn't think he had told his parents everything he knew or thought he knew.

"I need to talk to him. Unfortunately, right now," Robert said.

Quince grinned, as if in anticipation. "The good fellow went thataway." She pointed out the window toward the front of the house.

Robert started out of the kitchen but then turned back. "I'll meet you two on the court in forty-five minutes. Quincey, you and Puck against me and Thiz."

Tennis? Does he mean tennis? She used to play some women's doubles when the kids were babies and she had worked only part-time. She hadn't played for years, unless she could call hitting the ball with Marion last fall when she was getting ready to try out for the freshman team "playing." "I don't . . . I don't . . . ," she started to protest.

Anne overrode her, "I think I saw some clothes you left in your room that would work. I think you can find everything you need."

Everything I need. But I need a lot. More than one room could possibly offer.

Katharine found the monument that was Thisby's room. It was dark, shuttered up against the summer heat, and Katharine ran her hand up the inside wall, flipping the switch. The light gave the room a staged look — a teenager's room as envisioned by a mother. The clutter, the knickknacks, the whatnot, were all put away, neatly and symmetrically, the purple flowered wallpaper matching the quilt on the white canopied bed and the cushions of the window seat. A place for everything and everything in its place. Katharine knew the signs.

She stepped hesitantly to the windows, looking back toward the door, afraid that a cadaverous-looking housekeeper would suddenly appear and hiss, "It's a lovely room, isn't it? The loveliest room you have ever seen. Can't you feel her in here? Can't you? It's you who ought to be dead, not Thisby. Why don't you end it all and have done with it? Go on. Go on. Don't be afraid."

Her hand was on the window latch. Through the slats, she had an unobstructed view to the brick patio below her. *Go on. Go on. Don't be afraid.*

She grabbed the shutter knobs and threw the blinds open, letting the sunlight in to dispel the phantoms.

Thisby's room was lined with photographs, mostly her own, mostly unframed — just tacked up. Katharine recognized faces she had seen in the photo albums in TB's apartment: the girlfriend Maxie, the dog Snout, the boyfriends. There was a photograph of her parents taken many years ago; the caption read "UCLA Drama Department. *A Midsummer Night's Dream*, Spring 1962." Robert was crouched over a sleeping Anne. He was holding a sprig of what looked like heather.

On the bookshelves were a few stuffed animals: Gizmo the Gremlin, Chewbacca, E.T., but there were mostly books, and most of them by Shakespeare.

She reads?

There was a massive *Shakespeare: The Complete Works* in one volume, a leatherbound set of the tragedies, the comedies, and the histories, *The Quotable Shakespeare*, *Shakespeare's Insults*, *Acting Shakespeare*, the Arden edition of *A Midsummer Night's Dream*, the Twayne's *New Critical Introduction to A Midsummer Night's Dream*, the Cambridge edition of *A Midsummer Night's Dream*, and the Arbuthnot children's edition of *A Midsummer Night's Dream*. This one she pulled off the shelf, and it fell open to the Cast of Characters. Handwritten at the side was "To my Thisby Flute, May our love for this play be imparted to you as well. Love, Dad (the first Puck)."

Oh, God, I get it now. Puck, Thisby, and Quince. We've all been named after Shakespeare characters in A Midsummer Night's Dream. *No wonder Quince talks like she's in a costume drama.* Katharine pulled out her list of names from her back pocket. Snout the dog had his namesake in the play too. *Poor animal. Even he couldn't escape.*

She found a small carry-on bag and packed the *Complete Works*, which weighed a ton, then included a book called *The Quotable Shakespeare*, which arranged his most memorable lines by topic. *Maybe I can match Quince quote for quote.* She flipped a few pages. "Death once dead, there's no more dying then." Sonnet 146. *Shakespeare got it wrong, though, didn't he?*

She decided to continue collecting, so she ransacked the

desk set and found a diary, the word MEMOIRS printed in gold letters on the cover. The little brass catch was locked, but she easily forced it open with a pair of scissors. She glanced at it quickly and threw it into the bag.

She was just starting through the dresser when there was a pull on the door. A moment later she heard, "Let me in. Let me in. Or I'll huff and I'll puff and I'll blow your house down."

At least she quotes something besides Shakespeare.

Katharine unlocked the door, and Quince fell into the room. She glanced around, saw the bag, and peeked into it. "O you thief. You canker blossom." She paused. "The stuff to hock is in the living room."

"I'm heading there next."

Quince flopped onto the bed. She was wearing long shorts, a ragged T-shirt, and expensive-looking tennis shoes. "You're not ready for the great match."

"I got sidetracked."

"So I see." Quince looked around the room at the pictures on the wall. She got up and studied one closely. "I miss Snout," and she turned sideways so Katharine could see that she had been looking at a picture of the shaggy dog Katharine had seen in Thisby's photo book.

"I never told you this, but after Snout bit you and Dad sent him away, I was furious at both of you. You probably don't believe that I remember it, but I do."

Katharine nodded noncommittally and said nothing. This seemed to irritate Quince.

"I do remember. I loved Snout. He was my best friend. He'd come into my room when I'd get home from the hospital and sit by my bed. I remember. When I was around seven or eight, I rode my bike up Coldwater and tried to find him. I spent the whole weekend. I called and whistled, but I never found him. And you don't even live here anymore, and they still won't let me have a dog."

Katharine didn't know what else to do but keep nodding her head in a circular motion, neither definitely up and down nor side to side.

Quince turned away and after a bit sat down on the end of the bed again. "So, when can I come live with you?"

Oh, God. "Quince, I've been pretty sick." *That old excuse again?*

Quince immediately looked hurt and pissed off. "So, what's that got to do with it?"

A voice rose up the staircase. "Come on, girls. Let's go."

Quince slowly rose and tugged at the ends of her shorts. "Let the games begin."

"Tell him I'll be down . . . anon." Katharine sounded ridiculous to herself, but Quince didn't hesitate in response. "Anon."

It was the only Shakespeare Katharine knew. She remembered it from Franco Zeffirelli's film *Romeo and Juliet* — Juliet harking to her maid, "Anon, nurse," while kissing Romeo one more time. She obviously was going to need to know more than that to survive in this family.

Katharine followed the sound of someone hitting a tennis ball against a backboard. Beyond a pool and a sea of grass was only — *only?* — one court. Puck was volleying sharply against the forest green plywood backboard. He looked very good.

Maybe this isn't such a terrific idea.

Quince was pulling a racket from a cabinet that was hooked onto the outside of the fence; she then bounded onto the court to Puck's side. Watching Quince bounce about caused tears to pool behind Katharine's lower eyelids. How like Marion Quince revealed herself to be. Half child, half young woman. And able to somersault from one extreme to the other.

Robert Bennet took the other side and immediately started hitting the ball to Puck and Quince. Katharine was encouraged; Quince was not very good, and hopefully, Thisby wouldn't be expected to be much better. She opened the cabinet, and there were three rackets to choose from. She furtively tried the grips of all three — they all felt wrong — and took the last one in default. She walked onto the court and at the side bench carefully retied the tennis shoes she had found in Thisby's closet. Quince continued to be silly.

"Concentrate, Quincey," her father said rather irritably.

I see that he can get away with calling Quince "Quincey." What is it about fathers that they can do what mothers can't?

Quince hit a ball into the net and raced to pick it up. "My legs can keep no pace with my desires."

Her father responded seriously, "Question your desires, know of your youth, examine well your blood."

Quince stuck her tongue out at him, which he did not or chose not to see.

Puck was silent.

Katharine's apprehension grew. *I can't keep this up. I'll be unmasked.* She waited a moment longer and then forced herself to stand, hitching up the overlarge shorts. She moved into the forehand court, and Thisby's father almost reluctantly moved over to the backhand side. A ball rolled to Katharine's feet. She picked it up, bounced it, and sent it rather feebly over the net, though well within the court. Quince did not hit it back. Did not even try. She and Puck were staring at her. Katharine jerked her head and saw Thisby's father staring too.

Jesus Fucking Christ. What have I done wrong now? I just hit the goddamned ball over the net. What, Thisby never hit a ball over the net before? Her anger crosscut to panic. She searched frantically for clues to their surprise. She felt her brain begin to clot; soon all would be lost. Seconds seemed like hours — their questioning looks, time immemorial. Katharine looked at Thisby's father standing with his racket at his side . . . his left side. Katharine looked down at Thisby's arm, her right hand holding the racket and dangling at her right side. Katharine felt the proverbial lightbulb click on above her head. *Oh, my God, Thisby was left-handed.*

She started to fabricate some godawful story when Robert Bennet said, "Great Scott, Thisby, this is amazing. I never knew you could do anything right-handed. You never showed any signs of being ambidextrous before."

"It just happened," she said lamely.

"I wonder if there is any medical precedent for this." He stopped to consider. "I'll have to ask Bev the next time I see him." He frowned sorrowfully, but it was feigned. "We were the only lefties in the family. Now I'm the only one left." He smiled again. "Pun intended."

So much for strangeness. I suppose the truth that some body snatcher has invaded your dead daughter would be a lot harder to swallow than Thisby's waking up one morning having switched the dominant side of her brain.

"Ready?" Robert Bennet asked, and when the others nodded, he spun his racket. "Thiz, I'll serve," which was just fine with Katharine.

The match was a disaster. Quince refused to be serious. Her father refused to lighten up. Puck was silent, mostly playing the ball at his father. Katharine was too shook up to concentrate on the game. She was also exhausted. To move became agony, and she could feel slick sweat packing her face like a beauty aid.

She and Puck were facing each other across the net. He glanced at her, then stared. He held up his hand to stop Quince from serving. "Thiz, are you all right?"

The sound of genuine concern surprised her into the truth. "No," she croaked and lowered her racket. His solicitude seemed to tilt the court, and she slid off the edge.

They got her to one of the chairs by the pool, and Puck knelt in front of her.

"Her body's a passable carcass," Katharine heard Quince say.

Puck draped a wet towel over the back of her neck.

"Thisby never could take the heat," Robert Bennet declared.

Katharine saw Puck's jaw twitch.

Robert really doesn't want to get it, does he? This irritated her. She wanted to slap him out of his preferred blindness. *Your daughter needed help, needed some control exerted over her, and you didn't do it. Did you?* "I think it's more the years of abuse," she said louder than she had intended.

Puck shot her a look of surprise. Thisby's father ignored the remark and looked behind him.

Anne Bennet was coming around the hedge in a swim-wrap, carrying a towel. She took in the scene and hurried over. "What happened? Is she all right?"

"I'm fine," Katharine answered. "I just overdid it. I'll be all right in a second." She gently pushed Puck's hands away. "Thanks. I'm okay now," she told him.

He moved back. The other members of the family hovered around her until Anne waved them away and pulled up a chair beside Katharine. Soon Quince was dunking Puck in the deep end, and Robert Bennet had stretched out with eyes closed in a lounge chair.

"They like each other," Katharine said wistfully to Thisby's mother, indicating Puck and his sister. A montage of images of Ben and Marion flicked on and off in her brain.

"Puck can always get Quince worked up. You two used to be like that," Anne Bennet added.

Us two? Thisby and Puck? That was hard to imagine. Katharine could feel only animosity from Puck. It was a tangible dislike that slapped her in the face whenever she came near. Then she remembered the photographs in Thisby's earlier albums and the ones on the wall in the upper hallway. There had been a time when they had been friends, buddies, pals, cohorts. Something happened. Sibling rivalry, certainly. Maybe it was Quince, but Katharine figured Thisby was the instigator. She was the one who pulled away. Maybe Katharine could patch things up.

She got up and stood at the edge of the pool. "Can I join you?" she called.

"Gee, Thiz," Puck said, looking up at her and letting Quince out of a headlock, "my lifeguard badge expired last year. I wouldn't count on me saving you. How 'bout you, Quince?"

"Me? Hercules couldn't save her. She sinks like a navy."

"You gotta deathwish or something, Lady Ophelia?" Puck dunked Quince, and she came up sputtering. "I'm finished, you little squirt," he said. "I've got some things to do." He executed a jacknife under the water and swam to the other side of the pool.

Quince stroked to the other end, reciting as she went, "She

chanted snatches of old tunes till that her garments, heavy with their drink, pulled the poor wretch from her melodious lay to muddy death.''

Katharine watched them enviously; she really had loved to swim. But she somehow knew that Puck and Quince were right — although this body was thin, it was dead weight in water. *It would sink like a navy.* Katharine could remember, though, when she was young, cold mornings at the pool, steam hovering over the water like fog, the soft slap of flip turns and muffled voices, the lane lines bobbing against the wake. Swimming was the only time she ever felt light.

Fuck 'em — and she turned around.

With sudden clarity, she realized that swear words were appearing like teleprompted lines in her mind. She used to swear before she had kids — not a lot, but enough to decide to stop swearing, to even think in swear words, when Ben was born. She always hated to hear children swear, and she felt she should be a good role model. In the last couple of years, she had heard Ben swear like a longshoreman, and she had even heard Marion use expletives, but Katharine had practiced abstinence so long, she hadn't regained her fluency. Now it seemed so easy to swear. *Too easy.*

She moved to a lounge chair on the other side of Anne Bennet and lay down.

"So tell me," Thisby's mother said lightly. "Who's the current beau?"

Katharine always asked questions. Philip had cautioned her never to ask questions she was unprepared to hear the answers to, and she tried to be circumspect, but she often felt in desperate need to ask questions. Even when it felt as though she couldn't stop herself and, therefore, should stop herself, she asked, "Where are you going? Where have you been? Who are you going with? Is your homework done? How are you paying for that? What happened to the last five dollars I gave you? Who's driving? Do I know her? When will you be home?"

Katharine could tell that Anne Bennet really didn't want to know but couldn't help herself either. *I remember that perverse desire to know the worst.* "No one," and Katharine hoped to God that this was true. She didn't know exactly what would happen if or when the current beau — maybe it was the guy who had left all those messages — showed up, but she knew he wouldn't be current for long. Not that she had had any experience at dumping guys. She was dumped once, right before she met her husband. *Ex-husband, I guess I have to say. I am an unmarried woman. We were never legally divorced, but I guess death is the ultimate form of divorce.*

"Thisby. Are you all right?"

Katharine focused back and saw that Anne was leaning across the space between them. "Sure. I'm fine." Anne sat back in her chair.

If only that were true. If only Anne could truly believe it. Katharine knew exactly how glad Anne would be if it were true. She knew how she'd feel if it was true with Ben.

Katharine looked over and saw that Anne Bennet was crying, silently and discreetly, tears slipping off her high cheekbones and sliding down to the corners of her mouth.

Katharine sucked in her cheeks and held the spongy flesh with clenched teeth. *What we parents go through. And our children are clueless. To be fair, we were clueless when we were kids too. And I don't think kids ever really know what parents go through until they have children themselves. Only if you can live long enough as a parent — as a grandparent, really — to see it. Hal Holbrook said in the movie about Mark Twain, "When I was a boy of fourteen, my father was so ignorant I could hardly stand to have the old man around. But when I got to be twenty-one, I was astonished at how much he had learned in seven years." But I didn't get to live long enough for Ben and Marion to find out how much I had learned.*

I think I'd be better off dead. Really dead.

Katharine was dreaming. It was one of her recurring nightmares. She's back in high school, a new class schedule in hand. The backs of her fellow students are disappearing behind slowly closing doors. They know where they belong. She is frantically searching for T-2. She reaches a room numbered "2," but to her horror, it's S-2. Running through the fat air to get to the "T" wing, she sees that the numbers on the classroom doors are up in the hundreds. Time ticking by, and the tardy bell soon to ring. She can feel the second hand clicking over to the next minute. She will be late. She will be reprimanded. She will get detention. She will be noticed.

The tardy bell was ringing in her ears when she jolted herself awake, shaking. Her heart slammed off beat. She could still hear the bell and realized it was the sound of a Piccolo Pete firework, screaming and then dying in the warm air. The pool deck was empty, the sun low on the horizon. She had been asleep for some time.

She tried to shake the shards of the dream loose but then realized why her heart pounded so and why she was trembling. It had been the same old scenario — new schedule, wrong room, tardy bell. But the dreamscape had been different. The classroom she had been searching for had not been at James Marshall High School with its sprawling, barrack-style wings. She had been lost in a two-story building of white stucco and Spanish tile. She had been lost in Thisby's high school.

The dream still clung to Katharine like a sticky cobweb as she started up the steps to the back door. Through the window she could see Anne Bennet working at the center cutting board, the light in the kitchen rosy from the setting sun. Katharine wanted to stand there on the outside and watch forever, but Thisby's mother seemed to sense something and looked out to where Katharine stood. Katharine sighed, opened the door, and stepped into the kitchen.

"Did you have a nice rest?" Anne Bennet paused in midchop.

"Yes, thank you." Katharine felt awkward and formal again, like a first-time houseguest. *Well, aren't I?*

"We decided to just let you sleep. I'm sure you needed it."

"Yes, I'm sure I did. Thank you." Not wanting to stand there and do nothing, Katharine offered to prepare the vegetables. Anne moved to the stove.

As Katharine cut up the carrots, she picked at them. They were quite good, not store-bought but garden-fresh.

"Trying to change your eating habits as well?"

Katharine jumped. She had forgotten she wasn't alone.

"You used to love vegetables when you were a baby," Anne said, reminiscence in her voice. "I could never figure out just what happened. I guess it was trying to get you to work in the garden with me. But you preferred photography with your father. And you were so good at it."

Katharine turned; Anne had stopped stirring and held the spoon poised and dripping over the pot. She looked at Katharine. "I'm sorry."

Katharine was seeing with her own split-screen memory. In one corner was Ben coming home with his hair dyed a shocking chartreuse. She had made such a fuss about it. *Oh great,* she had thought, *now I'll be known as the mother of the boy with green hair.* She had dragged him like a baby to her hairstylist and stayed until the color was stripped and the hair was dyed back to near its natural shade. She had played every trump card she had over him. She didn't think he ever forgave her for that. He turned quiet and sneaky then. *I think he vowed he would get back at me. Well, getting bad grades and taking drugs was certainly a good way.* What was so awful about the hair? It would have grown out. It would have faded out. *Hair is such a transitory thing.* Maybe there would have been another battleground, and the outcome would have been the same. But maybe not.

Philip had tried to tell her that she had overreacted, but by the time he had come home from work, Ben was back in his room, hair back to normal, their relationship badly bruised. She had turned on Philip then. He had been in the catbird seat for so long. The kids had been preferring him. He had even gone to a rock concert with Ben. *Mothers don't go to things like that.* When Philip came back practically deaf, with soft-drink stains all over his shirt and reeking of cigarette and marijuana smoke, she wondered why she resented not being allowed to go, but she did. When Marion's school had called and asked her to chaperone a dance, Marion had almost cried with frustration. Katharine had wanted only to meet her friends, see them dance, see how they interacted. It was decided that Philip would go in her place, and Marion quickly recovered. *What did my children imagine I was capable of doing?*

"I'm sorry too," Katharine said contritely.

Anne paused and then said rather tersely, "Well, if you ever have children yourself, you'll do or say some things you'll be sorry for later too."

Katharine winced. "I didn't mean it that way. I . . ." She wanted to explain but knew it would be impossible. She reached out and lay a hand on Anne's arm.

Anne looked into Katharine's face, and Katharine made herself still — the split screen continuing to run in the corner of her mind — Thisby dead on one side, and on the other, Ben failing school and hiding marijuana in his fish-food containers.

What a pair we make.

Robert Bennet stood up at the head of the table, the dinner dishes having been removed by his wife with help from Puck and hindrance from Quince. Katharine hadn't been hungry and had forced herself to eat, Anne and Robert watching her take every bite. But dinner had been a more pleasant experience than she had expected. Puck had seemed to call a truce. Katharine figured it had something to do with the fact that he had come into the kitchen and had seen his sister's hand on his mother's arm, and the look of tethered hope in his mother's face.

Now the coffee had been poured. Katharine took hers black and strong. No one made the tiniest fuss. *Thank God, at least one thing TB and I have in common.* Robert Bennet seemed to be preparing to make a toast, but there was nothing besides the coffee to toast with. In fact, there had been no wine with dinner. Katharine had wanted some wine badly. *It would have helped. I could have used it.*

Katharine hadn't had to talk a lot through dinner, much to her relief. Robert did most of the talking, and she had been fascinated the whole time. He was a wonderful conversationalist, so articulate, so charming, so funny. She gathered from his talk that he was no longer an actor but one of the elite television producers in Hollywood. He was working on a miniseries project involving a remake of Hitchcock's *Notorious*. Katharine had seen the original not too long ago — *at least, not long before I died* — and they had a lively discussion about the famous crane shot from the staircase to the close-up of the key in Ingrid Bergman's hand and how that was to be duplicated without being mimicked. She could see that Robert Bennet was thoroughly enjoying himself. And so was she.

Katharine could feel that the rest of the family had been bored, and Anne more alarmed than bored. Perhaps Robert was telling stories that he had told time after time, and Katharine was being indiscreet in encouraging him. She realized the more animated she was getting, the quieter and more watchful Anne became — her scrutiny was intense. But Katharine was obtaining incredibly vital information about the family, and she stored it away like a squirrel hoarding nuts.

There was a definite sharpness in his voice when Thisby's father had asked her how the photography was going. Katharine had told him the truth — that nothing was going on and hadn't been for some time. She figured Anne couldn't object to that. It was the truth, or as much of the truth as Katharine could decipher. Robert pressed her, though. He had such great expectations, such high hopes. And now that she was better — *How he assumes the worst is over* — talent should not be squandered so; it would be so disappointing. *He would be so disappointed.* He would, of course, pay for the exhibit, as he had always said he would. This had the sound of an old discussion between them. Robert had to say it, though he didn't really believe she would hear it.

Katharine knew she did not have Thisby's eye, let alone her technical facility. It was the flicks she knew. She and the kids saw a lot of them — Saturday matinees, the early-evening shows, videos when Philip stayed late at the office. Before Ben straight-armed her, the two of them had fright-night video-fests when they were alone together; Marion and Philip didn't like horror films. Some of the movies did scare Katharine so badly that she couldn't sleep, but she felt it was a small price to pay to be able to sit in a room with Ben and share even a movie.

But the love, the pride, was so evident on Robert Bennet's face that Katharine didn't quite have the heart to burst his bubble completely. *Maybe photography's something I can learn.* . . .

Now Robert Bennet was addressing the family, but he had eyes only for his wife. He spoke simply, lyrically, lines that obviously had been memorized but were now a part of him. "It is said" — he looked around, mockingly resigned — "in a play we all know and love so well, that the course of true love never did run smooth."

Quince mock-gagged again.

He spoke now to his wife directly. "But, we are spirits of another sort. On this anniversary of the sealing-day betwixt my love and me, I'll put a girdle around the earth in forty minutes to bring my love her gifts.

> I know a bank where the wild thyme blows,
> Where oxlips and the nodding violet grows,
> Quite over-canopied with luscious woodbine,
> With sweet musk-roses and with eglantine;
> There sleeps Anne sometime of the night,
> Lull'd in these flowers with dances and delight."

He leaned forward over the table, and the candle flames danced up within his pupils. He whispered, "Am I thy lord?"

Anne remained seated, but she sat on the edge of her chair, her forearms stretched out on the table toward him. She was smiling, her eyes joining in on the dance. "Then I must be thy lady."

"Thou art as wise as thou art beautiful."

There was silence. They could have been the only ones in the room.

Quince quipped loudly to Katharine, "She's not well married that lives married long, but she's best married that dies married young."

The screen fragmented to a thousand pieces but, like a jigsaw puzzle, projected only one image.

All is pain. All is repulsion.

I am attracted to Robert Bennet as a man. I am thinking of him as a man. I am taking his love and his pride of his daughter and turning it into something perverse. She stared between them at the vase of red roses. *I am the unloved. No one loved me like that. No one ever loved me like that. No one will ever love me like that. My own husband couldn't even wait a year before he married someone else. I am twice dead.*

Katharine bolted upright, knocking the chair over behind her. She felt as if she were going to be sick, her dinner detaching itself from the lining of her stomach. She ran upstairs, leaving the babble of voices behind her. She made it as far as Thisby's bed and collapsed on it, holding down her threatening stomach. The sounds of sobbing that seemed to belong to someone else filled her ears. Over and over, again and again.

The door to the room was suddenly flung open. Katharine lifted herself up on her arms, and Puck seemed to explode into the room, slamming the door behind him. He was yelling as he came in, "You goddamned, self-centered bitch. I'm almost tempted to — " He focused on his sister's blotched face. "Jesus." He stopped a pace or two from her.

Katharine couldn't stop to say anything. The sobs wracked her body with a godlike hand.

"You weren't playacting." He sat down on the edge of the bed but didn't touch her. "Jesus, Thiz. I haven't seen you cry since you were fifteen."

He waited until Katharine could control some of the sobs. "Remember what you told me?" He didn't wait for her to answer. She couldn't have, anyway. " 'I have good reason for crying, but this heart shall break before I'll cry again.' You misquoted it, of course. Butchered it, actually. God, that drove Dad nuts. You were his little chip off the old block, but you couldn't get a quote right for your life." He shifted his weight on the mattress, and Katharine's sobs softened. "Maybe you have changed. You're crying, at least."

Katharine could feel herself fading, like disappearing ink on paper.

"Sleep. Let sleep, that sometimes shuts up sorrow's eye, steal you a while from thine own company," he commanded softly.

In her receding mind, Katharine thought she heard him add, "Bless thee, Thisby. Bless thee. Thou art translated."

Act 1, Scene 6 🐇

Was I part of this curious dream?

— FRANK PETTINGELL, *Gaslight* (1940)

The moon hung framed in the window seat of Thisby's bedroom like a huge klieg light suspended from the sky. Katharine felt reamed. *Again.* She wondered how many times she would have to go through this process. It was like trying to stay nourished during a vicious bout of the flu, hoping to keep something down — anything — crackers, 7-Up, clear soup.

It's just a matter of finding out what you can stomach.

For a long, melodramatic moment, she mentally swallowed all the pills in the plastic vials back in Thisby's apartment. *I can always finish what Thisby started,* but then she remembered Puck's last line before she fell asleep, "Thisby, thou art translated." The way he had said it made her wonder if, as opposed to having been translated into a more understandable form, he meant that she was somehow different — as in changed. *He would have meant Thisby has changed, of course, but so have I. I am no longer just Katharine.*

So what's the Plan now? What do I want? I know what I don't want. I don't want a Plan. I want to just be for a while. I want to find the right pabulum to stomach.

And if I die again, then how will I find out how this megillah ends?

Despite her aching head, she got up and leaned against

the pillows in the window seat. She looked down on the side yard off the kitchen to the tennis court beyond. The moon struck wicked shadows; it seemed otherworldly. She noticed a hedge that separated the house from the pool area. It had a shape to it. It was a beast. It reared up on hind legs, and its head roared as it cast a giant shadow, long and eager on the grass. Had it been shaped, this hedge, with just this purpose in mind — to be best seen when the moon was full and bright? *I wouldn't put anything past this family.*

There was a small reading light on the wall above her head, and Katharine reached up and turned it on. Its narrow beam highlighted the knees of her accordioned legs — *just where a book should be* — but didn't dispel the secret garden enchantment outside her window.

She leaned over and rummaged through the bag that she had packed, pulling out the *Complete Works.* She ignored the introduction and the background notes and turned to *A Midsummer Night's Dream.*

At once she was transported to the city of Athens and the surrounding forest, where lovers flee and are separated, mismatched, tested, and then put to rights at the end.

Katharine found the ending curiously interesting. Oberon instructs his fairy troops to bless the bridal beds so their children will be born without the despised blots such as moles, harelips, and prodigious marks. She wondered why Quince embraced this play, or Shakespeare at all, for that matter. *Wasn't she despised then?* The one line continued to chant through Katharine's head like a mantra. "Never mole, harelip . . . nor mark prodigious . . . shall upon their children be."

Katharine tried to imagine the Bennets in the various roles. Robert seemed more suited as the suave but rather domineering, self-righteous Duke than the Merry Prankster, Robin Goodfellow, aka Puck. The Duke smirked witty asides to the group of lovers, now newlyweds, as they watched the play *The Most Lamentable Comedy and Cruel Death of Pyramus and Thisby* performed by the workmen. Katharine laughed at one such remark, "Or in the night, imagining some fear, how easy is a bush supposed a bear." She looked down on the hedge again. The moon continued to illuminate the area.

Not a beast, but a bear. How easy is a bush supposed a bear. I'll be damned.

Like father, like son, Puck wasn't right for Robin Goodfellow. It was Quince she thought of when the Merry Prankster dashed about, streaking the eyes of Queen Titania and one of the lovers with the cupid juice. It was Quince she saw with elfin ears, crowing with delight as he gave the pompous workman, Nick Bottom, an ass's head.

She saw Anne not as Thisby, but as Hermia, one of the lovers — the one who was tenacious and resolute.

This whole family is miscast.

As she continued to watch the shadow play below her, she absorbed the tragic love story of Pyramus and Thisby, separated from each other by their families' hate and the wall that was erected between them. Their planned rendezvous is upset by Cruel Fate, and they meet — only to die in each other's arms.

Is it my fate, like Thisby's, to be separated from my love, to be reunited only in death? Only in death? In death?

There was a knock on the door, and a voice commanded through it, "Awake. Awake. The morning has chased away the night."

It took a moment for Katharine to orient herself; she was reclining stiff and sore on the window seat, the morning sun flooding in on her face. Then she called without hesitation through the closed door to Quince, "I'll be there anon."

Downstairs Thisby's mother was quiet and awkward, and Katharine had to remember why. She felt giddy and light. She was filled with lions, fairies, and bears. *Oh, my.*

Thisby's father was aloof, as if he wanted to let her know that he was not pleased.

Jesus, lighten up, you guys. "About last night . . . I'm sorry," she said to both of them. "I seem to have chronic PMS these days. The mood swings are incredible. Schizophrenic, even."

Anne stopped short with a knife in her hand. "You're not pregnant, are you?"

That stopped Katharine short too. The giddiness seemed to drain away like sand in a wide-waisted hourglass. "No, of course not."

Of course not? How would you know? You haven't been in this body long enough to know that.

Well, the way TB looked and lived, she probably didn't even have periods anymore. She can't be pregnant.

Breakfast proceeded. Her denial was taken at face value. *As if I knew for sure.*

The food smelled only okay to her stomach, but she knew it wasn't the disruption of pregnancy that made it that way. *She can't be pregnant. I can't be pregnant. This is not morning sickness.* During the entire first trimester of her two pregnancies, it had been a continual chore to balance the food going into her body and the food being unceremoniously purged from it. She remembered intimately the symptoms of morning sickness, and this wasn't it. *Or at least I don't think so.*

She didn't know anything for sure anymore. When she thought she had gotten a handle on things, it seemed only to mean she was kidding herself. The play was going on around her regardless of whether she knew her lines or not, and the outcome, though obscure, was already scripted.

Play out the play.

Puck came in and offered a general good morning. He looked tense. He sat down across from Katharine and awkwardly caught her eye. She smiled and tried to make it appear natural. That seemed to surprise him, but he relaxed noticeably.

Her smile had been sincere. She had gone to sleep the night before liking him. *He isn't such a bad guy.*

"So when are you two heading back?" Robert Bennet asked them.

Soon they were all outside, jumbled under the honeysuckle canopy. The sweet smell of the flowers pressed down upon Katharine. She hugged Thisby's father with much more ease than yesterday. *That was a short infatuation, I dare say.* She felt close to him, though. *A good old family friend.*

"Come back soon, Honeybee," he said as he released her. "I've missed you."

"I will. I promise." And it felt like truth. "Thanks, Anne." Katharine turned to Thisby's mother.

"God's mercy, maiden," Robert scolded from behind her, "Does it curd thy blood to say that she is thy mother?"

Katharine felt herself redden, and she fishmouthed. "I — "

"Oh, don't worry about it." Anne waved it aside. "I don't care what you call me. Just call me." She hugged Katharine and, as she was releasing her, added softly, "Think about the treatment center, won't you? Or, at least, seeing Dr. Mantle again. I'm worried about you."

Katharine looked around for an escape. "Where's Quince?"

She was nowhere to be seen, so Katharine excused herself quickly and went back into the kitchen. Quince was sitting on a high stool, her elbows on the counter, her head cradled in cupped palms. She looked up but said nothing.

"I wanted to say good-bye," Katharine said, lamely.

"Good-bye."

"So what's on tap?"

"What's on tap?" The left side of her upper lip rose in an exaggerated sneer. "Well, like the pelican, I'm all tapped out."

"Don't you have a job for the summer?"

"What would I want with a stupid job? Baby-sitting a bunch of spoiled brats? Being a lifeguard aide? I can't be a lifeguard cuz I'm not sixteen. Mowing lawns? Nobody wants someone who looks like me hanging around outside their house. Maybe if I was a Jap or a Spic or something, they wouldn't mind."

"Come on, Quince," Katharine said gently, as she realized that Quince was trying to impress her — impress Thisby — with her talk.

"What? Okay, okay. Asian or Latina. Shit, you sound like Mom."

Katharine stretched her mouth in an unspoken response.

"Maybe. . . ," Quince said slowly, not quite looking at Katharine, "Maybe I could find a job in Westwood, and then maybe I could stay with you."

Katharine stood very still, not even moving her eyes. *How am I going to get myself out of this one?*

Bluff.

"Okay. Will you let me look around first?"

Quince's face lightened, but not too much.

"Does it have to be for money?" Katharine suddenly thought to ask. *What are you doing? I said, Bluff — don't get serious on me.*

"A job without money? What kind of job is that?"

"Do you need money?" *Like I need money?*

Quince started to respond, but then shifted. "I guess not. Dad gives me a pretty good allowance. It's not as much as my friends get, though."

Katharine smiled. She had heard this complaint before from both her kids.

"But I don't want some stupid job taking care of kids or putting stuff on shelves or anything. And I won't change my hair. And I won't wear a uniform, like those pie places."

"Hey, you'd look pretty in pink. Okay. Okay. Pretty tough requirements, but I'll try."

"You'll call me?"

"I'll call you. I promise."

Hard promises.

No, it's okay. I can keep them and still do what I have to do.

Yeah, right.

Katharine hurried back outside and climbed into Puck's car before Anne or Robert could say anything else to her. She waved to Thisby's parents, and was off.

Act 2, Scene 1 🐀

I do perceive here a divided duty.

— DESDEMONA, *Othello*, 1.3.180

She was home alone.

She stood in the apartment at a loss for what to do. On the way home, she had asked Goodfellow to come over for dinner Thursday night. He was suspicious, but he agreed.

Katharine wasn't quite sure when she had started to think of Puck as Goodfellow. It happened before she even realized it. She guessed it was sometime after she had read the play, when she couldn't reconcile the character Puck with the brother Puck. For some reason, then, it was easier to think of him as Goodfellow.

There was nothing to clean up in the apartment. No one had been there to mess it up. She had never lived on her own before. She had lived with her parents and commuted to the nearby college. She was married after her sophomore year, and traded two parents for one husband. She graduated from college six months' pregnant. *A loner who's never lived alone.*

The tears that lately seemed always to be pressing against her ducts bubbled up and over. She used to savor the silence in her house when she was lucky enough to have it. But standing there in the silent emptiness, she realized that she had savored it because there had been balance.

Savor the silence because in just a little while, life will come sweep-

ing in the door — the kids, Philip — and the phone will start ringing, and the refrigerator door will open and close a hundred times. There'll be the sound of soda and beer cans popping, the rattle of chip bags. She swiped at the tears with the side of her hand.

Cry-baby. It doesn't matter whether it's silent or noisy. What matters is that there's not a damned thing to eat in the apartment — you gotta eat something — and I don't have a goddamned red cent. She had Thisby's checks, and she was going to have to bounce one if Thisby didn't have any money in the bank. She went into the bedroom, got the checkbook, and stared at the blank where the balance should have been. She flipped the ledger closed and saw, written in Thisby's hand, the five digits with the word "PIN" after them.

She listened, stunned, to the computerized bank teller as it recited Thisby's checking-account balance for the third time. Thisby had three months' worth of Katharine's household budget in just her checking account. This was real freedom. This was real independence. No wonder Thisby never kept track. *How could she ever run out? Where did she get it?* It was an outrageous fortune.

Katharine could leave now. She didn't need to wait to be resurrected by other people's money. She could call up right now and buy a plane ticket. *Bound for home.*

She picked up the bag she brought from the Bennets' and put it on the kitchen table, but then she let the handle slowly slip from her fingers. *I can't just show up. He's married. I can't just show up looking like this. What if Thisby got herself— ? What if I'm pregnant? What do I tell them? Where have I been?* The thought of the confrontation, the explanations, the required energy, deflated her. *Maybe I should wait a bit. Get healthy. Get strong. Hire a detective, maybe, to find out things. Then go. Okay. That's the Plan.* In the meantime, she would go to the store and buy food, various household products, and a home pregnancy test.

In the bathroom, she read the directions. When Marion was about seven or eight, Katharine had thought she was pregnant again. She had had a strange conflict of emotions. Pregnancy hadn't been easy on her, with the varicose veins, the morning sickness, the various postnatal infections, the neverending story of worry and sleeplessness. But even now, the remembered feel of having a life inside her — the kicks like karate jabs and the turning over like a slow-breaching whale — was incredible. If she had been pregnant again all those many years ago, then she would have had a reason to quit work, a reason to retrench. She didn't tell Philip but nursed the knowledge herself until it was a reality in her mind. She often thought that was the hardest thing for men to handle — the news. Women wrestle with the idea of pregnancy long before they ever become pregnant. By the time the woman gets around to telling the actual news, she's already dealt with it in some manner or other, and the man is always hurrying to catch up. But she never got to tell Philip anything. The home pregnancy test had been negative, and the final proof was the pale pink discharge heralding her period a couple of days later.

This test took five minutes and promised 99 percent accuracy, even one day after a missed period. The medicine strip that she had soaked with her urine showed the minus sign, and there were no conflicting emotions this time. The muscles in Thisby's chest loosened, and her lungs expanded with relief — and a bit of joy. She had just herself to worry about now.

Katharine had found some unopened birth control pills in the medicine cabinet, and as soon as TB had a period, she would start taking them. Or should she start taking them now and hope the periods would follow? She couldn't remember if it was okay to do that.

Better a couple of messed-up cycles than getting pregnant.

And just who are you planning to have sex with?

Katharine decided to wait for the period before she started the pills.

It was eight o'clock in the morning when she took up the phone and dialed the private investigator she had picked out the night before from the Yellow Pages. There were ads for decoy detectives who would entrap cheating spouses and for electronic debugging experts who would declare Thisby's apartment clean. There was even an ad for a discreet and confidential pet detective. She chose J. J. Mulwray for his modest ad, highlighting his expertise in child-recovery and adoption services.

It was early, but the voice that answered sounded as if the person had been up for hours. "Mulwray here."

"Oh, Mr. Mulwray. I didn't expect . . . I'm wondering . . . I'd like to make an appointment with you to talk to you about some . . . things."

"Some . . . things?" He didn't try to soften his sarcasm.

Katharine gripped the phone tighter. "I need some information . . . on some people."

There was a short pause before he spoke again. "Come over this afternoon. Tomorrow I'll be leaving for the next couple of days."

Katharine suddenly felt as though she were caught in a huge wave at the oceanside, forced along no matter how much she flailed her arms. The only thing to do was to ride it out and hope she didn't get slammed onto the sand with the breath completely knocked out of her. "Okay. Thanks."

Now what?

She sat and looked at her hands. They were beginning to look comfortable as they lay so innocently in her lap, as if she knew them — *as if they are someone to watch over me* — as if they would respond quickly to her commands, do little things for her, like pick lint off sleeves without being asked or massage her temples when the headaches got too bad. Katharine stood up quickly and shook them, as if she were flinging something foul off them. *They're not my hands. They're some dead girl's hands. They'll never be my hands.*

She paced the length of the living space and once more had mortal thoughts. *I could be dead again.* There were the bottles of pills in the cupboard. *I can still OD on them.* She always knew, for some strange reason, that she would die young. She used to think she was just being melodramatic — now it seemed she was clairvoyant — but she tried to tell Philip how she had always felt marked for an early death. She would not grow old with him. His family had hardy genes; he would probably live to ninety. She was tough, but she wasn't strong. It was just bravado and willpower. In everyday life, nothing knocked her flat, but she had always known that something — something big and nasty, something fatal — lurked just beyond the daylight. *Something wicked this way comes.* Maybe that was why she was always afraid of the dark. A grown woman who refused to walk into a dark room, who needed a light on in the bathroom so it would spill out into the bedroom, whose night shadows rose up immediately from the yawning netherworld when electrical power was lost.

I just didn't realize that I would be so hard to kill.

But now what was there to live for? She didn't even have the true grit to fight for what was hers. She had no family. No friends. She opened the cupboard and looked in. She had stacked the pill bottles in a pyramid so she could read all the labels easily.

Lioness, my ass.

Come on, I just need some time. Just a little time.

She backhanded the base of the pill bottles and sent them flying against the rear of the cabinet. She thought that she should be crying now, but this body remained dry-eyed, as if still on a different frequency. *Where are the tears now, when I want to cry?*

She was dead certain of one thing. It was suddenly clear in her mind, exposed and tingling like a raw nerve. *I want to live. I want to live anyhow, anyway I can. I can't do differently. I'm staying alive.*

So she did what she had always done when too many warring feelings threatened to overwhelm her. She pushed forward, pushed through. *You just keep going and get to the other side.*

She picked up Thisby's diary and started to read.

> . . . *Sometime when I am older, I am going to be a famous photographer. I am going to go all over the world and take pictures of famous people. I will be famous then too. Maxie and Puck can come with me* . . .

Katharine lay on the couch a couple of hours later. She had just finished reading Thisby's diary for the second time. She felt like a vampire who has just drunk in his latest soul. There was a sense of shared space within her, though the space was finite, as there would be no more growth for Thisby.

The diary was not long, and there were huge gaps between entries, often leaving Thisby's thoughts and concerns isolated and unresolved.

The first entry was dated when she was eight, the last at seventeen.

> . . . Daddy taught me how to use the telephoto lens. It's not that hard. I could tell D was proud I learned so fast. He made me memorize "Say, I taught thee." It's from one of the Henrys. I can't remember which one. Who cares anyways . . . Maxie and Puck took Quince Prologue — I secretly call her Kewpie — to the park. She's only a year old and can't even walk. Everyone feels sorry for her with her ugly lip. Puck's real weird about it. I didn't want to go, so I went into the darkroom. I spilled some fixer on the counter. I think I got it all up. I hope D doesn't find out . . . Not that he's ever around . . .

> . . . I'm supposed to keep a logbook of my photos. You know, of the f-stops and the shutter speeds and stuff. Dad says I have to. He's going to check it when he comes home from the road. It's an exercise in thinking about technique, he says. I'm doing it but it's stupid. Thinking just gets in the way. I don't want to be Ansel Adams. I just see something and react. If you wait for settings, the picture's gone. At least, mine are . . .

> . . . Puck thinks he's so cool calling me Lady Ophelia cuz he can swim and I can't. I try to swim but I keep sinking. Puck says I sink like an army . . .

> . . . I'm not doing very well in school. I thought junior high would be different. Puck tries to tell me what to do. Just because Dad isn't around much, Puck thinks he's the father and all. Yeah, right . . .

. . . Lunch. I hate it. You stand around in a circle and one by one everybody leaves and you're left alone standing there like some geek. Then you have to go break in on some other circle and sometimes people pretend that you're not even there. They make me so mad, I want to rip their heads off . . .

. . . I bring my camera to school now and take pictures at lunch and break. Now I can leave the circle and have a reason to go to another. It's amazing what fools do in front of a camera. Suddenly everyone wants to be a star. I do funny things to them in the pictures and they don't even know it. I take one good picture that I give to them. Some of them don't even say thanks. Then I take other pictures that make them look weird. It's easy. You just have to change the angle sometimes . . .

She felt a sudden twitch of envy. Katharine, being one of the outsiders, had watched that inner circle when she was a teenager. She had stood there many a time while it slowly collapsed in on itself and left her its sole survivor. Thisby had had her camera, but Katharine had had no buffer at all. Not even at home. Her parents needed her to protect them. She had never said, *Go ahead, lean on me*, but they did, pressing their weight on her as if she were the adult. At stores, she spoke for them while they stood a little way back, looking bewildered and bemused at this new and strange world and at this child who was their bridge. But her parents weren't Old World. Their ancestors had come to the United States generations ago. They were Americans raised on Fords and Quaker Oats and the righteousness of Uncle Sam. But for some reason they felt incapable of handling the outside world, and since there was nobody else to do it, Katharine did. *Good ol' Katharine.* They didn't even worry that she might get into trouble or why she was good. She just was. *I was.*

Thisby had lost herself and tried to find someone else in drugs and, no doubt, in sex, overlaying her alienation with synthesized bravado. What happened to Thisby that didn't happen to Katharine?

I never got into drugs, and I certainly could have, considering the times.

Bullshit, you were just chickenshit about getting caught. It wasn't that you were better than anyone else or knew something no one else knew. You were just scared shitless.

But Philip fell in love with her, and he was no Goody Two-shoes. He had been through a lot of bad experiences before her, though he probably would not call them "bad" — just growing pains. *Is that why the kids related better to him? He knew what it was like to dance with the devil in the pale moonlight, and I didn't?*

Philip saved pictures of himself: pictures taken at fraternity parties, at parties at the house he rented with a couple of other guys. There was one picture in particular that had always fascinated Katharine, though as the years went by, it became more of a *bothered* fascination. Philip is sitting in a camp chair, wearing only a pair of faded PE shorts and his ever present bandanna around his head. Sweat shines on his chest, and the waistband of his shorts is dark with moisture. He is in the backyard of his rented house — filling his navel, Philip liked to call it, collecting sweat until rivulets burst over the rim to run down into the waistband of his shorts. A cigarette is in one hand and a fat beer bottle is in the other — a Mickey's Big Mouth Malt Liquor, a brew that smelled like skunk to Katharine. Philip's eyes are unfocused, and there's a slackness, a vacuousness about his mouth.

Philip's roommate, Al, had bet that Philip couldn't drink eighteen Big Mouths in twelve hours without puking or passing out. Philip had taken the bet. On a hot summer Saturday at noon, Philip drank his first Big Mouth. Al brought out his tape recorder and played the event like a radio interview, thrusting the mike in her face as she put out food and drink. "Well, what do you think the odds are now? How's our boy looking?"

Philip sat outside in the hot sun, taking audience with the friends who came by to see how things were progressing.

Katharine hadn't been with Philip long and had watched, amazed and slightly horrified. It wasn't just that she had never been with anyone like him — she had never even *imagined* being with anyone like him. She didn't know what he saw in her — she knew his friends didn't know what he saw in her either — but for once in her life, she was willing to just go with it and not analyze it too much.

In three hours Philip downed twelve Big Mouths and, though a little buzzed, seemed to be holding it together. It looked like a sure thing. More and more people showed up, and Al greeted them to get their assessment of Philip's chances for posterity.

It was the dreaded thirteenth Big Mouth in the fourth hour that took out Philip, puking what seemed like gallons of skunky-smelling beer and then passing out on the lawn.

For years Philip lamented that his mistake had been a lack of pacing, that his strategy was off, and he often threatened to try the bet again.

Katharine often dreamed that Philip had returned to his wild life. The dreams had been quite frequent before she died. *Were things really bad between us just before I died? Had I already lost him to Diana, or the idea of a Diana, and didn't even know it?* Life was so stressful with the kids and her health and the job and money. She and Philip found things to do separately, but then they didn't talk about them when they were together again, each having lost too much background. *Together alone.* Then not wanting to leave the house at night for fear of Ben doing something stupid. *As if staying home would be some sort of protection against stupidity.* Not leaving on weekends. Hardly even going out. She would watch movies, and Philip would read and go to bed early. She would stay up until Ben would come home or lie awake in bed until she heard the rasp of his door opening while Philip slipped in and out of his card-flapping snores.

And what about this Bennet family? Just what was her responsibility to them? She might never know what had really happened to Thisby — what was hinted at in those last few diary entries.

. . . Uncle Roy told me why sometimes he's called Rob Roy and why that bugs the shit out of my dad. When he was a kid Uncle Roy read somewhere about a Scottish pirate named Robert Something-or-other whose nickname was Rob Roy. He raped and robbed his way up and down the countryside, taking what he wanted and making people pay for protection. That was the Rob Roy that Uncle Roy was attracted to, not the poor dude the movies are about. But somehow, the name got attached to Uncle Roy and my father. Uncle Roy and me laughed so hard. We thought it was the funniest thing, my father stuck with the name of a nefarious man and assumed to be a clone of another. In college, Uncle Roy said he lived up to the name because he liked to drink the cocktail called a Rob Roy — scotch, vermouth, bitters, and a maraschino cherry. That stuff is in our liquor cabinet. I'll show Rob Roy I can drink with the best of them. I always liked maraschino cherries . . .

. . . Spent a night in juvie. Got picked up on South Street for panhandling. Mom busted a gut. Q hanging around. Got to get rid of the little shit . . .

. . . What an old man you are, Puck. You're just like the parental units. The joke's on Thisby. Stupid old Thisby. Well, I know more than you think I do. I know better . . .

. . . I'm trying to hold it together. I can't seem to run fast enough to catch up with myself . . .

And the last entry . . .

. . . that fucking fairy kiss . . .

Was it important to know? It might have been that last thing or a series of things — or nothing at all — that set her slowly to kill herself. At least, to kill her brain. Do I really care? Is it my responsibility to save this family and leave my own to be saved by somebody else? Shit.

But Thisby was dead. Katharine had her own future to forge, and Thisby wasn't a part of it.

Act 2, Scene 2 🦎

Knowledge can be more terrible than ignorance if one can do nothing.

— JOHN JUSTIN, *The Thief of Bagdad* (1940)

She stood in front of the multistoried building with its green-tinted windows. She felt seasick just looking at it. As Katharine looked up and down the street, she realized this was not what she had expected. She had thought Mr. Mulwray's office would be in a weather-beaten brownstone, like the ones in the old cloak-and-dagger movies.

She glanced back at Thisby's Porsche, making sure she could see the bright-red Club clamped on the steering wheel, just as it had been when she found the car in the secured parking garage below the apartment.

> . . . Since he's goin' south, Uncle Roy says I can have his Porsche. It's his present to me. Uncle Roy is so cool. Yesterday he told Dad he was an old fart. Hard to believe Uncle Roy and he are twins. Dad says if I don't do better in school, I won't get my license or the FM2 and he won't let Uncle Roy give me his car. Shit, now he tries to get tough. I want that car. If I can transfer into yearbook or newspaper and take pictures, maybe I can make it. I've got to do some serious acting . . .
>
> . . . And they say I can't act. I got the Oscar for that

performance. He backed down like always. I knew he would.
I got my license. I got my car. I got the FM2 and I got my
freedom. Fuck yes . . .

Katharine had been prepared to detest the car. She had
noticed that Thisby liked expensive things, regardless of how
right-on and groovy she thought she was. Katharine had expected some sort of clichéd 911 Targa, black as death with
tinted windows, one of those spoiler fins on the back, and
chrome wheels with thick, squat tires. The car she found was a
1963 bathtub Porsche Speedster C, white with a black canvas
top. The paint was dulled with age, there was a dent or two in
the fenders, and the canvas top looked slightly dry and brittle.
It was the car Katharine had wanted the summer she was seventeen. "You don't want a car like that," her mother had said. *I
don't?* "You want something you can take all your friends in."
All my friends? Let's see, there's Eve and then there's Eve. And even
then, Eve didn't live long enough to ride in the car Katharine
bought — a boxy, four-door, pea green Plymouth Valiant that
someone pegged "the PG&E car." It turned out to be a great
buy, though, solid and long-term, surviving both kids and more
than 200,000 miles.

Katharine had approached the Speedster holding her
breath, but the key slid into the lock and turned. She had
smiled and slipped into the seat of worn leather that molded
itself immediately to Thisby's derriere.

Walking through the lobby toward the back of the building,
she continued to be disappointed. She had been expecting, at
least, a dark hallway ending at a door with J. J. MULWRAY, PI
etched in curved letters across the opaque glass. Instead, she
found a well-lit hallway and a solid door with a small plaque to
the right that read, MULWRAY INVESTIGATIONS. Inside was a
small reception room with a sliding glass partition separating
the other rooms in the back. Katharine was sure that J. J.
Mulwray had gotten a great deal on an old dentist's office. The
glass partition was open, and she could hear someone in a
back room.

"Hello?" she called out through the partition.

The noise of filing cabinets being opened and shut stopped, and a man's head appeared around a doorjamb. "You the lady who called this morning? Come on back."

Katharine's first glimpse of J. J. Mulwray was favorable. He did not look like he sounded. He looked pleasant. He was bald on the top, she knew, since he had leaned forward from the doorjamb and exposed the top of his pate. He had a good thick rim of gray hair, and Katharine wondered why he didn't let one side grow long and flip it over, the way most balding men did. She liked the fact that he didn't.

She walked through the door from the reception room, past a secretary's desk that was covered with papers, and into the room Mr. Mulwray had leaned out from. The office was as cluttered as the front desk. Papers and manila folders were stacked on the desk, the credenza, the wooden chair on wheels, and even the floor around the feet of the desk. He was standing at a filing cabinet, pulling a thick folder from the drawer.

"Take a seat," he said, and placed the folder on top of the filing cabinet. He looked around, closed the drawer, unearthed a chair that Katharine had previously missed, and placed it in front of the desk. He went back around the desk, lifted the files from his chair, dumped them on the floor, and sat down. Using both elbows and forearms, he cleared a space in front of himself, pulled a yellow-lined legal pad from the right-hand drawer in the desk, lifted a ballpoint pen from his shirt pocket, and looked up at her. "What can I do you for?"

This time Katharine was ready. "I need information on some people in northern California."

"Financial? Criminal? Personal?"

"Well, I guess you could call it domestic information." Katharine began to fidget with a piece of paper in her hands. *Am I deranged to be doing this? Could he get me into trouble?* She swallowed. *I gotta know.* "It's a family." She drew a deep breath. "I want to know about a family. I want to know how the kids are doing in school. I mean, I know it's summer, so how the last school year went." She glanced down at the paper, which had a list of items she had made out the night before. She felt as if she were walking on thin ice — but if she stopped, it was a sure thing that she'd fall through. "I want to know who their friends are, who they're going out with. I want to know what sports they're playing and how they're doing." She stopped for a moment, but he didn't interrupt her. She noticed that he did not write anything down on his pad either. "Their father has remarried. I want to know how he met her. When they got married. That kind of stuff. Their mother died a year ago. How did they handle it? What did they do for her funeral?" She looked at him squarely. "I don't know how much of this can be done."

He chewed the inside of his left cheek slowly. "Does the family move in protective circles?"

It took Katharine a few moments to understand what he meant. "No, they're perfectly normal."

"Will the family be expecting this kind of scrutiny?"

"No. Absolutely not. No."

"You want to remain anonymous."

It was actually a statement more than a question, but Katharine responded, "They can't know anything about me."

"Okay. What else do you have on that little piece of paper?" He gestured to her hands.

"I want to know if the kids are working. If they like their jobs. Anything and everything, no matter how small or trivial." She looked down to check again. "I'd also like pictures."

"Of the husband and new wife too?"

Katharine considered. "Yes, but not too many. I'd rather have more of the kids. Can any of this be done?"

"Some of it may be easy. Some, more difficult." He leaned back in his chair, elbows on the armrests, fingertips together. "I'll need to set up an informer and maybe a stoolie or two, to use an old police term. It may take a while to set up. Possible contacts may object because of loyalty, suspicion." He circled the air with one hand to suggest "et cetera." "Money may not be of any use. You sure the family and their friends won't already be setting up barriers?"

"I promise you, no. They're normal people."

"Well, Miss — ?" He pushed himself back farther in his chair.

Katharine was afraid he might topple over, and she imagined his legs wiggling in the air above the desk like some sort of overturned giant beetle. "Bennet. Thisby Bennet."

"Well, Miss Bennet, I would like to be honest with you. I do not like child-custody cases. Kidnapped kids, yes, but — "

"It isn't that kind of thing at all," Katharine rushed in. "I just . . . want to know about them. I just want to know what's going on with them. I don't plan to contact them." *Not yet, anyway, and not in the way you would ever understand.* "That's all."

Mr. Mulwray leaned forward swiftly and began writing on his pad. "Okay. It might take a while to set up. The bulk of the expenses will be in the initial transactions. Depending upon what is eventually put in place, the cost will level out and should continue at that price unless we need to add more informants. Now, if they are as normal as you say they are, there are advantages and disadvantages. I take it you don't care about investments or financial dealings?"

Katharine couldn't help but smile. *Philip with financial dealings? That would be a new one.* But she thought that maybe Diana might have money. "I don't think you'll find anything of interest there, but I don't know anything about the new wife. I guess I'd like to know what she brought to the marriage. I certainly need to know if they're destitute. See what you can find, and I'll tell you whether it's of interest and whether I want to know more." *This could be kind of fun.*

"All right. You'll need to write out as much as you know about these people: names, schools, family, friends, enemies. Addresses, phone numbers if you've got them."

Katharine had anticipated this and had written out most of it in Thisby's apartment. It was scary how little needed to be put down to sketch out a person. It did not, of course, include how Ben hated mustard on his sandwiches or how Marion wouldn't eat chicken unless it was boned. That Philip wouldn't clean the bathroom but would wash windows. That Ben loved babies, that Marion thought of wonderful things to do on

Mother's Day, that Philip had fallen in love with her when she thought no one else would. These things would not help the investigation but were the things she held close to her soul.

She wrote out a check for his retainer that was more money than she expected but less than she would have balked at. He promised to call her in a week to let her know what he had been able to get started.

And how about Thisby? It also had been so easy to narrow her life down to lines on a piece of paper. She could feel the wad of paper with the names of Thisby's family and friends in her back pocket. She realized she had been too hard on her just a couple of days ago. *But now I have a few things to hold close to my soul about Thisby too . . .*

. . . I'm sure he could feel the Kleenex in my bra. I could just die . . .

. . . Why do I always have to share my birthday with Christ and Kewpie? They promised this year it would be different but it wasn't . . .

. . . What if I ran away and no one noticed? . . .

She left exhausted, carrying the two souls, and with the added weight of it came a kind of stupor.

Act 2, Scene 3 🐿

You have a double tongue within your mask.

— LONGAVILLE, *Love's Labour's Lost*, 5.2.245

Katharine existed in a state of suspended animation. Time did not seem to move, yet the days slipped by without a ripple. She lay in bed until late morning and tried to take naps during the day. She felt like a teenager — not the teenager she had been, for sleeping in was something just not done in her family. Sometimes when she had been young, she stole into the living room to eat gumdrops from the cut-crystal candy jar with the chipped knob on the top. She would eat so many, heartburn would crawl up from her stomach into her throat and smolder there. She would tell her mother she wasn't feeling well, and her mother would allow her to be a daydreamer and lie on the couch. But not often and not for long. Philip always allowed himself to take naps as well as sleep in, which had irritated Katharine. Never weaken! That was the motto she had lived by as an adult. *Mothers have to keep going, no matter how tired or sick they are. Never weaken!*

But it was becoming hard to keep up with her emotions, and they constantly confused her. Sometimes she would catch a scent or hear a sound that reminded her of home and family, and a part of her would throb like an amputated limb that insisted it was still attached. Then, just as quickly, she would revel in the silence, in the aloneness. The phone didn't ring.

The TV was not on, blaring MTV and baseball games, and radios did not duel from separate rooms.

Never weaken!

But now she did.

Mornings found her on the balcony, a place in the sun, the corners of the unopened newspaper on the deck snapping in the sporadic breeze. She had planned on reading more than just the front page, the movie reviews, and the gossip columns, but she ended up reading nothing at all. She had also resolved to go farther afield in her walks around Westwood, but she found herself remaining on the balcony, both hands gripped tightly around a mug of microwaved water. It was the heat of liquid that she wanted — not the flavor of coffee — and holding something warm kept her hands from twitching. She just sat and thought and discovered that she missed the strangest of things. How, although Philip was gone by the time she got up, his presence lingered with the smell of his well-browned toast. How Marion would show her the Far Side cartoon to enjoy, but, in truth, to drop her a hint so Katharine would get it. That Ben, despite his cool and detached demeanor, in times of stress would often be betrayed by his own body — a cold sore blossoming overnight on the side of his mouth. Katharine remembered how she would receive this sight with almost maniacal glee — she realized that he indeed was not as nonchalant as he appeared.

It's a deception that being stripped of memories is the cruelest fate. Living with them is.

She often felt that she was her own contradiction. She sat at opposite ends of herself. What she loved, she hated; what she wanted, she didn't deserve; what she missed, she didn't want.

It was so much easier to go through the motions for a while and not think too much. *Play out the play.*

She continued to go through Thisby's things. Entries from her diary kept surfacing in her mind like cue cards. She looked through the pictures that were stacked on the bookshelves, seeing them with different eyes. She even found a photograph that Thisby had taken on a trip to New York with her father when she was fourteen.

> . . . I'm back. What a trip. We stayed at the Hotel New York in Manhattan. It was old and it had these gargoyle heads along the top corners that you couldn't even see unless you had a telephoto. I got some great pictures. I've already developed them and they look awesome. In one picture there's this woman looking out her window. You don't see her right away. And then when you do, you realize she looks like a gargoyle herself. She's got this fleshy face and she's mad, like the bellhop brought her coffee cold or she's been told bagels don't come on the menu. She's thinking about how to get back at him, like she's not gonna give him a tip or she's gonna write the hotel editor at the New York Times and tell them about the shitty service. Dad says it's good. Real good . . .

One day she systematically went through all of Thisby's drawers, pulling out each item and scrutinizing it. She felt like some sort of pervert even though she knew she couldn't get arrested for fondling essentially her own stuff. She found herself looking for something. Did Thisby have a hiding place where she put things — things like sexy lingerie that she would never wear because she looked ridiculous in it, or maybe a vibrator that was sold under the auspices of a weight-reduction miracle, disappointed on one front but satisfied on another, or — maybe, maybe . . . like . . . well — underwear she wore when she had her period? Old ones already so stained from previous leakages, she didn't care? *Am I sick? Is it just me?* But this wasn't the kind of thing Katharine would have asked anyone. Certainly not her own mother, nor her daughter. How did other women not let themselves bleed all over their underpants? *They can send a man to the moon but they can't make a good sanitary napkin. Dry weave, wings, flaps. You still bleed all over your underpants, waking up in the morning with crusty elastic along the crotch and your thighs flaking with red rust* — leaving the underpants to soak on the floor of the shower, or in the toilet like a diaper. Or was it only her old body? Was her old crotch not within the range of the anatomically average? Is Thisby's? Or was this something her mother never taught her growing up? Was it a learned skill? Marion never seemed to be concerned, using tampons or napkins with seemingly equal fluency.

Katharine never quite got over the toxic shock scare in the seventies. She was never fond of tampons to begin with, having inserted her first one in secret, incorrectly, with the cardboard sheathing still on, her mother having thrown away the directions. After all, she didn't need them, and who would have thought ten-year-old Katharine would start her period so soon?

Later on Katharine was tired of sticking things, or having them stuck, up her — the IUDs and speculums and cervical scrapers and fingers and even penises. The toxic shock scare took care of ever using tampons again, even when they were deemed safe. When Marion asked for her first tampons, Katharine had kept her mouth shut. She was proud of herself. To tell Marion of her fears was too much of a burden for a young girl, and anyway, what if Katharine was wrong? Maybe it was just her. It wasn't as if it were going to change anything anyway. She never saw Marion's underwear soiled. Did even her daughter know the secrets she didn't? Did Marion learn from her friends or just know — an inbred skill of which Katharine was ignorant, a certain gene that skipped a generation?

Katharine knew that Thisby had problems with her period —

> . . . I still haven't started my period. Maxie did this year. I'm getting boobs and there's a little hair under my arms. Everybody at school has started. I'm the only one who hasn't. . . .

> . . . My mother made me go to the doctor about my period. I've got pubes but no period. I had to lie on this table and stick my feet in these baskets so the doctor could stick his hand up my cunt. The doctor made some remark about my being a virgin, which pissed me off royally. Then he told me I didn't have anything to worry about and he

put me on the Pill, supposedly to bring on my period and regulate it. Well, I mind as well put it to its other use . . .

— and maybe Thisby's drawers would reveal something. But Katharine didn't find what she was looking for.

I guess I was a freak.

Thursday came, and she was glad. She felt that it was time for the sleeper to awaken, to come out of the coma. It was time to come back to the living.

She went out to buy food for her dinner with Goodfellow. He had called the night before to make sure it was still on. It was lovely to hear a real voice. She could carry on only so many conversations in her head.

As she walked to the store, that uncertain feeling of being at a perpetual masquerade continued, but she began to feel a sense of freedom. She was in costume, playing a part, and having had that part sketched in, she could now develop the character while remaining anonymous herself.

Katharine found herself looking at reflections of Thisby as she walked down the business section, her profile flitting from one windowpane to the next. As she headed toward a glass door, she framed Thisby in it and watched how she walked, how she held her head, what she did with her arms. Katharine used to make it a habit to walk straight at the seams around the doors so her own reflection would be sucked into the trough. She avoided mirrored walls at fast-food restaurants and washed her hands with head bowed in restrooms. She was always fascinated by the girls and women who could preen in front of mirrors in restrooms, applying makeup, brushing hair and adjusting skirts and pantyhose. She was still watching in fascination, for now it was an exterior that masked her interior.

And the mask was a young one. Here was an opportunity to be twenty-two again, though at twenty-two, Katharine had already been a wife and a new mother. Katharine had to admit to herself that she wanted a second chance at that young blood. Thisby wasn't a child: she was old enough to be on her own, with her own money and her own place. But she was still young and, therefore, attractive. Katharine noticed that about her children's friends too. Their naïveté, their energy made them beautiful. They all complained, boys and girls, about their bodies, big or small, and their skin, clear or pimply, and their noses and hair, but Katharine found them all adorable — that young flesh with all its imperfections. It glowed with — what? *The full flush of their youth?*

What is youth? She never knew. She was born with an old soul. Her parents recognized it immediately and took advantage of it. *Is youth the tasting of the infinite possibilities of being?* She definitely hadn't tasted that, since so many of the possibilities had been decided for her by other people. *What was my culpability in all of that? I was needed. I needed to be needed. But being needed is what drains youth, what pales the flush.* Katharine realized, after her long hours on the balcony porch, that it was not just time and gravity that sagged the butt, the breasts, the shoulders, but the weight of family, of tradition, of responsibility, of need. The roots, the tendrils of that weight slowly dig in over the years and settle firmly in one place, holding fast, holding firm, binding.

Could she avoid that weight now, in her new body? Did she really have another chance at youth? Or would it just be new trappings over the same old soul?

When she came home, the message machine was blinking. *Oh, God, what if it's Goodfellow, and he can't come tonight? What if he's going to be late for dinner?* She danced a bit out of frustration and then pushed the button. She was immediately relieved when the voice wasn't Goodfellow's, but then she recognized it as the man who had left messages before. "It's Hook. Gondorff said he saw you on the street the other day. When'd you get back? Haven't stung your old friends, have you? Call me."

She erased the message quickly and went into the kitchen to open one of the bottles of merlot she had purchased that afternoon. After a glass or two, she felt better and decided to start preparing dinner. She found that she was excited — her first dinner guest. She needed onion-chopping music, so she found something that had a good beat.

While stirring the spaghetti sauce, she stopped and set down her wineglass. "Number, please," she said in a caricature of a man's voice. She held the dripping wooden spoon to her mouth, and answered in a teenybopper's voice, "Well, Dick, I give it a nine cuz you can dance to it." She laughed.

The doorbell rang.

He's here!

Katharine opened the door without looking through the security lens, and Puck stepped over the threshold.

"Isn't it a little loud? I can hear it from the elevator."

She paused to listen. "Yeah, I guess it is." She walked back to turn down the music. "I'm so glad you came. Take off your coat and tie. Do you want anything to drink?"

He removed his coat and tie and draped them across the couch. Katharine noticed how long his fingers were as he unbuttoned the cuffs of his shirt and rolled up the sleeves to his elbows. "No, nothing. Not right now."

"I've got some wine."

"So I can see. No, thanks."

She recited, "Good wine is a good familiar creature." Puck looked stonily at her. "It's from *Othello*. So how was work?" she asked as she headed back into the kitchen.

There was a long pause. "When did you learn to cook?"

Katharine just looked back at him and didn't answer; she didn't know how to answer.

He shrugged and answered her question. "Work was good today. I actually got some things done." He leaned against the counter. "We have a case pending, and I tracked down some evidence to substantiate our claim of copyright violation. That's when the law works for me."

"It's like a paper chase, isn't it?"

"Yeah, I guess it is, but I like it. The rest of it, though? I don't know. But I gave Dad my word I'd stick it out for a year or two. I won't bail like some of the others. But it's not exactly what I'd hoped it would be."

Katharine thought about this for a while. "Yeah, I know. I was getting so bored with my job at the end, I felt sick. I mean, I had been doing all that jazz for close to — " Katharine looked at Puck, his face like granite again. *You know, this is really getting old. I was just talking about work. No big . . . Oh, bloody hell.*

"What's this, Thiz?" Puck said sarcastically. "Pretending to relate to the common working girl? Give it up. You're a slacker, and you know it. You haven't worked a day in your life."

"She must . . . I mean . . ." *What's wrong with me? Why can't I control myself?*

"A couple of weeks at Mom's store and filing papers in Dad's office is hardly what I call work. I think Mom is right. We should commit you."

Everything froze.

Puck walked over to the counter and lifted up the bottle of wine and tilted it. A finger depth of wine sloshed to the side. "Having a few drinks, are we? I thought . . ."

Katharine glared at him. Anger, at least, heated up the blood. "I'm not . . . I'm not . . ." She stopped to feel contact with Thisby's body, but it wasn't there. *Drugs. Drugs. I thought it was drugs. Not alcohol. Never alcohol . . . I'm not an alcoholic. I've never been one. I've never had any trouble with alcohol. Just a couple of glasses of wine at home. Margaritas when I was out.*

Puck still held up the bottle, displaying it. It seemed to throb. *I drank that entire bottle, and I don't even remember doing it. I was spilling my guts to Goodfellow about my other life, and I wasn't even aware of it. I may not be an alcoholic, but TB is. . . . And, therefore, I am . . . one . . . too.*

Katharine slumped down on the kitchen stool, the pressure building up behind her eyes. *I don't want to play the crying game.* But this body was taking over again.

"When are you going to figure it out?"

There was such self-righteousness in his voice, the Puck of old, that Katharine stood up, yanked the bottle from his hand and whipped it against the utility-room door. It shattered, and the red wine dripped down to pool at the base of the door.

Katharine was stunned, the anger immediately dissipating. She looked at the glass scattered over the floor. She was too petrified to look sideways at Puck. "I'm so sorry." Puck made no sound beside her. She got a broom, and Puck started to pick up the large pieces. Katharine saw the hard line of his jaw twitch.

"You know," she confessed slowly, "I've always wanted to do something like that. Just like in the movies." She ran a hand through her hair. "Funny. It helps too." She looked around again at the floor. "It makes a mess though, doesn't it?"

He didn't respond. Breaking a bottle like that was something Thisby would have done, and probably did, regularly.

By the time they sat down to dinner, Katharine was not feeling too terrific, but she didn't know whether it was the wine or the shock of almost exposing herself that soured her stomach. Puck seemed willing to fill the silence, and she was willing to listen as best she could through her raging headache. She did find out that he was a lawyer at his father's studio. His new girlfriend, Vivian Ward, was "a very pretty woman, but a hard-ass in the courtroom." The firm she worked for was prestigious and recruited only the best and the brightest and the most ruthless people. They both billed long hours and didn't see much of each other. "I admire her," he told Katharine. "She knows what she wants."

Puck refused wine with dinner, and the thought of it alternately called and repulsed her. The world was shrinking in on her. It was as if she were in a daguerreotype, and the edges of the image were being eaten away by shadows and fog. She tried to hide her distraction from Puck, and by the time he left, after she had silently handed him the unopened bottle of wine and he took it without comment, she was almost reeling but promised to call him "real soon."

Katharine slowly finished cleaning up, trying to shore up the barriers between her mind and this body. The distinctions were getting blurred, had been getting blurred, slowly, unevenly, but without her knowledge. She was losing the sense of what was her, Katharine, and what might have been Thisby.

There's a price. There's always a price. Maybe in order to be the exorcist — to get her out of my head — I must perform a sacrifice. Maybe before I can go home again, I must accomplish a feat, a labor.

Then maybe she'll leave me alone, and I can live my own life.

• • •

It was a little after 11:30 P.M. when she called Quince on her own line. Katharine figured she wouldn't be asleep, and the sound of the music in the background proved her correct.

"Are you doing anything this weekend?"

"Lie abed till noon, then I shall be dogged with company."

Katharine smiled weakly, not having the strength to respond out loud. "I was wondering if you could come over Saturday or Sunday."

"What? Hath your grace no better company?"

"I need your help."

"With what?"

"To go through some photos here."

"Why?"

"To help me pick out the good ones."

"Why?"

"Because I need your help."

"Why? Okay, okay. Can I spend the night?"

Christ.

Oh, go on. Why not? Play the sister act.

"Okay. I'll come pick you up around two o'clock on Saturday."

"I can get there myself."

"Okay. Thanks." Katharine was not overly anxious to see Thisby's parents for a while.

Katharine lay in bed. *It's been decided.* Katharine's family, no doubt, had given her body a funeral or, at least, a memorial service. *Some sort of last rites.* Even if they didn't, people knew she had died. They mourned her. *I assume.* But there had been no funeral for Thisby, no memorial. Not even any grief. *Thisby's dead, and no one knows but me.*

And maybe this would be enough for atonement. Maybe this would be the right offering to deflect all the Bennet women. She would take Thisby's father up on his offer of a photographic exhibit. It would be Katharine's memorial to Thisby. She would produce an exhibit, "The Photographs of Thisby Flute Bennet."

A posthumous retrospective.

Act 2, Scene 4 ❧

I will not permit you to have two families,

no matter what their problems are.

— SHANNON WILCOX, *Six Weeks* (1982)

Quince appeared about three o'clock, decked out in faded jean shorts and a T-shirt with SAVE THE WORLD across it and shod in purple sneakers. She had attached a chain from her nose ring to an earring, and it swayed across her left cheek like a jump rope. Katharine cringed as she imagined the chain getting caught on something, and the nose ring ripping apart all that cosmetic surgery.

Quince threw her overnight bag in the bedroom and looked around. "You've cleaned up."

Katharine was unsure whether Quince thought this was a good thing. "Yeah, I did. Did Mom bring you over?"

"Yeah, right." Quince gave her a withering look. "I hitched."

"You what?"

"I hitched. How'd you expect me to get here? By taxi?"

"There's a bus stop right out in front."

"Gimme a break."

"I never would have let you —" Katharine stopped.

A hitcher?

You are not her parent.

"I'll come get you the next time."

Quince shrugged. "So what are we doing?" she asked, eyeing the boxes lined up on the floor in the dining area.

"We're going to go through those and pick out the photographs we think should be exhibited."

Quince looked up sharply. "You changed your mind?"

"It just happened."

Quince shrugged and knelt down. "I never could figure why you were such a wench about it. You could be famous. The Lewis Hine of Slummed LA."

Katharine knew the name from Thisby's trip to New York.

. . . We took a flight to Rochester and saw the Lewis Hine Collection of Social Documentary photographs at the George Eastman House. Hine photographed a lot of immigrants at Ellis Island and the poor, the coal miners and stuff. He did a lot of action shots and liked weird angles, climbing up on things and shooting down.

They had other photographers, too. I'll never forget this one photo. It was of this narrow street lined with tall apartment buildings and dead trees. It was taken from above, at least three stories up. There was an ambulance in the street. The guys were bringing someone out on a stretcher. The lights on the ambulance were flashing and lighting up the area around the car. That was it. But it wasn't. If you looked closer, you could see people like storefront dummies at the windows in the apartment building across the way, barely visible but backlighted by the TV screens behind them. It was really eerie. I liked it . . .

Quince opened up a box and looked through the top layer. "You've marked up a lot of these contact sheets." She pointed to hand-drawn lines that cut across the tops and sides of the exposures. "Did you print these up with the new crops?"

"I . . . I don't know. I don't remember."

She snorted and shook her head. "Okay, so what do you want me to look for?"

"Let's just separate the 'like' from the 'dislike' for now."

"So you're adding to your portfolio?"

Portfolio? What portfolio? I haven't found that. Shit. "Yeah."

Quince grunted, then folded and rocked herself into a comfortable lotus position.

"Do you want a Coke or something before we start?"

Quince had stacked photographs and contact sheets in her lap. "No, I'm okay." She began to spread them out around her like lily pads until she was awash in a pond of pictures. Katharine watched Quince study each photo critically. This was another incarnation of Quince Katharine would have to get to know. *And she seems knowledgeable about photography.* Katharine picked up her own stack and started going through it, but very slowly; she kept checking the photos Quince was interested in.

Surprisingly, it was Katharine who asked if she could put on some music; Quince was completely absorbed. But about five o'clock, Quince straightened up and announced, "Cigarette break. Smoke 'em if you've got 'em."

Katharine sensed something sit up excitedly in this body, but she quickly tamped it back down. "I don't smoke anymore, and you need to go outside if you do."

"Outside?"

"Yes. You can go out on the balcony. I'll bring you an ashtray."

"Shit, soon you'll be going to church."

Katharine snorted and pulled open the sliding glass door to let Quince through. Quince jammed her hand in her shorts and fished out a crumpled pack and a book of matches. She lit up with practiced ease and blew out a puff of smoke. Katharine's nose began to quiver and her hands trembled; she shut the door tight.

Katharine had always hated cigarettes, and when a neighbor told her she had seen Ben smoking downtown, Katharine was sick with embarrassment. She could hear Philip's voice even now, that reasonable, logical, experienced voice, "How can I tell him to stop smoking when I smoked for ten years? You fell in love with me, married me, when I smoked. How can I tell him his life will be completely ruined if he smokes? When it isn't true. Yes, it will be hard for him to quit later on in life, but it can be done. Don't sweat it. There are worse things." Why was that kind of objectivity so easy for Philip? Why couldn't she have it too? So now as she searched her mind carefully, she realized that she held no emotional condemnation that Quince smoked. There was none of the tightness in the stomach, the ache in the jaw. It felt good. It felt light. *No roots of responsibility starting to take to this soil. Is this what it's like being an older sister, as opposed to being a mother?*

They worked and sorted for another hour until Katharine declared, "Enough. I can't look at another depressing building. Or used people. Let's go out and eat. What do you want?"

Quince leaped up like a frog from its pad. "That pizza place you took me to last year. Pizza Man, right? And then let's go to that candy store. You know, the one with the rum balls."

Katharine had seen the Pizza Man restaurant on one of her earlier walks through the neighborhood and, though she had seen numerous ice cream, candy, yogurt, and cookie stores, thought she knew which candy store Quince had in mind — the one whose front-window display was a confection in itself — Sugarbaby. Katharine hoped her instincts were correct.

Quince was as animated on the street as she had been silent in the apartment. She jump-shifted between personalities so fast, sometimes it was hard for Katharine to keep up. Quince rattled on about wanting a dog, and then about some all-day concert she and a friend had gotten tickets for. In the pizza parlor, after they had been seated, she cried, "O look, sir, look, sir! Here is more of you," pointing to deep grooves in one of the corners of their wooden table. It read "Thisby" in stiff lines like Greek letters.

It must have taken her a long time to cut that deep.

Katharine suddenly saw Thisby at the table, her pale face and light eyes hooded by makeup and hair. *She has a Swiss Army knife. A pitcher of beer and glasses sit in wet rings on the table. A pizza tray is shoved to the side, napkins balled up in mounds like cannon shot. The restaurant is crowded, and although there are many waiting for a table, Thisby and her friends aren't aware of it or, if they are, ignore it. When she* and her friends leave, they won't bus any of their mess, though there is a sign hanging above the ordering desk requesting such help. The friends wait, talking about nothing in particular, while Thisby methodically chisels out her name, deeper and deeper. She has nowhere to go, nothing to do, and she's determined that it will take more than a mere pass with a sander to obliterate her. Some of her friends begin to feel uncomfortable. The management glares at them; after all, they hadn't bought that much food. But Thisby ignores them all and keeps on carving. The friends are forced to wait; they will not leave until she's finished. When she's done, she deliberately closes the knife, hands it back to the person she took it from — a stranger from the next table over — slowly drains her beer glass and stands up. The rest follow, and the busboys pounce on the table, sweep up the remains, and seat others by the time Thisby and her friends reach the door. It's as if they were never there — but for the name, gouged out like an injury.

Katharine traced the letters with her left hand, and all of a sudden felt odd. Thisby's past overlapped Katharine's present and superimposed its existence onto hers. The waitress eyed her suspiciously, and Katharine had a sudden fear, mixed somehow with perverse anticipation, that the waitress would turn and yell to the cook, "Nick, it's that girl again," while desperately seeking to invoke the right-to-refuse-service disclaimer on the menu. But she just took their order sullenly and left.

Katharine mentally punched through the thin membrane that was Thisby and picked up her water with her right hand.

When their order arrived, it came with the attention of two young men at the next table. Katharine supposed they were nineteen, twenty — too old for Quince.

They began to discuss Raves, the bar Katharine knew from the message on Thisby's answering machine. But there seemed to be more than one rave; they were all over the LA Basin. She slowly realized that raves were roving portable nightclubs whose whereabouts were spread by word of mouth. Katharine began to despair that she would ever learn this foreign language fast enough to protect her double identity.

"Thisby's been to a lot of raves," Quince volunteered, and

the boys turned toward her expectantly. Katharine shrugged noncommittally. The conversation sagged until Quince picked it up again.

Katharine watched the interplay with fascination. It was a verbal dance, sashaying in and then bowing out. One boy, with his sad eyes and scraggly facial hair — *oh, Ben, have you shaved off that awful stuff yet?* — tried to redirect the conversation toward her, but Katharine was content to hang back and watch.

When they were finished eating and back outside, Quince rolled her eyes. "What a couple of punk rampants."

"They were?" *I didn't think they were total . . . punk rampants. Their awkwardness was kind of endearing.*

Quince pulled the corner of her lip up in a sneer. "Not Hercules could have knocked out their brains, for they had none."

Katharine laughed. "You mean, you've known sheep that could outwit them? You've worn dresses with higher IQs?"

Quince laughed with her. "Okay, so they weren't that bad."

They walked on, and Katharine forgot about the boys. She worried about how she was going to entertain Quince after dinner — she was afraid Quince had some sort of trouble in mind. But on the way back to the apartment, after Quince filled up on Sugarbaby rum balls — Katharine had nothing, though the sweets called to her like sirens — they rented a movie. It was a slasher film that neither of them had seen before. It was so bad, they hooted at it with great pleasure, throwing popcorn at the screen. "Don't go in there, you triple-turn'd fool," Quince yelled at the heroine.

It seems like old times.

The next morning they weeded through the photographs they had chosen the previous day. Quince indeed knew a lot about photography and had Thisby's eye without the despair. In the beginning, Quince was hesitant to give her opinion, as if Thisby had disparaged her too many times before. But, bit by bit, Katharine was able to coax Quince into offering it.

"Shooting any pictures lately?" Katharine asked, taking a leap of faith.

Quince looked at her with so much suspicion, Katharine was worried she had risked too much. "Not much. My camera's acting up."

"It is? Why don't you use . . . mine?" She jumped up and fetched the Nikon FM2 from the box in the utility room. She placed it and all the paraphernalia in front of Quince. Quince stared at it, looked back up at Katharine, and then back down at the camera hungrily. Katharine rushed on, "I mean, I'll be so busy getting this exhibit ready, I won't be taking any pictures. It's just sitting around not being used. And it should be used."

Quince reverently unsnapped the cover and lovingly took out the camera. Katharine grimaced, remembering how roughly she had handled it before. "Rich gifts wax poor when givers prove unkind," Quince murmured.

"It's okay. Really. I'm not going to use it." *Ever.*

"Dad'll get mad."

"Oh, the hell with Dad. I can get mad too." Katharine saw a flash of fear in Quince's eye. "Hey, it's my camera," she said to quiet Quince. "I can loan it to whoever I want. To be really honest, I'm not sure I can ever take another picture. I want to do this exhibit, but then I think I'm finished. I've got to move on to something else. Really. I want you to have the camera. Think of it as a loan. You just gotta take good pictures as payment."

Quince didn't say anything but tucked the camera back into place and set it and the accessories case by her stuff. Katharine watched her with growing, but unasked for, affection.

Act 2, Scene 5 ⟊

To live a second life on second head.

— SONNET 68,7

Katharine continued to spend time walking around Westwood. It wasn't as odd as she thought it might be, or as uncomfortable. Knowing her geographical base anchored her, and it also made the days go by faster as she waited to hear from Mr. Mulwray.

Coming home from the grocery story on Monday, Katharine passed by and then backtracked to an innocuous-looking building. The sign painted on the window read:

THE ANIMAL HOUSE:
LOW-COST VETERINARY CARE
BOARDING KENNELS
ABANDONED, SPAY, AND NEUTERING SERVICES

Katharine felt that if Quince could volunteer there, it would be a perfect match. *I doubt the animals would care what color hair she has and how many earrings she wears.*

She went inside. The young man at the front desk looked exactly the way he should have looked: tall, thin, with a calm, gentle face — even the stripes of his cotton shirt were muted and soothing.

"Do you need any volunteers here?" she asked.

He took her back to meet the office manager, Pepa Marcos, who looked like . . . *a woman on the verge of a nervous breakdown.* She was mucking out a dog kennel whose resident had given birth to nine puppies three weeks before. Pepa was ecstatic about a volunteer. "Your timing is perfect. One of our boarders"— she gestured to the kennel —"gave birth sooner than expected. And for some reason this summer, we haven't gotten the student help we usually get from the University. We could use another person to handle the odd jobs. Maybe then I could finally catch up on my paperwork." But as Katharine watched her affectionately scratching the head of the German shepherd mother, she wondered.

"It's really my sister who I'm asking for. She's fifteen. A hard worker, very focused."

They did not look so pleased then, and Katharine could see Ms. Marcos framing some well-we-thank-you-for-your-kind-offer rebuff. Katharine knew this was where Quince should be, so she recklessly added, "She can work two or three days a week, and she'd be staying with me, just down the street. She could walk here."

What the hell are you doing?

The office manager eyed the other kennels that needed to be cleaned and agreed to hire Quince on a trial basis.

As they were walking back to the front room, Katharine felt compelled to add, "There's one more thing you ought to know." The other two tensed. "Quince looks a little different. I mean"— Katharine self-consciously put a hand through her hair —"she has colored hair and a lot of earrings."

They visibly relaxed. "Oh, that's okay," Pepa said, waving it off. "The animals don't care as long as she's good. And like Conrad here, I don't hire just ordinary people."

"I think you'll really like it," Katharine added lamely for the third time the next morning. Quince wasn't saying much as they walked to the clinic, and Katharine couldn't tell what that meant.

She didn't have to worry long. As soon as Quince saw

the puppies with their blunt little faces, butterball bodies, and mewling voices, her tough demeanor melted. Pepa and Conrad watched Quince closely as she carefully made her acquaintance with the mother. Only when the mother was comfortable and settled did Quince approach the puppies. Knowing looks were exchanged between Conrad and Pepa, and Katharine felt like shouting, "Bingo. We've got ourselves a winner."

Pepa explained to Quince the mutual trial basis, and she had to agree to be punctual, reliable, and hardworking.

One of the last Girl Scouts.

"And I understand you'll be staying with your sister on the days you work here," Pepa remarked as they were setting up the first two weeks of her schedule, beginning Thursday.

Quince looked at Katharine, puzzled but hopeful. Katharine hadn't quite gotten around to mentioning that part to Quince.

If you ever were.

"Yes, that's right," Katharine conceded.

Come on, it won't be that bad. She's a nice kid.

"Cool," Quince said, and Katharine felt the downside tug of responsibility.

That afternoon, after she had dropped off Quince at home, Katharine drove down to Melrose Avenue, where, according to the phone book, there was a profusion of art galleries.

The Ziegfeld-Zelig Gallerie, its logo two large intertwined Zs, was just off the main street. Its inside paid homage to its humble beginnings as some sort of sweatshop, with tube railings on the spiral staircase, exposed steel buttresses, and skylights with their metal-encased panes propped skyward.

The photographs along the first exhibit panel were all contemporary and were split evenly between color and black-and-white. Most of them were either abstracts or landscapes, but there were a few documentaries.

She was halfway down the second panel when a gentleman approached her. He was in his mid-forties, dressed in pleated black pants and a white shirt. His hair was pulled back in a long and luxuriant ponytail, one diamond stud in his left ear.

He had beautiful teeth and nice eyes, but Katharine figured later it was his manners that had made her pitch Thisby's exhibit. He had taken her purse, her bag of Farmers Market bread and set them aside as if he were a butler. He brought her some good coffee, and it tasted like Philip's. She missed being waited on.

She had not brought any of Thisby's work, nor had she planned to ask about exhibiting. She was going to appear only as a potential contributing artist, but she found herself spilling her plan to him almost before they finished touring the gallery.

"So you'd like to have an exhibit of your own work, and you're willing to pay for it. Or at least," Max von Mayerling corrected himself as he noticed Katharine beginning to interrupt, "your father is willing to pay for it. Publicity included."

"I know it sounds like my father is just paying for a hobby. Poor little rich girl. But the photos are good and local and provocative. There's a surreal feel to them that's hard to explain" — *damn straight* — "but I think you'll be impressed." She could see that he was interested, so she gave him Thisby's best smile.

"Okay, okay." He smiled back. "I give up. Bring by some of your work."

Katharine could tell he was humoring her — flirting with her, but humoring her. *Why didn't I bring any of Thisby's work? Stupid. But maybe I can convince him. Thisby would have been able to convince him, I'm sure. I could try it, but nicely.*

"What's your name?" he asked.

"Thisby. Thisby Bennet. I really would like —" She stopped; something seemed to shift in him, but Katharine couldn't tell what it was. There was certainly some sort of recognition, but she didn't know what kind. It made her nervous, and she could feel a prickle of cold sweat between her shoulder blades. The smell of her strange self filled her nostrils.

"You're Robert's daughter? I know your father." Katharine relaxed. "He may remember us more from our studio on Sunset Boulevard." He considered her again. "Did he suggest our gallery?"

"He doesn't even know I'm thinking about exhibiting."

Max nodded slowly. "I think we can work something out. Can you come back tomorrow morning with your portfolio? Say, around ten?"

"Sure," she said hesitantly. *There's that portfolio again. Where would Thisby have put it?*

Katharine left feeling excited but a little guilty. Thisby's father's name had certainly turned the tide, but after thinking about it awhile, Katharine didn't care. She didn't care if it was his name and his money that got this exhibit going. She didn't even care how good Thisby was, whether she had been a talented amateur or something truly special. *It just doesn't matter.*

She was back the next day with Thisby's portfolio. She had found the large, zippered case propped up behind a filing cabinet in the darkroom. Inside were twenty mounted photographs of varying sizes separated by large sheets of thick waxy tissue paper. Thisby had signed the mats, and Katharine recognized the photos as the results of Thisby's tramps around the city.

> *. . . I've been spending a lot of time at Venice Beach. Me and my friends. What a scene. One night we grabbed the flyers some asshole born-again was passing out, the one who drags a cart behind him with the dummy in it. Weird shit. We preached to the tourists. When we got some money we let the old chink man rattle his bones for us. He told me I was a bright hot spark but would be extinguished soon. Fuck yes. Party hardy and leave a good looking corpse . . .*

> *. . . the little black kids thought I was some reporter come to put their picture on the front page of the Times. They got in the way of my shoot but then . . .*

> *. . . the suits were out in force today. What empty architecture they wear . . .*

Max looked silently through the entire run, sometimes scrutinizing them with a magnifying glass. "You print these yourself?"

"Yes," Katharine lied.

"Hmmm . . ." He shuffled a couple of them. "Some of these are good as is, but one or two I'd like cropped differently. This one, for instance." He held up a photograph of a squat structure made out of concrete blocks — a beach bathroom. There was a sandwich board on the ground in front of the entrance, PLEASE USE OTHER BATHROOM. It was foggy, or maybe it was late. The sky was gray and so was the sand and the building and the man who stood at the side with his back to the camera. There was a faint sheen to the wall in front of him, waist high, that dribbled down to the base of the building. "If we crop a bit more on this side, the pisser is even more diminished. Could be very effective. How many have you pulled for the exhibit?"

"Oh, around one hundred and fifty."

He laughed. "Archival-quality printed and matted? Like these?"

"Oh, no. Not like those." *Like those?* How was she going to print them properly? *I doubt the local photo store is appropriate.* "Just ones my sister and I liked."

"Okay. Well, bring them down, and we'll have a look." He glanced up at her and grinned, humoring her. "One hundred and fifty is a bit much. I mean, that's a lifetime's work, and you're not even dead yet."

Katharine dropped her eyes. "But they're okay? You'll show them?"

"Absolutely. They're wonderful."

"I think so too," Katharine said wistfully as she looked at them.

They grow on you. Maybe I didn't like them at first but . . .

She started. "I mean . . ."

"I know. I understand. Sometimes we wonder how we did it. It's like we were a different person. I think of it as a form of divine inspiration, so when we're back in our own bodies, it's not from egotism that we compliment ourselves. We're complimenting the inspiration that flowed through us for a time."

She nodded as if she understood, and said nothing.

"So you've got twenty here, and another hundred and fifty to look through. How 'bout Friday?"

Katharine thought two days ahead. "Friday's okay."

"Wonderful. Say, four o'clock. My assistant will be here by then."

It had been an eventful week so far. *I bear a charmed life. Sort of.*

The goals she had set, the feats she had to accomplish, the promises she had made, the wheels she had set in motion, were being realized. In order to be able to go home — when she was ready to go home — these things had to be completed. She had found Quince a job, and she would have Thisby's exhibit.

It was almost scary how simple it seemed to be.

Act 2, Scene 6 🦎

Some of us are cursed with memories like flypaper.

— ROBERT STEPHENS, *The Private Life of Sherlock Holmes* (1970)

Quince was over at eight o'clock the next morning. Katharine wasn't ready. She had thought she would walk Quince to the veterinary clinic as if it were her first day of school, but Quince barely leaned in, dropped her overnight stuff by the front door, waved good-bye, and said she'd be back around five.

Katharine felt hurt by this dismissal.

For God's sake, don't be like your mother.

She had a flashback to her mother on the sidewalk in front of their house, watching Katharine walk the length of the street to the corner. There Katharine would meet a classmate, and they would walk the rest of the way to school together. She remembered the feel of her mother's eyes on her back. Katharine would have to physically stop herself from turning around. It always felt as if her mother were right behind her; she could practically feel her mother's breath on the edge of an ear. Katharine would walk straight ahead, without one unnecessary movement. Her arms hung straight at her sides, her hands keeping the lunchbox and book bag from swinging, her head level. It wasn't that her mother ever said anything about her demeanor; she never did. But Katharine didn't want her to see, didn't want her to mark any part of her. When she reached the corner and had to turn around, she wished that once — just once — her mother would have already gone back into the house. But no, now it was Katharine's turn. She had to watch and make sure her mother got to the front door and into the house safely, her mother's last little wave another tug on the knot.

Katharine walked nervously into Mulwray's office later that morning. He had called the night before and said he had some information for her; she had fretted and fidgeted ever since, as if she were truly awaiting the ghost dentist with his bite blocks and drill bits.

This time there was a young woman dressed like a European model behind the sliding glass window. The desk in front of her was clean.

Katharine gave her name to the receptionist, who picked up the phone and said into the receiver, "Miss Bennet is here to see you."

A voice bellowed from the back office, "Kelly, just send her back."

Kelly stood up and leaned toward the window and Katharine. "My name's really Sabrina, but Mr. Mulwray says he calls all his temps Kelly. Isn't that cute?"

"Darling."

Sabrina let her in and escorted her back to the office. "Miss Bennet, Mr. Mulwray," she announced at the doorway and turned away.

Mulwray waved her in. Katharine could see all the furniture, and the files were in neat manageable stacks on the low bookcase. He got up and closed the door behind Katharine and motioned her to one of the two chairs in front of the desk. He sat down again and looked at the top file tab on a stack of folders at his right elbow.

"So"— he centered the file squarely in front of him —"preliminary information was rather easy to find, as you intimated." He lifted up the top single sheet of paper. "On Tuesday, June twenty-first of last year, at two twenty-two A.M., Katharine Rachel Ashley suffered sudden cardiac death."

"Sudden cardiac death?" TB's heart seemed to cramp, and

Katharine tried to relax it by breathing methodically. "Is that different"— she breathed —"from a heart attack?"

He took a minute to silently read further and then read out loud, "Sudden cardiac death is an electrical phenomenon that throws off the rhythm of the heart. It's different from a heart attack, which occurs when a clot inside the artery causes a blockage of blood flow. Scientists believe that high anxiety and intense psychological stress may trigger episodes of irregular heart rhythms that lead to sudden death." He looked up. "I didn't know what it was either and asked my researcher for clarification." He then continued reading. "Mrs. Ashley was cremated Friday, June twenty-fourth, at the Sultenfuss Mortuary. Interred privately, and a memorial service was held in the Berlin Funeral Chapel, Saturday, June twenty-fifth. Reception followed at the deceased's home. The death notice is in the file." He patted the folder. "Is this the kind of information you wanted?"

Katharine nodded, her neck so stiff, the nod was almost imperceptible.

"You'll get a copy of all this, but I like to go over it verbally. Then we both know whether I got the right stuff or not." He looked back down, one hand silently tapping the blotter pad. "Philip Burton Ashley married Diana Christensen, Saturday, May twenty-seventh of this year, at her home on Hanover Street, where the couple and the two children now live."

"They moved? But I . . ." *But I called them. I called my own number.* She couldn't believe it; her old number now rang through to this Diana's house. She had never imagined them in any other place than familiar surroundings, at the kitchen table looking out on the planter boxes filled with the current flowering annual, or Ben leaning back in the one of the precarious dining-room chairs, watching Japanese spy shows on cable TV for the heck of it, Marion and her homework littered across the table. She felt her grasp on them slip.

"Yes, but it's in the same school district, so the children don't have to change schools."

"Is it a big house?" *Jesus, I can't believe you asked that.*

"I have pictures." He gestured to a manila envelope in the

file but didn't bring it out. "They had their honeymoon in Vegas."

You gotta be joking.

"The children stayed with friends, though our contact did find out the son spent a great deal of time in the house at Ten Navarone Drive under the auspices of getting it ready for rental. He did have a large house party, and the police were called out to disperse it."

Katharine couldn't help but smile wryly. *That's my boy.*

"The new couple seem to be financially stable, though Mrs. Ashley is still paying off the last of her college loans. There was a good life-insurance policy out on the former Mrs. Ashley. A double indemnity, in fact."

I took that out.

"We're working on getting a contact in the school or the district office with access to the computer. I'm optimistic that we'll be able to get you a copy of their transcripts. As far as the more personal items, like copies of letters sent home? I don't know. That will be iffy. We'll try, but we'll need to go slow on that. At least, until the school year is closer at hand." He seemed to wait for Katharine to say something, but she couldn't trust herself to open her mouth. "As for their current activities, the daughter isn't doing much that's organized this summer. She isn't working or going to summer school, though she is taking tennis lessons at the club."

"The club?"

Mulwray glanced through the file and found another sheet of paper. "They belong to Club Paradise Swim and Racket. Mrs. Ashley had a single membership and now, of course, it's a family membership. Nice place."

"Oh."

"The boy, Ben, has a part-time job at Federal Security Bank."

"He has a job at a bank?"

"Yes, he works nine to five three days . . ."

But he would have to wear a tie! I couldn't even get him to wear a clean T-shirt. What is this? I die, and my children turn into Republicans?

He checked his notes. "We don't know when or how the

current Mrs. Ashley and Mr. Ashley met, but I'm encouraged that we will. People have been very free with information so far." Mr. Mulwray picked up yet another sheet of paper. "Diana Ashley was born Diana Faye Christensen, thirty-three years ago —"

I knew she was young.

"— in Santa Ynez, California. She graduated from CalPoly in communications and got her MBA from UC Berkeley. She works for United Broadcasting System. It's quite a large network. She's a member of the American Association of University Women, Business and Professional Women's Foundation, Women in Cable, and Women in Broadcast Technology. She also belongs to one of those local businessman's — excuse me, businessperson's breakfast clubs. This is her first marriage, and she has no children of her own."

Yeah, so she had to go out and steal mine.

"You should be receiving the local newspaper soon — let me know if you don't — and when school starts again, we'll get you the school paper. Well"— he leaned back with a decided air of satisfaction —"I would say that was an auspicious beginning. Don't you agree?"

Katharine nodded.

Well, you asked for it.

Mulwray seemed a little disappointed that she didn't say anything. "Do we agree to continue on the projected course, then reevaluate after school has been in session for a few weeks?"

She nodded again and paid him for the information.

"I know it seems like a lot of money," Mr. Mulwray said with some chagrin.

The price I'm paying now is not monetary.

Mr. Mulwray said he'd call her in a couple of weeks, and Katharine took the file and the envelope of pictures, nodded to the temp, and went out.

After she cried, arms over the steering wheel, head pressed against the spokes, wishing they would slice and dice her brain like a Veg-o-Matic, she sat in Thisby's car and looked at the manila envelope in her lap, her stomach roller-coastering though her lower intestines. Her hands shook when she pinned aside the brad, raised the flap, and pulled out the photos. They were all 8 x 10 black-and-whites. In her newly acquired knowledge Katharine thought that they were rather sterile but well taken, balanced and focused with good contrast. The top photo was of Ben and Marion coming out of a ranch-style house, heavily landscaped with low-maintenance junipers and evergreens. They were laughing, Ben's arm outstretched toward Marion as if he were in the process of playfully jabbing her in the shoulder. Ben was indeed in a tie, white shirt, and slacks, Marion in tennis gear. They looked older, taller, more mature than Katharine remembered them.

They look glorious.

The next picture was of Philip and, presumably, the new Mrs. Ashley, also coming from the house on their way to work. Katharine could even see it. He has just kissed her good-bye, holding her left hand with his right. They are leaning toward their respective automobiles, but their hands are still clasped just before the moment of release. Philip looks happy, relaxed, full — rich in love. Diana is tall and thin, wearing a tailored suit and tasteful gold jewelry that gleams even in the black-and-white photo. *When did this kind of woman attract him? With her good clothes and her good connections? He never commented on this type. He never followed them with his eyes as they wove their way around tables in downtown restaurants carrying their practical briefcases and expensive purses.*

There were a couple more photographs of Marion at the club, of Ben going in and out of the bank. There was a picture of Philip and Diana at a restaurant. They have been given a window table, and the shot is taken from outside. They are talking earnestly, hands held across the table. Katharine imagined the cameraman hiding somewhere across the empty outdoor patio, huge telephoto lens glinting in the dying sunlight.

She jammed the pictures back in the envelope, feeling dirty, as if she had just bought a *National Enquirer* featuring her own family, the paparazzi relentlessly dogging the happy couple. *Voyeur.* She felt drugged — Thisby's body heavy and dull, her mind slow and stupid. *One year* — and Ben and Marion already had lives she had no part in anymore. They were moving away from her so fast, she had no way of keeping up. As if from a long distance, she heard sounds — the pulling up of stakes, the snapping of roots — and she listened until there was nothing left to hear.

That night Quince came home with a puppy in a box. It was a sad little thing with barely opened eyes. "You remember the puppies from the clinic? Well, the mother died," she explained quickly. "She got something called eclampsia, or milk fever. The vets tried to save her, but they couldn't. It was awful. We couldn't just let the puppies die. We got all of them homes except one. This one. I couldn't just let him die. I have to feed him with a baby bottle every four hours. He would have died if I hadn't brought him here. No one else could take him. I couldn't just let him die. I . . ."

"It's okay, Quince." Katharine soothed her. "I don't mind. I'm not sure the super would be too happy if he knew, but I doubt"— she looked down on the barely moving mass not much bigger than her hand —"this one is going to be racing around and pissing on the carpet."

"What's with you these days? I thought you've always hated dogs."

"Me?" she asked incredulously and then realized who the "me" involved was — she had forgotten; she was no longer feeling such an identity crisis in this body. She ached to tell Quince how she loved dogs, how she knew just the right spot to scratch with just the right pressure, how she could correct Rathbone with one well-stressed word. "People can change, you know," she said lamely. "I don't mind as long as you're the one who gets up to feed him. I hope you're a light sleeper. What kind of dog is he? I know the mother was a German shepherd."

"Conrad thinks the father was a Malamute."

"Oh, a small dog."

"He won't get real big for at least —"

"It's okay, Quince," Katharine assured her again.

"I'm the only one who's supposed to handle him. Too many people, and he might get sick."

"Okay, he's all yours." But the scent of the puppy made her want to scratch his little head. "Can you manage dinner?"

"I plan to eat you out of house and home. I'm starved."

"A starved body has a skinny soul."

Quince looked perplexed. "I don't know that one. Falstaff?"

Katharine smiled a little self-consciously. "Marlon Brando." Quince continued to look puzzled. "Marlon Brando in *Viva Zapata!*" Katharine trailed off. "It's a movie. From the fifties."

"Umm. I like it. I wonder if Shakespeare said it first? I'll check the concordance."

Over take-out dim sum and tampopo noodles, Quince told Katharine about her day, the temperament and known history of the animals currently at the clinic. "Because we're so close to the University, we get a lot of animals that have just been abandoned. You know, the students leave for the summer or graduate, and they figure the animal can stay with the house or apartment, and the next guy will take care of it. It doesn't always work out that way. The vets are really nice. They do a lot of stuff for free, and we try and adopt the animals out, so they don't have to go off to the Humane Society, or to Animal Regulation. That's where they get put down." Quince visibly shuddered. "We also have a big program to spay and neuter animals. Real cheap, too. Sometimes we even get weird animals like snakes and birds and wild things. Conrad has a six-foot python at home that someone lost at a frat house and was found a couple of months later in an old Raiders' football helmet. He was so weak, he could hardly constrict enough to eat. Now he's fat and happy and named Reggie."

Quince, in turn, listened intently when Katharine told her about her meeting the day before with Max von Mayerling of the Ziegfeld-Zelig Gallerie, or the Zweimal, as its nickname appeared to be. "The Zweimal has good stuff," Quince said knowingly. "I like it there. So when are you telling Dad?"

Katharine had truly forgotten that she needed to do that. It was hard to remember that, as Thisby, she needed help from other adults for the exhibit to happen.

"Now is a time to storm. Why art thou still?" Quince asked. "If this Max guy knows Dad, he might find out before you tell him."

Carpe diem?

Katharine snapped apart the fortune cookie, the white strip of paper sticking out from one half like a tongue — "You will be fortunate in the opportunities presented to you."

"Hi . . . Dad. It's Thisby. Yes, Quince is here. She's fine. Yes, she's had quite a first day. I'll let her tell you about it later." Looking over at Quince, who was feeding the puppy in her arms, she added, "She's made a lot of new friends. . . . I'm fine. . . . Well, that's kind of why I called." *Jesus, don't you think about anything else?* "I've decided to take you up on your offer of the exhibit. . . . Yes, well, I changed my mind. . . . I — I already did that. I've got it set up . . ."— *we know what we're doing* —"Max von Mayerling at the Ziegfeld-Zelig Gallerie . . . Yes, the Zweimal. He says he knows you. . . . I'm glad you think so"— *not that it would have mattered if you didn't. Well, maybe it would. You're controlling the money* —"I meet with him again tomorrow. . . . Dad, please, if you don't mind, I'd like to take care of that part myself. I understand, but . . ."— *back off* —"Quince is helping." Quince looked up, rather surprised. "Okay, I'll call you this weekend." *Like hell.* "And . . . thanks, Dad."

Katharine handed the phone to Quince and felt guilty and glad at the same time. How unfair was it to ask Thisby's father to pay for the exhibit but not let him become involved and unknowingly help in his own daughter's memorial? Katharine felt territorial, and she was afraid that if she let Robert Bennet help, he would end up taking over the whole exhibit. He had that way about him, that going-overboard way. But who had more claim to Thisby's work, her father or Katharine's parasitic brain? Katharine didn't want to think about that too much.

Quince had hung up the phone and gone out on the balcony to smoke. Katharine watched her light up and suddenly felt the old loathing. She wanted to snatch the cigarette out of Quince's mouth and shake her until her earrings rattled like Yahtzee dice in a cup. She wanted to thrust Quince back in time three years and three hundred miles north, where, after a lifetime of smoking, Katharine's mother lay in bed waiting to die. "I'm so sorry to put you through all this," her mother is saying, while holding up a cigarette for Katharine to light. "It's my only pleasure left in life, and I'm not going to give it up. You can understand that, can't you?"

Katharine realized that her previous indifference to Quince's smoking had nothing to do with being a sister as opposed to a mother; she simply hadn't cared enough. A stake drove down, a root tendril dug in, and Katharine felt pinned. *There is no escape. You care; they can hurt you.*

Act 2, Scene 7 ❧

Do not give dalliance too much the rein.

— PROSPERO, *The Tempest*, 4.1.51–52

It was after nine o'clock on Friday evening. Norma, Max's assistant, had said good-bye and closed up a few minutes before. Katharine was tired, and the incessant headache made her eyes scream. But the exhibit was definitely coming together. They knew generally which photos they wanted, in what sizes, and in what broad categories. They had even discussed the layout of various flyers and brochures. Katharine was sure of a quote she wanted both on the brochure and enlarged at the entrance to the exhibit. She had found it among Thisby's photos. "If you expect to be supplied with beautiful and reassuring pictures which do not raise any problems in your minds . . . don't rely on me." Someone named Louis Aragon had said it at a 1959 meeting of the Young Communists in France, and it obviously had affected Thisby strongly.

"Let's have dinner to celebrate," Max suggested. "Hungry?"

Katharine wasn't, but the thought of another evening alone made her lie. "Sure. But I've got to go home first, if you don't mind. I'd like to change." She had been sweating through her clothes every day — this day was no exception — and the odor of perspiration that she still didn't recognize as her own irritated her.

"Okay, I'll follow you, and then we can go together in my car."

She left Max in the living room looking at some of Thisby's more whimsical photographs that Katharine had hung up. She walked into the bedroom and saw that her answering machine was blinking. She pressed PLAY.

"It's Hook. What the fuck's goi —"

Katharine punched the NEXT MESSAGE button. He had been calling for the past couple of days, and she had either hung up or erased his messages. She tried not to think about him, and concentrated on the next message.

"Hi, Thisby. This is your mother. Would you have Quince call me?" *Beep.*

"Thisby, is Quince with you?" *Beep.*

"Damn it, girls. I think one of you could at least call me if Quince is staying there again tonight." *Beep.*

"Thisby, Quince, don't make me go through this again. I don't think I could survive it."

Katharine called to Max in the living room. "I'm almost ready, but I need to make a telephone call first."

"Take your time. I'm fine."

She called, and the receiver was picked up in the middle of the first ring.

"Quince?" Anne's voice sounded balanced between anger and concern.

"No, it's Thisby."

"Where in the hell is Quince?" The white heat of Anne's anger sparked over the concern. "She was supposed to be home hours ago. I swear, Thisby, if you think for one minute I'm going to stand by and watch you try and turn Quince against me, then you've got another thing coming —"

"Wait a minute. I just got home. I don't know where she is. She went to work this morning and then was supposed to go home afterward. I haven't been here all day. Her stuff is gone." *Goddamnit. Why am I responsible for this one?* She rubbed her forehead, her eyes shut. "With that puppy, she can't be far."

"What puppy?"

"Oh, shit." *Oh, shit.* "She didn't tell you?" Massaging a temple, she tried to think. *Jesus. I guess I'm in it whether I want to be or not.* "Listen, don't panic. I think I might know where she is. I'll call as soon as I know. I promise."

Katharine went hurriedly back into the living room. "I'm sorry, Max. I've got to take a rain check on dinner tonight. Something's come up."

"Problem?"

"My little sister is missing. I've got to go see if I can find her."

"Need any help?"

"No. No, thanks. I might have to play the ref even after I find her. Thanks anyway."

In the elevator, just before the doors opened at the lobby, Max said, "We did good today. You work on the brochure and then call me." He leaned over to kiss her on the cheek.

Katharine was surprised, but was more surprised that she responded by quickly turning her head so his lips matched her own.

She drove to the veterinary clinic and parked in front. There wasn't a light on in the lobby, but Katharine could see a crack of light underneath the door leading to the back room.

Katharine pounded on the door and yelled, "Quince, it's Thisby. Open up!" There was no response, but Katharine banged and called again. The crack of light widened and rose up the doorjamb until Quince was silhouetted in the doorway.

"Would you open the goddamned door?"

Quince, looking thinner and more forlorn than usual, let her in. They walked silently into the back room. Quince had made a makeshift bed on the floor with her clothes and towels from the clinic. The puppy was hunkered down on a towel placed next to Quince's jacket pillow.

"Why didn't you go home?"

"I just couldn't leave the puppy. Conrad said he'd take him, but he knows only me."

"Okay, but why didn't you just take him home with you?"

Goddamn you, you've ruined my whole night.

"They'd never let me keep him. You know how Dad —"

"You didn't even ask?"

"No. But I know they'll say no. They —"

"What did you say to me last night? Something about time to storm. Why does it pertain only to me?"

"But what if they say no? What if —"

"For Christ's sake, Quince. What were you going to do? Be a runaway? Spend the rest of your life living here instead of going home?"

"No."

"You know I can't have animals in my building. Were you expecting me to hide a hundred-pound dog in my bathroom?"

"No." Quince sat down next to the puppy and lightly rubbed his toes. He twitched.

Katharine tried to rub out the creases in her forehead. "Okay. Call Mom and Dad and tell them what happened. Tell them — tell them it'll be just for a little while. You know, until the puppy can survive on his own." Katharine saw the angry but miserable look on Quince's face and sighed. "I know you want to keep him. I know that." She saw Quince shutting down, closing off. "Okay. Call Mom and Dad. Tell them what's happened. Tell them you're responsible for the puppy until he's big enough to be adopted out. Then let them get used to him. Get them to see that you can take care of him all right. Figure out a way to keep him out of the living room and the gardens. I can help you with that. I know a few tricks."

Quince sneered and started to speak. Katharine realized her mistake and cut her off. "They're not ogres, Quince."

"That's not what you used to say."

"For Christ's sake, Quince. People change. All the time. They change." Katharine felt that she was losing control of her act — and didn't care. "Go on. They're waiting for a call, and each minute you wait will only make them more mad and less rational."

"But so happy I'm alive, they'll say yes to anything?"

"Don't bet on it. And don't try and make them feel guilty about Snout. Guilt has a nasty backlash." *I should know.* "And another thing"— she could not seem to stop herself, did not want to stop herself—"you've got to let them vent their anger." Katharine could feel the weight of parenthood settling back down on her shoulders. "You've gotta listen to all of it. That's really your punishment. It's a pretty small sacrifice on your part, if you think about it. They'll feel better afterward too, and there'll be less hard feelings. Trust me."

"You're the professional?"

Katharine finally laughed. "Well, something like that."

So Quince went in the other room and called. Katharine heard her apologize, and then there was a long pause, then more apologies and soft agreements, and then a muffled explanation and more long pauses.

Parent time. There's nothing as screwy as parent time. There's nothing as wearing as parent time, and children are the time bandits. The shortest minute in the universe is when a baby is taking a nap, and you've got a million things to do. The longest minute in the universe is waiting for a child to come home, sectioning off increments of time like rungs on a ladder. At this step, I'll be mad. At this step, I'll be furious. Past this rung, I'll be ready to wring his neck. At this step, I'll be calling the other parents. Here, I call the cops. The hospitals. Then he comes home with some excuse like, I forgot or There wasn't a phone around or I was with some people who didn't want to stop or I didn't want to wake you or I told you I'd be this late — you just weren't listening. And your anger is like a pearl, layers and layers of irritated secretions compressed into a satiny orb. And you string these pearls around your neck to be burnished against your skin and sometimes to be unknotted and flung back at the oyster child, pelting him with beads of anger as fresh as the day the pearl was created. *I remember.*

After a while Quince returned, smiling. "She says I can care for him until he gets bigger, and then we'll see. It worked. I think. She was pretty mad, and I had to listen a long time. But she finally wound down, and I told her about Oberon. That's his name. Oberon. Wait until she sees him. How can she resist? She's coming to pick me up. You don't have to wait."

"I'll wait."

"At least I had to hear from Dad only once," Quince said as they packed up her stuff. " 'Sharper than a serpent's tooth it is to have a thankless child.' "

Quince put Oberon in his box, and they waited just inside the front door for Anne.

When Anne arrived, she roughly hugged-strangled Quince and then peered into the box at the sleeping puppy. "You say he's going to be a hundred pounds?" she asked incredulously.

"Well, not all at once."

"Good heavens, I should hope not."

They put Quince's stuff in the back of the Range Rover, and Quince waved happily to Katharine and climbed in.

Anne walked Katharine up to her car. "You got her to call, didn't you?"

Katharine nodded.

Anne's eyes narrowed as if she were trying to see what her daughter's ulterior motives were but couldn't quite figure them out. Katharine watched her exercise control over her suspicious mind. "You surprised me. I never thought you'd . . ." Anne sagged her weight against Thisby's car. "I'm . . . I'm sorry about what I said on the phone. It's just that tonight brought back so many memories, and I just couldn't . . . I don't think I could have . . . Never mind. I can handle a puppy." She straightened up. "Maybe you're ready to hear this now. I don't know. I don't believe in giving my children everything, but I like to think I know when it will hurt them not to be given something."

Then you know a hell of a lot more than I do.

Katharine lay in bed thinking about Max and perhaps kissing him again. The mere thought of it made her trill. She wondered whether it was Thisby's body or her own mind responding. She hadn't noticed that she felt starved for sex, but maybe this body was just a bit more demanding. *Is there such a thing as that?* She certainly knew or had read of people who desired sex more often than others, but she had always assumed it was their mind that desired it. Maybe it was their body after all.

She thought of sex with Max and, if it was anything like kissing him, didn't find the idea objectionable.

Objectionable? That's the only reason you can think of why not to have sex? What about commitment? Your marriage vows?

She had never been unfaithful to her husband. He was her first and only sex partner. The last time she worried about the dangers of sex was long before AIDS and even before herpes became a common problem. Her friends back then sometimes worried about pregnancy, but since almost everyone was on the Pill, there wasn't even much of that. Guys would have been embarrassed to put on a condom. The thought of using one to protect from much, much worse things than unwanted pregnancy paralyzed her. She had heard that people were now carrying around in their wallets results of their HIV tests to share before initiating sexual relations. So chastity was the best bet. Abstinence the safest sex. The safest sex . . . *single sex.*

Katharine shyly ran her hands down Thisby's breasts and felt the beginnings of a shape, nodules presaging a second puberty. She followed the curve of her waist to the spread of her hips, discovering the twin dimples at each side. They had been hollows two weeks before, she realized. She rubbed down her thighs, coming up between them, skimming across the material of her underpants.

She imagined Max kissing her, and her breasts tingled as if milk were coming in. Her hand planed her belly button and then slipped into her underpants. Her fingers ran through the pubic hair, curlier than her own had been. They flitted by the clitoris, and her body pulsed as the nerve endings sprang to the surface like escaping bubbles.

She jerked her hand away.

This isn't me. These feelings aren't mine. I didn't have to do things like this. God, I wasn't even fantasizing about Philip.

Her hand strayed over a breast, and the nipple pecked at it.

Someone was kissing her, his face too close to see clearly. She imagined his lips against hers, gentle at first but then harder, more insistent, his tongue exploring the depths of her mouth. She lost all shyness and stroked Thisby's body. It seemed to rise off the bed, her nerve endings afire, sparking and spitting, her breasts straining against her T-shirt, even the soft cotton stimulating the nipples to hardness. She rubbed her fingers back and forth over her pubic bone and across the hard knot of Thisby's clitoris, her other hand encircling one breast and then the other in an ever tightening circumference ending at the nipple. She could feel this body heat up — the pores, the veins widening to accommodate the surging blood. The focus narrowed under her fingers, gathered pressure, and consolidated. Her muscles clenched almost to cramping, and then her clitoris seemed to recede into that fearful place before orgasm. In this body, the agony was a trench, so low and deep that Katharine feared she would die again. Then the ascent toward ecstasy came, so fast and swift that Katharine lost her breath, and the spasms of coming arched her back. Noises came from Thisby's mouth that didn't seem to come from Katharine. She had broken out in a sweat, and she panted shallowly. Reconnecting with the bed, she slowly dissolved into it. Something had been released. Something once locked, now unlocked.

My God, what would it be like with a man?

Act 2, Scene 8 🐿

I don't know who I am anymore. I don't know what I remember
and what I've been told I remember.

— INGRID BERGMAN, *Anastasia* (1956)

Puck's apartment was at the back of a rather modest quadplex.
There was a small patch of deep green lawn outside his door,
flanked on all sides by flowers in planter boxes. *It seems that
Goodfellow was the one who took after Anne.* On a cement patio was
an umbrella table and aluminum washtubs filled with bottles
and cans of beer, wine, soft drinks, and water. The door was
open, and Katharine could hear music coming from inside.

It was seven-thirty Saturday night. Puck had called her
earlier in the week and invited her over to meet some of his
friends, including his girlfriend, Vivian. "There'll be alcohol,
but a lot of my friends don't drink, so there'll be water and
juice and Coke as well." She had assured him it would be okay
and then offered to come a little early to help. He was surprised, but he agreed.

She placed her hands on the door frame, leaned her torso
into the entry, and called loudly, "Goodfellow, it's Thisby."

His voice floated to her from a couple of rooms away.
"Come on in, Thiz. I'll be out in a second."

The apartment was neat and utilitarian, the carpet a cream-
colored shag that horrified her. *How could anyone keep that clean?*

She went into the kitchen to see what needed to be done and started to chop the vegetables that were draining in a colander. Puck came in, buttoning his shirt. Katharine noticed that his chest was tanned and defined, but not in that muscle-bound way she detested.

He gestured to the vegetables. "Looks like you've found yourself a job. So," he said as he opened the refrigerator to take out some dips in plastic containers, "I hear Mom and Dad not only got their daughter back but a canine companion thrown in as well."

"Did you talk to them today? How's it going?"

"Good, I think. Dad's resigned, and Mom's learned to feed the thing since Quince wants to go somewhere tonight. God, you'd think, though, that she'd pick another name. Oh, well. Mom's already taken with him. Dad's having a bit of a hard time, but I don't think he's going to be able to pull off with this dog what he did with Snout. Mom won't let him. Actually, I think Mom would have let us bring home all kinds of things if Dad hadn't been scared to death something would hurt his precious couches."

"His couches?" It was out of her mouth before she could flick it back with her tongue.

Puck looked at her askance. "Jesus, Thiz. Don't you remember how he lectured us about proper furniture behavior?"

Robert's the interior decorator? She had assumed it was Anne. But when she thought of Anne's kitchen, she realized that it was workable and livable, whereas the other rooms were too beautiful to be comfortable. *They were Robert Bennet's creations.*

She had to get Puck onto a different subject. When he had invited her over, she had already visited the Ziegfeld-Zelig Gallerie, but she didn't tell him of her intentions. "Goodfellow, I wanted to tell you in person, so I saved the news. I'm going to have an exhibit. In late fall, if we can get it set up that fast."

A voice came from behind them. "Set what up, RB?"

Katharine turned to see a rather petite woman with long, wavy dark hair, still damp, in high heels and silk stockings.

"It's Thisby. She's going to exhibit her photographs."

Puck bobbed his head in contemplation. "And it's about god-damned bloody time."

The woman smiled but seemed a little unsure.

Puck stepped forward between the two women. "Thisby, this is Vivian. Vivian, my sister, Thisby."

"Nice to meet you," Katharine said, holding out her hand. "Goodfellow has told me great things about you." She had a vision of Quince standing behind Vivian, sticking her finger down her throat.

"I've heard a lot about you too." She had a soft handshake that would have made Marion cringe. Katharine had expected something completely different from a female lawyer who was "a hard-ass in the courtroom." Vivian stepped back and added, "I'm a great admirer of Ansel Adams."

Puck laughed. "Thisby's photographs are a bit different from Adams. Maybe Adams on LSD." Immediately he looked liked he wanted to take that back.

Vivian turned sideways and nodded toward the bedroom. "I've got to finish drying my hair, but I'll be right out to help finish up."

Puck turned back to Katharine. "So, who's setting it up?"

"Max von Mayerling at the Ziegfeld-Zelig Gallerie. We worked on it yesterday."

"I hear he's good. The Zweimal's got a great reputation. I'm really glad you've decided to do this, Thiz. It's like real recovery now. I always felt that would be the sign. I don't know why, but I always did. It turns out I'm right or close to it. If you need my help, just ask. Though you'd do better asking Quince. She's much better . . ." He stopped and looked at her closely. "Was that what you two were doing last weekend?"

Katharine nodded.

He grinned. "This is great. This is really great." He seemed to go off into his head for a few moments, the grin still on his face.

Katharine stared at him and felt good.

He focused back on Katharine and noisily blew air out of his nostrils. "Quince worships you, you know."

"She worships you," Katharine retorted.

"Yeah, but in a different way."

The good way.

There was a halloo from the front door, and others began to arrive. Vivian reappeared with her hair piled up on her head and with small, square diamonds in her earlobes. She and Katharine finished the dips and put them out on the dining-room table while Puck offered drinks from outside. After a while Katharine had to admit that Vivian, though extremely overdressed, wasn't as bad as she first appeared. She spoke well of Puck or RB, as she called him, though she thought he could do better than studio law work. Katharine realized that Vivian was just very reserved and, *well, a bit cold. Funny, when I first met Goodfellow, I would have thought they would be perfect to-gether. But he isn't cold at all. They're a bit of an odd couple now. Nothing in common.*

Puck introduced her to most of his guests — the women appearing magically at his side, their real intentions only thinly veiled. *Vivian doesn't even see it, or maybe she doesn't care.*

> . . . *All the girls love Puck. They show up at my house supposedly to say hi to me but I know better. They come to see him. They say, "Oh, is your brother home? I'm supposed to give him a message from my brother. Is he in his room?"*
>
> *And then I never see them until they have to leave. Ta-ta. Puck says he doesn't want them hanging around either, but I know better.*
>
> *He's so good-looking and nice. I can see why they all love him. I just wish he'd stop playing father knows best . . .*

Puck seemed to take less care in introducing Katharine to the male guests. One was so handsome, Katharine could hardly stop herself from staring, since such good looks had always simultaneously repulsed and captivated her. His opening line, after Puck grudgingly introduced him as Benjamin Caine, was "First off, we shoot all the lawyers." He seemed to wait for the punchline, but Puck barely laughed. It must have been a very old exchange between them. Katharine wanted to correct this Benjamin Caine, as she had just read that quote from *Henry VI, Part II*, "The first thing we do, let's kill all the lawyers," but she could sense from Goodfellow that it would be too much trouble.

"RB says you've taken some time off from UCLA but will probably be going back in the fall," Benjamin said, as if they were old friends, after Puck had left them to greet some new guests. "RB and I were in SAE together, though he was older. Now I'm in law school too. Soon to be another one of the legal eagles. But, shit, we were the original animal house. Pledge night was killer. Did you ever go to our Paddy Murphies? Now there was a lost weekend."

> . . . *Puck is graduating. Or RB, as he wants to be called now. Yeah, right. He'll be off to UCLA next fall. He's even talking about rushing the SAE frat. I hope he doesn't mind me coming to the Paddy Murphy party. A whole weekend of partying. I'm sure as hell not gonna miss that . . .*

"What a killer party. Not that all of them weren't. We used to have these luge run parties. Remember them?"

Katharine shook her head.

"You know the luge. Like the bobsled but without the sides. Well, we'd get this big block of ice, put it on a table at a slant and chisel out a twisty, turny course. Then one person would pour a shot of whiskey or whatever at the top of the run and another person would be waiting at the end on his back with his mouth open. You'd get this awesome iced shot. We sure'd get pissed on that easy. Cocktail?" he pointed to her empty glass.

She wanted him to go away. "Thanks. Orange juice."

"Just orange juice? No tequila?"

"No."

"I'll be back," he said without much conviction, and took her glass.

I sure as hell hope not. Katharine was about to disappear into the bathroom when a voice paralyzed her. "I was named after one of the most famous pitchers in baseball. My dad's a real baseball nut. He even gave himself his own nickname. Hank, after Hank Aaron . . . Me? No, I hate baseball. Can't stand the sport. But it's a great name for a lawyer, don't you think?"

Katharine turned around to visually confirm what her ears already knew. It was him, all right — True Young Denton, son of Henry Denton and wife Emily, née Emily Ashley, sister to Philip Burton Ashley of northern California. This was her nephew.

Puck appeared at her side with some orange juice. "Benjamin asked me to bring this to you. I never did like him, but he's here with a good friend of mine. Benjamin's the kind of guy who thinks that with a flawless profile, a perfect body, the right clothes, and a great car, he'll get to the top. And in this city, who's to say he's wrong?"

Katharine took the glass from him absently, hardly taking her eyes off her nephew. She had forgotten how much he looked like Philip, the compact body, the thick, coarse, technicolored hair, the smile that transformed the quiet-looking face into something bordering on luminous.

Puck followed her gaze. "Haven't you ever met True?"

Katharine shook herself. "No," she croaked, and took a sip of orange juice.

"Come on. I'll introduce you. You'll like him. We were in the house together and then law school. He talks a lot, but he's a good guy." He turned, and Katharine was too stunned to do anything but follow.

"Hey, Puckman," True called when he noticed them approaching. "Nice party. Thanks for inviting me."

"I didn't. But I knew you'd come anyway. How's it goin'?"

"Same old, same old."

They shook hands.

"True, this is my sister, Thisby."

"We know each other already," he said, eyeing her critically from over the rim of his raised glass.

I should say we do, True Young Denton. Remember, I'm the one who sent you the Darth Vader light saber. You burned out boxes of flashlight batteries because you were afraid of the dark, all huddled under the covers, the light saber clutched between your knees. I'm the one who told your parents to leave you alone about it too. If it helped you with your nightwars, it was worth it. He continued to watch her, and Katharine grew suddenly uncomfortable. *What did he say? "We know each other already." He doesn't mean in the biblical sense, does he? Carnal knowledge?*

"We met at one of the Paddy Murphies. You might not remember. You were pretty wasted."

Katharine could feel Puck growing uncomfortable beside her. "No, I'm sorry. I don't remember you, but — hello, again."

"You look a whole lot better now than you did the last time I saw you."

She wanted to grab him by the collar and shake him. *Watch it, mister. I know your mother.* Katharine had always liked her nephew's directness, but at this moment she wasn't so sure. She hadn't seen him too much in the past couple of years. His parents lived in Long Beach, and although she usually saw them at Christmastime up north, True was always coming from somewhere and going off to someplace else. Some years they were lucky if he stayed through Christmas dinner. And if he did, he would get the whole family to play charades, even getting his mother, Emily, to stand up and mime movie titles, Philip laughing at her like any other younger brother would. When Katharine and True were paired, nobody could beat them.

"Did you ever finish up at UCLA?" he asked.

Katharine blinked, and her eyes felt tight. "Not yet." It felt odd defending her life. *Thisby's life, you mean.*

"Still optimistic." It was somewhere between a question and a statement.

True looked up at Puck and grinned. "I was just making conversation, RB. So whatcha been doing these days, Thisby?"

Puck answered for her. "She's finally going to have an exhibit. Remember when I used to brag about her photographs?"

"God, how could I forget? No, really, congratulations. When is it?"

"Late fall, I think," Katharine said.

"I'll be sure to make it. RB always said you were good."

"Our father is paying for it," she couldn't stop herself from adding.

"Paid for or not," Puck said, "the Zweimal has a reputation to uphold. Even paid for, they're not going to let some shit show in their gallery."

A thin and dramatic young woman with alligator eyes and a striking widow's peak came over and dragged True off to meet someone she had been talking to.

"He's really okay," Puck said, rather apologetically.

He was called away, and the circle collapsed in on itself to leave only her. She wanted a glass of wine badly. She found herself outside near the washtub with the alcohol, people around her busily laughing and talking. Her body moved closer to the table, as if something were gently prodding her from behind. Her skull clamped down on her brain. It was going to squeeze her cortex like an orange.

She sensed a presence. "How ya doin'?" Puck asked. "You okay? You're not mingling. Where is our usual manager of mirth?" He then looked embarrassed, as if the latent image of Thisby as the usual manager of mirth was not what he really meant.

But at the sound of his voice, Katharine found that she could think again, and the white knuckles around her brain relaxed. "I'm okay. How you doin'? I haven't seen you slow down once." She also noticed that he never had a drink in his hand.

"I'm the host," he said matter-of-factly.

When she left, one of the last to do so, Puck walked her out to her car. "I'm glad you came," he said. "Thanks for all your help."

"Thanks for asking me."

"I'm really glad about the exhibit. I think it's great."

She unlocked the car door. He held the door open for her, and she slid past him into her seat. He smelled of cologne, laundry soap, and warm body.

Act 2, Scene 9 ᥰ

What's gone and what's past help should be past grief.

— PAULINA, *The Winter's Tale*, 3.2.222

She started to feel uncomfortable in Thisby's apartment, uneasy, as if she were being watched. There was always something just beyond the corner of her eye, a presence, a smudge that slipped beyond her vision but never quite left. It wasn't necessarily friendly, but she thought she knew it. At least, it was not completely unfamiliar. It made her think of home when the kids were younger, of evenings before dinner, when she and Philip would sit down — he with a beer and she with a glass of wine — and talk. They might discuss work or the kids or what they had read in the newspaper that morning. Katharine wanted to wallow in the memory, but when Quince returned for her second stint at the clinic, the smudge disappeared so completely that Katharine convinced herself she had imagined it altogether.

One late afternoon in the middle of the week, after she had been diligently working on the exhibit brochure all day — bearing the weight of her labors, thinking how this must be, had to be, enough to appease the gods — she felt desperate to get out, to get her blood moving.

From the moment she stepped out on the street, she had the feeling of being watched again. She kept glancing behind her, but she couldn't see anything. She was walking home with her groceries past Willie Bill's Bar & Grill, the laughter and raised voices spilling out from the opened windows. A low, rather pleasant voice whispered to her, *Slush margaritas with lots of salt.*

Katharine whirled around, but nobody was there.

The voice continued whispering, very reasonable, not dark or sinister at all, and with an accent of familiarity, *Fresh chips in baskets. Chips and margaritas. Like old times. Just go inside and look around. No harm in that.*

She stopped spinning. She listened, but there was only silence. She must have been imagining things. But it wasn't a bad suggestion.

It was a noisy place with three suspended TVs tuned to a sports channel. In the center of the room was a square wooden bar with a brass footrail that wrapped around the base like a heating duct. Tables and booths filled in the remaining area to the walls. A waitress passed her, balancing a large tray of beers and margaritas in frosted mugs, wide red straws sticking out of the margaritas like candy canes. She placed them one by one in front of a booth of chatting professionals, their ties barely loosened, their suit jackets neatly draped across the vinyl padded back. When she put the last drink down, she added, "This is the nonalcoholic one."

Katharine felt her head jerk sideways as if she had been slapped. She clutched her bags and hurried out. Back on the street, she blinked.

What had she been thinking?

She called Goodfellow. Just to hear his voice made her fears seem silly.

"So are you going up to Ashland with the folks?" he asked, his opinion on the matter evident in his hopeful voice.

Anne had surprised Katharine the night before. "I'm calling you because your father and I are wondering if you'd like to come up to Ashland with us this year."

> . . . *Ashland. Shakespeare's Theater of the West.* "I like this place and could spend time in it.". . .

"Just think about it for a day or two," Anne continued, not waiting for Katharine to answer. "We're flying up Monday and staying through Saturday. Quince will be coming too, of course. Puck can't get away, but we'd love it if you'd come. It's been so long since you've come up."

. . . Every fucking summer it's the same. Ashland with the old farts. The plays aren't so bad but, shit, having to go out with the parental units every night sucks. I'd rather stay with Uncle Roy. He says I can . . .

"I don't know." *A week with Thisby's parents? I don't know.* "I'll need to think about it."

While they're away, I could be stealing home. I could be home in a couple of days. I could sit down and have that glass of wine with Philip.

But then I can't drink anymore, and he's got a new wife.

"Of course. I understand. Just let us know in a day or two, so we can include you in the flight."

It could be a good way to get a crash course in Shakespeare. "What's being performed?"

Anne hesitated. "Well, *Midsummer,* for one. I don't know if that interests you or not. Then there's *Hamlet* and *Much Ado.* But there are also a couple of good contemporary plays this year I'm looking forward to, Ibsen's *Wild Duck,* a new Fugard . . ."

Maybe I could make a play for Philip as Thisby. Then he'd have a really young wife. And I'd have an old husband. "Well, I don't know."

And Katharine still didn't know. "I hear you can't go," she said to Goodfellow, trying to keep the disappointment out of her voice.

He scoffed. "I've had enough of that. Hey, did True call you?"

"No. Was he supposed to?" *What does he want?*

"Well, he asked for your number. I hope you don't mind that I gave it to him. I figured if you didn't want to see him, you'd tell him. You were never very shy about that. But I hope you do see him. He's a fun guy. Light-years beyond that guy I heard you've been seeing lately. That Johnny Hooker guy."

She almost burst out laughing. *That's his real name? Or is that his occupation?*

Saturday night found her awaiting her date — *my nephew* — in a small Thai restaurant in Santa Monica at Zabriskie Point. She almost got up and left, but she told herself that she was being stupid. What was it going to hurt? What was she afraid of? True might think that it was a real date, but it was doubtful he was going to make an indecent proposal right there in the middle of the King and Thai Restaurant. And he could take a rebuff if she gave him one.

True arrived fifteen minutes late, still in his suit, tie knotted and squared perfectly over his top shirt button. "Sorry. I had to take a last-minute phone call."

They sat down. True seemed distracted and wasn't the brash, almost smirking young man from Goodfellow's party. He looked at the menu but couldn't seem to focus on it.

"Is something wrong?" she asked, a little hurt that he was so preoccupied. True did so look like Philip, though Philip would have never been caught dead in a suit and tie at the same age. That compromise would come later.

He looked up and was shaking his head as he answered. "No. No. Everything's fine. I just . . . I'm just thinking over this conversation I had before I left. That's all." He shrugged.

"Work?"

"What? Oh, no. It was something else. It was Holly. You know Holly? The girl at your brother's party. It was her."

He was silent, and Katharine waited. She remembered True couldn't stay silent for very long. If he changed the subject, then he really didn't want to talk about it.

"I don't understand her," he said, after only a moment or two. "She was the one who wanted to go lightly. Just friends, she kept saying. I thought we had something, but she wouldn't admit it. I thought we should admit it and see where it went. But no. She wouldn't do that. Now, all of a sudden, she gets jealous. Like I'm the one stepping out. I told her you and I were old friends. But . . . I think she's heard something about you. Probably about your rages. They're still legendary, you know."

Katharine bristled but kept her temper under control. "I'm not the competition. We're just old friends. All of that and nothing more."

True looked closely at her and visibly relaxed. "You don't mind, then?"

"I could use a friend." It was true. *I just didn't know how true it was until I said it.*

"Good, good. Friends are good."

Katharine felt the hinges in her jaw creak as she tried to loosen them up.

"You know, though, you always did intrigue the hell out of me." True grinned his devil smile. "Shit, you were something wild."

Yeah. That's me. Wild thing.

The image of seventeen-year-old Thisby swam into view. She's with True. It's the Paddy Murphy weekend. The moist smell of beer with a hint of vomit permeates the fraternity house. Thisby and True have staggered up the two flights of stairs to True's room at the top. He makes a vain attempt to kick the clothes on the floor underneath the bed, but they just pile up against the mattress. Five beers, still attached to the six-pack plastic ring, hang from his index finger.

Thisby laughs as the bed trips her up, and she falls back on it heavily.

True launches himself beside her and fumbles at her shirt, the buttons proving to be uncooperative. He bites the top button, trying to tug it off. Thisby's eyes burble behind their closed lids, and she goes limp. True looks up at her, the button still between his teeth. "Thisby?"

"Thisby?" True called her back. He took a sip of his beer and watched her. "It's still there. The wildness, I mean. It's just a lot more subtle now. More under the surface, you know?"

What a smoothie you always were, True Young Denton. Nevertheless, she felt this body heat up, and her face flushed with the
energy of it.

Soon they were sparring, feinting, jabbing — flirting.

The vision of Thisby passed out on True's bed stroked by
her.

*What in the hell am I doing? Would you please get your damned
signals straight. True could be the brother I never had.*

What about Goodfellow? What's he?

*Goodfellow? What? Oh, he's Thisby's brother, not mine. Anyway,
that's different.*

"Holly seems nice," she said abruptly.

True didn't look like he wanted to talk about her but
seemed to sense the shift in Katharine as well as in the conversation. "She is. We've known each other for a long time. You
sure you don't want some wine, a beer?"

More than anything else in the world.

Then go ahead, whispered a voice.

"No, thanks. I'm trying to quit." She clutched her teacup
with both hands.

Trying?

Oh, shut up.

"Why don't you tell me about one of your cases," she
added — *while I figure out a way to ask you about your relatives.*

Katharine ended the evening rather early. True seemed disappointed, but she was the one who was dissatisfied. She had
tried everything she could think of to get him to talk about
Philip and the kids. She had conjured up a phantom aunt who
had died recently, and told him how affected by her death she
had been. He almost reluctantly offered that an aunt of his had
died the year before and he was sorry, but he didn't elaborate.
She asked him how the aunt's husband took her death. He
couldn't have taken it all that badly, True told her, he's already
remarried — but he wouldn't elaborate. Katharine's heart
ached as it strained against its pinnings.

Then she told him about her aunt's son who had gotten
into bad company — her throat constricting as she spoke —

and True sympathized but seemed to be innocently ignorant of any problems his own cousins had.

True effectively ended the entire conversation by remarking that Puck hadn't mentioned that his aunt had died. They had just been talking about death a few days ago, and True was a little pissed that Puck didn't bring it up. Katharine changed subjects but remained frightened that True would confront Puck about it. *How would I explain this one away?*

Katharine realized, as they walked into the parking lot, that she had had a good time, though. *He could be a good friend.*

"Maybe we can see each other again," he said as he stood next to her while she opened her car door. "I can get tickets for some good concerts at the Forum. The partners take ones for the Lakers and Elton John, but they give us younger guys the tickets for the rock concerts."

"I don't know." She turned toward him, and he kissed her. She thought she should pull away, but it was like kissing a brother, so she didn't. Then the kiss went on a little too long, and it started to change; she started to change. She backed him off with a hand on his chest, and got into her car.

Katharine stepped into Thisby's apartment, trying to disentangle the tendrils of Thisby's life that were grafting onto her own, and she pulled up sharply just inside the door. A young man lounged on Thisby's couch, a trail of cigarette smoke above his head like a question mark, a tall beer bottle on the coffee table. It was inevitable, Katharine realized, and she didn't even cry out at the shock. Perhaps she wasn't even shocked. Maybe she had always known it would happen, and a part of her was just waiting for it. It couldn't be anyone else. It had to be Hooker.

He uncrossed his long legs and stood up languidly. He was tall, and as he got closer, she realized how coolly handsome he was with his dark hair, olive skin, and night eyes. He was dressed in black, just a pair of chinos and a long-sleeved shirt, but he looked designed.

"So you *are* back. What's going on? Why didn't you return my calls?" His voice sounded concerned, yet Katharine thought she could hear something else, something hard, underneath.

"Nothing. Nothing's going on." She felt beguiled, but she was proud of Thisby's voice. Her mind was quavering, but her voice was steady.

Katharine walked past him, the hair on her arms spiking with static electricity, her nostrils flaring to suck in his smoky odor, and went into the kitchen to put some water on to boil. She was trying to focus on something, anything, to ignore the screaming in her head and the writhing of this body. *What is going on?* She scanned this body, the hardening nipples, the tightness in the lower abdomen. *I can't be attracted to him. What am I? Insane? A nymphomaniac?*

"How'd you get in? That's unlawful entry, you know." She squeezed her voice so flat, it was just a thin stream of words.

His eyebrows pulled together. "The same way I always get in. With a key."

Deadbolts don't keep anyone out when you're not here to bolt them.

"What do you want?" Katharine was surprised at how controlled and defined she sounded.

"What do you mean, what do I want? I came to see you. I came to see why you haven't returned my calls." His voice reverberated, and the feedback dizzied her. He took a step toward her, and she stepped back. "What's going on with you? What's happened to this place? And you?" He eyed her with such possessive intimacy that screams began to gurgle in her throat.

"I'm clean." Katharine didn't know what else to say. *What else is there to say?*

"You clean up pretty good." His smooth talk washed over her.

"I mean, I'm really clean." The flatness was beginning to fill up with fear. The kettle whistled, and she wanted to cry as she watched her shaking hands move it to a cold burner.

"So you said. So where do I fit in with all of this?" He moved oh-so-slightly closer to her.

"You don't." She could smell the beer yeast on him. Part of her wanted to suck it out from his pores. "I'd like you to leave, and I'd like my key. Now."

"Leave?" His eyebrows lifted, and his clear, moonless pupils fixed on her. The whole sky was in his eyes. "But I just got here. I haven't seen you in a month." He spread his hands apart like a preacher. "And you probably don't even remember that. You weren't looking so good."

"I wasn't? What happened?" She leaned toward him unthinkingly.

He seemed genuinely confused. "Nothing *happened*. You just got some pretty strong shit. I don't know."

"Did you give it to me?"

"No, it wasn't any of my stuff." He looked insulted. "I don't know what you were taking that night. There wasn't much you *weren't* taking, as far as I could see. You're one vicious dope fiend," he added with affection.

"Was," Katharine said and felt the anger deflate and sag. "I was."

"Well, hell, now that you're clean and sober, let's go out and party. My treat."

"Go away." She brushed past him into the living room, trying to ignore the charge that spiderwebbed across her exposed skin.

He followed and stopped her by pulling back on her upper arm. His fingers were deceptively gentle. "I'm sorry, go away?" *Is that genuine hurt in his voice?*

"Wait a minute. Come on. Let's go out." His hand caressed her arm now. He was so close. So claustrophobically close. She could feel the approaching flashpoint on her skin.

Katharine jerked away from him. She was scared now. *Scream for help?* Would anyone come if she did? The front door tunneled away from her like a nightmare. *No one's ever in the corridors. The elevator takes too long. I don't know where the stairs are.* "I'm not going anywhere with you. Leave me alone." Could he even hear her? *Am I speaking out loud or only in my head?* His expression remained still. *Am I on tape delay?*

Noises off in the seeming distance brought them back in sync, and they turned toward the sounds. Quince was walking in the door, pulling out her key from the lock, another young girl in wrinkled cotton following behind her.

Quince looked up and didn't seem surprised at the two in front of her. "Ah, it's the bended hook. Whose slimy jaws are you piercing now?"

He hesitated for a long moment, looking from one girl to the next. "I guess I'll see you later then, Thiz." He reached out, took Katharine's hand and pressed a key into its palm. He then lightly etched her arm down from the shoulder with his fingernails, her skin puckering in farewell. He went over to the coffee table, picked up his beer, and drained it. Katharine watched spellbound as the backdraft pulsed in the bottle after each gulp. He walked by her, and she tried not to acknowledge his parting glances.

He appraised Quince as he went by. "Hey, Kewpie doll. How's the harelip?"

"Fuck you," Quince drawled and emphasized it with a thrust of her chin.

"In a year or two," he said calmly and walked out.

Katharine jumped at the door, shut and deadbolted it. Her knees turned to straw, and she wobble-danced to the couch and collapsed into it.

"What an asshole," Quince said blithely as she stood in front of Katharine. "I never could figure out what you saw in that king of codpieces."

He left too easy.

Quince patrolled a short route in front of Katharine. "Me and Gert have something to ask you."

He gave up his key too easy.

"Remember I was telling you about that all-day concert I got tickets for?"

Does he have another one?

"Well, I kinda got the wrong tickets. I thought I was getting ones for here in LA, but I was really getting ones for the show up north near San Francisco."

I'll have to change the locks.

"But we've got this idea. Gert's brother, Michael, was gonna go, but he can't now 'cause he wrecked their mom's car backing out of the driveway. So we've got this extra ticket."

What a fool I was. Why did I think he would just fade away when I didn't call him back.

"So we thought . . . well, I thought, maybe you could take his ticket and drive us there."

I gotta get out of here. I'll really go stir crazy if I don't.

"We could ask Mom for her Range Rover and then — I know you haven't said yes yet — we'd be halfway to Ashland, and we could meet them up there on Monday. Gert has some cousins up north, and they're going to the concert too. We got it all worked out. She could go home with them and then fly back to LA later. Michael can take care of Oberon. He's taking care of him right now actually."

But where to go?

"The problem is . . . I mean, it may not be a problem, but the concert is tomorrow. We'd really, like, have to leave early tomorrow morning."

Katharine stood up. "Tomorrow morning? No, we'll leave tonight. We'll leave right now. I'll throw some things together, and we'll drive over to Mom's and get the car."

It wasn't that easy, of course. Quince hadn't mentioned that Anne didn't know about this arrangement; neither did Gert's mother. The mothers agreed after some strong persuasion from Katharine and a lot of pleading from the girls. Katharine thought privately that Anne said yes only because of her own ulterior motives. It was obvious that Anne wanted Thisby to join the family in Ashland, and this would be the trade-off. Well, Katharine had a hidden agenda of her own.

There's no place like home.

What happens, though, when you don't know where home is?

Act 3, Scene 1 🐿

I think you people have proven something to the world — that a
half a million kids can get together and have three days of fun and music and
have nothing but fun and music, and I God bless you for it.

— Max Yasgur, farmer, *Woodstock* (1970)

The LA heat tried to smother the dying sun, but rays managed
to escape and ricochet off the swath of thick, gray smog, turning the sky a rose-orange. It was Saturday night, one week
after Katharine had driven out of the city limits. Now she was
returning, crawling along the 405, wedged in by automobiles
whose occupants would just as soon wish she was not there
either.

Ah, to live and die in LA. Is that also my fate?

Anne, instead of Gert, was now in the passenger seat,
dozing, and Quince was in the back plugged in to her Walk-
man. For Katharine, nothing had changed. She felt stunned.
She thought that somehow she would have escaped from this
dreamworld, that somehow on this road trip she would have
awakened.

Here she was, a week later, awakening — but awakening
into the same dream. She was meekly resuming the rhythm of
someone else's life, having given up her own with hardly a
whimper.

Lioness, my ass.

She had felt different up north, though. She thought she had seen a way. She had felt young and vibrant at the concert, and in Ashland the full flush of youth glowed within her. She was Merlin the magician, aging backward.

The week clicked in and out of focus in her mind like slides in a projector.

This is what I did on my summer vacation. This is the parking lot of the Shoreline Amphitheater, where the concert was. See those twin peaks? That's the tent over the main stage.

You're not going to bore us with the whole thing, are you?

I might.

It was her intermezzo, her interlude, up north. Time stopped, shifted, and restarted in a different direction — and at a different speed.

I forgot who I was and who I had to be.

From the moment they pulled into the concert parking lot at high noon, the swimming ripples of the summer heat so high off the macadam that Katharine felt as if they were going under, she knew that it would be no ordinary day. And when she stepped from the cool, rational confines of the black-and-white interior of the Range Rover into a world, odd and unpredictable, with its wide-wale spectrum of heat and smells and noise and colors, inhabited by the strange and unusual, she knew she was leaving normal behind. She fought it for a long time. It threw off her senses and her equilibrium. Nothing was as it seemed.

A huge tailgate party surrounded them — hatches of cars elevated, coolers perched on the lips of opened trunks, the smell of coals and lighter fluid, hot dogs, hamburgers, and an occasional chicken, mostly teriyakied.

It took her nasal memory a second or two to identify the softer but more acrid smell of marijuana, and she feared that she had made a mistake letting the girls footloose at something like this. She could hear Philip's voice, swirling around her, trying to soothe and caution her, "You agreed. Now let it go. Don't make it miserable for them just because you said yes."

• • •

Driving the long, dark miles of highway from LA to the concert, she had discussed and argued with herself about what she should do when she got close to home.

Katharine had always carried on conversations in her mind. They were the normal discussions most people have with themselves. At least, she assumed they were normal. This was another question she had always been too afraid to ask anyone. But now it was as if the different personalities in her brain had been given speaking parts, and it was getting crowded inside. Certain voices were easy to distinguish as the residue of people in her life. She could recognize her mother's gentle and sometimes needy voice — *Take care, Katharine, watch out* — Philip's logical, unflappable voice — *For God's sake, Katharine, it's not as if the world is going to end* — and her father's often irritatingly optimistic voice — *It will all work out; it was all meant to be. It just means that there's something better on the horizon.*

There were other voices that she didn't have names for. There was the sarcastic one that was always trying to tell her what to do, as if it knew better than she did. Then there was the voice that whispered with its ingratiating, persuasive, chummy lilt. It was a shadowy presence outside herself that felt familiar enough to be disconcerting. It was as if it sat on her shoulder, just tall enough to lean over and whisper down the length of her ear canal.

I'm hearing voices. Maybe I should be committed.

At first, she was going to turn off onto the exit to her hometown. *What are you going to tell the girls? How are you going to explain this one?*

As the sign for her city flashed above her, her hands stayed still on the wheel, and the exit slipped by.

All right. I'll drop the girls off and then come back.

In the parking lot, she was torn. *You can't leave them alone. They're your responsibility now.*

Maybe Ben and Marion are here. Maybe I'll see them. It's something they might do together.

You're here. You might as well try to enjoy it.

As they walked to the entrance, Katharine thought she saw Ben or Marion a dozen times. She hurried the girls along this way and that, to pull up alongside someone wearing a shirt similar to one of Marion's, or walking pigeon-toed like Ben in those black, high-top boots that looked so terribly hot and uncomfortable. But they were not them.

At the entrance, she got frisked.

A hip-looking security guard with round sunglasses reminiscent of John Lennon's stopped her to check the backpack that she had stuffed full of needful things from Thisby's apartment — clothes and sunscreen and hats and Band-Aids. When the guard returned her pack, she started forward, but he stopped her again. "I'm sorry, but I have to pat you down."

The girls were disappointed that they didn't even get stopped.

It had been kind of fun to get frisked. It was almost as if she were a . . . *a dangerous woman.*

At the midway, they split. They made arrangements to rendez-vous there every three hours, unless a band was playing — then they would meet right after it finished.

A mother couldn't have said it better. But I didn't say it. Philip would have been proud of me. It was Quince's idea.

To the right was a flea market, the vendors selling a hodge-podge of concert wear and accessories, silver and beaded jew-elry, East Indian–inspired baseball caps studded with dime-size mirrors and other sparklies, and anything in Rastafarian green, yellow, red, and black. The temporary tattoo and body-piercing booths were doing a brisk business. Katharine watched a girl get her nose pierced. The young woman almost fainted when the gun went *pop!* through her flesh; her friend teased her for being a wimp.

The cloying smell of burning incense spread from punks that lined most of the booths' tables and shelves. A tendril of smoke spiraled right into her brain, and Katharine tripped back in time to Ben's room, rancid with stale incense, the punk burning holes in the carpet, Marion complaining of the smell, and Katharine wondering what other smells the incense was covering up. She regressed deeper into memory. She was a sophomore in high school. There was a party at some senior's house. She had gone with a girl who lived on her block but who normally hung around with a faster crowd. They drank tequila sunrises at the girl's house beforehand, the only time Katharine had ever been drunk in high school. The backyard, full of the in crowd, and full of marijuana smoke, had tables covered with food for when the reefer madness hit them and they got the munchies. Katharine saw a guy who she had always thought was cute, a football player two years older and with all the right moves. *God, I even remember his name. Stef Djordjevic.* Before she even knew how she had done it, she found herself backed up against the patio wall, making out with Stef Djordjevic. She remembered the incense burning — sandalwood — and his tongue, his body pressed up against hers, his crotch matching hers, hard and pressuring, his insisting they go to his car — her resisting — his urging. She had gotten scared and bolted, the alcoholic fog dissipating in the anxiety. She remembered finding her friend intertwined with some other senior and demanding that they go home.

The next day she had felt that the scarlet letter A — for Alcohol — was seared across her forehead, but her parents continued in their befuddled ignorance. She had a hangover but was sicker with the memory of being prodded by Stef Djordjevic. She felt way over her head and had vowed to never give up control like that again.

Katharine continued down the concourse hung with banners spelling out various political causes: safe sex, abortion, Greenpeace, Amnesty International, animal rights, marijuana legalization. She scrutinized those collecting literature who had the contours of her children. She was mad if they were standing at the marijuana-legalization booth, frightened if they were at the abortion-rights table, proud if they were supporting Amnesty International, and disappointed when she realized that none of them were her children.

This is ridiculous. I don't belong here. I have no reason to be here. My children aren't here. And even if they were, what would I do?

She could never think past the image of spotting them, walking along together, Ben protecting Marion from the sleazoids who appeared to be all around her. The frame always jammed up and then melted, the center curling back until there was nothing left to burn.

On a patch of grass half a dozen people were sitting on folding chairs, holding large purple viewfinders like snorkeling masks over their faces. A man in his late forties, in tie-dye from bandanna to drawstring pants, was pulling more viewfinders from a large cardboard box and speaking softly to the vendor next to him. "My distributor really blew it. I could have sold two thousand of these today." He turned and addressed the group. "This is an LSD flight simulator, and I'm your pilot . . ."

Katharine turned away — *what suckers* — and retraced her steps to the entrance. She continued on to the left of the split; the scent of food was so heavy, she could walk on it: grilled chicken and beef over open pits, frying onions, garlic, curry, saffron, and hot barbecue sauces. People were walking around with corn on the cob, meat and vegetables on skewers, huge turkey legs that they were tearing with their teeth and fingers like Tom Jones.

In front of a small stage off to the left, a large group of people periodically crowed with approval. It took Katharine a while to realize that the person on the stage, who was dressed in a G-string and an unbuttoned leather vest, was picking up cement blocks attached to chains that were hooked to rings threaded through his nipples. The ringmaster was explaining how Mr. Lifto was next going to use the ring through his penis to lift — The announcement of what exactly he was going to lift with the ring through his penis was lost as Katharine turned away from the trajectory of sound and went up the ramp to the amphitheater.

The amphitheater was bowl-shaped, funneling to a stage that looked impossibly tiny, where roadies were setting up for the first group. At the separation between the grass seating and the rows of orange-colored chairs, large video screens puffed like sails.

Along the lip of the stage ceiling there was a computerized message board espousing all manner of politically correct statements:

RECORDS DON'T KILL KIDS — BULLETS DO

and

THE EARTH IS NOT DISPOSABLE

Most of it was hip trivia, though, meted out in short phrases like sound bites:

AVERAGE LENGTH OF SEXUAL INTERCOURSE —
   IN HUMANS IS —
      TWO MINUTES

75% OF AMERICAN WOMEN —
   WEAR THE WRONG —
      BRA SIZE

PERCENT OF NUTS SQUIRRELS LOSE —
   BECAUSE THEY FORGET WHERE THEY PUT THEM —
      50%

Everything was whirling around her. It was overkill — the sounds, the smells, the Hardbodies, the Winter People — that's how she thought of the two groups of young people who surrounded her.

She watched a Hardbody — a tanned, shirtless young man — pull a Ziploc bag from inside the waistband of his jeans. Amber-colored liquid sloshed from side to side, leaving gold droplets clinging inside. He poured a third of his large soda into the grass and, after slitting the seal of the bag, tipped the alcohol into the cup. He took a sip, the hard, flat muscles of his stomach shivering, and passed the cup to a young friend, who grinned and sipped and passed it to a third member of their group, a girl in low-slung shorts, her underwear rising high over each sun-bronzed hip, and a crop top with SOME LIKE IT HOT printed on it.

The Winter People — their wraith bodies clad head to toe in black with silver accessories, their pale skin already reddening — passed around a conch shell no bigger than their palm, a Bic lighter held over the length of the lip.

Thisby had been one of the Winter People, Katharine realized, seeing Thisby in her mind's eye. She's at an event similar to this one. She's wearing the bell-bottom jeans and the denim halter top Katharine had found in the bedroom. She even has an authentic Woodstock necklace on, the silhouette of a bird perched on the neck of a guitar. A narrow thong of rawhide is tied around her forehead, the beaded ends tickling an earlobe. A roach clip in sunflower filigree is clipped to the inside of her halter top. She's out cold, unconscious, on the lawn. Her friends have ditched her, leaving her to sleep it off and afraid to be in the vicinity when she wakes up to find her face almost blistered by the sun — the roach clip gone. And she has missed the concert.

Chords crashed, and the first band began to play. Katharine watched as a group of kids down the slope started running in a clockwise circle, a haze of kicked-up red dust hovering overhead like a familiar. Every once in a while, a body was hoisted over the running mass and passed on shoulders until it was sucked back into the maelstrom.

The boys in the band tried vainly to incite the crowd. "Don't let the deciders decide for you. Fuck the deciders. Your anger is a gift." The crowd in the orange seats responded dutifully, but the grass crowd seemed too busy with their alcohol and their drugs and their hair to react at all.

A voice floated from the loudspeakers. Katharine tried to see the miniature human on the stage. "I'm Dr. Timothy Leary," the voice said. "Am I having a flashback to Woodstock?" The crowd yelled. He introduced the next group, an all-girl band, and ended with the admonition "Learn how to program your brain." The crowd nodded collectively at such sage advice.

Katharine sneered. *The sixties are gone, and here's another generation trying to rip them off.* She wanted to spell out another item across the computerized message board:

GET A LIFE — GET A FUCKING GENERATION OF YOUR OWN

Oh, knock it off. You're just feeling sorry for yourself. What did you have in common with the Woodstock generation? You weren't a hippie or anything. Hell, you just watched. The movie. The news. Where it was safe and easy. Just because you were such a Goody Two-shoes doesn't mean everyone else has to be. It doesn't make them degenerate or future drug lords.

But it takes just one time. One damned time. I know. I lost Eve that way.

That was an accident. This is an Event. They're busting out. Give 'em a break. Tomorrow they'll be back at their jobs or back to school . . .

Tightly compressed images battered at her neurons like blipverts, overloading her system, and she feared that she would spontaneously combust.

She got a hand-drawn henna tattoo above her heart. She thought it would distract her.

"That one." Katharine pointed to the zodiac sign for Gemini, two identically beautiful, fair-haired women joined back to back, their hair twined around each other's throats. She didn't like the crabby sound in her voice, but she *felt* crabby. "But different. I don't want them to be twins."

The artist fiddled with his tools. "Opposites, then? One dark, one light? One Jekyll, the other Hyde?"

"No," she said, immediately horrified, and was startled at her own strong reaction, though it somehow softened her mood. "Just different. Not opposites. Just different." *Just different. Because if we're opposites, who has to be Mr. Hyde? Am I so sure that it's Thisby?*

When it was done, no matter how she craned or ducked her head, she couldn't see the tattoo properly. She fought her way forward in one of the restrooms to see her image in the mirror. Thisby's elfin features stared back at her, her pale brown hair beginning to flatten. Katharine ran a hand through it to spike it back up. She realized that Thisby had been essentially right; darker hair would probably be a better color for her, more dramatic with her pale skin and light eyes.

She changed into Thisby's halter top and bell-bottom jeans — they were some of the things she had on impulse stuffed into the backpack — and the curve of the halter top delicately framed the tattoo of the two-faced woman. Both faces were young and attractive, but one seemed stronger, the other smarter. She could see the tattoo only in the mirror, and therefore only in reverse.

"Great threads," said a girl who looked like Elvira, Mistress of the Dark, with her black hair, black makeup, and white skin.

"Yeah, they are." Katharine took a last look at her reflection; it was almost with affection. *Okay, Thiz, let's try this again.*

"Shit," Quince commented approvingly when she saw her sister at their next meeting. "Where'd you get that outfit? Is that a tattoo?"

"I had the clothes. The tattoo is temporary. You guys having fun?"

The girls were sweating as if they had been in a race, but they wiggled with yet unexpended energy. Quince was bare of face — no earrings, no nose ring, no chains — and she looked somehow strangely exposed, almost naked.

"The pit's bad. There're some crazy guys out there. Gert lost her balance and almost got trampled. I need something to drink. Can you get us a beer?" Quince pointed to the red bracelet around Thisby's wrist.

Katharine had felt strangely obligated, after she donned the new clothes, to approach one of the many ID stations where, after a rather cursory perusal of Thisby's driver's license, she had been equipped with a hospital-style plastic bracelet that identified her as a legal drinker. She had waited for the whispering to begin, but she heard nothing.

"Why not?"

She waited in line. Perhaps she would get a beer for herself too. Maybe the silence was a sign. Maybe it meant she could drink again.

Hey, this is an Event. I'm busting out. Tomorrow I'll be back to safe, old, boring Katharine.

She was next up to the counter. She suddenly didn't feel so good. She had that sense of being stretched again, as if something were pulling at her, tugging at her, driving at her. Spores of anxiety popped like sweat in her brain, and the rhythm of her heart became irregular. She started to tremble.

"Thisby, are you all right?" Quince pulled her from the line and sat her down in the shade. "You're shaking like crazy. Are you cold?" Quince took a sweatshirt from Thisby's pack and wrapped it around Katharine's shoulders. Quince and Gert waited silently until she stopped quivering.

The sun had set, and although it was still light, the blue sky was darkening to shades of gray. The relentless energy of the crowd had mellowed. The frenetic edge had softened, and people moved more deliberately.

Katharine came upon a pentagon-shaped structure called the Rhythm Beast made with a life-size Erector set. At the five corners hung speakers draped with animal pelts, and from the crossbeams remnants of a civilization dangled down: hubcaps, washtubs, inverted pails, a car radiator, a bed frame, and various lengths and widths of sheet metal and tubing. It was a vision of the Apocalypse — now the salvaged technology is good only as junk, and it is crowned by the real trophies of life: skinned and scalped prey.

Katharine stood there and watched. She had stopped looking for Ben and Marion in every step, dress, face that passed by. It was as if she had had double vision all day long — always stepping awkwardly, afraid she would lose her balance. She now felt strangely light. She weighed less. Gravity eased. Her vision cleared.

Five men approached the Rhythm Beast, ringing its perimeter. They picked up the drumsticks that hung from wires and hammered out a rhythmic pattern on the metal in front of them. Katharine could feel the syncopated pulsebeat like tremors burrowing up from the ground and grabbing her bones. Her heart, her blood pressure, pumped with the tempo, the cadence. She wanted it to go on forever, but a young man with lank hair barked, "one-two-three-four," and the drummers jumped to the next panel and began a different rhythm. Her body shifted easily enough and conformed to the new pulse. It felt right again, but then the leader yelled once more. Another shift, another rhythm, another beat. Each time Thisby's body seemed to adjust and achieve synchronization immediately. Katharine could have stood there all night, but the group abruptly stopped, leaving the last tremors to slowly ripple through the soil — tangibly — and her body to continue to throb like a sustained note.

She sat down heavily on the nearest chair, and the tie-dyed LSD flight simulator pilot handed her a viewfinder, a tube jutting out from the bottom. The top of the mask went up to the hairline, the sides to the ears, the tube in between the lips. Recessed in the cut-out eyeholes were whirling, multicolored disks. She blew gently into the tube. The circles passed the open eyeholes like softly flickering strobe lights. They made her high and dizzy, and her stomach started to cringe. "Blow harder," she heard the man say, and she increased the shutter speed. Her eyes stopped trying to catch the circles, and her stomach settled back down, the sustained throbbing from the Rhythm Beast still humming through her ears. Instead of the air escaping out the tube, it felt like it circulated back into her body, expanding it. She didn't feel connected with the chair or the ground under her feet; the slightest puff of wind would send her off like an escaped helium balloon. The sounds, the smells dissolved around her, and she swelled until she thought she was going to explode. At the instant of explosion, she collapsed in on herself, the extraneous parts of her hurled away and the essential parts coalesced.

What was left was a new pulse, a new rhythm, but this time it was her very own.

Nothing is as it seems. And that's okay. Thisby did not kill me, and I don't have to hate her.

There was a tap on her shoulder, and a voice said, "I'm sorry, but you really do have to give it up this time. You can buy one. Only twenty-five dollars."

Katharine pulled it from her face with a sweaty sucking sound. She stumbled up — he steadied her — and handed the viewfinder to him wordlessly.

"Are you all right?" he called after her.

The headline group was playing when she returned to the grass, their images projected on the giant screens. The rhythm was still with her, a descant to the meter playing from the stage. She was feeling drunk, stoned, out-of-bodied, but not isolated. She was suspended among a larger entity. *Maybe I am stoned. I . . . I feel so big.* Her arms stretched out across the whole amphitheater. *Oh, the things I can sense.*

She could almost see anticipation taking shape in the audience. The pit continued to circle in the dark like molasses while the rest of the crowd stood, singing and dancing, but they were waiting for something. When the music seemed to be over, and the band had walked off the stage, the audience yelled and clapped and demanded attention. The promise was unfulfilled, the anticipation not satisfied.

The group returned to the stage for the encore, and when the opening guitar riff was played, the entire assemblage screamed. This is what they had been waiting for. The crowd began to sing along, and Katharine found herself listening to the lyrics:

> Today I'm gonna live the life I never had.
> Play the adult I'll never grow to be,
> Pray like the child I'm never gonna have.
> I think I deserve to take that trip,
> So that I can connect the two and create me.

The last chords died out. The curtains closed, and the lights came on. The multitude was satisfied. They would leave now.

Katharine stood still as the crowd collected its possessions and drained down the walkways. She watched the people leave, and she felt satisfied too. It was almost love. She smiled at the Winter People with their seared red skin and their silly outfits. She wanted to pat the Hardbodies on their goosepimpled brown arms. She felt a part of all of them, part of the pattern. They had shared something. An Event. Community. Peace. Love. *And understanding.*

Maybe their generation isn't so bad.

It was after midnight when they drove out of the parking lot, the taillights of the cars in front of her strung out like a centipede crawling toward the freeway. They had already transferred Gert and her luggage to her cousins' car, and Quince was curled up in the backseat, her eyes closed.

Katharine was glad Quince was quiet, because she was occupied elsewhere — having a conversation elsewhere.

Katharine had died. Thisby had died. But Katharine still had a life. Her own family were like shape-shifters; she couldn't seem to hold them long enough in her mind to know what she wanted from them. Maybe she had a life with the Bennets; she and Quince were forging something good. But maybe not.

Maybe it was just a life for herself.

> "I think I deserve to take that trip,
> So that I can connect the two and create me."

Act 3, Scene 2 🪶

All the world's a stage
And all men and women merely players:
They have their exits and their entrances;
And one man in his time plays many parts,
His acts being seven ages.
— JACQUES, *As You Like It*, 2.7.139

She had felt the immortality of a teenager as she drove north from the concert with Quince, sleeping a couple of hours at the Dunnigan Pit Stop, which was just off what Katharine remembered from childhood as Temp 505, which connected Highway 80 and Highway 5. She had no idea when the 505 had gone from a two-lane country road to this four-lane highway with its sides blasted clean of anything human, no billboards or signs for gas, food, lodging. She missed the reptile zoo in the run-down barn, the nut-and-dried-fruit stalls and the Burma-Shave signs.

> DON'T LOSE
>   YOUR HEAD
>   TO GAIN A MINUTE.
>   YOU NEED YOUR HEAD
>   YOUR BRAINS ARE IN IT.
>   BURMA-SHAVE.

She had felt invincible, the darkness rolling around her, Quince laid out and softly snoring in the backseat. Maybe it was the strength that the concert had left her with — or the release it had given her. Maybe it was the speed and power she felt through the steering wheel of Anne's car.

Or maybe it was just the height.

She remembered cruising her hometown's version of Sunset Strip with her high school friend, Eve White, in Mr. White's beat-up GMC truck, country music blaring from the tinny speaker. Eve had listened at home to acid rock on the local FM station like every other self-respecting teenager at the time, but sitting high up in her daddy's truck, she seemed to put on a different face, singing along with Tammy Wynette and novelty songs like "Dropkick me, Jesus, through the goal posts of life, end over end, neither left nor to right." Sometimes Eve would scream out the window at someone who had pissed her off, "Don't fuck with me, bubba. I got two fuel tanks and a fourth gear that'll turn you into roadkill."

It had felt a little like that.

Ashland overlooked a valley of patchwork farmland, and the mid-morning heat had the smell of mountain elevation. Katharine had been too restless, too energized to sleep after they had put all their stuff in their room at the bed-and-breakfast where Anne had made reservations, the Cowslip's Belle. *In a cowslip's bell I lie.* Quince, who was not under the same restraint, fell into the daybed and was asleep again within minutes.

Katharine walked the two blocks lined with red-and-yellow banners on the lampposts into the center of town, passing by stores with names like Puck's Doughnuts, All's Well Herb, and a restaurant called Quinz, which made her laugh. She climbed a long stretch of stairs into a bricked quad framed by festival buildings. A wooden sign proclaimed an oddly roofed edifice surrounded by ivy-covered walls as AMERICA'S FIRST ELIZABE-THAN THEATRE.

There were people standing silent in the quad, many holding cardboard signs. Katharine stopped by a gentleman whose sign read WANTED: 2 FOR HAMLET. TOMORROW and asked what was playing that night.

He looked at her blankly. "It's Monday," he replied after a moment's hesitation.

Katharine didn't see how that answered her question, so she waited.

"Monday's a dark day," he tried again, but Katharine was still confused. "There are no plays," he said, and then added with some irritation, "Never on Monday."

So she crashed a tour group that stood near her and was told again that there were no plays on Mondays, that the area they were in was called, appropriately, the Bricks, and before each evening performance, there was something called a Green Show, where performers danced and sang in the Renaissance style. She learned that a vomitorium was not a place to get sick in but a ramp underneath the audience that actors entered and exited the stage from. Rumble pots produced fog, squibs were tiny explosives to simulate gunfire, and gels were colored plastic filters placed in front of lights to produce colored beams.

I'm ready for my quiz, Mr. DeMille.

Robert and Anne arrived sometime in the late afternoon while Katharine was sleeping. Quince tried to get her up with temptations of dinner, but Katharine just waved her away. She awoke again sometime later, the evening fading. It took her a while to remember where she was, but she got up with an air of expectancy once she did.

She walked back to the town square and beyond it to a grassy area, heralded by a sign that said LITHIA PARK. Night was falling, and people were packing up their picnic baskets and blankets. A creek ran chorusing alongside the park, and Katharine could feel the humidity rising up from the lawn as she walked farther in. She took a turn on the swings, something she hadn't done since Marion was a toddler and needed to sit in Katharine's lap while they gently swung back and forth. She could feel the phantom weight of Marion on her thighs and felt oddly comforted.

The old-fashioned lampposts that lined the walkways around the park had diamond-webbed, wrought-iron shades. They gave the park a timeless, magical feel. She wouldn't have been surprised if they were gaslight and a lamplighter had appeared in top hat and waistcoat and lit each one, wick by wick. Or even if Mr. Tumnis, the faun from the books *The Chronicles of Narnia* both she and Thisby had read as children, popped up and waited under one of them, his long tail draped over an arm that held his umbrella. It would start to snow, cold and soft, and if she turned around, she would see the wardrobe she had spilled out of into his magical kingdom.

And all things would be possible.

She blinked and shook off the fancy. The electric lights in the lampposts that had turned on simultaneously steadied in their 500-watt incandescence, the sound of automobiles could again be heard from the street, and the moist heat of the ground rose up around her.

But that night in her dreams she had a sense of softly falling snow.

"Will you come with me to the Exhibit Center? I want to see what costumes they've put out this year," Quince asked Katharine after their breakfast with the other guests of the Cowslip's Belle. The two other couples, a gregarious brother and sister and their quieter spouses, met at the Cowslip's Belle every year. The brother and sister looked a great deal alike, their salt-and-pepper hair binding them inexorably to the same gene pool, and Katharine imagined Ben and Marion meeting like this in the future. The short cuts in the siblings' language, the shared experiences, the towering faults in one's memory when the other remembered better, made Katharine wistful.

Maybe Quince and I will sound like this someday too.

The owners of the bed-and-breakfast, Sybil and Basil, seemed to be old friends of the Bennets. Basil even kissed Anne, called her "fair Helena," and launched into who was playing her part in this season's *Midsummer*. "She's not the best Helena I've ever seen, but she's not the worst."

Anne played Helena, not Thisby?

Sybil turned to Katharine and asked, "So what do you think of Ashland after so many years?"

" 'I like this place and could spend time in it,' " Katharine recited from Thisby's diary.

Quince huffed. "Jesus, Thiz, it's 'willingly could waste my time in it.' 'I like this place and willingly could waste my time in it.' Can't you remember anything?"

Robert looked embarrassed, and Anne was angry. "Be quiet, Quince."

But that's what Thisby wrote. I know it was. I got it right. I guess I just can't be sure Thisby did. But then, getting quotes wrong seems to be in character, so no one is suspicious.

The Exhibit Center turned out to be a museum of memorabilia: furniture, set-design drawings, props, and costumes.

Katharine heard laughter above her and climbed up to the loft area to investigate. The loft was low-ceilinged and contained a lounge chair, a dressing table with a mirror, an end table with a simulated bowl of fruit on it, and a straight-backed chair with worn crimson fabric riveted to pale-colored wood. A profusion of theatrical costumes hung from wooden pegs, and people were playing dress-up with them.

She saw Quince standing at the opposite wall, tossing a crushed velvet hat onto the faux gold-leaf chaise longue. Two women and a man were watching her. Quince had assumed a supercilious attitude to address them. "If we offend, it is with our good will. The actors are at hand and by their show, you shall know all that you are like to know."

The man was checking a piece of tape at the nape of a heavy red cape with gold braid. "*Julius Caesar*, it says." He threw the cape to Quince, who caught it and swung it up around her suddenly erect shoulders with practiced ease.

"Cowards die many times before their deaths; / The valiant never taste of death but once. / Of all the wonders that I yet have heard, / It seems to me most strange that men should fear: / Seeing that death, a necessary end, / Will come when it will come."

The man took away the cape, and a woman handed her a beaded shawl. *"Taming of the Shrew."*

Quince draped it across her shoulders and haughtily addressed the air in front of her. "They call me Katharine that do talk of me."

She stepped forward, spun, and lectured her ghost with sarcastic patience. "You lie, in faith; for you are call'd plain Kate, / And bonny Kate and sometimes Kate the curst . . . / Hearing thy mildness praised in every town, / Thy virtues spoke of, and thy beauty sounded, / Myself am moved to woo thee for my wife."

She spun back, all fury and emotion. "Moved! In good time, let him that moved you hither, remove you hence."

A couple of people clapped.

"Hamlet," someone called out from behind Katharine.

"Oh, God, too many," Quince gasped, dropping the shawl to the chaise longue. "Brevity is the soul of wit." The audience laughed.

"Cleopatra."

Quince looked around, grabbed the bowl of brightly painted fruit and held it on her head like Carmen Miranda. "My salad days when I was green in judgment."

Katharine called out like a teenager requesting a song from her favorite group, *"Midsummer,* Quince. Do *Midsummer."*

Quince looked at her oddly but then shifted into a grinning prankster and said ingratiatingly, "If we shadows have offended, / Think but this, and all is mended: / That you have but slumber'd here / While these visions did appear. / And this weak and idle theme, / No more yielding but a dream . . . / So, good day unto you all. / Give me your hands, if we be friends, / And Robin shall restore amends."

Her audience blinked and seemed to yawn and wake up as if they had indeed been asleep. Katharine looked behind her and found the staircase packed with staring faces, two of them being Robert's and Anne's, peering over the loft floor. Quince suddenly looked self-conscious and began returning the costumes to their pegs.

"What a show," said one of the men as he passed Katharine. "They ought to put her on the stage and let her do all the parts."

Katharine found herself grinning and bouncing around Quince like a fawning groupie. "Quince, you're amazing. I had no idea you were this good. You should come up to that youth program here next summer." On the backstage tour, the guide had mentioned a two-week seminar in August at which high school students learned firsthand the workings of a performing theater company. "You're the right age, though you probably could teach it. You should be on the stage. God, I was transfixed." Even as she spoke, Katharine realized it probably wasn't something Thisby would have said, but she didn't care. Out of the corner of her eye, she could see Anne and Robert Bennet standing there, watching her, their faces stone still. But still she didn't care; she hadn't cared since she had gotten to Ashland, and it felt good not to.

Don't fuck with me. I've got a full tank, and the road is mine.

Quince glanced at her parents, and they silently turned and left.

Katharine and Quince went downstairs — the Bennets were nowhere to be seen — and out onto the sidewalk. Quince was quiet until she stopped and turned to Katharine. "They want me to have another plastic surgery next summer."

It took Katharine a while to understand her. "Why? You look great."

"Right." She turned and walked on. Katharine followed. "They think my face has stopped growing, so they want to try and put the divet back."

"The divet?"

Quince brushed angrily at her upper lip under her nostrils. "You know, the shape in your lips. The divet. The dip. The one you have. The one I don't. Shit, Puck's got two of them." She flopped down on a bench. "I'm tired of surgeries. I'm tired of hospitals. I'm tired of them thinking that my face has stopped growing but not being sure. And I'll just end up with the same old nose. All for nothing."

Katharine stared at Quince's profile, set off by the pearl blue of the Ashland sky. *I never knew so young a body with so old a head.* "So what do you see when you look in the mirror?"

Quince mimed a scarface with a slashing hand.

Katharine fished for something to say. "I think you're a very attractive young woman, Quince. You're smart. You have wonderful bones, great eyes. And you dress really interestingly."

Quince gave her a scathing look.

"No, I didn't mean . . . It's a line . . . Oh, never mind."

They sat in silence for a long time until Quince said, "Why didn't you ever like me?"

> *. . . Kewpie was in the hospital again, so we didn't do anything. She's got something wrong with her kidney now. Mom was gone a lot and Granma spent Christmas Eve with us. It wasn't the same. She called me a spoiled brat and didn't I care about my sister? Puck got after me too . . .*

"Maybe it was because I was jealous. Mom spent a lot of time with you."

"But you had Dad. You always had Dad."

"I think Mom was harder to please. Dad was too easy."

"Yeah, well, easy for you. Dad always liked you best," Quince said quietly.

If that's true, God knows why. "But, Quince, it doesn't matter who liked who better. It doesn't matter whether I liked you or not. It doesn't even matter if I like you now, though I do. You're good at this acting thing. I can't believe Mom or Dad would mind if you pursued it."

"You really think I'm good?" Quince asked plaintively.

Katharine grabbed her around the throat and throttled her gently. "Would you stop with the February face. Why do you think I've been dancing around for five minutes? Yes, I think you're good. Truly, madly, deeply. You're radiant."

Quince blushed and smiled and radiated until she was transparent around the edges.

· · ·

Katharine visibly wiggled in her chair in the outdoor Elizabethan theater. The seats were incredible — fifth row, front center. "I don't like them," Quince had said as they sat down. "Remember in the old theater how we could get so close they'd spit on us?"

Funny how different the stage looked from her seat; on the tour the day before, she had only looked out into the empty house from the backstage curtains. Now Katharine realized the facade of the theater looked a great deal like the Bennet home, chocolate brown half-timbers on the walls and diamond-paned casement windows in the gables. The pools of light seemed to wait expectantly for someone to appear in them.

The Bennets and Katharine had gone to dinner before the play at a restaurant built beside the Lithia Creek. The elder Bennets seemed tense and wary. When Robert ordered a pitcher of margaritas, the waitress asked, "How many glasses?" Robert answered quickly, "Just two," and then looked almost apologetically at Katharine, "That right, Thiz?"

Katharine had been distracted, not really taking in the nuances of the exchange. She had been waiting for the whispering to begin, but there wasn't a sound. Not even one murmur of temptation. She laughed. God, she felt good. She laughed again.

"Not for me," Katharine told the waitress gaily, "but can you bring me a virgin margarita with lots of salt?"

The waitress could.

Anne looked at Katharine again with that puzzled expression, but Katharine felt invincible, immortal, aglow. And what was Anne's problem anyway? *She's got her daughter back and I'm not drinking, am I?*

It was child's play. She could do this. *No sweat.*

From there they had gone to the Bricks to watch the Green Show. Katharine had never seen or heard anything like it. The young musicians, singers, and dancers were having so much fun, she couldn't help but clap and laugh and grin idiotically with the rest of the audience. The troupe was dressed in period costumes — warm, cinnamon-colored pantaloons and skirts with soft-soled shoes. Sometimes the musicians played instruments so curled and twisted with teeny, tiny reeds that Katharine wondered how any sound came out of them at all. Quince took pictures and seemed removed, even bored, as did Anne and Robert, until they turned their gaze on Katharine, and then their gaze became scrutiny. Their faces swam with concern, fear, and worry and then anger and suspicion. Katharine tried to appear more aloof, the way Thisby would have been, but then she didn't care what they thought.

This is my holiday.

Nor did she want to maintain any aloofness in her seat, craning her neck this way and that to look around her. There was a roar, and Katharine noticed everyone looking up. At the uppermost part of the theater, someone was hanging out of a paned window and hoisting a flag on a pole mounted there. He waved and closed the casement.

The play began.

It was as if they were performing the play only for her. It made so much more sense now. Of course Anne had been Helena, one of the women lovers, and not Thisby. That part had to be played by a young man, preferably a goofy one. She didn't like the Duke — she hadn't expected to — but she felt differently toward Oberon. She decided that Quince was right. He was not to be judged against human morality. It was true he wasn't especially nice, and when he told Puck to streak Titania's eyes with the juice that would make her fall in love with the first thing she saw — in her case, the ass-headed Nick Bottom — Katharine wanted to slap his smug face. She wouldn't have dared, though. She knew she would have been in the middle of something she didn't understand. This was between loftier beings. Puck was mischievous just for the fun — or the nastiness — of it, but, like with Oberon, the normal rules didn't apply.

When the play was over, she stood up and clapped madly with the rest of the audience, ignoring the waves of anxiety lapping at her body from Thisby's parents and Quince's hiss. "Shit, it's not as if you haven't seen this a gazillion times."

• • •

For the next couple of days Katharine felt as if she had indeed gone through the wardrobe and come out into the magical kingdom of Narnia. Sometimes Quince and she hung out like friends, Katharine acting as silly as any teenager. Other times she just took off, not caring whether she was supposed to be somewhere, coming back to shrug off the Bennets' equal mix of anger and confusion. She forgot that she was miles from home, that she was Katharine, the good wife, the good mother. She forgot that she was Thisby, the bad seed, the problem child. And she loved it. It was a self-centeredness, a selfishness she had never allowed herself to indulge in. She *deserved* this.

One of the plays she saw with the Bennets was Ibsen's *Wild Duck*. It struck Katharine as an odd coincidence that the main character visits a family and thinks the truth — as he knows it — is going to help them. He believes that revealing the truth will set them free. But the truth only ends up destroying them. All of them. Katharine tried to have a deep, philosophical conversation with Anne and Robert about it, but, God, they were so uptight. They kept looking at her as if they didn't recognize her, and it drove her crazy. It was useless to try and talk to them.

It was easier to talk to Quince, who didn't look at her so weirdly. Sometimes Katharine wanted to spill everything to her — reveal everything — but then everything didn't matter anymore. She didn't care who she had been. And the truth wouldn't necessarily set anyone free.

In some ways she felt more solidly herself than she ever had, but not solidly her old self. It was a self she could have been if events had been different in her life.

Friday evening some older guys tried to pick up Quince and Katharine by inviting them to participate in an old Ashland tradition: consuming mulled wine while enjoying some outdoor hot-tubbing. When they finally ditched the guys, Katharine laughed so hard, she thought she was going to pee in her pants. Quince stopped her by putting both hands on Katharine's shoulders.

"Thiz, you better be careful."

"What do you mean?" Her laughter died out quickly; she didn't like the tone of Quince's voice.

"Whatever you're on, can you be more careful about it? I don't mind, but Mom and Dad are worried. Now they think you're some sort of manic depressive."

"I'm not on anything. I haven't been on anything. I'm just having a good time." She shook off Quince's hands and stalked forward. "Goddamn it. This really pisses me off. I'm just having fun. What do they want from me? A drug test?"

Thisby's mother was waiting for them on the porch when they got back. Since Anne could drive back with the girls the next morning, Robert had taken the opportunity to fly home early.

Quince went inside, and Katharine sat down at the umbrella table.

Katharine found it ironic to be under suspicion for the wrong crime. She decided it would be best to take the offensive. "Quince says you think I might be taking drugs. Well, I'm not. I don't know how to make you believe it unless I take a drug test. And I will, if you want me to."

"I might ask you to. But for the moment, I'll take your word for it."

Katharine tightened. *So this is the way it's going to be, is it? Guilty by suspicion.*

"You have been acting very strangely this week."

That's your evidence? "I've just been having fun," Katharine said with some desperation. She could feel this body weighing down into the chair.

Anne looked at her, right through the pupils.

What do you see?

"I have not seen you have 'fun' since you were a teenager. 'Fun' has not been a part of your repertoire for years. It's not something I recognize easily."

"Me either." Katharine leaned forward on the table and struggled against the air that was pressing down on her. "But I feel like a teenager. It feels wonderful. Is there anything wrong with that?" There was almost a whine of panic in her voice.

"No, of course not. It's just not like you."

Guilty as charged.

"I'm not like — her — me . . . anymore." Even to Katharine it sounded feeble.

"I realize that. And that's why I think you need help."

The air was oppressive.

Here it comes.

"I know your father and I haven't been a part of your life for a long time now. You haven't asked for anything from us for years either. Now you have. And now I ask for something in return. The exhibit in exchange for going back to Dr. Mantle. Your father and I are worried that this exhibit might be more than you can handle right now. We think going back to Dr. Mantle will help you level out the ups and downs. We love this new expressiveness you have, but it's as if you're trying too hard. We're afraid . . . We want . . ." Anne wavered as she must have seen the animal panic in Katharine's eyes, but she pushed forward in cold blood. "As Puck would say, this offer is nonnegotiable and final. Should you not keep up your end of the bargain, you lose the exhibit. High stakes, I know."

The lightness of being that Katharine had felt all week deadened and the weight clamped down over her.

Anne stretched her hand toward Katharine but didn't touch her. Her voice lost its steely resolve. "I love you. I want you to be well. You're an adult. But that doesn't change anything. You need help, and I'm still your mother."

Denial flared up in Katharine, then sputtered and died. She knew she owed Thisby the exhibit; she had promised Thisby the exhibit. The gods were just going to make the feat harder, that's all. Katharine knew *she* needed the exhibit. It was the one thing, the one concrete thing, the future held for her.

Anne pulled back her hand and hid both of them under the table. "Sometimes I can't sleep. It's almost like I'm waiting. I'm waiting for the doorbell to ring. And there'll be a policeman standing on the step. 'Mrs. Bennet? There's been a terrible —' "

Katharine's brain, from long rehearsal, joined in, — *accident. I'm sorry, Mrs. Ashley, your son —*

" — your daughter — "

— is *dead.*

" — is dead."

Now she was coming back into LA — a fugitive from her old life, and a defeated participant in her new one. On the dashboard of the Range Rover was a picture that Quince had taken and gotten developed of Katharine standing enraptured, watching the Green Show. Katharine hadn't seen a picture of herself in Thisby, and she had scrutinized it minutely to see if she could see any of herself, superimposed on Thisby like an aura. As she took the Santa Monica exit, Katharine looked at it now and didn't know either of them.

There was no way out.

Yeah, I'm a real lioness. Unless you make that cowardly. None of it got me anywhere. She was back where she had started from. She didn't deserve anything.

There may be no place like home, but what happens when you don't have one?

Act 3, Scene 3 🐇

What we've got here is a failure to communicate.

— STROTHER MARTIN, *Cool Hand Luke* (1967)

It was full dark by the time Katharine pulled into Thisby's parking garage. She had declined the offer of dinner at the Bennets' and dropped an anxious Quince off at Gert's house to see Oberon.

Her body felt as though it weighed a thousand pounds; there didn't seem to be enough left of her northern self to keep her afloat, her thoughts sinking into an abyss.

She was heading for the elevator, pulling her suitcase by its strap, when a body stepped out from behind a pillar and blocked her way. She raised an arm in reactive defense, and Hooker grabbed her wrist and held it above her head. He didn't say anything, but stared at her; she felt pinned down in the headlights of his eyes. He smelled of warm yeast, cologne, and cigarette smoke.

Things began to separate. Katharine could feel the ribbons of her mind, body, and soul unraveling. *Parts is parts.* She tried to wrap herself back up, keep herself together, but it was too hard, and she was too tired. The resolution of her surroundings blew up into a grainy blur. Sound distorted to a roar. She could see the body heat between them. It glowed with effervescence. Her skin bubbled like champagne.

• • •

She kissed him, her whole body in her mouth. Her free hand scrabbled at the buttons of his shirt; she wanted to scratch her name in bloody letters on his chest. He let go of her wrist, and she slid her hand between his legs, feeling through the cotton and silk. She burrowed her head down and started to bite at his clavicle. He moaned and exposed his neck.

I made a guy moan? was Katharine's last coherent thought.

She would have taken him right there in the elevator, but he held her off while he pushed the third-floor button. She got the door of the apartment open, and it slammed solidly behind them as he pressed her up against it. She toed off her leggings, and he held her up to him with his arms under her butt and her legs wrapped around his waist, the core of her centered over and around him. He swore as he tripped on the puddle of clothes around his ankles and lost his grip on her. She slid off, and howled in frustration. "Hold on, hold on," he yelled as he skipped out of the quicksand at his feet and kicked off his shoes. In his stocking feet, he dropped down on the floor and pulled her on top of him as he lay back. He pushed her denim shirt down her arms and yanked her tank top over her breasts and suckled her. "God, I love it when you eat," he muttered and bit at her nipple, setting off a series of squibs that shook them both.

She loved his pectorals and his rib cage and stomach, and she kneaded them into submission, fighting his hands at her buttocks as he tried to direct her thrusts. *No.* He let go and cupped her breasts. She slid farther up his stomach and ground against him. *Ah, there's the rub.* She laughed. He moaned.

They fucked again on her bed. This time he pinned her down while he went at her, the compressed air popping like flatulence between their bodies. She bit at his hands, his wrists, drawing blood in numerous places. She sucked at the swelling wounds, feeding on him.

He flipped her over and entered her from behind. He had her in a half nelson with his right arm, pinning her head down sideways on the bed. She struggled and butted back at him, coming twice this way before he did, his other hand cupped over her pubic bone as if to stifle a scream.

Katharine awoke groggily when a silhouette leaned over her and stroked her down the length of her side. "I left you a job. I'll call you." The silhouette straightened and moved away. From a distance, Katharine thought she heard it say, "I love you," though it was barely audible, as if the speaker were unsure whether he wanted it heard or not.

The front door closed. A moan of protest escaped from her body, and with a sudden fear that she had OD'd again, she took inventory and realized that although this body was sore — incredibly sore — the stomach, the innards were clean. She felt as if she had been Rolfed, massaged so deeply that every muscle felt separated and reamed. And then she remembered. Sort of. It was filtered through a smog-colored gel, but it was clear enough to inspire a gasp of horror, which when expelled, hung above her like a cartoon bubble. The rising sun illuminated the bed, and the covers were twisted and clumped. *Last night . . . was it only last night?* She played it back in her mind, the tracking on the screen jerky. She winced. *I couldn't have done that. It must have been someone else. A body double. I'm incapable of doing something like that. I couldn't have liked it. It was so . . . so . . . It hurts too much afterward.*

She swung her legs over the side of the bed, stood up — *how can the soles of my feet hurt?* — and hobbled into the bathroom. A smell clung to her, the pheromones burred into her skin like Velcro. *My offence is so rank, it smells to heaven.* She stepped into the shower, and urine ran hot and stinging down a leg into the drain. She turned the water on as hard and as hot as she could possibly stand it. She expected some sort of chemical reaction, purpled bruises like images developing from an emulsion bath spreading across her skin.

I lost it. I goddamned lost it. No control.

She tried to patch herself back up and soaped and scrubbed with the washcloth until her skin felt raw.

I'm acting like I've been raped and trying to scrub it away.
And exactly whose act of rape are you trying to obliterate?

Feeling scourged, Katharine walked gingerly into the kitchen. She had a cup of coffee in her hand before she noticed the brown wrapped package the size of a loaf pan on the counter. She frowned and poked a finger at it. She lifted it — it felt like a bag of flour — then dropped it as if it had bitten her. A napkin that had been under the package drifted lazily to the floor. She picked it up and made herself concentrate on the leaden lines that someone had written on it. There was an address — a number and street name in Bel Air — and underneath was scribbled, "After the delivery, meet me at Potters at 9." She scrunched the napkin in her hand. *Messages on napkins. I get more like Thisby every day.* She took a knife, flipped the package over cautiously, again as if it might attack her, and slit the tape on the underbelly. Inside was a plastic bag of white powder.

"I've got a job for you." Isn't that what he said? Isn't it? Now I've got the big picture. This is how Thisby made her money. She was a goddamned drug runner.

She stabbed the package with the knife, and it stuck there like a quivering arrow shaft.

Oh, great. Get mad and stab the damn drugs. Now what are you going to do?

I'll tape up the goddamn bag. Like I give a shit.

Yeah, but Hooker's gonna give you more than shit when you give him back the package with a hole in it.

"Shit," Katharine swore as she found some Band-Aids and pulled the knife out very gently and quickly covered the wound. She replaced the wrapper and flipped the package on its back to keep the seams together. "Shit."

I gotta get this back to him. I gotta tell him I can't do this. There's probably a time limit on this kind of thing. He'll come after me when the client calls him and says the stuff didn't show up.

"Shit."

• • •

At exactly nine o'clock she arrived at Potters, a downtown bar on a long skinny corner lot. Hooker's package was in an oversized shoulder bag; she didn't dare leave it in Thisby's car with that flimsy canvas top. It was a hot night, but she had soaked through her clothes with fear, not heat. The smell of her kept her thinking that she was standing next to a stranger, and it wasn't hard to imagine the feel of Hooker's blade running across her own throat.

It had been the longest day. She couldn't concentrate and keep the voice that whispered quiet. She prowled the apartment, trying to outdistance her own smell, and took three long showers and paced again — the voice that whispered incessantly murmuring in her ear. She had gone to the store as early as possible to buy packing tape, to patch up the knife wound. She expected the police to come barging in her door any second. And Quince? Was this her day to come? She couldn't remember. Would Quince let herself in with her key, hurt and then furious at the sight of her seemingly strung-out sister and a loaf of drugs on the kitchen counter?

When she taped the hole and a bit of the powder dusted her fingertips, she swore they tingled as if they were having an allergic reaction.

Just lick it off your fingers, the whispery voice cooed. What's the big deal? Hooker's not gonna know, and it's so little, it can't hurt you.

She had her fingers up to her tongue before she curled them back into her palm, marking her skin with her nails. She washed the cocaine off, and a fleshburn dotted the tips of her fingers.

She left the house at eight, strung so tight, she thought she might snap. And all day she had not allowed herself to hear that other voice again, that voice that floated across the room like a poltergeist, "I love you."

He was playing pool and looked like a hustler; he had just missed what looked like an easy shot. When he saw her, he smiled, and Katharine felt her chest ease a bit. He walked her over to the opposite wall.

"It go okay?"

She opened the bag that she had put the drugs in and held it up to him so he could see inside. He closed it quickly, a frown on his face. "Shit, Thiz, whaddya doin' bringing it here?" He looked around quickly and took her back into a storeroom filled with cases of beer and hard liquor. "What's wrong? I gave you the address, didn't I?"

"Yes, it's not that." Her throat felt dry, and she wanted to guzzle the entire contents of the room. "I can't do it. I can't be your runner." She suddenly needed breathing lessons. "I can't do it ever again. I'm out."

He looked surprised, and then his eyelids narrowed. He grabbed her wrist, and she struggled but couldn't release herself. "What's gotten into you? First you disappear for a month, then you treat me like shit, then you jump my bones, now I'm shit again. What gives?"

"Last night was a mistake. I meant what I said"— *and I said what I meant. An elephant's faithful . . . my God, stop it* —"I meant what I said last week. I'm clean, and I want you to leave me alone."

Hooker let go of her and just stood there. Then his whole body seemed to coil up and tense. "Are you dumping me?"

It was Katharine's turn to look surprised. He'd said it in such a way that it sounded like, Was she really giving back his frat pin? "It's not as if we were engaged or anything," she said, and then flinched at the look on his face. *Were we?*

Katharine suddenly had a vision of Thisby and Hooker, in perhaps a rare quiet moment, curled up on Thisby's couch. She's snuggled against his chest, her head tucked up under his chin. "My parents would have a shitfit if I married you," she says to his collarbone. His voice comes to her softly from above. "My parents wouldn't be so pleased either, but that wouldn't be the reason I'd marry you."

Hooker's body shifted, and Katharine jumped back, slamming her hipbone into a corner of shelving. She straightened slowly and, gently taking out the package, put in on a stack of J & B cases. "Here. You'll need to rewrap it. There's a hole in it."

He stepped toward her, but she moved out of striking distance and said hurriedly, "I didn't take any. I swear. Weigh it or whatever you do. I stabbed the package with a knife when I realized what you had left me."

He smiled, and chuckled. Katharine relaxed. He did have a way about him. "That's my Thisby. Come on back into the bar, and I'll buy you a beer, and we'll talk."

Is he the voice that whispers? He sounds so reasonable but . . . but they're not the same. "No, I can't. I mean it. I'm out. I'm sorry." *Why am I sorry?* He closed in on her. "No, don't touch me." She slid around to the door. The skin around her wrist tingled and sang. Then she was sorry. *In more ways than one.*

She stumbled through the door and out of the bar, limping slightly. He followed her out but didn't cross the street where her car was parked. Her hands shook crazily as she tried to open the door, watching him watch her. He put his hands on the roof of a white Lexus two-door, and a mechanical voice spoke loudly from the automobile, "Please step away from car." Hooker pressed the entire length of his body against the passenger door, stretching his arms across the moonroof. "You have three seconds to step away from the car before the security system is engaged," the voice monotoned.

Katharine got the door open but watched him in fascination until the shrill horn blew. A group of well-dressed people on the corner turned toward the sound, and some came running. She swung herself into the seat, locking the door behind her. As she drove past Hooker, he followed her with mild, confident eyes, ignoring the protestations of the car's nervous yuppie owner trying to get him to back off the paint job.

Act 3, Scene 4 🦎

What, must I hold a candle to my shames?

— JESSICA, *The Merchant of Venice*, 2.6.41

She knocked on Goodfellow's door, and his voice called out from inside, "Who is it?"

"It's me. Thisby."

"Come on in. I'm on the phone with True."

He was standing in the kitchen with a towel tucked around his waist, holding the phone. He wasn't dripping, but his hair was damp and his chest had a soft, moist look to it. Katharine tried to look elsewhere, but the look of his newly showered body kept drawing her back. The towel was slung low on his hips; she could see the tan line from his shorts. He and Hooker were about the same size, and although Hooker spent more time in the gym (had, no doubt, more time to spend in the gym) she liked the shape of Goodfellow's torso, which was slim and — *what am I talking about? I can't believe I was so petrified that I had to get out of the apartment, and now I'm calmly comparing their gross anatomy.*

She had come over ostensibly to bring him the new set of keys to her apartment and her unlisted phone number, but it was the idea of spending another night alone that had really made her visit him unannounced. She sat at the dining-room table and traced his profile against the backdrop of the cabinet doors.

"I'll ask her." Puck dropped the end of the receiver away from his mouth and spoke to her. "True's inviting us over this Saturday afternoon to his parents' house in Long Beach. He was going to call you after he called me, but since you're here . . . Can you go?"

Her heart thumped erratically, but then her mood lightened. *Emily and Hank.* Yes, she could handle them. She could even get them to talk. *Well, Hank anyway.* She hadn't known what she should do next about her family and had been feeling guilty because she had been so inept, so waffling, so undecided. But now she was back on track. She felt calmer, more at ease about them than she had in days. She nodded her assent.

When Puck turned to hang up the receiver, the cord, which had gotten hooked under a corner of the towel, pulled free the tuck at his waist. He grabbed at his hip and managed to catch one side of the towel, but the other dropped down, exposing his right buttock and the port wine stain that was slanted across his skin, from low to high. It looked like a cattle brand; it was elongated with symmetrical curves and had . . . *a divet.* It was as if he had been seared by a bright-red pair of lips.

Goodfellow disentangled the cord and rebound the towel around his waist. He saw that Katharine was staring at him. "Yeah, the ol' fairy kiss." He rubbed the spot. "I used to think it would lose its shape or, at least, lose its color as I got older, but the ol' mark prodigious just grew right along with me."

The mark prodigious. She remembered that from *A Midsummer Night's Dream.* In the end the fairies bless the bridal beds so their children shall ever be fortunate. No harelips or skin blotches for them. *None of the Bennet children were so fortunate, were they? Thisby's defect just wasn't visible, that's all.*

Puck left and came back wearing a pair of cotton drawstring shorts. He had run a comb through his hair, which lay slicked back over the top, though the waves, refusing to stay straight, curled back on themselves. "So why the unlisted phone number? The new locks?"

"Oh, that." She gave him the short version, leaving out

the X-rated parts, but no matter how she edited it, the censors were still squirming in their seats.

He was silent for a long time.

Say something. Say anything.

He was silent for a bit longer. "Well, I'm glad you've dumped this guy, but I gather you're still scared that he won't leave you alone."

"Yes."

"So spend the night here. Maybe we can think about something else — some other way to handle it — later." He came over and stood near her. She could feel the moist heat coming from his naked torso. She leaned back, feeling uncomfortable. "We'll figure something out." He touched her hesitantly on the shoulder. His fingertips, like the cocaine, caused her skin to feel hot.

They really didn't talk much more that evening. Katharine was waiting for him to go to bed, and Puck was, no doubt, thinking about his troubles with Vivian. He and Vivian were fighting. "Not really fighting," he told her, a little too cavalierly. "She just gets silent." He massaged his kneecap. "She's good at that. Silence." He folded his arms over his chest and looked at Katharine, his forehead bunched up over his eyes. "I know most people think she's a bit stiff, but, really, she can be different. We haven't been together for all that long, but I like her. She hasn't had an easy life. I really respect her."

"What's she mad about?"

"Oh, I don't know. I'm pretty good at the silent part too."

"You're talking to me, aren't you?"

"Well, sure. You're easy to talk to."

Katharine had to hold down the corners of a silly smile.

Puck shook his head. "You know, I don't know. There are a lot of times when I want to talk to her. Really talk to her. About my job. What I don't want. What she wants. I think I must go about it the wrong way, though, because the more I try to get her to talk, the more she clams up.

"She calls me the yin-yang man."

"Does she?"

"She says there's not much gray in me. I want to talk. I don't want to talk. I'm serious. I'm not serious enough." He stood up. "I don't know."

Puck's leatherbound copy of *A Midsummer Night's Dream* lay open in Katharine's lap, her fingers tracing Oberon's instructions to his fairy minions to bless the children of the newlyweds and keep them from the despised blots of birth defects. Katharine was in that innerspace where she seemed to be able to mind-walk within Thisby's life. It scared her, how easy it was to imagine herself standing at the bottom of the stairs at the Bennet house, her right hand on the newel post, her right toe tap, tap, tapping on the first step. She's on her way out to meet some friends downtown. Her parents are in the living room discussing Quince and one of her many illnesses. God, her parents like to jabber. Always in the kitchen or the living room, gibbering. She doesn't normally care enough to eavesdrop, but her father's voice catches her. "The fairies missed Quince, didn't they? Sometimes I think she is despisèd."

The anger that has simmered under the bedpan of her brain for years suddenly boils over. *That fucking play. Our fucking lives have been scripted by that fucking play. Puck is despised. Quince is despised. So what does that make me?*

She stomps into the living room. Her parents are surprised; they didn't even know she was home. She screams and yells at them. *Why can't you just accept me as I am — not as a fucking character in a fucking play. Why are we performing our lives against some moldy text?* Her parents' faces are studied masks; she wants to slap them. Things then start to get jumbled. She's losing her focus, but she can't stop the words. *And if Quince is so despised, how come she got all the attention? How come she got the dog and Puck and all the attention? And Puck's despised too, isn't he? Poor Puck. Poor Quince. You can feel sorry for them, can't you? But me? I'm not despised, or I'm not supposed to be.*

Well, she'll show them how to be despised. They ain't seen nothing yet.

Act 3, Scene 5 🐿

He told me I would forget. But how could I not remember?

— JANE FONDA, *Old Gringo* (1989)

Anne was making coffee in the kitchen, and Katharine and Robert were left in the dining room, the crumbs of their dinner still scattered over the tablecloth. Quince had gone off with friends, but promised to be back for Oberon's next feeding.

Katharine had driven Quince and Oberon home after her work at the clinic. Thisby had been invited to stay for dinner and spend the night — only if she wanted to — and Katharine had accepted, much to Anne and Robert's surprise and wariness.

This was the length to which Katharine would go to avoid being alone, though it was a deceptive aloneness — her mind was alive with the company of thought, fear, and voice.

She had spent one more night at Goodfellow's, making dinner for them. It was the least she could do. She had returned both days to Thisby's apartment and found it undisturbed — no strange marks on the lock, no obscene messages shoved underneath the door, no blinking lights on the answering machine.

Goodfellow and she had talked a lot over dinner, the bowls of their repast covering the small table. Goodfellow was a good storyteller — like his father — making a soap opera out of the daily happenings at work. Katharine's husband had always cut to the chase, and it drove Philip crazy when she wanted to stretch out the telling with prefaces and digressions and background information. So it was with great pleasure that she had told Goodfellow, in lengthy detail, about her escapades at the concert and in Ashland, even pulling aside the neck of her shirt to show him the now-faded tattoo.

Then Puck had gone to see Vivian. Katharine thought he would certainly not come home that night, but he did — and she was glad. She wasn't afraid in his apartment, but it was nice to have someone else around, someone to talk to. It kept the whispering down and kept her from thinking too much about the party at the Dentons. She didn't want to think about how it was going to feel seeing Emily and Hank. It was enough to know that it was going to happen.

"I think we're okay now," Puck told Katharine when he got back from Vivian's. "She's leaving for a few days to visit her parents in Paris, Texas. She says she does this every year. It's not unusual. I think when she comes back, everything will be back to normal. She just needs to get away for a while. I think it will be good for the both of us. Don't you?"

Anne returned with the coffee, which seemed to prompt Robert into speaking. "Hey, how's the exhibit going?"

"Great. Good." Katharine bobbed her head. "It's going good."

"Anything I can do, just let me know."

"No, we're fine. We've got it under control." But then Katharine remembered her last conversation with Max; he was pressuring her about printing up the other photographs. "Well, actually, I take that back. You can help. I'm going to need some help with the printing. Would you mind?"

Robert's face shone.

He's so easy to please.

"Of course. I'd love to. No problem. Just tell me what you want done."

Katharine nodded. Max had essentially told her what she wanted done.

"I got an e-mail from your Uncle Roy," Robert continued. "He's coming up for your exhibit."

"I know. I got a postcard saying he'd be there with bells on." The postcard was of a Central American version of the jackalope, half turtle, half alligator, the amateurish pasteup oddly affecting.

"Oh, God. With Roy that probably means he'll have bells on. Literally."

From the corner of Katharine's eye, she saw that Anne was watching this exchange as if she were the chair umpire at a tennis match, following the ball with incredible powers of concentration.

"Roy always did consider you his kindred spirit." The way he said it made Katharine feel that Robert didn't think that was such a special distinction, though he was trying to disguise it. He turned sideways in his chair and crossed his arms and legs. "My brother was not an easy person to live with. I always thought you blamed me when he left the country — as if I had something to do with it. Actually, he felt he could manage his investment business just as easily from Belize as from here. He certainly could live cheaper." He shook his head. "I've stopped worrying about what you kids are going to accuse me of, because I figure it's going to be something I had no control over anyway. It's all in your perspective."

Katharine wondered if Robert ever lectured for UCLA extension courses. She could see him at the lectern with his light pen, emphasizing certain paragraphs on the overhead projector.

"I'm not being self-righteous. I was the same way as a kid too. I thought Roy got everything, and I got nothing. Roy might say differently. No"— he paused —"I take that back. Roy would say he got everything too." He smiled at Katharine as if to convince her he was just trying to lighten everybody up.

Anne measured out her sugar with infinite precision, folded it into her coffee, then set the spoon on the saucer without a clink. She picked up the cup with both hands and sipped carefully.

Robert glanced at Anne, but her eyes were looking into her cup.

"Puck carries this heavy burden of responsibility that he won't allow himself to give up, and somehow I'm responsible for that. I guess he thinks I was never home when you kids were growing up. But that's not true at all. I was just gone the wrong time — for him anyway.

"When you left home at eighteen, we know you hated us. Blamed us. For whatever. We could never quite figure out what you were accusing us of. Did we, Anne?" Katharine could see that he wasn't really asking Anne for a response. He leaned forward. "I don't know how to tell you this so that it will make any sense to you. You really have to have kids to understand. We found out, perhaps too late, that we had to treat each one of you children differently. You were such different people. With Puck, the parenting hand had to be so light, just a touch here and a touch there. We made the mistake of thinking that you were like Puck, and we could treat you like we treated him. By the time we realized we shouldn't, you were on a road we couldn't follow, couldn't even conceive of. We were chasing after you, and you were on one of those airport walkways, striding along faster than we could ever run."

He seemed to be on his own airport walkway, straining to keep up with his speech that was running along faster than the rest of him. His weight returned to the chair, the belt of his speech slackening. "There was always a crisis — Quince being born with the cleft lip and not being very healthy — and we were putting out small fires without realizing that the entire forest was burning around us. Sometimes we thought the fairies had indeed missed us, but we thought we were doing a good job making you all realize you weren't despised. How you ever thought that we — How absurd!" He drew his lips into a straight line. "You . . . You slipped through our fingers, and we watched you fall. For years. In slow motion. I thought I would die. But I didn't. And you didn't. And somehow it seems to be turning out okay. Is it going to be okay?"

The frustration that had been growing in Katharine while

Robert lectured threatened to make her reckless. *What do you want from me? From Thisby? Why didn't you parent a little harder? Make that hand a little stiffer when she needed to be put on her ass a couple of times?* The parental part of her knew that Robert wasn't solely responsible for Thisby. Thisby did what she did, was what she was, because of the choices she made. But that was Thisby, not Katharine. She did not owe Robert. *You have the gall to demand retribution from me!*

Both parents looked at her, and Katharine could see that Robert wanted an answer. She wasn't sure what Anne, who remained silent and closed off at the other end of the table, wanted. Katharine shrugged her shoulders and made a noise in her throat that could have meant anything — anything they wanted to hear.

Katharine was annoyed, but she also knew what Robert was talking about. She had wondered about it too. What things would her own children accuse her of?

I was too hard on them. I was too easy on them. They're too uptight. They're too easygoing. My fault. My fault.

Maybe they would blame the rest of their lives on her death.

"So, Thisby," Anne said, too casually after her long silence. "Have you had a chance to make an appointment with Dr. Mantle?"

Yeah, they want to believe that everything's hunky-dory, but they want the added insurance. Now they're grasping at control when it's too late. Too late for Thisby anyway.

"It's a week from today. I made the appointment all by myself." Even to her own ears, she sounded like a sullen sixteen-year-old.

It had been a strange call. The receptionist had been very pleasant in the initial stages of their exchange. "Actually, we have a cancellation next week. This always happens in August, what with vacations and so on. Now you say you're a former patient of Dr. Mantle?"

The phone line iced over when Katharine gave her Thisby's name.

"Could I put you on hold? I need to check this appointment with Dr. Mantle. He might have a conflict." She was gone a long time. "Miss Bennet? The doctor says he will see you."

Oh, goody. But Katharine would go. She would see it through. She kept her word. Dr. Mantle for the exhibit. She hoped it would be the final task, the final payment. *These three.* The first had been to agree to the exhibit, the second to go to Ashland, the third to see Mantle.

And the old saying is The third pays for all.

Katharine could sense that Anne was skeptical whether Katharine had really called Mantle — or if she did, why she had acquiesced so easily. Katharine was worried why she had done it so soon too. *The third may pay for all, but . . .* Was it really that? Or was it just to get it over with? There was also a nagging in her brain that she really did want to see him, to see a shrink. Did she think he could help her? That maybe she could talk to him, tell him all? That maybe he could stabilize the swings she was going through — of who she was, of what she wanted, of who she wanted?

Spending the night at the Bennets, and in Thisby's bed, surrounded by her childhood things, her parents securing the house downstairs, Katharine couldn't help but somehow feel — even when she was irritated at them — connected to them. *Isn't that what family is — connection?*

Katharine was beginning to realize that the connections for Thisby were not strong. She did not receive her signals straight; she processed them differently and got a lot of them wrong. *Or skewed.* The family thought she didn't get the subtleties of Shakespeare, but she did — she just saw them differently. She did know better, as she always wrote, but she didn't know enough.

The world according to Thisby. It makes me sad.

So what about Katharine's own world? What were her plans now, her strategies, her goals?

She thought she knew. She used to know. She would use Thisby and her family to get back to her own family.

I still want that, but the only thing I can imagine is the way we were. Things aren't the way they were, are they? Not for me. Not for anyone.

She felt as though she were on one of those airport walkways. But she was trying to go against the flow, the ramp rushing her forward faster than she could run backward.

And I have no idea what awaits me at the end of the line.

Act 4, Scene 1 🦎

You speak not as you think. It cannot be.

— HERMIA, *Midsummer Night's Dream*, 3.2.191

Katharine had to force herself to get out of the car, stand up, and walk, almost reaching out for Goodfellow's arm to steady herself.

She hadn't been to the Dentons' house in years, and it looked different. Katharine noticed that the willow in front of True's bedroom had gotten bigger, and there were tiered brick planter boxes along the front of the house where Emily had finally replaced those awful evergreens — *like the ones Diana has* — with a full-color range of New Guinea impatiens.

True opened the front door. "Hey, what are you doing here? The party's tomorrow."

"Out of my way, Young Denton." Puck pushed past him. "Your mother invited us."

They went through the living room and the family room and into the kitchen too quickly for Katharine to see what changes had been made. Emily was at the counter dicing onions. She looked the same. It was almost a disappointment. Katharine felt that somehow Emily should look different — more gray, more bowed from having lost a sister-in-law and gained a new one in less than a year. But she still had the Ashley hair, curls spilling all over her head in so many different shades of blond, brunette, and auburn that gray would be embarrassed to show up. She wasn't thinner or fatter, or younger or older. Just Emily.

Katharine shook her hand. Had she ever shook hands with Emily before? Probably not. The first time they met, Emily had hugged Katharine. Katharine had been seeing Philip for a while, and they had already talked about marriage. Emily seemed to have been well acquainted with that. And well pleased.

"Thanks for having us."

She could hear Goodfellow behind her asking True, "So, who's here?" and True answering, "Oh, you know. All the players. Griff Mill, June." There was an implied "hubba hubba" in the way he said her name. "Even Thisby knows . . ."

True's words faded as Katharine's ear picked up another voice and seized on it. "Aunt Em, we need more guacamole."

Katharine suppressed the urge to laugh, as she knew hysteria wasn't far behind. What would start out as a chuckle, then a huff in her stomach like a bellows, would grow into a howling.

The gods must be crazy, and they're having a shitload of fun with me.

The voice belonged to Marion, and for the first time, Thisby's body felt like it was Katharine's very own.

Now I know I've got a heart, because I can feel it breaking.

Katharine turned around and feasted. It had been twelve months dead and six weeks alive — *sort of* — since Katharine had looked at her daughter. Marion was tanned, and her brown hair was streaked with startling blond. *It must be all that time in the sun at the . . . club.* She couldn't tell if Marion had grown any taller, but she had certainly filled out more, having lost the boyish frame to feminine curves. She was in blue-and-green plaid shorts and a white T-shirt with the slogan of some tennis tournament on it. She wasn't wearing any makeup, whereas a year ago she had been experimenting with foundation and lipstick and all the eye stuff. Katharine also saw that Marion's fingernails were natural; again, a year ago she had spent hours each night changing polish to match the next day's outfit. But Katharine noticed that Marion's toenails were painted candy-apple red — the same color as Emily's.

True came alongside Marion, grabbed her shoulders, and pulled her off balance. She almost dropped the bowl she was carrying.

"Aunt Em!" she protested.

True let go of her, brought his hands up to his face, and wiggled them over his cheeks in glee. "Auntie Em, Auntie Em," he screeched in the witch's voice. He smoothed out his features, straightened up, and spoke to Puck and Katharine. "This is my cousin, Marion, from up north. She's nothing but trouble, but I gotta put up with her."

Marion gave him her if-looks-could-kill face, which he successfully ignored.

Oh, look at me that way!

"This is RB," True told Marion.

Puck held out his hand to her. "Nice to meet you, Marion."

Marion looked up into his face with shy admiration.

"And this is my sister Thisby."

Katharine stepped forward, and her entire body shook from the need to gather Marion in her arms. "Hi" was all she could say, and she kept her hand down, not convinced it wouldn't do something stupid.

"Come on outside," True commanded. "There's a helluva lot of stuff to drink and eat."

Not without my daughter. But Marion neatly stepped around Katharine to the counter, and she and Emily started talking. True took Katharine by the arm and led her outside. She forced herself not to jerk away from him and flee back to the kitchen.

True introduced her around. There were a couple of people from Puck's party to whom Thisby nodded, but as soon as Puck and True were engaged in conversation, she drifted back to the kitchen.

Marion was sitting on the counter, her feet tucked up under her Indian-style, her hands resting on her knees. Emily was cutting up tomatoes for the guacamole. Katharine stood just inside the back door and watched them. Marion seemed to be telling Emily about some guy at the club and this other girl who liked him but he didn't like her and Marion thought he might like her, which was okay because she thought he was pretty cute too and he was one of the best players on their summer interclub team and they might get to play together as a mixed doubles team, though she wasn't nearly good enough to be partners with him but maybe they could play for fun. . . .

Marion talking to Emily. Well, I guess nothing's changed here.

Emily noticed her standing there, so Katharine came quickly into the kitchen. "I thought I'd come see if you needed any help."

"No, I think we're pretty well squared away here. I'll be done with this in a second."

Marion was beginning to unfold her legs.

Don't go! "So, where are you from?" Katharine said it so quickly, she wondered whether Marion could even understand her.

"South of San Francisco. Sunnyvale."

Katharine nodded. "Just visiting?"

"Well, I was hoping to get into a tennis tournament too, but I didn't get accepted."

Katharine gestured to Marion's T-shirt. "Was that a tournament you were in?"

Marion looked down and pulled the shirt away from her waist as if to read it for the first time. "Yeah. I even won a couple of rounds, but then I got bageled big time."

"Bageled?" Emily asked.

"Yeah, you know." She held her hand up and made a zero with her thumb and forefinger. "I lost six-love, six-love."

Mulwray didn't tell me this. "But it's good you won a couple of rounds, isn't it?"

"Sure. I'm even better now, now that I can play at this club we joined. I'm gonna win a lot more."

A lump lodged in Katharine's throat, and Emily handed Marion the bowl of guacamole. She hopped down in one fluid motion and took it outside.

Katharine turned to go outside after Marion, but Emily stopped her. "So, Thisby, what do you do?"

Katharine turned back reluctantly.

Live off the sales I made drug running and fuck drug lords in my spare time. You wouldn't mind if your niece spends some quality time with me, would you?

"I'm preparing an exhibit of my photographs."

"Are you? That sounds wonderful. Here in LA?"

"Yes. A gallery on Melrose. The Ziegfeld-Zelig."

Emily nodded, though Katharine thought not out of recognition. Katharine didn't remember that Emily was much of a gallery-goer. "What kind of pictures do you take?"

"Well, they're a little hard to explain. Did you ever get that magazine *Highlights for Children* when you were a kid?"

Emily thought for a moment, and then her face brightened. "No, but my eye doctor did."

"Okay. There was always a puzzle game, called Hidden Pictures, where you had to find, say, the outline of kitchen appliances hidden in a drawing of a forest scene or barnyard animals in a cityscape."

Emily laughed. "The knot on the tree trunk was also the lid of a pot? I remember desperately trying to do that one just after my pupils had been dilated, and I couldn't see a thing."

"Yeah. Well, the photographs are a bit like that."

"Umm. I was never very good at that puzzle, even when I could see." Emily wiped down the counter.

I was great at it. Hidden Pictures was my favorite game.

"Well, make sure you send us an invitation. We'd love to come."

Hank Denton walked into the kitchen with two grocery bags in his arms. Katharine suddenly realized she hadn't noticed his absence — and she had always liked Hank.

"Okay, I got wine, two more six-packs of sodas, limes, and another thingie of orange juice. The limes aren't very big, but that's all they had." He put the groceries down on the counter and turned toward Katharine, halting in his self-introduction as if something had thrown him off. Katharine could see him mentally shake his head, and then his face cleared so completely, she thought she hadn't really seen anything at all. "Hi, I'm Hank Denton, True's dad."

"I'm Thisby Bennet, RB's sister."

"Oh, yeah, right. He's got another sister, doesn't he? One with a weird name?"

Katharine laughed. "It's Quince. But I think we all have weird names."

"Well, of course, people think that True has a weird name. Do you know who Denton True Young was?"

Emily swept him back with her hands. "Henry, go get the rest of the groceries. You can tell Thisby all about Cyclone Young later. I'm sure she's just dying to hear it." She rolled her eyes at Katharine, who laughed even though she had seen this scene played out many times before.

"I know I'm in big trouble when she calls me Henry." He called to Katharine as Emily pushed him into the family room, "I let her boss me round, cuz she's so cute. But as soon as she loses her looks . . ." He made a slicing motion against his neck.

Emily chuckled as she emptied the contents of the bags. Katharine always admired husbands and wives like Hank and Emily. They really seemed to like each other.

She felt like a wrangler trying to maneuver about stubborn livestock all afternoon. She wasn't very successful at it. Katharine would almost have Marion cornered when she would suddenly slip out of range.

Hank was better at wrangling than she was and nabbed Katharine to tell her the story of True's name with great relish. He flirted with her a bit, and she flirted back. It meant nothing — she knew it — but it was fun. It was a game they had played as Hank and Katharine, and it made her feel as if she were still participating in her old life.

While they talked, Katharine kept an eye on Marion, and half a brain on the conversation. *Did she always part her hair on that side? Look how she rocks back and forth from one foot to the other. Philip did that for hours, holding her when she was a baby and wouldn't sleep. She's charming the pants off that guy.*

By seven o'clock most of the guests had gone home, leaving the Dentons; True's girlfriend, Holly; her roommate, Tiffany;

Puck; Marion; and herself. They were all outside, some dangling their feet in the Jacuzzi, the others sitting around the picnic table. The sky was softening overhead, the sun having dropped below the line of the eaves.

"I'm hungry," Marion said to the assembled.

"Me too," Katharine agreed; she had been too keyed up all afternoon to eat. There was a hollowness inside her stomach that she knew she couldn't fill, but she knew what Marion would say next.

"Pizza," they said simultaneously, and then laughed.

"What kind do you like?" Marion asked her.

"Canadian bacon, not ham, and pineapple. The big chunks, not those little canned pieces, and a few bell peppers, but not too many."

Marion's eyes got big and sparkly. "That's my favorite too."

"Well, why don't we go down to Mystic's on Second Street and order one. We'll order something else for the others. Not everyone has such refined taste in pizza. Goodfellow — RB — will let us use his car. You'll love it."

Katharine hated Canadian-bacon-and-pineapple pizza, but tonight maybe it would taste like ambrosia.

"So, do you get down to LA a lot?" Katharine asked as they got into Goodfellow's car. She knew Marion would have liked the top down, but it was hard to talk in a convertible.

"Lately, yeah."

Already shuffling her off, are we?

"Are your parents divorced?" She couldn't believe how casual she sounded.

"No, my mom died a year ago."

"Oh, I'm sorry. I bet that was pretty hard."

Marion shrugged and said nothing.

Well, what did you expect?

"You get along with your stepmom okay?"

"Yeah, okay."

"How about your brother?"

"Oh, he likes her. He gets along better with her than he did with my mom."

Bam! straight through the heart. Well, you asked for it.

"But he was being a butthead when my mom died. Even he'll admit that." Marion rubbed her knee. "They flirt a lot."

"Excuse me?"

"My brother and stepmom. They flirt. Like they pretend to be mad at each other and all, and he says she isn't his mom and he'll get a tattoo on his butt if he wants to, and she says she wouldn't want to be his mom but she'll paddle his behind, tattoo or no tattoo. It's all pretend, though. She doesn't act like a mom with him, and she can't decide with me."

"What do you mean?"

"She can't decide whether she wants to be my friend or my mother."

"What do you want her to be?"

"A dog." Marion said it so softly that Katharine wasn't sure she'd heard correctly. "No, really." Marion grinned. "She doesn't like dogs. She's scared of them. You know." She demonstrated, wrapping her arms around her head like an octopus and squashing herself against the car door. "That kind of thing. Got bit as a kid, I guess." She readjusted herself in the seat, arranging one arm in her lap, the other resting atop the door. "My mother loved dogs. Our dog died two months after she did."

Rathbone? He died? Katharine felt the prickle of tears. How she loved that dog. Philip used to tease her that she loved that dog more than she loved him. In a way it was true. She desperately needed Rathbone's unconditional affection, the kind she had gotten from her kids when they were little but she lost as they grew older—*and wiser.*

"I thought he'd pine away because it was my mom who took care of him, but I think he died just because he was old." Marion plucked at her collar. "I wanted another dog. A puppy. My mom and me both wanted our next dog to be a German shepherd. His name was going to be Atwill, after this guy who played Dr. Moriarty in the old Sherlock Holmes movies. My mom and dad had a dog before I was born named Nigel. He played Dr. Watson. Rathbone was the guy who was Sherlock Holmes."

She remembers that?

"Dad wouldn't let me, though. Get a dog, I mean. And then he started seeing Diana, and I think he knew pretty soon that he was going to marry her, and she couldn't stand a dog."

"Not even a puppy?"

"No, can you believe that?" Marion shook her head. "So sometimes I'd like to turn her into a dog."

"What kind of dog? A rodent?" It was out of her mouth before she could stop it.

Marion stared at her. "My mom used to call little dogs 'rodents' too."

Katharine felt sweat build up just under the layers of her skin, but Marion continued. "No . . . She isn't that bad. She can be okay. She lets me borrow her clothes. I don't want to hurt her. I miss a dog, though. My mom hated small dogs, you know. It got so we all thought we hated small dogs too. Dad included. But I wouldn't mind a small dog. Maybe Diana wouldn't mind a small dog either. It wouldn't have to be big."

Katharine felt an idea take shape in her head. "How long are you going to be down here?"

"I don't know. A week. Maybe more. Depends on how busy my aunt is."

"My little sister — she's your age — works at a veterinary clinic near where I live. She comes and stays with me at night and goes to work during the day. She works a lot with the dogs. Perhaps you could go with her one day, spend the night at my place, and then I'd bring you back to your aunt's."

"I don't know," Marion said slowly, but there was a spark of interest in her voice.

"Well, think about it. I'll talk to your aunt. She seems like a nice person. You seem to be real close to her."

"Yeah, she's cool. She never had a daughter, but she knows what I'm going through."

"And, of course, without your mom to talk to —"

"Oh, I always talked to my aunt, even when my mom was alive. My mom . . . she didn't grow up like me. She never worried like I do. She always knew what to do. She was always so sure of herself. She never messed up as a kid." Marion shifted a bit in her seat. "She wouldn't have understood. I tried to be like her, but I couldn't. I can't. I didn't want to let her down, so I didn't tell her a lot about the things that bothered me. So I talked to my aunt."

Ah, truth. It is a thief of hearts.

"So you and your brother getting along okay?" Katharine asked when they got back into the car with their order. She felt like a cassette tapehead — pressed on RECORD only, letting the words flow over the magnetic strip unheeded. Later, much later, she would play it back, and then, maybe, she would let herself feel.

"Me and Obi? Okay."

"OB?"

"Yeah, Obi. For Obi-Wan Kenobi. After my mom died, we were talking about how much she liked the movies, and how she named everything after movie characters."

Not everything.

"Like the dogs and other things. She called her car the Predator, after that Schwarzenegger movie."

That was just a joke.

"We even had rats named Bert and Ernie."

All right already!

"Did you know that Bert and Ernie — you know, the *Sesame Street* puppets — were named after two characters in that movie *It's a Wonderful Life?*" Marion's voice dropped down a notch. "We'd always watch it at Christmas. Diana hadn't even seen it before. I think she got confused. Well, anyway"— her voice rose again —"we figured we were named after somebody too. We tried to think of movies around the time we were born. We figured Ben was named after Ben Kenobi — Obi-Wan Kenobi — from *Star Wars.*"

Katharine watched her out of the corner of her eye. "And you?"

"I'm harder. I mean, we blew off Maid Marian right away. It just didn't seem right. Then we were watching *Raiders of the Lost Ark* again, and the girl in that is named Marion. She spells her name with an O, and she'd be someone my mom would like me to be. Taking care of myself and all. And my mom had this thing for Harrison Ford. He was, like, one of her heros."

He is not.

"He was in both movies, you know."

"I know," Katharine said with something like resignation in her voice. It was all beginning to feel like too much, this dichotomy of her existence.

They drove up to the Denton house, and Katharine had to fight the urge to push Marion out on the parking strip and keep driving. *Dump the kid and drive straight as piss up to Frisco and beyond. And farther beyond that. Then beyond that.*

But she got out of the car and ate the pizza that tasted like cardboard. She watched her daughter laugh and make jokes with her aunt and uncle, punch her cousin repeatedly in the upper arm for teasing her, and quickly develop a crush on Goodfellow, who looked so handsome in his khaki shirt with the sleeves rolled up, following him with her eyes, asking him questions about his job at the studio in such a way that was endearing and irritating at the same time.

Katharine felt like the Monster in *Frankenstein*, who is taught to speak — *and his only profit on it is, he knows how to curse.*

Act 4, Scene 2 🦎

Youth! Stay close to the young and a little rubs off.

— MAURICE CHEVALIER, *Gigi* (1958)

Katharine bumped the waiting tape cassette into the car stereo. There was some static and then Mr. Mulwray's voice poured into the car. "Taking care of business, Miss Bennet. I'm not sure whether I told you that sometimes I'll be sending taped reports. When I'm on the road, like now." Sounds of fast-moving vehicles periodically threatened to overpower his voice, and there was a loud backfire like a gunshot. "I've found the only way my reports get done is to tape them. Kelly will be sending you a transcribed copy in a few days."

The tape had arrived in the mail that morning, and although Katharine could have listened to it in the apartment, she waited until she would be driving; it would be easier to listen to the tape when her arms, legs, and subconscious were engaged elsewhere.

"I don't have a tremendous amount of new information for you. The girl — what's her name?" There was the sound of pages being shuffled. An irate horn from a nearby car burst on the tape. "Yeah, yeah," yelled Mr. Mulwray away from the microphone. "Freeway maniac," he murmured. "Where was I? Oh, right, the girl — Marion — is down in Long Beach, visiting her father's sister and husband. I'll be sending out one of my operatives to watch her for a few days. There'll be an additional charge for that, but it won't be too bad. Don't worry. Let's see. The girl continues to play a great deal of tennis. She was in a tournament two weeks ago and won a couple of rounds."

A little late, Mulwray.

"Mr. and Mrs. Ashley are vacationing in San Diego for a couple of days. I won't be assigning anyone to follow them. You said the children were your primary concern. I understand the boy has been hired as a housesitter for a neighbor while they're all gone. And there appears to be a young lady in his life. Her name is Allie Fox."

Katharine didn't know anyone by that name, anyone who went to Ben's school. She felt something like jealousy flare up and smolder.

"She works at the bank as well. She's an older woman. Nineteen. They went to that new Harrison Ford film on their first date. She drove. After the show they went back to his house and talked for quite a while in the car. 'Round midnight, he kissed her and got out of the car. From the sidewalk he waved and called to her to drive defensively. I'll keep you informed as things progress. Mulwray out."

As Katharine pulled up in front of the Dentons' house, she was warmed by the thought that her words, her admonitions, her warnings of love — *drive defensively* — were being passed down by her son. It was a legacy of sorts.

In the three days since True's party, Katharine had managed to spend each night alone in Thisby's apartment, although she made sure she was safe and locked up before nightfall. She would make herself wait until dark before pulling the blinds and turning on every light. She couldn't expect Goodfellow always to be there to bail her out. Like now. Vivian had come back from Texas, and Katharine realized he would spend his time with her.

She had hardly slept. She didn't really feel tired — more like wired, and that stretched sensation was beginning to feel something like normal. But she also felt attuned, as if she were listening in on everyone else's lives, their bandwidths chafing her skin to irritation.

The voice that whispered in her ear was more subdued. It wasn't silent, but it didn't nag at her. Sometimes, when she had so many Classic Cokes that dingleballs swelled up all over her tongue and she knew with every fiber of this body that wine would smooth out the phoofums, the voice would begin to hum, building up a wall of white noise against which it would broadcast its next message: *Eat Me. Drink Me.* She would try not to listen, though often trying not to listen only made her listen harder, and she would waver from an affirmation of another life to a resignation of a second death. It sounded so peaceful.

She had been surprised when Puck came over the night before. He didn't call first; he just showed up. She hadn't seen or heard from him since True's party.

She froze when the doorbell rang. She didn't want to look through the security lens, as if whoever it was would nightmarishly liquefy like mercury right through the hole and gobble her up.

After he came in, and she stilled her beating heart, she was not sorry for the interruption. A UCLA fall schedule of classes had come in the mail that morning, and she had been looking it over when the doorbell rang. The descriptions of the classes confused and frightened her. She had no idea how she should start. She didn't even know what interested her anymore. Here was the opportunity of a lifetime — actually, twice in a lifetime — college, again, with years of adult experience behind her and youth in front of her. But it just made her feel bad. She should be desperate to take advantage of it. Why else had this whole thing happened?

She had slipped the material under the pillow on the couch, but Puck was preoccupied and wouldn't have noticed anyway. He was upset and wanted to talk. Vivian, again. She had come back from Texas even more unsure of their relationship than when she had left.

"What does she want from me?" He circled the furniture in the living room. Katharine could see the tension in his neck and jaw. His hair fell forward into his eyes. She watched his long fingers comb it back over his forehead. "I don't know what she wants from me."

"What happened?"

"Nothing happened," he said, exasperated, thumping down hard on a chair. "It's the same old thing. We're too different. We don't think alike. I'm never happy. I'm —"

"Are you happy?"

"Me? Shit. I don't know. Look who's talking. Are you?"

She was taken aback. Her mother used to say when Katharine was growing up, "I only want you to be happy." It wasn't until her twenties that Katharine realized what a crock, what a set-up, that was. She was always feeling guilty before then because she wasn't happy. At least, not all the time. When she was happy, she would try to wrestle it into staying, but it never would. She would feel worse — she had achieved that mythical state but just couldn't sustain it. Then she realized that it couldn't last. Shouldn't last. *Because in order to know when you're happy, you have to know when you're not. You have to get the reverse.* It was the natural reaction to an unstable state. Action-reaction. Yin-yang.

"On and off," she answered. "But I don't go around trying to be unhappy."

You don't?

Katharine ignored that voice. "What about your job?" she asked impulsively.

Puck's face clouded over. "What about my job?"

"It makes you miserable. Anyone can see that. Everyone does see that. Your parents. Your father — Dad — especially." He didn't even notice her slip. "Even Vivian. What are you doing it for? Vivian's not stupid. She sees it's more important for you to stay in a job that makes you miserable than to leave it and get a job that might make you happier. Maybe she thinks she has something to do with that."

"Vivian? She has nothing to do with my job. You don't know anything about it."

Don't I?

He had resumed his widow's walk pacing around the coffee table. "I like to finish what I start. And, unlike some people, I like to keep my word and honor the commitments I make."

One of the lords of discipline. How I know the signs.

"I know what I'm doing," he said curtly. He slowly sat down in the chair again and seemed faraway for a long time. He drummed his fingers noiselessly on the table, his forehead deeply ridged. He raised his head after a while, his forehead smooth. "Okay. I take your point. You know, I think I even know where the problem is. I think I know what to do now." He stood up to leave. "You know, I'm really glad you're here. You've been a lot of help to me lately." Katharine watched — when he twisted to look for his car keys — how his shoulder blades were defined by the creases in his shirt. He turned back around and looked at her with some confusion. "But sometimes it's like you're a completely different person. Sometimes I don't think you're really my sister. Quince says you're a changeling." He gestured forward with his hands. "You even look different. I've never seen you look"— he stopped in embarrassment and ended lamely —"so good."

Katharine felt confused too. She knew what he meant, though. She had been filling out like Marion, the boyish lines softening into slight curves, and she was feeling more womanly. But it scared her. It was the first time she had ever been thin, and now she was putting on weight.

At the door, she touched him, the tips of her fingers spread out lightly along his forearm. He turned toward her and awkwardly hugged her, one hand pressing her head lightly against his chest.

Katharine strapped Marion's small overnight bag on the luggage rack over the Porsche's trunk. They were going to pick up Quince at the Bennets and then go back to Thisby's apartment. It had been easy to get Emily to agree to the scheme, and Quince, though not overly enthused, did not vehemently object.

Katharine and Marion made sporadic small talk over the street noises. The top was down on the Porsche, since Quince was going to have to scrunch herself in the space behind the seats. Katharine desperately wanted Marion and Quince to be friends, just as she had wanted her parents and Philip to like one another when they first met. Katharine could tell that Marion was nervous too. She remembered that Marion had never really liked going to playgroups, knowing uncannily of parents' odd belief that, by virtue of being a kid, she'd automatically get along with all the other children. *Play nice, now.* But Marion had always been a self-contained, self-sufficient child who didn't need to be surrounded by playmates — unlike Ben, who needed constant outside stimuli.

As they pulled up in front of the Bennet house, Katharine wondered whether an automobile was discreetly sliding past the driveway while the driver jotted down, *At two-fifty, the two females exited the automobile, the elder self-consciously tugging at her shorts.*

She forgot about it when she saw Marion at a standstill, awed by the structure and grounds in front of her.

"Wow," Marion said.

"My sentiments exactly." *I always wanted to give you something like this. At least, I always thought I did.*

They walked around the side to the kitchen. Katharine loved the fact that the Bennets didn't enter through the front door. In her childhood neighborhood, friends always entered one another's houses through the back door, no matter how long the driveway or how many windows they passed by.

Going to the back door somehow connected Katharine with this house.

No one was in the kitchen. Katharine went through the swinging door into the dining room and called, "Quince. We're here." Then she heard the stereo upstairs. "I'll go get her," she told Marion.

She returned with Quince, who was dressed in her finest down-and-out-in–Beverly Hills look, an oversized T-shirt, baggy jeans, and military-looking boots. They found Marion almost comatose in the living room, perhaps overcome by the warring perfume of the roses.

"Your house is very beautiful," Marion whispered, as if she were in a museum.

This did not impress Quince, who, no doubt, would have

preferred to hear that it was decadent and ostentatious. She grunted.

Katharine hustled the two girls quickly into the car, and the conversation on the way to Thisby's apartment was strained and stilted. *Whose idea was this anyway? I must have been demented.*

They parked in the garage, and Katharine put the top up while the girls gathered their stuff and waited over by the elevator. She kept an eye out for Hooker, as if he would drop down from the max headroom sign swinging across the exit. It made her feel faint just to imagine it.

When she joined the girls, Quince was exclaiming, "You mean you actually saw them? In concert?"

"In this small theater, the Circle K. It was so cool. I could practically touch Ted Logan. What a hunk. I'm sure he winked at me. I even got a guitar pick he threw out."

Quince turned to Katharine. "Marion got to see Wyld Stallyns." She swung back. "You're so lucky," she said enviously, and the two girls proceeded to name-drop groups and concerts they'd been to.

"I went to Shoreline too," Marion told her. "Which day did you go? Sunday? Me too. We could have seen each other. My brother took me."

They were there? I could have seen them!

"Did you see that fight when Led Astray was playing?"

"Yeah, that was cool. The guy with blood all over his face. His nose was really busted."

What fight? I didn't hear anything about a fight.

As it turned out, Katharine never did get a word in edgewise before the two left for the veterinary clinic, hardly waving to her as they went outside — Marion in her squeaky-clean catalog wear and Quince in her bag-lady couture.

Katharine was making the girls root beer smoothies after dinner. Marion sat on a kitchen stool watching her, and Quince was in the shower. Katharine poured a small amount of soda into beer mugs, then added the ice cream and stirred the mix into a thick pudding. Then she slowly poured in the rest of the root beer, stirring constantly.

"My mom did that." Marion broke the silence. "She made smoothies like that."

Katharine clattered the spoon against the side of the mug.

"It's funny. Sometimes you remind me of her," Marion added.

Katharine stood still against the counter and looked into the grain of the kitchen cabinets until the lines separated and floated away. She closed her eyes wearily.

"I mean, you're not at all alike, but . . . oh, I don't know. You talk like her sometimes." Marion paused a moment, then offered, "I don't think she would've liked you, though."

I wouldn't? "She wouldn't?"

"Nah, I don't think so. For one thing, you're too different-looking."

Katharine looked down at herself. She had never made it to the Goodwill to drop off Thisby's clothes. She found herself raiding the piles in the closet but didn't think she looked all that different. Yes, she had dyed her hair a couple of days ago, but it wasn't the flat black color Thisby's had been, but a deep, rich, glossy brunette. Katharine thought it looked good.

"She was weird like that. Anyone who didn't look, you know, right, she was suspicious of. She cared too much about stuff like that. It was hard on Obi — you know, my brother, Ben — because he didn't know what he wanted to look like."

Katharine turned around slowly. "Do you miss her?"

You just keep flogging yourself, don't you?

"I have good memories of her when I was a kid. You know, taking us to the park, reading to us. My friends liked to come over to our house because we could pile cushions from the couches on the floor and dive on them. Our couches were really old and ugly, and my mom didn't care. Your house is beautiful, but it made me sad. I bet you guys didn't get to jump on the furniture."

"No."

"Then something happened when we got older. She got different. Nervous. She suddenly had all these rules, and we couldn't do anything right. We were always messing up something. It was like she was scared. Scared of our friends, of strangers lurking outside the door, of the music, the clothes . . . of us. I was okay with it. I mean, it didn't bother me all that much. But it bothered Ben, you know. I talked to my dad about it after she died, and he said when we were younger he was the one who worried, you know, about us climbing trees and running with pencils in our hands, and she wasn't. But then they made a switch, Dad says. He said it was because she didn't have much of a life when she was a teenager, and she saw a lot of people change with drugs and stuff. She grew up when there were hippies. Her best friend died while they were still in high school. OD'd and Mom didn't even know she was a junkie."

Eve wasn't a junkie! Philip ought to keep his goddamned mouth closed, especially about things he doesn't know anything about. She wasn't a junkie. It was just that one time. That one damned time. It took only one time, and I lost her. And that's just it. Can't you see? If you mess up once, just once in a lifetime, you could die!

"Thisby, is something wrong?"

Katharine turned her physical attention back to the smoothies. "I lost a friend from drugs too. She wasn't a stoner, though people thought she was. She died — it was an accident — and suddenly people — her so-called friends — started talking about her. They said things like they knew she was a junkie all along. That was so much bullshit. She wasn't a junkie. They just liked being part of the rumor mill. Maybe it was the same with your mom's friend."

Katharine could almost feel the offhanded shrug that Marion must have given. What did it matter to her? It was just some long-dead friend of her dead mother. It wasn't as if it meant anything to her.

I'm losing them — my children. No, I've lost them. I could have done real damage to Ben. I could have forced him on the very road I was so petrified he was going to go down. And this is probably as close to Marion as I'm going to get.

Act 4, Scene 3 🦎

I am almost out at heels.

— FALSTAFF, *The Merry Wives of Windsor*, 1.3.32

Katharine drove resignedly from her appointment with Dr. Mantle to the restaurant where she was to meet True — *and the rest of them* — for dinner. True had called and explained to her that Philip — Marion's father, True added in case she didn't know who he was referring to — and Diana — his new wife, he inserted again — had invited Katharine out to dinner with them and the Dentons to thank her for entertaining Marion.

Katharine said yes, as if that were the only response left in her vocabulary. *Hell, it doesn't seem to matter which path I take. They've all got out-of-control, well-fueled vehicles on them, and I'm the designated roadkill.*

It had been such a strange day, noticeable even among so many strange days. And it started early.

Mulwray called in the morning, waking up Katharine and sending her heart into arrhythmia — calls at odd hours still held the panic of potential bad news regarding ailing parents and driving teenagers.

"What a surprise it was," he began immediately, "to find in my operative's latest report that the very person who hired me to keep tabs on the family is spending time with the daughter right here in LA. Now how did this come about?"

"By accident most strange." *What does it matter? I'm paying you, aren't I?*

"I thought you said you weren't going to contact these people."

"It just happened."

"It just happened," he scoffed. "I'm nobody's fool, Miss Bennet. You're not the shining example you present yourself as. In fact, you've got yourself quite a little rap sheet. Several truancy, loitering, panhandling infractions in your teenage years. Three counts of possession with intent to sell within the last three years. Charges dropped. Inconclusive evidence. You seem to have a knack for being in the wrong place at the wrong time. Or do you? Or do you think you're above the law? Is that it?" He paused. "Just what is your interest in the Ashley family?"

She twisted the phone cord around her hand like a garrote. "It's nothing bad. You wouldn't understand. If you're uncomfortable about it . . . ." She pulled the cord tighter. "In fact, why don't we just call it quits. I don't think I need the reports anymore."

He was silent, but Katharine could feel his annoyance and suspicion coalesce into anger. "If you change your mind, I'll charge you all the set-up fees again. Every single one of them." He waited, but Katharine didn't respond. "I'll send you my bill," he said in dismissal but then added, "If I hear about anything happening to the Ashley family, even remotely odd, you'll be hearing from me. And the police. On this one I'll make sure you'll be doin' time."

Katharine was about to ask him if he would send her a copy of his file on Thisby when he hung up.

Katharine and the girls went down to Venice Beach later that morning. Katharine was trying to avoid thinking about her afternoon appointment with Mantle, and Marion was trying to be cool and not gawk. She wasn't very successful, her head snapping back and forth. "Did you see him? He was tattooed all over his chest. Look at her! She's got a bone through her nose."

Katharine felt strangely at home. She didn't let the people in Venice bother her, anymore than they had bothered Thisby.

> . . . it's so fucking great down there. Weirdos and pricks and crazies. Everybody's got a story. Musicians who were gonna make it big but some asshole stole their song or stole their lyrics or stole their voice.
> The con artists, the showmen, the vendors — all ready to snap. Supposed to be so laid-back, but nobody is.
> O brave new world peopled with such as these . . .

Thisby got the quote wrong, of course: "O brave new world that has such people in 't!"

Katharine let their cons and their makes and their curses roll off her like oil, the residue just building up a tougher hide; her skin was thickening exponentially.

The girls and Katharine had their fortunes told by an elderly Asian man with long, wispy chin hair, whose sun-bleached, brocaded jacket was too long in the sleeves, the frog buttons frayed and misshapen. He rubbed small, ivory-colored bones in his hands and rolled them out on a faded black felt square. Katharine wondered if this was the Chinaman who years ago had told Thisby that she would be dying young.

He wouldn't let them hear one another's fortune. "Tell each other later, if want."

Both girls were surprisingly quiet about what the old man said. Quince, who had gone first, kept looking at him suspiciously while Marion sat there, hovering over the bones as if she could read them too. The only thing Quince offered was that his incense sucked. Marion came back, white-faced. Quince shrugged. "He just wants his money, so he says that all that good shit is going to happen to you." Marion didn't respond.

It was Katharine's turn; the walk over to his cardboard table seemed to take a long time.

Will he see more than I'm willing to reveal? Reveal to him or even to Mantle.

The fortune-teller had her blow on the bones in his hands

and then cascaded them onto the felt. He considered the pattern for a long time and then rolled them again. He stared at the bones even longer this time. He finally looked up and spoke past her left ear. "Too many paths. Very different fortunes on each path. Choose carefully." He quickly gestured to the next person who waited.

"What'd he say?" asked Marion, who appeared to have recovered and was too curious to keep quiet.

"I have no fortune," Katharine replied simply.

Or I have too many. What the hell.

On the way to her appointment with Mantle, Katharine drove Marion and Quince back to the Dentons'. The girls decided they didn't want to go out to dinner with the grown-ups, so they planned a fast food–videofest at home. Marion might have reconsidered if Puck had been invited, but he wasn't, and Katharine was glad all around.

She wanted to say good-bye to Marion before her father and stepmother arrived, and Katharine hugged her, perhaps a little too long for such a short acquaintance, but everyone thought it was so nice of her to be so sad that Marion was leaving. Katharine didn't know when she would see Marion next — school was starting soon — and didn't know how to arrange herself to be of importance. *I am not her mother anymore.*

She overheard Quince and Marion making plans to visit each other sometime in October or November, so she kept telling herself she would see Marion then. Perhaps she shouldn't have been so rash in firing Mr. Mulwray; it was painful to be around Marion, and knowing about her through Mulwray, despite his threats, might have been a less wrenching way to get information.

Hank Denton walked Katharine out to her car, even though she really didn't want his company. He stopped her before she climbed in and drove away.

"You don't remember me, do you?" he asked.

Katharine froze, her hand on the doorlatch.

"I didn't think so. It took me the longest time to place you too. I thought I knew you from somewhere when I first saw you in my kitchen, but I wasn't sure from where or when."

Katharine just shook her head.

"Over a year ago? Downtown at the Cabaret?" he prompted.

Katharine continued to shake her head.

"It's okay." He then looked at her stricken face. "Oh no, it was nothing like that. Nothing happened. Though we were both pretty drunk. We just talked. Maybe I talked you into a stupor, which is why you don't remember me." His laughter sounded canned, and it didn't suit him.

Katharine tried not to bolt.

"I had just lost my sister-in-law, and I was pretty upset."

Katharine stared at him incredulously.

He didn't seem to notice. "I talked to you because you seemed so sympathetic. You seemed so interested. You asked so many questions, and I talked so long. . . ." His voice trailed off, but then he seemed to collect himself. "I told you that evening that I was a little in love with her, you see. She didn't even know, mind you, but I took her death hard — harder, perhaps, than a mere brother-in-law should have, and I came out here to see if you ever did remember who I was and where you met me, and ask you not to say anything. You know, to Emily. She might not understand why I was crying in my beer in a downtown bar. Alone. She might not believe there was really nothing to it. That nothing ever came of it. She might not believe that."

"It's okay," Katharine barely croaked out. "I won't say anything. I believe you. Really."

Hank nodded and let her go without another word.

Katharine pulled out into the street, barely missing the rear bumper of the car parked in front of her.

Thisby knew me? Thisby was interested in me? She didn't think I was just some boring middle-aged woman who died? Hank said she was sympathetic; she asked so many questions.

Thisby knew me!

She wanted to wrap her arms around Thisby and hug her.

· · ·

Dr. Mantle had barricaded himself behind his huge mahogany desk for their meeting. He pointed to a chair and, when she was seated, pushed a business card across the expanse of desktop. Katharine leaned over and took it up — HELEN HUDSON, PH.D., PSYCHOTHERAPY AND CONSULTING.

Dr. Mantle sat up straight in his chair, playing leapfrog with his pipe and lighter on the desk blotter. He was good-looking, in a stuffy British sort of way, his thin, blond hair carefully combed across his forehead. He looked like someone who had prepared a speech and had been practicing it all morning — he was anxious to get it over with.

"I agreed to see you only because your mother called and asked me to. And only because I see most of her social peers and their children." He pointed to the card in her hand. "That is the name of a colleague who has agreed to see you from now on. You can tell your mother that it was a mutual decision, that we decided it would be best for you to see someone who specializes in your kind of trouble. Dr. Hudson *used* to specialize in serial killers, some of the smartest psychotics out there, so your little tricks will have no effect on her. Try as you might."

This sounds like a challenge.

"I fulfilled my part of the bargain. I owe you nothing more." He tapped the bowl of his pipe on the desk and waited. "You have nothing to say to me?"

I'm sorry? No, I don't think so. Thisby would never want me to say that. "I'll just leave then." She stood up.

Dr. Mantle stood up too, rapping his thigh hard against the center desk drawer. Katharine could tell that he didn't trust her to leave easily anymore than she had trusted Hooker to. His fingertips were on top of the desk, not resting lightly but seeming to force the desk to its knees. He breathed deeply, showing signs of anxiety that he valiantly tried to mask. "I will go to the police if you ever threaten me again. I have enough on you to make your life miserable too. I'll get you."

Over my dead body.

Katharine thought she could imagine what Thisby had on

him. Sex with a client. Perhaps with an underage one. Prescribing drugs she sold or shared or hoarded for herself.

The showdown reels forward in her mind.

She just appears in his office. Out of the blue. She's dumped him some time ago, but he's never gotten over her. She's his drug, his addiction, his magnificent obsession. He'd do almost anything to get her back, and for some reason she needs him now. She teases him, staying just out of reach, but still tantalizingly close. He aches to touch her skin. It calls to him. His fingers twitch. He feels an erection beginning. He knows that will only give her more power, but he is standing and to sit down would unbalance him even more. She grins when she notices the bulge in his pants. He smells her. He can hardly breathe. She's so thin, he could crush her. But he knows better. She can be as impenetrable as Kevlar. He needs her cooperation. He can hardly understand what she is saying. Something about a drug bust and an alibi. She needs him to say that she was here. As a patient. That she was with him in a special follow-up session. All evening long. She needs him to be her alibi. He agrees. He would agree to anything. She comes up to him and rubs herself against him. He tries to inhale her through his mouth. He can't help it. It's been too long. He slamdances his erection against her and comes. She holds him as he spasms but lets go as soon as he stops. She backs out of the office, the ultimatum hanging between them like a noose — or I will tell your wife, the psychiatric board, all my mother's friends who see you too, how you raped me. How you fed me drugs and then raped me. How you continued my treatment just to keep me accessible. I can damage you. As he looks down at the spreading stain of spent semen on his tan slacks, he realizes just how damaged he is.

Act 4, Scene 4 ⚬

The fates are against me. They tossed a coin — heads, I'm poor;

tails, I'm rich. So what do they do? They tossed a coin with two heads.

— JOHN GARFIELD, *Four Daughters* (1938)

Katharine stood with True in the restaurant lobby and watched her husband approach them. She wished she could turn to True and say, "He looks weird, doesn't he? He looks really weird. He looks very weird. Really. I think he's retaining water." But she couldn't. He looked good. He looked really good. As Mr. Mulwray had told her, Philip and Diana had been down in San Diego playing golf. *Golf? Philip never liked golf.* He was tanned and looked relaxed. The Ashley hair was brighter on his head than she had seen it in years. *Even his hair is happy?*

She had dressed for dinner with the utmost care but realized it was all for naught. Thisby usually handled casual well, but Katharine couldn't cover up the fact that she had been sleepless for days — and worn through.

Diana looked dressed to kill. She wore white, which showed off her slim body, her blond hair, and her tanned skin. She had too much makeup on in Katharine's opinion, her teeth were too big — *and her breasts don't look like they're all that big a deal* — but she was definitely a looker.

Philip shook Katharine's damp hand. "I see the family resemblance. Quince looks like you. Actually, True says I might have met you once before. If I did, I'm sure you've changed since then."

At our last meeting, I died. It alters the appearance.

True had arrived at the restaurant by himself. Hank was not feeling well, and Emily had stayed home to nurse him. *Did Hank not believe me? Did he think I was going to tell his family that he lusted in his heart? Lusted after . . . me? I don't understand. A secret admirer. I never saw it. Never felt it. I mean, I loved him as a brother, but why would he be in love with me? When he had Emily. The person my own daughter would rather talk to than me.*

The four of them sat down at their table, and the men launched immediately into the glories of golf. Philip was in a good mood, talkative, jovial, like he used to be when Katharine first met him.

Strangers in good company.

Katharine sat there, stubbornly quiet, and watched Diana through slitted eyes. Katharine was conscious, as never before, of the shared space within her. It was almost as if she could tap directly into Thisby. *And Thisby knew me. She knew me.* They both decided that the worst punishment would be to make Diana talk. She might be a terror in the corporate world, but it was obvious to them that she was feeling uncomfortable in her new role as wife and stepmother. And Katharine knew things about Philip that no one but an intimate would know. She could make it very uncomfortable for all of them.

Does Philip still leave his used dental floss by the bathroom sink as if there might be a dental floss drive some day?

Is he still so ticklish under his right testicle that when you touch even near the spot, he is torn between agony and ecstasy?

"So, do you like golf so much too?" Thisby's voice boomed in her ears.

Wow, way to go for the jugular.

Diana laughed a little deprecatingly. "No. It's all right, but I'd rather play tennis. So we split the days, tennis one day, golf the next. Phil's not a bad tennis player for not playing a lot."

Phil? He lets you call him "Phil"?

The waiter came by and took their order. Philip selected a bottle of Chianti for them, and Katharine let the waiter fill the four glasses at the table. The blood-colored liquid held shadows that flickered darkly against the glass. The phoofums in her mouth exploded into cotton balls, and suddenly she thought the inside of her mouth would crack like overdone skin. She took a swig of water.

Katharine felt perverse. Mad and perverse. There was a stirring in her center that started to take on bulk and shape. "I understand you two haven't been married long." She directed this toward Philip.

"Two and a half months. It's just flown by." He glanced quickly at Diana and then turned to Katharine. "You probably know that my wife died over a year ago." He paused. "I didn't think I could fall in love again so quickly." He reached for Diana's hand and covered it with his.

Katharine looked at their hands as if they were mating toads.

"We got quite a bit of grief from friends and family, including him" — Philip pointed to True — "for not waiting longer."

Katharine couldn't help but lean closer to True.

"But . . . I hope Katharine understands."

Katharine felt a hysterical chuckle tickle her throat. *You talkin' to me?*

"Didn't Aunt Katharine always say that if she died first, she wanted you to remarry?" True asked and then saw Katharine looking at him dumbstruck. He blushed and turned to Diana. "I'm sorry. I didn't mean to be rude."

"No, it's okay. You weren't being rude at all," Diana said quickly. She glanced back and forth from True to Philip. "I wish he would talk more about her. He never talks about her, her death, what she thought. I'd like to know things like this."

"I talk about her," Philip protested rather weakly.

"No, you don't. You barely mention her in passing. Sometimes I want to bring her up, but since you don't, I don't feel right about it."

"I don't bring her up because you don't."

"But I don't . . ."

The newlyweds smiled and made up in a microsecond.

"Okay" — Philip pretended to hunker down as if to do business — "I've been instructed by my wife to talk. So what do you want to know?"

It was almost too good to be true. Katharine could see Diana forming a question. *No, this is going to be my quiz show.* "Her death was sudden?" The corners of her mouth felt as if they were about to split. She fingered the stem of her wineglass.

"Completely unexpected. I thought it was stress. She hadn't been getting along with the kids for a while, and I thought it was that. And then there was her job. We weren't getting along real well for that matter either. We would have gotten through it, though. Marriages go through stages like that." He looked solemnly at Diana, as if to impart some well-earned knowledge.

"Mom said Aunt Katharine hadn't been feeling well for a long time," True remarked.

"Well, yes, but she had been to the doctors, and they said she was fine. I'm afraid I kind of brushed it off. I don't know. I don't think she knew what was happening either." He tapped the handle of his fork and the tines bounced off the table. He quickly put his hands back in his lap. "I'm wondering if she didn't just give up. Maybe she had just had enough. She had a long haul with her parents. They were sick for so long, and she was an only child. They relied on her a lot."

I took it. I always did.

"She took care of them. Always did, I think. Even when she was a child. Always responsible. Always there. I think that's what attracted me to her. I was a bit of a fuckup, pardon my French, before I met her, and she was always so steady, so strong, so solid. Someone you wanted to attach yourself to."

Jesus, I sound like some sort of fucking, pardon my French, rock.

"But I don't think she had much fun in life. She never could understand why someone would do something for no good reason, let alone for a bad one. But to her credit, she never expected our kids to be like her, and thank God, she wasn't like her parents."

They weren't so bad.

"But Katharine just didn't understand the kids."

Oh, and you did?

"At least as teenagers. I think they would have gotten along well as adults."

But I never got the chance.

"But they never got the chance." Philip focused back on the faces around the table. "I'm sorry. I didn't mean to dominate the conversation. Even if I was instructed to." He cast a glance at Diana, who was looking at him without expression but then smiled encouragingly.

Katharine felt like a real junkie now, having been deprived of a drug just long enough to be mad enough to kill for a fix. She was going to murder him if he didn't talk, even if she hated what he said. She was going to stand up and drive her fist under his solar plexus. *Talk, you polygamous bastard, or I'm going to push my fist right up to your heart and rip it out from under your ribs and shove it still beating into your face. Then I'm going to eat it in the marketplace with fava beans and this nice Chianti.*

"No, really, I'm interested." She almost laughed at her ridiculously pedestrian-sounding tone of voice. "And you? How did you handle her death?"

"Oh, me? I fell apart. Simple as that. It was incredible the little things she did that I didn't even know about. The whole house fell apart too. I remember one day" — he moved his silverware — "standing outside in front of the garbage bin, holding a milk carton in my hand. We're on this so-called voluntary recycling program. You know, where supposedly the only things left to go in our garbage can are used lightbulbs and toothpaste tubes. Now was this" — Philip mimed the carton in his hand — "supposed to go in the mixed paper or the catch-all recycling bin?" He looked up. "Katharine took care of all that stuff. What did I care? So I'm standing there with this miserable carton in my hand, feeling totally stupid and useless, and I'm crying. How am I supposed to figure out life when I can't even figure out the damned recycling bins. I'll tell you that was a low point in my life."

Katharine watched as Diana took her other hand and covered his hand that was covering hers. She wanted to slap her own hand on top of both of theirs. *I win.*

"So what was it?" True asked.

Philip looked up, puzzled. "What was what?"

"The milk carton. What was it? Mixed paper or catch-all?"

Philip stared at him. Diana looked horrified. Katharine started to choke, the laughter a lodged pit in her throat. True looked innocently about him.

Philip began to chuckle. "Catch-all. But I didn't know I was supposed to rinse it out first. They get a little rancid after a while if you don't."

I hope you got fined.

Diana relaxed.

"It was Ben who saved me and, ultimately, saved us," Philip continued, after a moment.

Shit, now how do you shut the fucker up?

"Ben was a rock."

Another one? A chip off his ol' mother?

"You haven't met him yet."

Not this one.

"Marion says he's changed quite a bit," True offered. "I'm not sure if that's a good thing or not, coming from a little sister."

"No, it's good, it's good. From my point of view, it's good. From our point of view," he amended, leaning slightly to include Diana. "Ben was into stuff he shouldn't have been into and not going to school. But he's getting back on track." Diana watched Philip with fierce maternal protection. "He's still a teenager, of course. He knows everything, and he's absolutely right. All the time." He paused again, and no one said anything. "In fact, it was Ben who talked us into getting married."

O wonderful son, that can so stonish a mother!

Philip nodded to her as if he had heard. "He told us, Why wait? We knew we were going to get married sooner or later, so why not sooner? We took a lot of grief for that. If I hadn't had Ben's backing — and Marion's, for the most part — I would have never done it." He turned to Diana, who nodded.

"I think Marion is still taking it kinda hard. She and Diana get along pretty well, considering, but she misses her mom."

The membranes in Katherine's mouth felt like they had been squeegeed. *They won't care if I drink. They won't even think it's strange. They'll think it's strange if I don't drink. True doesn't know all of it. Goodfellow wouldn't have told him everything. That's family business.*

Philip looked at her squarely. "I really appreciate you taking an interest in Marion. I can see how much happier she is after being down here just a couple of weeks. I'm not sure about the hair, though." He laughed. "But even I remember how important it is to go back to school after the summer looking totally different."

They had dyed Marion's hair the same color as Katharine's, laughing and giggling and getting dye all over the bathroom, the towels, their clothes. When Marion came out of the bathroom, after having rinsed and dried her hair, Katharine was quite shocked. The darker color made Marion look older and more sophisticated, something Katharine couldn't quite figure out whether or not she liked. But she loved the fact that she and Marion now shared a physical attribute.

"But hair grows out," Philip said. "I try and be open."

Well, aren't you Mr. Wonderful.

"Katharine went crazy one day when Ben dyed his hair. Something she regretted, I think."

Katharine had held her breath the day before, wondering whether Marion would bring up the fiasco with Ben dyeing his hair. But she didn't, and Katharine was eternally thankful. She didn't want Quince to hear that story. She didn't want Quince to think badly of Marion's mother.

"Marion can't say enough nice things about you and your sister."

"She's a great kid," Katharine managed to say, when what she really wanted to do was pick up the glass of wine and . . . and . . . throw it in his face.

Diana looked at her, chagrined. "I'm jealous, though." She paused. "I'm still feeling my way around Marion, and I'm having a hard time deciding whether I should be a mother or a friend to her, or whether she'll allow me to be either. We do like clothes. One of the things we have in common."

"Except that one time," Philip prompted.

"Oh, that." Diana now looked embarrassed. Everyone waited, and she reluctantly continued. "I told her she could wear anything of mine she wanted to. She said the same. So once I went into her closet when she wasn't home and found an outfit I really liked. A simple A-line skirt and short jacket. It was a little snug on me, but not too bad, so I wore it. I thought Marion was going to either faint or kill me when she saw me. You see, the outfit had been one of her mother's. Marion liked it and had kept it for herself. I will never forget the look she gave me. Of course, I had no idea, but . . ."

That outfit was snug on her?

"But Diana and Ben get along famously," Philip said. "Don't you?"

"Yes, but with Ben, it's different." Diana turned to Katharine, as if only another female would understand. "He doesn't need me to be a mother right now. Maybe later, but not now. I can get away with being a pal. We've got too many years left with Marion, I think, for me to be a pal. But I'm jealous anyway. I'm jealous that you can be her friend. She obviously needs one."

The waiter came by and notified them that dinner would be just a few more minutes. Diana stood up and announced that she was going to the bathroom. Katharine realized that Diana was one of those women who liked a mass exodus to the powder room, but Katharine pointedly ignored her, and Diana left slowly.

"Sometimes," Philip said, drifting along, "I hear Katharine's phrases coming out of the kids' mouths. It's the strangest thing. Maybe they were saying them before, but now that Katharine is dead, it's very startling. I don't say anything to them about it, because I don't want to make them self-conscious. Plus I like to hear them. It keeps her alive.

"That doesn't mean I don't love Diana," Philip continued after a pause, looking guiltily around to make sure Diana hadn't returned. "I do. Passionately. It's wonderful. I feel like a teenager again. Katharine was a little solitary for me, now that I look back on it. I didn't know then how much I like being needed by my partner. Katharine never asked for help. Ever. She was so used to doing things for herself, she seemed to even resent my asking. So I stopped."

I did need help, even though I always did everything by myself. I just had trouble asking for it. Then I'd get mad at you for not realizing that I needed you to just do whatever it was I wanted or needed you to do . . . though I probably would have resented that too. . . .

She picked up the glass of wine, and the white noise in her head muffled the conversation between True and Philip. Her eye caught several dark presences at separate tables. She looked to her right, and a shadowy shape raised a glass and took a healthy sip. "Good wine is a good familiar creature," she heard it whisper.

She gripped the bowl of the glass tightly. *I want this. I want this so badly, my blood simply sings with it.*

Another voice, so familiar, yet never so clear, came up from the depths of this body. It implored her, *Don't. It's not what you want.*

But it is. It is.

Diana returned, dinner came, and the conversation eased into small talk. Katharine didn't say much. She didn't care. She felt uprooted. She realized then that she had hoped, more than just a little bit, that at the moment she and Philip met again, he would look into her eyes and would see Katharine shining through. In a moment of passion, the room would fade away and they would be the only ones in existence, locked into each other's heart and soul. Theirs would be a true romance, an undying love that withstood time, death, reincarnation. Mate for life; mate for eternity.

Always. Happily ever after.

What a lot of Harlequin romance bullshit.

She watched Philip and Diana, their heads touching as they spoke quietly to each other.

Does he play DJ for you while you're doing the dishes? Does he come into the kitchen and dance for you — the Funky Chicken, the Frug, and a very bad but energetic Running Man? He could make her laugh so, grabbing her hands encased in soapy, industrial rubber gloves. "Here comes the dip," he'd warn her.

It had been years since he'd dipped her, and washing dishes had become yet another drudge.

Do you bake him chocolate chip cookies?

Katharine rested her fingertips on the inside of her other wrist and thought she had flatlined again. There seemed to be no vital signs at all, but then she realized there were entire oceans between her heartbeats. She had to do something, or she would drown.

"Marion would like a dog."

Everyone started, and Philip blinked, trying to digest this bit of information. "Diana's afraid of dogs."

Diana's mouth opened.

"All dogs?" Katharine upstaged her, ignoring Philip.

"I . . . Big dogs scare me." No one spoke, though Philip appeared to be wrestling with himself in order not to elaborate for her. Diana looked trapped, and struggled to explain. "I was bitten one summer when I was about seven. We had rented a cabin up in the mountains." She spoke directly to Katharine again, as if she were the most important person to convince. "I got surrounded by a pack of dogs. They weren't wild or anything. Not always, I mean. I was walking around the small lake, and they charged out from the trees. I had been told to stand still around charging dogs, so I did. They ringed around me. It made me dizzy, trying to keep all of them in my sight. And they kept moving, circling to the right, then to the left, weaving from side to side. Then one jumped at me." She bent up her right arm, and there was a jagged edge of puckered skin. "He drew blood, of course. Even at seven, I knew the smell of the blood would drive the others crazy. I screamed. That backed away all of them except the one who had bitten me. He was crazy. Not rabid. Just mean crazy. He was going to bring me down, and I was going to die. I knew it, and I didn't know how to stop it."

True shuddered next to Katharine. "Shit."

Philip sat silently, holding Diana's hand, watching her closely.

"Then one of the neighbors came and scared them away. He drove me down to the county hospital with his shirt wrapped around my arm. Forty stitches. A couple of days later I had to pick out the dogs that had attacked me. A doggie lineup." She tried to laugh. "I couldn't. They all looked alike, and the dog that had bitten me wasn't there. Him, I would have known. My mother was told later in the summer that they had found him. He'd gone completely feral, and they destroyed him."

Philip looked up at Katharine with a see-I-told-you-so challenge.

"I know Marion would really like a dog. . . . I don't think I'd mind a small dog," Diana finished softly, and Philip swung his head around to make sure he had heard right.

"A small dog?" Philip exclaimed. "I don't think so. She wouldn't stand for it."

Who in the hell is he talking about? Marion or me? Marion was right. I had the whole family convinced that the only dogs are big dogs. "It doesn't have to be a rodent, you know." At Katharine's choice of words, Katharine noticed Philip shiver. *Good.* "As a matter of fact, there's a Sheltie to adopt where Quince works that's full-grown but only about twenty-five pounds. She's the sweetest thing. Marion already loves her."

Diana smiled shyly at Philip. "Maybe we could go by tomorrow. Just to look."

He shrugged and looked almost threateningly at Katharine. She stared right back at him.

Take that . . . Phil.

He looked away.

Tears welled up in her eyes. *So that's it.* She wasn't even worth a sarcastic retort. He had no connection with this young woman across the table from him. Why waste energy on her? She was not part of his family.

Philip had indeed been a bit of a fuckup when she first met him, and he had wasted energy on so many useless or impossible things. Admittedly, that was what had initially attracted her. But he turned solid on her — so respectable and responsible — it was as if being a fuckup were only a passing fad to be dragged out at appropriate times to show her up in front of her own children. *See how right-on and groovy I was?*

But maybe it was all her doing. Maybe it was she who took all the fun out of Philip.

She picked up the glass of wine and tilted it to her mouth. It was like swimming: once learned, never forgotten. The wine burned her throat, and the voice that whispered was roaring gleefully in her ears.

The evening was over, and the four people stood up, gathering their individual belongings and their individual thoughts. Katharine felt eroded; parts of her had been forever sluiced away.

The men were a little ahead when Diana stopped her. "Thank you for bringing up the dog. Phil wouldn't talk to me about it. I really think I can handle a small dog, and Marion knows so much about them already. She really would like one. And maybe she would feel more comfortable in my house. Maybe my house would seem more like a home to her then."

Katharine barely looked at her.

I don't give a rat's ass about you. I did it for Marion, not you. You can make your own fucking way with Marion.

As Katharine was driving home, the evening whirled and barked around her like Diana's dogs, snarling and encircling her, making her dizzy as she tried to keep all of them in her sight and under control. They herded her toward the dark waters.

I was too proud, too stubborn to let people know when I needed help. What an image I projected.

Oh, fuck the self-pity.

My daughter wouldn't talk to me because she thinks I never made any mistakes. My own husband felt unneeded and unappreciated; I could do it all with or without him.

You did the best you could. What else can you expect?

My family was falling down around my ears, and I wasn't going to change. I couldn't see a damned thing. I was too busy hanging on to what I thought was the only way — rigidity, rules, conformity, rightness.

Don't worry. It will turn out all right. It always does. It was just meant to be.

I can't be strong anymore. I don't want to be strong anymore.

Never weaken! That's always been your motto.

What a joke. What a theater of the absurd.

She gave up and slipped into the drowning pool, letting the voices close in over her head.

The best thing I ever did for my children was to die.

Act 4, Scene 5 🐎

Love looks not with the eyes but with the mind;

And therefore is wing'd Cupid painted blind.

— HELENA, *A Midsummer Night's Dream*, 1.1.234

She knocked on his door. It opened so quickly, she jumped back. It was only him, but he looked crazed, and it took a moment for his eyes to synchronize and focus.

"God, that was fast." He blinked myopically. "I just left the message. I didn't know what else to do." He wandered back into the apartment, leaving her to follow.

She had to shout down the voices that continued to thunder in her head. "What's wrong?" she said, now frightened. "What's happened? I haven't been home yet. I didn't hear your message. Is everyone okay?"

He turned and looked at her blankly for a second. "No, everyone's okay. I mean, yes, everyone's okay. No, I don't mean that either. I'm not okay." He sat down heavily on a kitchen chair, almost missing the seat. There was a nearly empty bottle of Jack Daniels on the table. "I called because Vivian left me. Irreconcilable differences." She watched him fill his glass, how the tawny-colored liquid gathered and reflected the light. "That's what she said we had. Irreconcilable differences." He had trouble with the word "irreconcilable," and it came out "irrecable."

"She's moving up to San Francisco. She's leaving this weekend. Just like that. Already subletting an apartment. Has a job. She probably already has a fucking boyfriend. What do I know? She says it's best this way. She says she was dying in my arms."

It felt as if she were suffering from hypothermia, stripped down and exposed, shivering from the center of her being. One voice that she had kept so successfully dampened, the voice that had watched and studied him — the way his hands looked while buttoning his shirtsleeves, how the line of his jaw changed when he was thinking, the curve of his pectoral muscles — that voice now had access and came forward softly.

Then I envy her. If I were to die, there's nowhere else on earth I'd rather be.

"Thiz, whaddam I gonna to do?" He took a small swallow from his glass, and she watched the muscles in his neck constrict. He stood up, the chair almost upending, and looked at her desperately.

She went over and hugged him, her face in the hollow of his throat. He smelled warm and smoky, and she drank him in. It was better than wine.

She stroked his back. She could feel how tense he was, how the muscles across his shoulders were ropy and strained. She kneaded them blindly with her fingertips, using the muscles' feel and dimension to guide her, and slowly, ever so slowly, they softened, and he began to feel like a man again instead of a cyborg encased in thin epidermis.

"I-I don't feel so good," she heard him groan through his throat. She stepped back, and his face had a satin finish.

"Come on." She put her arm around his waist and led him into the bedroom.

She sat him down on the bed, pried the whiskey glass out of his hand, and put it on the nightstand. He fumbled with the belt of his khaki shorts. She helped him undo the buckle and slide off the shorts. He curled up on the bed in his boxer shorts. She started to leave, but he stopped her. "Don't go."

She closed the bedroom door, and the room was in total darkness.

"Don't go," he called louder.

"I'm here."

She heard him settle back down.

She sat on the bed. He wiggled more into the middle, and she lay down beside him. She continued to shiver.

"You smell good," he said.

She had gone out and bought some of Katharine's perfume before her dinner with Philip, thinking it would trigger some sort of response in him, but Philip's nostrils never even quivered.

He pressed closer to her and seemed to fall asleep for a while.

She could feel his hand like a hot iron on her shoulder blade, and she started to cry.

Propped up on one elbow, she held the whiskey glass under her nose, the fumes whirling her brain. The wine she had drunk had taken the edge off for a bit, but now it was back. She imagined the whiskey in the glass, like amber syrup, smooth and medicinal. She tipped the glass back and took a sip. He stirred, and she replaced the glass on the stand.

"Thisby?" he said drowsily.

"No," she whispered. "Katharine."

"Katharine?"

"Yes."

"I know you?"

"Yes."

She slowly leaned forward and with lips still stinging with alcohol anointed his eyelids with kisses. His mouth opened, and his breath, smooth as the smell of softened caramel candies, fogged over her. She lowered her mouth and reached into him with her tongue and her soul, and like Queen Titania with her ass-headed lover, she sang his anxieties to sleep.

She sat on a chair next to the bed and watched him sleep. She wanted to be smoking. It would have felt so right. She had even gone unsuccessfully through his dresser drawers to find a cigarette. So she sat there, legs crossed, leaning one elbow on the topmost knee, the closed fist holding up her head, watching him and wishing for a cigarette. He was so beautiful, lying on his stomach, his head turned toward her. His features were smooth, almost porcelain, his morning beard barely noticeable. His hair was tufted around his ears and curled over his forehead. The sheet barely reached his waist, and she had gently pulled down a corner to reveal the fairy kiss. In the gray, it looked like a mere smudge. A flexed knee struck out from under the covers toward her. She wanted to touch that knee. It had fit in her palm so well before. His right arm was relaxed and gently curved, almost groping for something. For her? She could touch it if she just reached out. How she wanted to reach out. He wasn't snoring now, but he had been before; she had nudged him under the shoulder blade to turn him over, and then she had begun to cry.

It was the morning after. The sun was up, and even though she had opened the curtains to let in the light, the rays hadn't yet reached the level of the rear window. She was glad. She didn't want him to wake up just yet. She wanted to watch him. One of his pillows was at her feet. They had knocked it off last night. She rocked it back and forth with her dangling toes and then flipped it over, rotisserie-style. Over and over again.

She remembered everything. This time. *One potato, two potato.* It was just that she didn't want to think about it. *Three potato, four.* But she didn't want it to be like a Harlequin romance. *Five potato, six potato, seven potato, more.* They kissed and then it was afterward . . .

Katharine had kissed him. It was true; she had started it. But she hadn't come to his apartment to do that. She hadn't. She wasn't quite sure what she had come for — she just wanted a little kindness, a little sympathy, a little closeness.

And when he lay in her arms in the dark, so warm and alive and needing, she wanted to be closer. She wanted to lay bare her soul, open up to him. Thisby was only skin deep, and Katharine was right there.

I'm not the person you think I am. If you could just see me out of this body.

And he seemed to sense it. He was truly seeing her for the first time.

He kissed her back, didn't he?

Their lovemaking hadn't been elegant. The skirt of her dress was already around her waist, and he worked off their underwear with fumbling hands. He pulled her buttocks toward him and then turned heavily over into her.

He murmured into her hair, but she didn't understand what he was saying, and she didn't want to know. She was fighting her own battles. They were all in her head, all yammering at her.

Thisby's own flesh and blood. Even she wouldn't do something like this.

Disgusting. You could be his mother.

Such dexterity to incestuous sheets. Have you no shame?

Come on. Come on.

Shut up! Shut up! All of you. This has nothing to do with Thisby. I'm Katharine. And I . . . and I . . . and I love him.

He came quickly, and she had been glad of it. She had excited him to a point where he had no control; he was swept along; she had pulled him out of himself. Then she had held him in her arms, stroking his head as it lay on her shoulder. His arm and hand rested lightly around her stomach, his ankle hooked around hers. He quickly quieted and seemed to sink alongside her. She held him up long after her arm began to numb. He then rolled away, and with it came the voodoo stabs of returning circulation. She would have held him all night if he had let her.

Now she was sitting there, watching him. She felt like Oberon's mischievous henchman, Robin Goodfellow — having latched the wrong lover's eyes with the Cupid juice — now forced to undo the spell to see what remains.

With eyes open and in the light of day.

She took another sip of the whiskey on the nightstand. It made her shudder. With moist lips, she streaked his proffered eyelid. It fluttered.

Will he wake up and be thought he was enamoured of an ass? Will his eye loathe this visage now?

Act 4, Scene 6 🐿

Life is a thief.

— KATHARINE HEPBURN, *Suddenly Last Summer* (1959)

She stood in the hallway, the morning sun hot on her back, and through the slit between the bedroom door and the jamb, she watched him slowly come to consciousness. She had all her belongings in her arms, the key to her car between her thumb and forefinger.

Whom had she been kidding? She couldn't face him. This wasn't some damn play, where everything comes out all right after the exchange of a few simple lines. She couldn't stand to see the realization explode across his face: he had just made love to his sister.

She watched him open his eyes, grimace, and shut them again, covering his forehead with a hand to block out the light. "Too bright," he moaned, but slowly like a contortionist bunched himself into a sitting position. He held his head in his hands, his elbows propped up on his knees. "Have I laid my brain in the sun and dried it?"

He sat there and seemed to deliberately reconnect his various body parts. He finally looked around him, and she saw him take in the disarray of the bedclothes, his semi-erect penis. He took a handful of the sheet, brought it to his nose, and smelled it.

The skin on her shoulders was on fire, and she thought she might throw up.

He turned his torso toward the bedroom door, but didn't get up. "Kath — ? Katharine?" he called softly.

She didn't move. Her skin blackened, and hairline cracks webbed across the surface.

He frowned. "Thisby?"

Flames licked up the length of her body. The hard casing around her, impervious to so many elements, finally succumbed to the intense heat and split apart, falling away to be left among the cinders.

She pulled back, and her movement caused the bedroom door to sway. She ran.

As she closed the front door behind her, she heard him call from the bedroom, "Wait . . ."

Act 5, Scene 1 🦎

Believe me, if a man doesn't know death, he doesn't know life.

— LIONEL BARRYMORE, *Grand Hotel* (1932)

Katharine snaked another glass of champagne off the waiter's tray, spilling some on the marbled floor. Shit. She was getting a tad unsteady and thought perhaps the tequila poppers she had slammed down before going to Thisby's reception hadn't been such a good idea. She had felt increasingly frantic as the afternoon wore on, and the tequila had calmed her down — as she knew it would — but now she felt herself rushing too fast toward the oblivion she sought each night.

It was a late Indian summer evening with the promise of cool just a few blocks away. The elephant doors in the back of the Zelig-Ziegfeld Gallerie were open, and inside the skylights were jacked open. A breeze was sneaking in and rippling the flower arrangements that Anne had made for the two long trestle tables now covered with platters of manicured food.

Katharine stood a little way from the front door, but within the sight line of the entering guests. She felt like a bride but with no groom beside her — hers was the only hand to shake in the reception line. Max had positioned her there, and since this was also in the flight pattern of the waiters with their full glasses of champagne, she didn't protest.

• • •

She watched Puck as he took his right hand and molded it against Vivian's right hip, his fingers almost cupping her buttock. They had come straight from the airport, having flown down from San Francisco where Puck had gone to live in September to see if things could work out between them. Their backs were to Katharine, but she thought she could see their studied but mannered concentration as they took in the exhibit.

Puck had called Katharine a couple of times after the night they were together. That Night — that's how she thought of it. Like a movie title. It Happened That Night. Both times he was so hesitant and confused, she almost felt sorry for him. He seemed to be trying to dismiss it — That Night, That Woman, Thisby, Katharine, whoever, whatever — as a dream, a figment of his drunken imagination. He was trying to act normal, but the uncertainty was a breach between them. He didn't ask her anything, and, although half of her wanted to confront him — make him writhe in shame and remorse — the other half swallowed their joint culpability and guilt and was mute.

The last time he called had been to tell her that he was moving up to San Francisco, that she, his sister, had been right, he had held himself hostage with his job; that he wasn't satisfied or fulfilled in it; that it was time to strike out on his own, away from his family, to begin anew, to commit to Vivian, if she would have him; and that he owed this realization all to Thisby. She had steered him toward it. He was beholden to her for everything.

She found it almost funny; in all her mother-life, one of the things she had always wanted was for someone to confide in her — choose her to be their confidante, draw on her years of experience and well of wisdom. Someone did and then took her advice, but it wasn't even necessarily right. *Or true. It was really the fear, the uncertainty, of what actually happened That Night that forced him to act. I'm sure it was.*

And now Puck owed her for it; Vivian had taken him back.

So Vivian owes me big time too, though she doesn't know it. She owes me because I taught Goodfellow the thing we both wanted him to learn. I have given him the gray area. He is awash in the nethertones.

Never again will the resolution be clear or definite. Never again will things be black and white, yin or yang. I forced Goodfellow away from me and have sent him to her an altered person.

Vivian owed her all right.

It's just . . . it's just . . . It just wasn't what she had wanted to happen.

She took a sip of champagne and saw that Anne was pinning her down yet again with a disapproving eye. At the beginning of the reception, Anne had tried subtle hints about not drinking too much and staying focused. She brought up how Thisby's father had bailed her out — yet again — by not only paying for the exhibit but basically doing all the work for her. Anne then escorted people over to divert Katharine. Robert and Anne had asked the entire dramatis personae of their lives, and it seemed to Katharine that they all showed up. Anne and Robert prompted her, "Thisby, you remember Peter Hoskins and Rita Boyle, don't you?" She didn't, but all she had to do was smile, shake their hands, which was often a prelude to a perfunctory kiss, and say, "Nice to see you again. Peter. Rita. Thanks for coming."

Now Anne just shot darts at her, and the disapproval and disappointment were thick on her face. But so what if Katharine had been drinking? So what if Anne got upset? *What does she know about hardship, about pain, with her big fucking house and her perfect husband?*

Katharine had developed her own thick skin.

Goodfellow said the magic word as I ran out the door —"Wait . . ."

But nothing happened; I'm only waiting to die.

I went home by way of a liquor store, on the road to ruin, the voice that roared riding shotgun. I owed it to myself to get drunk.

I didn't look back.

Robert Bennet had done his dead daughter proud, evinced in the way he had printed, framed, and hung her photographs to their best advantage. He had even come up with the name for the exhibit —"Chameleon Complex"— and the tagline —"Images of the Scurry of Human Lizards Who Have Blended into Their Inanimate Surroundings."

He had happily and sympathetically taken over from Katharine weeks ago. She had let it drop one night over the phone that she felt overwhelmed and had lost control of her time. *As if I had any fucking control of anything in my life.* She then let Robert's running commentary about how the photographs were going to be cropped, framed, and hung wash over her while he did it all. It washed across her ears, across the planes of her cheeks, across her mouth. It was only fitting, only right that she step back and let Robert handle it. What did she know, anyway? She was a parasite in his dead daughter's body, and Katharine's role, her goal in life, the feat, the gift to poor, dead Thisby Bennet, was to allow the exhibit to exist.

And now it did.

Quince stood off to the side of the gallery, purposely ignoring her, it seemed to Katharine. She hadn't seen much of Quince in the past two months. Actually, not at all. Katharine supposed it had something to do with telling Quince that she couldn't spend the night anymore when she came down to work at the clinic. Katharine had tried it a few times after she started drinking, and it was just too hard. If she didn't drink, she was so taut that her muscles ached the next day from the isometric strain. If she did drink, it was hard to stop, and she wanted to slap the mad and disappointed look on Quince's face. *What does she know about pain?*

Since That Night two and a half months ago, Katharine had sat long hours on Thisby's balcony, baking in the late August sun, a glass of cheap white zinfandel in her hand. At first she had tried to salvage things. She tried to go back to that place where everything she did seemed right. But the harder she tried, the worse everything seemed to become, and the stronger the call was from the balcony and from the glass of wine. The restlessness was like an infection in her, drawing her tight in the body and crazy in the head. The relief, the antidote, was that glass of wine and the balcony, its railing giving in to the soles of her feet, cradling them. There she could think and plan and scheme. *And do nothing.*

She used the telephone. That was something she could do — sit on the balcony, the receiver's cord stretched out from the dining area. She called Quince, and Quince would be coldly civil and get off the line as fast as she could.

So Katharine sat on the balcony, drinking and using the phone. She called home — the Ashley home — when no one would be there, just to hear the greeting, just to hear Marion's voice. She didn't leave any messages, though she filled up the tape day after day with her soft sobbings. Then it was Philip's voice on the recorder, and Katharine stopped calling.

Katharine followed Puck and Vivian with her eyes and couldn't help but imagine the look on Puck's face if she had been showing by then, the rounded curve of their baby defined by Thisby's thin body. Thisby probably would have shown so much earlier than Katharine, who had been able to absorb the growth of new life in her womb, camouflage it, embrace it. A pregnancy in Thisby would have stuck out like an offense. But Puck wouldn't have acknowledged it either. Just as he hadn't acknowledged their union at all.

Puck said, "*Have I laid my brain in the sun and dried it?*"

Blame it on the alcohol, why don't you? Gimme a fucking break.

Have I laid my brain in the sun and dried it? Falstaff, of course, said it before him. In The Merry Wives of Windsor.

She had discovered she was good at remembering quotes. So much better than Thisby had been. She had a whole slew of them at her disposal. She could have responded with "O God, that men should put an enemy in their mouths to steal away their brains."

Cassio said that, not Falstaff.

Or she supposed she could have said, "Take a flying fuck, Puck, at a rolling doughnut. I could carve a better man out of a banana."

Shakespeare didn't say that, of course. Paul Lazzaro did in

the film *Slaughterhouse-Five* — Valerie Perrine's movie debut of her impressive physical endowments. Valerie Perrine certainly had no trouble passing the pencil test.

But Katharine said nothing.

There's something to be said with silence.

Even before Puck left for San Francisco, Katharine knew she was pregnant; there was no mistaking the rolling nausea of morning sickness. Even when she woke up sick from the previous night's alcohol, she knew what was underlying the hangover. *Prithee, do not turn me about, my stomach is not constant.*

She had taken three home pregnancy tests in her life — in her and Thisby's life. The first two were negative, the last was positive.

Primo, secundo, tertio. The third pays for all. The baby's mother, however, is a drug addict and an alcoholic, and the father is either a drug pusher or the mother's biological brother. Okay, fans, there's the whistle. You make the call.

She aborted it.

It was a Saturday when she went to the women's clinic for the abortion. Operation Rescue was there in full force, lined up outside in the gauntlet of righteousness.

To save me from myself. Christ, if they only knew.

Katharine had been there a couple of days before to have her required meeting with a family-planning counselor. She felt she had to be sober, or they might not give her an abortion, but it hurt to be sober, the white noise quieting to a mere wail. She liked the solid wall of roaring sound. Then she didn't have to listen to anyone — especially to herself.

The counselor was a motherly-looking woman with soft padding around her body. The effect was amazing. A part of Katharine wanted to climb up into her lap and cry. But another part, all fire and ice, sat firmly in her chair and answered all the counselor's questions rationally and straightforwardly and lied masterfully, when she had to.

No, she was currently not taking any drugs, which was true. Yes, she did drink, but only in moderation, which was not. Yes, the father knew — NOT — but no, he would not be accompanying her to . . . to her . . . to her *appointment with death.*

They allowed her to keep her clothes on from the waist up, and they draped a pale blue cotton sheet over her stomach and raised knees. The feet stirrups were padded, and there was a poster of an emerald forest on the ceiling above her.

The doctor patted her on one knee and told her it would all be okay. They had given her a pill to relax, but it only made her nauseous. She could feel the speculum inserted into her vagina and the turn of the screw to widen the opening.

"You'll feel a pinch now," the doctor said, his voice coming up right through her body.

Her abdomen cramped, and she gasped.

"It's okay now. It's all over now."

She lay down on an army cot in a room packed full of army cots, a dormitory for the recently unpregnant.

I was a fool to weep at what I am glad of. Hey, so I'm living prime-time stuff. A soap opera couldn't have written a better script, a tabloid a better headline: GIRL IMPREGNATED BY ASS-HEADED BROTHER. INCREDIBLE PHOTOS INSIDE.

Roy Bennet arrived an hour into the reception. Roy and Robert were not identical twins, but they were slightly distorted fun house mirror images. Katharine wondered vaguely whether Robert ever thought about a Jekyll-and-Hyde connection. Roy seemed to Katharine a little younger, a little wilder, and a lot hipper, but maybe, she decided, it was the tanned, relaxed, kept appearance about him.

He walked up to Katharine and took her hand that held the champagne glass. She thought he was going to kiss her fingertips, but instead he brought the glass to his lips and took a sip. "Not as good as I'm accustomed to, but I doubt my brother is serving Rob Roys. I guess this will have to do, won't it?" He looked Katharine up and down and said, "So how's my favorite niece?"

Roy stood with her then, taking up the role as host, or groom, nodding and greeting people as if he had been her

Svengali all her life. He cast his voice in her ear like a ventriloquist, his mouth barely moving underneath the disarming smile that he gave as people appeared in front of them to *ooh* and *aah* over the exhibit.

Katharine wondered if this was how he really made a living, not as the international investment broker he claimed to be. This was how he really paid his bills and kept himself in the style to which he was now accustomed. He was an American gigolo, and he entertained his patrons by making them laugh, by dealing gossip, by telling tales and offering up bedtime stories. He kept his head by playing Scheherazade.

"Those two," he said, his voice a narrow beam between his easy smile and liquid voice. "Ellen and Annabel Andrews. Mother and daughter."

She watched the two women, who were dressed not identically but enough alike for it to be a little bit weird, approach her.

"They used to be in the waterskiing show at Sea World. It was quite an act, I hear. They can hardly stand each other, but they're so used to being a team, they can't break it up."

After they extended their greetings, the women moved into the gallery and Roy gestured to a handsome man with an extremely wicked grin who was leaning over some batting-eyed blonde. "That's Charlie Sorel. He's a writer for your father's studio, making the switch from bad novelist to mediocre screenwriter. He's also a horseplayer. I hear he's playing the ponies close, real close. One bad bet, and it's goodbye, Charlie."

"And those two?" Katharine asked as Anne and Robert were making their way over to Roy, once they finally realized that he was not going to come to them.

Roy was surprisingly quiet, and when he spoke, his voice had lost its mocking quality. "My better half and his lovely lady." He then turned to Katharine and said, very low, "But he's so tight, if you stuck a lump of coal up his ass, in two weeks you'd have a diamond."

Robert shook hands rather stiffly, which made Roy laugh. "Don't worry, I'm not staying long. I finished my business here in LA. I'm taking a flight out tonight." Roy turned to Anne and took her hand. "Still hanging around with this bum, are you?"

Anne gave Roy a kiss on the cheek with real affection and said, "Nice to see you, Roy. I'm so glad you could come. Thisby's done well, hasn't she?"

Ah, yes. Well done, that's us.

Roy took a turn around the gallery, leaving her at her post. He returned, offered his congratulations on the show, kissed her on the mouth, and then waltzed back out of their lives to do some deep-sea fishing off the coast of Mosquitia — *ta ta.*

Katharine was sorry to see him go and accepted another glass of champagne, though she knew she was moving from that state of euphoria to that hollow where it was dark and the night monsters sprang at her back from the doorway and the ceiling.

Things were beginning to pile up on her. *Dead heat on a merry-go-round,* she could hear Philip's voice saying to her. In the beginning, the alcohol had buoyed her, but now she felt as if she were being squashed by it all — sinking underneath, like water under oil.

Well, it had been a bitch of a two months, considering.

Considering. Concerning. With respect to. Oh, yeah, and regarding. Regarding Hooker.

Katharine called him after the abortion and after Puck had left. She suggested that they meet for drinks. She could almost feel his eyes narrow over the phone line and wonder what the sting was. But he agreed, and when they went back to his place, she thought he would whack her around a few times for dumping him — *I bet he's hell at whacking* — but he didn't even twitch a finger to scare her. She was almost disappointed.

They had some good times. She snorted a few lines of cocaine, smoked a couple of iced cigarettes, but Katharine found that she was not really interested in feeling wildly euphoric. She was interested in not feeling at all, and she liked the rush to be slow and numbing — *and loud.*

He ended up dumping her after a couple of weeks.

They were at Potters. Katharine had arrived earlier and had

already downed a couple of margaritas. *Well, margaritas of sorts — I'll have a slush margarita, hold the ice, hold the triple sec, bring the tequila with lime and salt on the side, and I want you to hold the straw between your knees.*

She was propped up against the bar and clumsily lit a cigarette, watching the ring go up in smoke. She did that too now — smoke. There had been no cough of surprise when she inhaled that first cigarette, only relief. She had always heard that nicotine is the most addicting substance known to man, but no one told her how good it could taste.

Fuck you, Surgeon General.

On into the evening, Katharine noticed that some young woman in tight jeans and three-inch heels, with boobs the size of honeydew melons, had draped herself against Hooker's back as he was leaning over the pool table. She was biting at his earlobe, and his elbow kept jabbing her in the tit as he practiced his stroke at the cue ball. They were laughing.

Katharine unsteadily got to her feet and grabbed the girl by her arm and yanked her off.

"Hey," the girl protested, rubbing her upper arm.

"Why don't you go home?" Hooker said in precise tones to Katharine.

"I don't wanna," she said, or that's what she thought she said.

Hooker nodded to one of his friends. "Take her home."

When she woke up, Hooker was there, sitting on her bed. "You're boring me," he told her, his voice strung tight with control. "You used to be fun — even when you were stoned or drunk. Now you're just drunk." He stood up and looked down on her with . . .

Disappointment. He's got the fucking gall to be disappointed in me.

"Don't call me," he said bluntly.

He turned to leave, but she grabbed his pant leg and tried to think. "You can't leave me. You can't." She held on tighter. The panic grew in her. Tears choked her throat. She wanted to say to him, *Everything I love, I lose. I had a husband, kids. I lost* them. *I don't love you, but I thought I could keep you.* But no further sound came out, and she only tugged harder.

Hooker pulled away, rather gently, and left.

Emily and Hank Denton walked into the Zweimal. They caught sight of Quince, waved to her, and then gestured quickly to someone who was entering behind them. Katharine was surprised that they had come. After Hooker had dumped her, she went out with True a couple of times. *Hey, if I had no compunction about fucking TB's brother, why should I worry about my nephew? We aren't even genetically related.* But it had ended badly. True informed her that she wasn't the fun drunk she had been when she was younger and suggested that she get some professional help. For his troubles, she had told him to fuck off.

Katharine saw Quince smile as she shook hands with the third person in the Denton party. Katharine was almost shocked to see how pretty she looked. Had Katharine never noticed it, or had something changed, had something happened to Quince?

Yet another person moving on without me.

Hank stepped forward to give Quince a hug, and Katharine had her first clear view of the stranger. Her mind sent Thisby's heart leaping into her throat.

It's Ben. Ohmigod, it's Ben.

She reached out to steady herself, found nothing, and stumbled. The Denton party and Quince turned toward her, and Katharine thought she might faint or throw up. Emily gave her a tentative smile. Hank's was warmer. Quince's face was like granite, and both Katharine and Quince watched Ben size up Katharine with interest. Quince's face almost solidified.

Katharine narrowed her sights to focus only on Ben. He looked so handsome, so mature, so tall, so grown-up, so like Philip when she first met him, with his multicolored hair and hazel eyes. Her baby boy. But where were the torn jeans, the soiled T-shirt with the hole in the back of the stretched-out neckband where the manufacturer's tag had been cut out — and part of the shirt with it — because it irritated his skin?

Not there. His slacks were baggy, but they were intact and clean. The shirt was funky fifties, but it had a collar and was buttoned all the way up. Katharine recognized him, but she realized that she didn't know him.

Katharine set her champagne glass down on a passing tray and walked toward him. She had dreamed about this so often, the reality of it was surreal. She watched herself approach him from so many angles, she felt dizzy. From one angle she was so controlled, she looked robotic. This was her own son, for God's sake. Didn't she feel anything? From another it looked as though she was having trouble breathing. Why did she still care — considering how she had given up on her old life? Another part of her just felt numb. She had no great expectations. The previous two close encounters with the other members of her family had not produced any momentous results; her life had not essentially changed.

After scarcely returning the greetings of Emily and Hank, she was in front of him. "Hi, I'm Thisby. You must be Ben."

"Ahh, the cause célèbre. How's the fifteen minutes been?" He turned to Quince and said, "Fifteen minutes of fame. An Andy Warhol quote."

"Gee, thanks for the explanation." The edge in Quince's voice sliced right through his veneer, and Katharine could see how thin and how freshly laid it was; he was trying on this aspect of his personality and seeing how it fit, just like the new clothes.

She saw her own boy then and wanted to gather him in her arms. Pretty soon she was going to be crying. She *was* crying. Why had she drunk so much?

She stopped a waiter, lifted a glass, handed it to Ben, and then took one for herself. She took his arm and leaned into him, feeling how his body compensated to take her weight. She steered him down a panel of Thisby's photographs. "Here, I'll give you a personally guided tour."

Quince kept up with them; Katharine could feel her.

Go away.

"Marion says hi." Ben directed this somewhat toward the both of them, but then said to Katharine, "She couldn't come down this weekend. Some school thing. Homecoming float or something."

"How is she?" Katharine knew she couldn't hide the wistfulness in her tone, so she didn't try.

"She's doing good. She's having a good year. She made the tennis team, third or fourth doubles."

"Third," Quince informed them curtly.

Some loud woman tried to waylay them, some relative by Quince's salutation, and Katharine deftly sidestepped her and allowed Quince to run interference.

They pulled away from the sound of the gushing relative. "So, Ben, I've heard a lot about you." Katharine dropped her voice to imply intimacy.

"I've heard a lot about you too."

"All good, I'm sure."

He looked boyishly uncomfortable, and she laughed. God, she felt good. Wasn't life good? "It's okay. Sometimes it's fun to be wicked."

His reaction almost sobered her. He looked pained, and sad, and oh-so-guilty.

Katharine suddenly had a wild urge to pull down his pants to see whether he had gotten the tattoo he threatened Diana with. She didn't do it, but then they talked about tattoos. They talked about a lot of things, wandering up and down the aisles as if no one else were there. They talked about life and college and career.

And death.

They talked a lot about death.

And his buttoned-down look.

They're related, you know.

That buttoned-down look was for her. His dead mother. He thinks he caused her death. He thinks he was responsible. If only he hadn't been fucking up. If only he had been more responsible. Had seen things from her point of view. Had seen what it was doing to her. The stress on her heart. Then she would have lived. And he wouldn't have to carry around this guilt.

So he's trying to clean up his act. Stay on the straight and narrow. A good son. He is what he thinks his mother would have wanted him to be. He's trying to be responsible, clean-living, hardworking, and self-sacrificing. What mother could be unhappy about that?

Me. I am.

"So now I'm taking a couple of night classes to make up for the classes I fucked up when I was younger," Ben continued, refusing a third glass of champagne. "I'll graduate okay, but I'll have to go to community college before I can go to a four-year. I'm working at a bank part-time, and hopefully next summer they'll give me full-time hours." He stopped and stared at a photograph, but Katharine could tell that he wasn't really seeing it. "I've got this chance to go to Wyoming next summer with a friend of mine to work on his dad's ranch, but"— he turned to her —"I guess it's really just a stupid idea. I don't know, though." They walked on. "I know I'd be doing grunt work for a while, but I've always loved horses, and maybe I could learn something. I've always wanted to be a cowboy." He paused again. "But I guess it's just a stupid idea."

A cowboy? I never knew this about Ben. A quote skittered across Katharine's brain like a spider. "It is a wise father who knows his own child." *Maybe Will got it wrong. Maybe there aren't really any wise parents out there.*

He finished talking, and she, unexpectedly — even to herself — lit into him. He might have thought she was nuts. She did kind of go off. But how could she not? She'd seen too much. She knew too much. She'd felt too much.

"Your mother did not die for your sins." She could feel him stiffen under her hand, but she squeezed back and leaned farther into him. "She does not want your penance. You do not need absolution. Don't you know a life spent for someone else is just an imitation of life?" She felt impassioned. *Because I believe it.*

Ben did not respond, and Katharine could feel a space growing between them. She did not know how to make him see, if he would not look.

I'm trying my personal best here. Why go through all this if you can't tell someone, help someone go through it too? Are we always doomed to go through it alone? What good does it do to be a parent if you can't help your children with the tough problems in life? What good are you? Oh, it's easy when they're young. The advice is easy. Don't play in the street. Don't talk to strangers. Don't run with sharp objects in your hand.

They barely made a pretense of looking at the photographs, each of them inside their own thoughts.

Later on, it's all different. Don't you even dare think about drinking. But if for some unforeseeable reason you do, then please feel free to call home. We'll be happy to jump in the car in our pajamas and come get you. No questions asked. No recriminations.

And sex? Well, it should be enjoyed, but it can kill you. Wear a condom, insert a diaphragm, and wash up thoroughly afterward.

Question authority . . . but not mine . . .

God, she was doing it again. Giving advice. Was any of it any good? She had told Ben to follow his heart. Did she really mean that, or was that just Thisby talking? Thisby, who followed nothing but her own heart and wants and needs and desires and demands? Who had no regard for anyone else. Who didn't sacrifice. Who didn't put others before her. Who didn't allow others to take advantage of her and then resent them and send them spiraling away from her.

She wanted to grab her head and twist it off, unscrew it like a bottle cap. She really was going crazy. All the simple truths she thought she had captured in her life were splitting off and rearranging themselves. All the thoughts she thought were only hers didn't seem to be following along the paths she thought they should take.

Who was she these days?

I am Katharine. I am a mother. I am a wife. I am Thisby. I am independent. I am alone. I am nobody.

I'm afraid I am not who I think I am.

They came around to the front of the gallery, where Emily and Hank were waiting for them. Katharine felt tired beyond time. She couldn't see anymore. She couldn't think anymore.

Ben gently shifted her weight away from him, and immediately her body felt as if it were going to break through the floor. "Thanks for the guided tour and the talk. Maybe I can call you the next time I come down. I'll be sure to send you a postcard from Wyoming. Maybe I will go." He gestured with his shoulder toward Quince, who was also waiting. "I gotta go. I promised my sister I'd take her little friend out for coffee. You know." He dug into his pocket for his keys, reassuring his aunt and uncle that he knew the way back to Long Beach and that he wouldn't be late, eyeing Katharine to see if that made any difference to her. The silence fattened between them. "Well, nice to meet you, Thisby. I hope to see you again." He went over to Quince and they left, Quince's grim little face lightening a bit as they walked out the door.

Hank chuckled. "There's good news waiting for Ben when he goes back up north. We got a call from his father tonight, but Philip wants to tell Ben in person. Diana, you know, Marion's stepmother, is pregnant. She's having a baby."

Katharine could feel the memory of the speculum being jammed into her vagina and the wrench of the screw to widen the opening.

"You'll feel pain now," the doctor says, his voice reaming right through her body.

Her abdomen seizes up, and she screams.

"It's finished," the doctor says.

She jerks her feet out of the stirrups, gets off the table, and stands up. She stands up, and she stands up in what she knows is her own aborted fetus. The nurse is too slow to pull away the plastic sheet that the doctor scooped it out on. She doesn't wince. She doesn't shudder. She doesn't do anything but walk on, ectoplasm stuck to the soles of her feet.

The shaking started in the core of her solar plexus and radiated out. A waiter stepped in front of her, his tray laden with champagne glasses. The cool liquid shimmered, and the bubbles that escaped from the sides of the glasses sent baby plumes of spray over their lips. The voice that whispered now laughed, its glee translating into words that it poked and jabbed her with. *You need a license to buy a dog or drive a car. You need a license to catch a fish, but they'll let any buttweeman-asshole be a parent.*

She saw her arm come up like a backhanded slap and felt

it connect with the bottom of the metal tray. The horrified look on the waiter's face hung in the air like a hologram.

She didn't remember much after that. She remembered the sound of breaking glass, someone pinning her arms to her side, and voices — oh, *so many voices* — raised in surprise and concern and anger.

Was one of them hers? Were all of them hers?

Act 5, Scene 2 🐿

. . . we are not ourselves

When nature, being oppress'd, commands the mind

to suffer with the body.

— LEAR, *King Lear*, 2.4.107

They all appeared at her door the next afternoon: Anne, Robert, Quince, and — *surprise* — Puck. Actually, Katharine wasn't all that surprised that they had come, though she had heard that Vivian and Puck were leaving for San Francisco that morning. She knew she had gone too far at the reception, that there were going to be repercussions. Sometime during the night she had thrown up — which was unusual for her — on the bathroom floor, and the irony was not lost on her. Her whole head was as tender as a bruise, and she felt hollowed out, but the showdown was coming and she thought she was ready for it.

Thisby's family walked into the apartment, and before Katharine could close the door behind them, *who else should arrive, making a grand entrance? Why Dr. Mantle. That quintessence of dust. That pigeon-liver'd ape-dog. That diffused infection of a man.*

Katharine was furious. It changed the balance completely. This was supposed to be a family matter. "What's he doing here?"

Robert Bennet answered her. "Your mother and I asked him."

They sat down in the living room in a circle, and Katharine felt surrounded, ringed by so many snarling dogs masquerading as a loving family.

The accused presumed innocent until proven guilty? No way. They're out to get me.

"Thisby, we're all here, your family," began Robert Bennet, "because we love you. You are a member of this family. You mean a great deal to this family, even if you think at this time in your life that doesn't matter to you. We felt the only way to make you understand this is to confront you. All of us. However, your mother and I felt that we — and you too — needed some professional guidance. We felt the only way to get through to you is to have an intervention, and we asked Dr. Mantle to come because he has had quite a bit of experience with interventions."

Only Quince had the decency to look uncomfortable.

"We want you to know we think you're killing yourself. You're killing yourself as surely as if you held a loaded gun to your head. But we believe you can take your finger off the trigger. You can save yourself. Maybe if you think of it as being possessed by some alien thing, you can fight back. You've got to stop the drinking and get yourself clean. Then the old Thisby will come back. Then our own Thisby will return."

Katharine looked at their frightened faces and almost spat at them, *Fat chance. Can't help you there, guys.*

It was so orchestrated — their little speeches like Academy Award acceptances. Puck read a letter he had written. "To my sister, Thisby" it began, as if he needed to make sure it was addressed properly. He dwelt on their younger days, before Quince was born, when he and Thisby were buds.

As if that means jack shit right now to either me or Thisby.

Quince's contribution was achingly curt, full of hurt and love and confusion. She didn't know which sister, which personality, she wanted back; she just wanted a sister she could talk to and who would remember the conversation the next day.

Anne's was hardened over with tenets of tough love worked out from a handbook or an afternoon TV talk show.

But not that shallow. Never that shallow. Anne also had seen too much, knew too much, felt too much, to be shallow. "I am concerned for you. I love you, but in the last couple of months we have opened up our hearts to you again, only to have you shred them. I will not let you drag the emotions of this family down the self-destructive path you've chosen. I will not let you. I will fight you, and then I will let you go. But if you let me, I will fight *for* you. Fight for you in every way I can. But only if you let me. The choice is yours."

Katharine was staring down at the rug, hearing Quince, hearing Anne, hearing her own voices from so many dedicated speakers.

Then Anne asked Mantle to talk, and Katharine's head snapped up and stared at him.

He's holding the family's trump card. And isn't he just loving it. So caring. So concerned. And doesn't he just have me over a barrel cuz he can damage me now. He's muscled his addiction into sweet revenge, and he's playing for keeps.

He spoke evenly, softly, but letting the edge of his voice separate himself from Thisby's family. He was concerned too, but after this intervention he would do what had to be done, if it came down to that. With the approval of her mother and father, he would certify her as mentally incompetent and commit her, for her own good, of course, but commit her nevertheless. Again, the choice was hers.

Katharine realized he wanted her to fight back. He wanted a reason, wanted justification, to certify her, right then and there, bullgoose looney tunes and commit her. Into the snake pit, the madhouse, with all the other lunatics. For her own good, of course. The choice was hers.

So who gave him all the best lines?

Katharine looked away from Mantle's mean, pasty face into Robert's hopeful one, to Anne's waiting one, to Puck's skeptical one, to Quince's. Quince was looking down at the rug, the shadow of her nose broken by the scar above her lip. She looked utterly miserable, wishing she could be anyplace but here.

I know how you feel, kid.

Katharine closed her eyes. She knew what she feared most. She had been fearing it all morning. She could do this, get sober, but there was a good chance that nothing would be any different, nothing would change. Life could still be no better than it was. She would still be alone. She would still be in a stranger's body and she would still be living a stranger's life. And, without the alcohol, it could be worse; it had been worse. It was so easy to drink; it was so easy to keep drinking. It was going to require so much energy to stop. *And for what?*

The Bennets wanted Thisby back, but she was dead. *She's dead!* And who was Katharine? Who was Katharine now? *I can't go back, but how can I move forward?* Robert was right; she was never going to figure out who she was until she excised all the alien things.

It's just that I'm not sure who'll be left.

Katharine kept her eyes closed, and while the Bennets silently watched her, she mentally flew away north to her home. Except it wasn't her home, it was Diana's home; and her family lived there, without her. They had moved on, without her. And they were going to be all right, without her.

She thought of her advice to Ben — live your own life. It seemed so trite, so sixties, but that didn't diminish the truth of it, and it sounded as though Ben really might go to Wyoming. She hoped he would. *Philip would hate it if he did.* Maybe she'd visit him there. *I hear Harrison Ford has a ranch in Wyoming too.*

She knew that Ben really did feel responsible for his mother's death — that he wasn't just auditioning another personality — and she could imagine what a truly awful burden that must be. But if he could move on, then she could try to move on from her own guilt too.

No, there was no going home again. Not that home anyway.

In the back of her mind, she knew she had always expected she would be transformed — somehow, some way — back into her old body and her old life, and all this would be as a dream. After all, that's the way it always happened in the movies and books and plays. *You learn what you're supposed to learn and then you always get to go back — eventually.*

But there was no going back, she realized, and there weren't too many other choices. She was tired of fighting her battles alone. Never weaken! hadn't helped her. Maybe she needed to give up a little of herself, give up a little of her power to someone else, to allow someone to help her. Maybe life wouldn't be better, but understanding might be. Was that worth the energy it was going to take?

That was the hope. Wasn't it?

Katharine opened her eyes in Thisby's apartment, watched over by Thisby's family, and nodded to them. "Okay," she said.

Act 5, Scene 3 🦎

To sleep, perchance to dream — ay, there's the rub.

— HAMLET, *Hamlet, Prince of Denmark*, 3.1.64

June 20. Midsummer Night. Witches and fairies will be abroad after dark, granting wishes or causing havoc as they choose. Tomorrow is the summer solstice. She has come full circle. Her father used to say, "If we lived here, we'd be home now." But she didn't live here, and . . . *I'm far from home.*

In her head, she has erected a garden wall made with heavy rectangular stone bricks, the cracks mortared and sealed tight, dense ivy springing up the sides. The wall closes off a dark and overgrown path, one she doesn't want to go down or even peer into. When she can't stop herself and steps a foot closer, a faint voice from behind the wall calls out, "Wait. I can help. Please."

She shrinks away, and the voice cries, "How can you be so callous, so heartless, to ignore me?"

Easy. Easy.

Katharine has been getting straight for 245 days. It hasn't been easy, nor is success assured. Anne and Robert are keeping their hope close to their chests this time. *As is Quince. No question now that I'm not the blessèd child.*

She sits in Thisby's window seat, a thirty-two-ounce plastic coffee mug by her side. The moon is pale-bright, and in honor of Midsummer Night, the Bennet house is bedecked with greenery and hanging lights — Thisby's room in rosemary for remembrance, pansies for thoughts, and violets for faithfulness. Katharine has checked for columbines and rue, symbolizing ingratitude and repentance, but finds none.

Supposedly if she places the flowers under her pillow tonight, she will dream a little dream — about her true love.

When she received the invitation to Midsummer — the first time in eight months to the day she would see the Bennets outside their family-therapy sessions — she accepted it with as much wariness as it was probably given.

And when she knocked on the front door instead of going around to the kitchen entrance, it did not surprise them. And that did not surprise her.

Quince answered the door and took her bag quickly, as if to avoid any attempt at a more physical greeting. Katharine didn't dare touch her.

Anne and Robert received her in the living room, surrounded by their cool and perfect world. They exchanged their greetings pleasantly enough, but there was no mistaking that even though she had been clean for eight months, this last fall from grace had hit Anne and Robert hard. Real hard. Katharine couldn't remember feeling more awkward, more unsure, more tentative around them.

Anne and Katharine prepared the Midsummer dinner together. Katharine felt her first déjà vu in this body. Quince sat on the stool, with Oberon curled up like a tricolored snowball at her feet. Katharine hardly petted him, so clearly was he Quince's dog. It made her want to cry.

"I don't want to go to UCLA," Quince told her mother for the third time. "I don't care if they have a great drama department. I wanna go someplace away from here. My own school."

"Quince, for heaven's sake, no one's going to say, 'Aren't you Robert and Anne Bennet's daughter? Gee, I saw them in that play twenty-five years ago.' No one's going to say, 'Aren't you Puck Bennet's sister? He sure was a great pre-law student.' "

"They might."

Aren't you Thisby Bennet's sister? She sure was a fuckup.

"Yes, they might, but they won't. UCLA's a huge school. You'll make your own mark."

"But I don't want to go to UCLA."

Anne sighed. "Quince, we'll talk about it later. I'm sure Thisby isn't interested in listening to us argue."

Quince turned squarely toward Katharine. "Well, what do you think I should do?"

She squirmed. "I don't know, Quince."

Quince got up and left, Oberon leaping up after her.

Watching the shadowplay outside the window, Katharine leans farther back into Thisby's seat cushion and takes another sip of coffee from her mug. She has discovered something else recently. She is no more capable now than she was when she was a mother of telling Quince, or anyone else for that matter, what to do. *You're doomed to go through it alone. You don't go through something so you can help someone else avoid it. You can't tell anyone anything. You're on your own.*

She couldn't believe how self-righteous she had been last summer, how incredibly arrogant. She thought she could save everyone. Quince, Goodfellow, Marion. Ben. Yes, even Thisby. She could make it all right. With age and experience and perspective, she could make it come out all right in the end.

But life is messy. *And noisy.*

Katharine tried to repress the voices in her head when she first went to see Dr. Hudson, but like so many times in this body, once she gave up, let go, things went easier. She realized that she could use her life and Thisby's life and her life as Thisby as a kind of metaphorical existence. The truth, the facts weren't important. They would only end up destroying her and both her families. She realized that by using the voices, giving them audible speech, their power over her waned. That left the voice that whispered. It wasn't going to be bound and gagged so easily. It became even more forward, more determined, *louder,* making her offers she could hardly refuse. It offered to take away the hurt — a drink would file down those rough edges so easily. But Katharine was beginning to believe that listening to the voice that whispered was treachery and that trying to avoid pain was really the art of dying. Feeling pain was a sign that she was alive, Dr. Hudson said, and Katharine was open to that possibility.

Katharine has an image of Anne and Robert after she left the Midsummer dinner table, collapsing into their seats, too exhausted to move, asking themselves how they are ever going to get through the next day, and lamenting that it is so awkward, so tiring to be around their own daughter. They are also thinking about the remark Puck made to them the day of the intervention, after Katharine had agreed to a daily drug-and-alcohol test, to see Dr. Hudson, to get clean. "Mom, commit her, for Christ's sake. How many more times are you going to be taken in?"

Then Katharine has a different vision after she left the table: Anne and Robert look at each other and sigh, but it's more a sigh of, *Well, that wasn't so bad, was it? We've weathered the worst of it. We did the right thing.*

Whichever scene really happened, Katharine knows that in the back of their minds, there's a small voice that constantly cries, *What did we do wrong? What didn't we do right? What could we — should we — have done to save her from all this pain?*

This will. This will save her. Katharine's going to let their love and loyalty and responsibility for Thisby save Katharine. She's going to take their love and use it for herself. That's why she's here.

Katharine hoards this knowledge like a squirrel stockpiling his nuts.

But 50 percent of all the nuts hoarded by squirrels are lost because they forget where they put them . . .

Recovery had the comfortableness of routine. She had her sessions, the daily journals Dr. Hudson made her write, her exercise classes at the local gym. And she got through the day.

She had been right, though; her fears had been real. Her life isn't that different. She's sober, and that's all.

If only I could be dreamless too — because something is happening. She's under siege, and she's afraid to be alone. It's getting increasingly harder to stay away from the wall she has erected, the one she has so carefully built up to protect herself from the things that were destroying her — the one she now fears is keeping her away from something else that she might need. But to acknowledge that need, to open herself up to it — isn't that opening herself up to this body's other demands? Isn't denial of all the appetites her safest bet?

But she can't get away from her dreams.

She's been dreaming a lot lately. The dreams are often about Thisby, and they are always a variation on the same theme. Thisby stands in front of Katharine in Katharine's old body, only now it's roast-meat for worms. The skin sags, scarred and flaccid under her eyes, and the bone sockets are showing. Her lips are stretched back in a sneer, exposing the rotting gums. She shouts expletives. They spew from her mouth like so much filth. *You counterfeit module, you monstrous malefactor, you triple-turn'd whore, you dissembling harlot, you measureless liar, you hag of all despair, you pernicious bloodsucker of sleeping men, you inexecrable dog, you deformed and vile thief. I want my body back.*

She's afraid to go to sleep — to sleep and then to dream, alone.

The coffee has grown cold in the mug. Katharine realizes that she has been waiting for the sound of Quince's knock on her door, but it hasn't come. It's late, and she slips between the sheets of the bed but keeps on the night-light.

She hears footsteps and the muffled voices of Thisby's parents coming down the hall. The sounds stop in front of her bedroom door.

"Thisby? Are you awake?" asks Anne, softly enough so as not to wake Katharine if she isn't.

"I'm awake."

The door opens, and the blurry silhouette of two people blocks out the faint light of the hallway. "We're glad you came this weekend," Anne says. "We just wanted you to know that."

"Thanks. I'm glad I came too."

"Well, good night."

"Sweet Midsummer Night dreams," Robert says, and as the door closes them off, he adds, "about your true love."

Katharine lies on her back in the semi-darkness. She realizes that she had forgotten how nice it is to have parents, to have that feeling of having a buffer, a higher authority — *if you so need it* — in her life. She did feel safe here — and loved, as much for being Katharine as for having been Thisby.

Suddenly she sits up and grabs a fistful of petals from the flowers on the bed stand. She lifts up her pillow and lets them drop like tears to the bedsheet.

Act 5, Scene 4 ঔ

The web of our life is of a mingled yarn, good and ill together.

— FIRST LORD, *All's Well That Ends Well*, 4.3.84

She wakes up in the morning to the smell of crushed rosemary and violet. She nuzzles under the pillow to cloud her face with the scent. The dream comes back to her, so vivid, so bright, she thinks she might have fallen asleep again and, like a natural dream state, is in the dream and inside the dream, around and outside it, victim, master, slave to its course.

Katharine stands in front of her garden wall, the mortar green- and gray-tinged, warning of disintegration. A voice calls from the other side of the wall, and even though Katharine knows it comes from just a few feet away, it sounds faraway and from the depths below.

It says, "Katharine, Katharine, let down your hair." The voice is familiar; Katharine knows she knows it but she doesn't want to acknowledge it.

She responds, "Not by the hair of my chinny chin chin."

"Then I'll huff, and I'll puff, and I'll blow your house down," it says suddenly loud enough to make Katharine jump.

A small hole appears between the stones. Something is growing stronger on the other side and wants through. She knows now who it is. She knows who the wall is separating her from. It's her true love, just like in the myth of Pyramus and Thisby. She envisions Goodfellow, then Philip, True, even Hooker, then an embodiment of all of them. But she's afraid. For some reason, she's scared to come face-to-face with the person on the other side.

Katharine jams her finger in the crack, and the wall tightens around it, causing it to ache with such a familiar pain that it feels normal. But someone is poking at her finger from the other side. It's like a rat nibbling at her fingertip. She pulls it out; the wall tries to patch itself, but someone punches through the hole, and the wall, like a soft avalanche, crumbles.

Thisby stands on the other side, in her own body, a singular smile on her face. The wall that lies in chunks between them — the wall that was once the voice that whispered — is now silent. Thisby prods a stone as if to make sure it is truly detongued and looks up at Katharine with a beatific smile that makes Katharine want to simultaneously laugh and cry.

Katharine gathers up her quilt and sits wrapped up in the window seat. The dawn has barely broken, but there is a clarity to the morning that predicts the fairness of the day. That same sense of transparency illuminates her mind. She feels on the edge of sanity.

And it hurts. But it's a razor's edge kind of hurt, so clean, so thin, the blood wells in tiny popbeads along the score; it aches, but it's bearable.

The loathing I have felt for both of us . . .

The cut throbs, and she thinks about retreating, a part of her wishing she could edit her life as she sees fit, splicing, retouching, so everything is beautiful and nothing hurts.

But another part of her says, That that is, is. There is a new strength in her, a combined resolve. *Thisby is not mad at me; she does not begrudge me this body. She never has.*

She pulls out Thisby's diary from her overnight bag. Every day she writes in her own journal, but it's Thisby's diary that she has taken to carrying around with her wherever she goes, like some sort of talisman. She hasn't read it since the beginning of last summer, almost a year ago, but now she looks at Thisby's last sentence in the last entry

that fucking fairy kiss

and knows she can turn the page over.

> *June 21.*
>
> *It wasn't Thisby in my dreams who said all of those horrid things to me in my putrefied body. I should have figured that out long ago. All the quotes were correct. I should have realized what that meant. All the quotes were correct; Thisby would have never gotten them right.*
>
> *But I would.*
>
> *I also used to think the voice that whispered was really Thisby, as if she resided like some dark half in my brain — if cut open, they'd find another pair of eyes staring out from the skull.*
>
> *But no. That wasn't Thisby either.*
>
> *It was me. It was me who wanted to be the fuckup — and blame her. What a convenient alibi. I was tired of being good, of being there, of doing the right thing. I just didn't want to acknowledge it, admit it.*
>
> *Thisby isn't dead and stagnant; she isn't some malignant eyeball in my brain. Thisby is still alive and speaks to me. She has always spoken to me.*
>
> *I just didn't know it was her.*
>
> *I thought she had nothing to offer, nothing to say, nothing to teach me. But in many ways, she was my best conscience. She did know better this time. She certainly knew better than I did.*
>
> *Now I see she speaks to me directly with her blood, her skin, the very filaments that make up her connective tissue. I don't know where the one of us ends and the other begins.*
>
> *I find I can write as easily with my left hand as my right.*

We are truly blood sisters — and we are truly ambi-
dextrous.

I thought that it was like the tragedy of Pyramus and
Thisby, a wall separated me from my dream lover — part
Philip, part Goodfellow, yes, even part Hooker.
But it was Thisby the wall separated me from.
And the wall was the voice that whispered.
And the voice that whispered was me.

There's a tentative knock on her door, and Quince softly calls through, "Thisby, are you awake? Can I come in?"

Would it be more humane, Katharine thinks, to sever all ties, now that she knows what she is going to do, what she now has the strength to do? Would it be better to cut off the Bennets completely? Now instead of later? Would it be better for all of them in the long run?

Perhaps, but she realizes she can't cut herself off completely from them any more than she was able to cut herself off completely from her own family. Yes, she is going to have to live her own life, just as Ben should — but not as selfishly as Thisby did, and truer to one's self than Katharine did.

She had given Goodfellow the gray tones; perhaps now she's found them herself. The yin-yang was a nice concept, but it was only a concept. Nothing is so definite, so separate, so defined in life. And Katharine was beginning to think there was a certain strength in that.

"Come on in, Quince. I'm wide awake."

Act 5, Scene 5 🐁

As you grow older, you'll find that the only things you regret are the things you didn't do.

— ZACHARY SCOTT, *Mildred Pierce* (1945)

> *"Would you tell me please, which way I ought to go from here?"*
> *asked Alice.*
> *"That depends on where you want to get to," said the Cat.*
> *"I don't much care where," said Alice.*
> *"Then it doesn't matter which way you go," said the Cat.*

She's taking the feline's advice; she's hitting the road and it doesn't matter which way she goes.

The Chinaman was right. A plethora of paths. A phantasm of forks. A congestion of crossroads.

Katharine realized she had tried to parent Thisby herself, but it hadn't worked. She was going to have to let go of Thisby as a parent. As any parent would. Growing up, letting go, and moving on. Wasn't that the way it was with everyone? Why had she forgotten that?

She could stay, the Bennets would have her, Quince would have her, but this is the price she will have to pay — for sanity, for a life forged for Katharine and Thisby, in all their strengths and their weaknesses.

Letting go to survive. But surviving didn't mean reinventing herself, it didn't mean rediscovering herself. It meant opening herself up enough to be able to embrace Thisby. It meant integration and then, ultimately, invention, for wasn't she creating something — somebody — entirely new? For neither extreme — Thisby/Katharine, black/white, yin/yang — was healthy or honest. *It's somewhere in between. It's in searching for the balance.*

She traded in the Porsche and bought a Jeep Renegade with a detachable hardtop. Yes, she'll admit it. She half bought it because of its name. *Assume a virtue . . .*

Don't fuck with me, bubba, I've got a dog, two gas tanks, a tattoo, and a fifth gear that will turn you into roadkill.

She adopted a dog from Quince's veterinary clinic, an attack-trained German shepherd she named Moriarty. He takes his role as the bodyguard very seriously. She is now loved enough to die for.

She had the tattoo of the two-faced woman permanently inked above her heart. The artist explained to her that it was in actuality a Janus symbol, one face looking back at the past, the other looking forward into the future. Janus is also the god of beginnings, of gates, doorways, and entrances, so her tattoo is now the portal into her new heart.

She has money. She sold off most of Thisby's possessions to the pawnbroker. If she's frugal, she can go a long way before she gets down to the seeds and stems. *Seeds and stems. Drug lingo. From the Woodstock generation.* Maybe they'll go north toward Ashland. She hears there are communes in Oregon. The same ones that were started during the sixties. Maybe she'll drop in.

But she hopes they have grown up too, because the Woodstock generation didn't have it right either. "If it feels good, do it." "Love the one you're with." *All of that disregarded the connections you have, must have, with the people around you. If you can defy those connections, then that only erects the wall that separates you from everyone else, including yourself.*

She may not know which way she's going to go exactly, but another thing she's discovered on this excellent adventure of hers is that *you cannot do everything you want to just because you* put your mind to it. *You can't have everything you want just because you want it. You do not always get what you deserve.*

Katharine wanted to go back to her family, but she found out there are just some things she couldn't change and had to let go of the idea that she could. *You learn what you're supposed to learn, but you don't get to go back — not always. No matter how much you wish it.*

But she also realized that she couldn't give up, let the winds of life batter her back and forth. She began to understand that people are reactive creatures, but if they're not careful, they'll live in reaction, as characters in a play within a play, never taking over and commanding a starring role in their own lives.

My starring role now, so to speak, is to live — and to connect.

Quince will be going to the Ashland summer seminar for high school students in a few weeks. Katharine will drop by and say hello, and then she'll go on to Wyoming. Ben's got a summer job there, mucking out horse stables and mending fence posts. Just what he asked for. Marion is planning on visiting him too.

She'll see the both of them.

Harrison Ford is his neighbor, and maybe she'll meet him, him and his second wife and their couple of kids. By his first wife, he has two grown sons — Ben and Willard.

Yes, like the horror movie rat, Ben, and his twitchy human master, Willard. Ford didn't name his kids after characters from a movie any more than I did. But it makes for a good story, doesn't it?

Hidden stories. Hidden lives. Hidden pictures. The MacGuffin. Kitchen appliances drawn into the scene of a forest. The knot in the tree trunk is also the lid of a pot. Things are hardly ever what they seem.

And that's okay because I'm making this up as I go.

Epilogue 🦎

They called her Katharine that did talk of her, but she lied, in faith, for they also called her plain Kate and bonny Kate and sometimes Kate the curst, and now they will call her KT. No, not Katie. KT. Katharine/Thisby. An amalgamation. A comingling. A grafting.

Sometimes she still can't help but wonder whether this other existence is but a three-second dream before she really dies in that bed of hers next to Philip, her heart exploding in her chest. It's just seconds long as she mounts a short but steep flight of stairs, almost a ladder, entwined with clusters of bright blue flowers, imagining a lifetime, only to feel the hands of Death once more.

You may ask, will she try her word again? It's always there in the frontal lobe of her brain. She doesn't know. Two bodies may be enough. Two lives may be enough.

She doesn't know.

Maybe I should know better, but I don't.

Say the magic word, KT.

Wait . . .

FADE OUT

Laurel Doud on writing
This Body

The first question many people ask me is "What is your book about?"

When I tell them it's about Katharine, a working wife and mother of two teenagers who dies suddenly and wakes up a year later in the body of Thisby, a twenty-two-year-old drug addict who has just overdosed on her Los Angeles bathroom floor, and in that year Katharine's husband has remarried and her children have seemingly moved on without her, *invariably* the second question people ask is "Good heavens, how did you think of that?"

My stock answer is the honest one: it had been a really bad week.

My children were fifteen and thirteen at the time — difficult ages in anyone's book — and I woke up one morning feeling poor, unattractive, and unappreciated. I thought that I would just like to die and start all over again. But then I realized that I didn't want to be reincarnated with a clean slate for a mind and a baby for a body. I also realized I didn't want to do junior high or high school again. (Shudder.) So I decided I would like to die and come back in the body of a twenty-two-year-old (and, therefore, perfectly legal; *I'm much more Katharine, I have to admit — sometimes more than I'd like to admit — than Thisby*) with all my memories intact, and I would be thin, rich, and desired by all kinds of new and interesting men.

That's my romantic side.

My pragmatic side said, "Be careful what you wish for. You might just get it. You want to be thin? Okay, we'll make you so thin you look anorexic. You want to be rich? Well, then we'll make your money come from drug dealing. You want to be desired by all kinds of new and interesting men? We'll make sure they're *really* interesting."

And suddenly I had the idea for a story — an idea that could perhaps sustain me through the length of a novel.

In the beginning, my audience consisted of two: my daughter and my son. I thought that if this fantasy/nightmare were really to happen and my children were left motherless, I'd want them to have something in writing about how I felt about raising teenagers, growing older and hanging on to youth, about love and lust, longings and addictions, and about knowing "best" yet letting people make their own mistakes and learn their own truths.

My publisher calls *This Body* "a novel of reincarnation," but it really isn't. It's a novel of transmigration, which is defined by the *Oxford English Dictionary* as "the passage of the soul at death into another body." (I *am* a research librarian by profession!)

It's a minor point, and it really doesn't matter whether it's technically reincarnation or transmigration. For me it was a plot device to explore issues I find much more interesting. If you had a second chance at youth — with all your knowledge, experience, and "wisdom" intact — would it make a difference? By putting Katharine's brain and soul into Thisby's body, I could play with all kinds of questions: Where is our love? Our lust? Are they in the mind or the body? What controls our addictions? If our mind isn't addicted, can it overpower its drug-dependent host, or are there demands of the body that ultimately cannot be ignored? Does the body hold memory? Are our experiences imprinted into our very synapses? Can we tap into them? Would Thisby's memory cells start to break down the barriers to Katharine's mind? Would the two separate entities start to merge, or would they fight — each demanding exclusive control of the body?

I had the first and last words of the novel in my head that morning. I knew generally how it was going to end; I just didn't know exactly how I was going to get there. I started writing, and the story started to tell itself.

One aspect of the story that just seemed to happen was the incorporation of Shakespeare, and notably his play *A Midsummer Night's Dream,* into the plot. This came about after searching for an appropriate name for my young body and finding it in Thisby, a character in *A Midsummer Night's Dream.* I'm not a Shakespeare scholar, but annually I visit the Shakespeare Festival in Ashland, Oregon, and I have acquired a love for his work. Rereading *A Midsummer Night's*

Dream, I realized there were similarities between the play and the story that I wanted to present: being forced to wear an ass's head and not knowing it, fighting authority with naïveté and bravado, lovers being mismatched, and, most of all, going into the forest and coming out changed.

This Body was my first attempt at writing a novel. After spending a month completing the first draft at a writer's retreat, I decided I would see how far I could take the publishing process. It took me five years to get the manuscript into good enough shape to send out to a literary agent. I didn't know anyone in the publishing or creative writing field, and I found my agent the good old-fashioned way, using *Literary Market Place* to send out sixty cold-query letters over a six-month period. My manuscript was the first one my agent had ever accepted out of her agency's slush pile of unsolicited material, and she sold it to Little, Brown in two weeks. The system does work, and I am proof of it.

This Body has been optioned by the film studio Fox 2000 *(A Thin Red Line, One Fine Day)*. The director is George Armitage *(Grosse Pointe Blank, Miami Blues)*, and the producer is David Friendly *(Courage Under Fire, My Girl)*. It's a long and hazardous process, but perhaps *This Body* will be showing at a local theater near you someday.

Thanks for reading *This Body*. I hope you find truth and honesty here.

Reading Group Questions and Topics for Discussion

1. Katharine's situation might strike some readers as a dream come true: the chance to start one's life anew. Put yourself in Katharine's shoes for a moment. If you were to find yourself awakening as someone else tomorrow morning, what kind of person would you want to be?

2. At first Katharine has a hard time seeing her predicament as an opportunity. How does she eventually manage to use this "reincarnation" to her advantage? Do you think that, in the end, this mind/body switch was an enriching experience for Katharine?

3. At the heart of *This Body* is a constant struggle between the

responsibilities of parenthood and the recklessness of youth. Did the novel instill in you a new appreciation for either youth or middle age?

4. Katharine was allowed to peek into the future — to see her husband with his new family. Would you want the opportunity to see how your family survived without you? Why?

5. We hear so much today about the importance of the mind-body connection. Does it seem even remotely possible that one person's mind could thrive within another person's body? Take Thisby's addiction as an example; Katharine initially dismisses it, but then falls prey to the physical cravings herself. What does this suggest about the mind-body connection? Have Katharine's mind and Thisby's body made peace with each other by the end of the novel?

6. There are times when Katharine seems to enjoy being in Thisby's young, thin, attractive body — most notably during her sexual encounters. What do these encounters suggest about the mind-body connection?

7. Quince seems to accept the "new" Thisby with surprising ease. She is apparently so starved for a sister, any sister, that she doesn't even ask questions about the "new" Thisby's attitude and approach to life. What is the significance of this relationship? What do Katharine and Quince learn from each other?

8. In the course of the novel, Katharine makes choices about what is right for herself, for her family, for Thisby, and for the Bennet family. Do you agree with Katharine's choices? Do you think she should have been more honest with the Bennets? Do you think Thisby's parents had the right to know that their daughter was dead?

9. The Shakespeare play *A Midsummer Night's Dream* figures prominently in the life of the Bennet family. How does Katharine use her knowledge of Shakespeare's play to better understand both the Bennet family and herself as a member of it?

This Reading Group Guide to Laurel Doud's *This Body* is available also at www.twbookmark.com